THE VEILING OF THE MOON KINGDOM

CAITLIN ZURA

THE VEILING OF THE MOON KINGDOM

CAITLIN ZURA

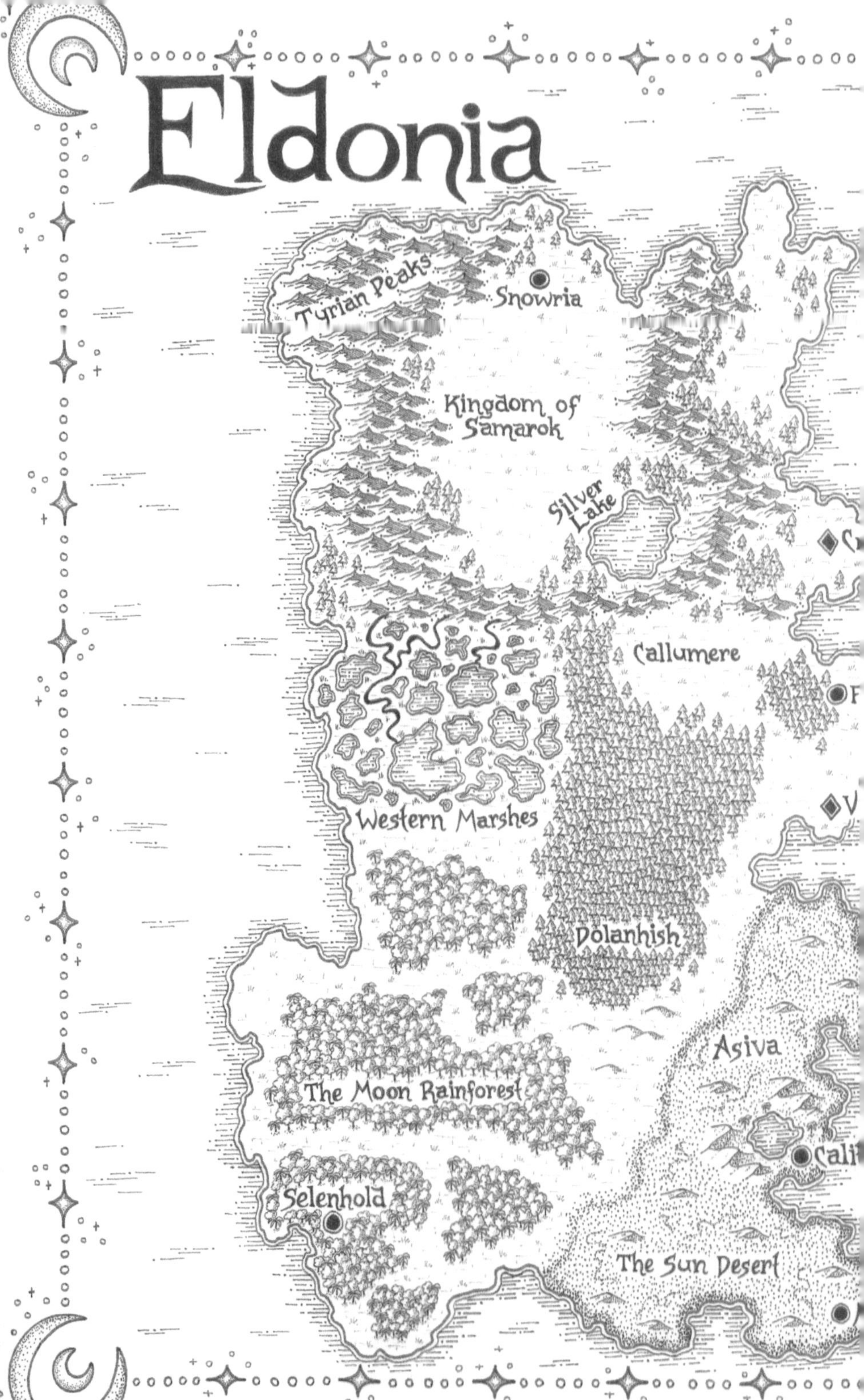

Eldonia
Tyrian Peaks
Snowria
Kingdom of Samarok
Silver Lake
Callumere
Western Marshes
Dolanhish
The Moon Rainforest
Asiva
Selenhold
The Sun Desert

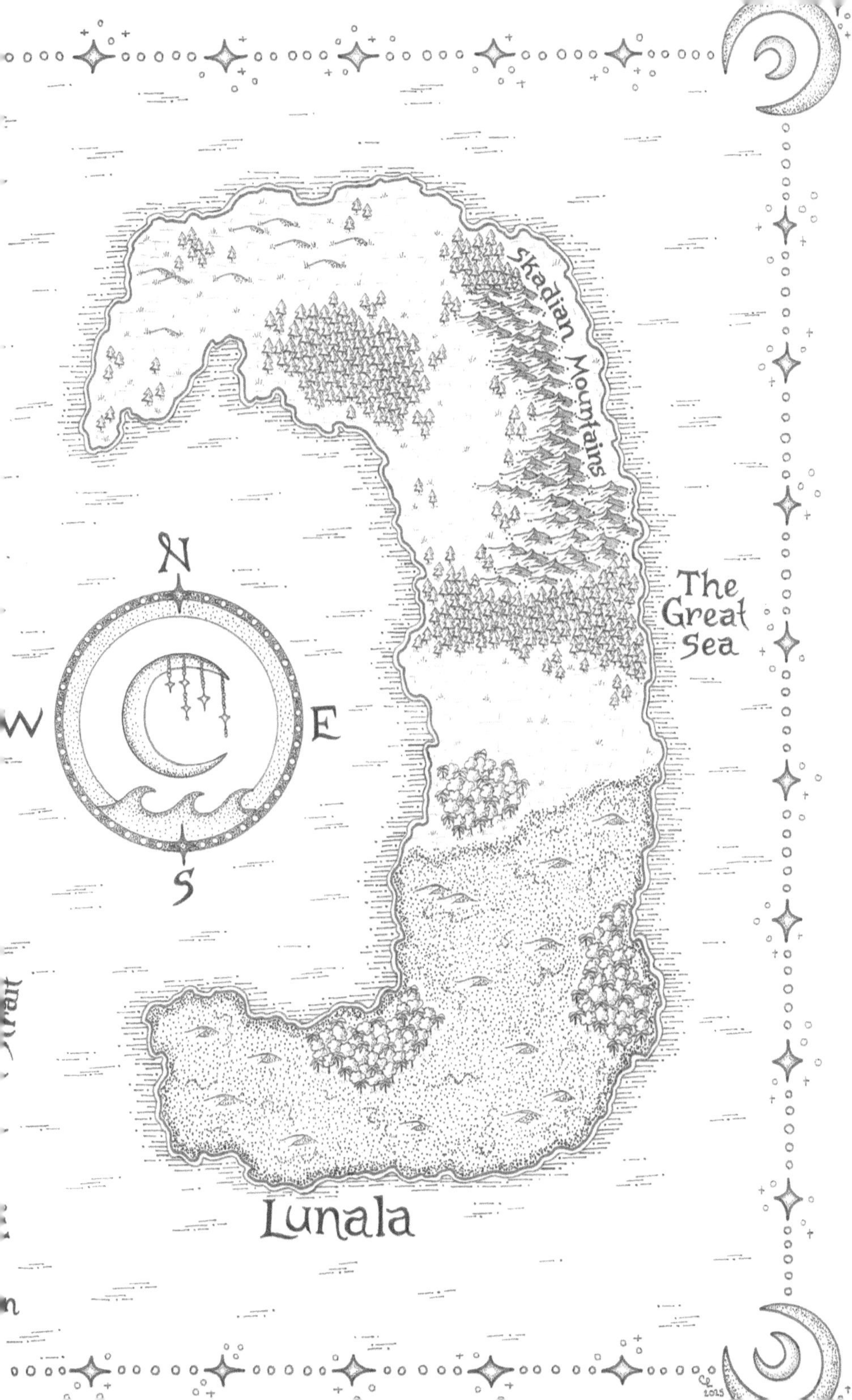

N
W
E
S
Skadian Mountains
The Great Sea
Lunala

Pronunciation Guide:

People:
 Elodae Kenton - (el-uh-day) (ken-ton)
 Irelia Hailwyn - (ur-eh-lee-uh) (hale-win)
 Vanor Hailwyn - (van-or) (hale-win)
 Alden Einar - (all-den) (ay-nar)
 Charon Einar - (care-on) (ay-nar)
 Lillianna Einar - (lil-ee-ah-nuh) (ay-nar)
 Finn Draethen - (fynn) (dray-thin)
 Warren Torvus - (war-in) (tor-vus)
 Astrid Marlow - (ass-trid) (mar-low)
 Vincent Marlow - (vin-cent) (mar-low)
 Orion - (oh-ry-in)
 Fornax Branton - (four-nax) (bran-ton)
 Hadeon - (hay-dee-in)
 Atlas - (at-liss)

Places:
 Dolannish - (dole-un-nish)
 Asiva - (uh-sea-vuh)
 Callumere - (kal-uh-mear)
 Eldonia - (el-doe-nyuh)
 Lunala - (loon-all-uh)
 Cronanth - (crow-nan-th)
 Samarok - (suh-mar-rock)
 The Oreithyians - (or–ee-thee-in)
 Tyrian Peaks - (tier-ee-in)
 Amphian Strait - (am-phee-in)

Vastolis - (vah-stole-iss)
Felidell - (fell-ih-del)
Calith - (kal-ith)
Selenhold - (suh-len-hold)
Mauwen - (maw-when)

*To the readers who keep their hearts in a cage—
don't throw away the key.*

PROLOGUE

Thirteen years—that was as far back as Elodae Kenton's memory went.

Hair white as the moon, the young woman sat on her balcony, sipping from a steaming cup of tea. She had woken mere moments ago in a sweat-soaked panic and sought the comfort of the stars.

Elodae spoke to herself of her dreams: nightmares they were more like. She pondered aloud if the nightmares were truly her memories or simply a figment of her imagination. Wishing on the twinkling lights above, Elodae asked, begged, for answers.

Too many holes in her memory kept her from knowing truth from fiction.

The young woman gritted her teeth, frustrated that she couldn't remember anything about her life before the cold, brutal shores of Samarok. It was the same after every dream.

Irritation ate away at her night after night when her mind would give nothing but the barest glimpse.

She fidgeted with her necklace, as she did every night, turning the two center circles so they were perpendicular to the outer one. Running a thumb over the center-most circle, over the eight-pointed star that rested atop a crescent moon, she relinquished a sigh that was felt through the stars.

With a glance skyward to constellations and vast galaxies that brought her comfort in her times of need, her eyes searched and searched for her favorite: a man holding a shield in his right arm and a raised sword in the other. The sword was outstretched as if pointing to his next opponent. The tip of the sword always faced eastward.

The Warrior. Or so she called it.

The stars had always fascinated Elodae. She could spend hours gazing up at them, reading about them in the castle library or at the Astronomers, even creating her own constellations out of the shining dots in the darkened sky. But tonight, even the stars couldn't keep thoughts of the nightmare at bay. As she gazed at the speckles of light, her mind wandered.

She remembered only three things from the day she abruptly arrived in Samarok thirteen years ago. First, her name was Elodae. She had no last name that she could remember; just Elodae. The king had given her the last name of Kenton during the blur of days that followed, graciously taking in the stranded, frightened little girl who had washed ashore after a shipwreck. The name had belonged to the late queen's sister after she had married a duke from western Samarok, making Elodae a duchess, as well as the king's niece.

To this day, she never truly knew why the king had taken her in, lying to his court, and made her a part of his family.

The second thing she could remember was that she'd been ten years old. She could still feel the terror within her as she regained consciousness in the arms of the gentle woman who brought her to the towering castle along the shore.

Lastly, she did not hail from the kingdom in which she'd landed.

A noise sounded from beyond the door to her bedroom, pulling her from her thoughts. She went still, straining her ears. When all remained silent, Elodae drained the rest of her tea and set the cup on the small table that separated the two lounge chairs on the balcony. She stood, wrapping her blankets tightly around her shoulders, and walked over to the railing. A breeze lifted the ends of her hair as she leaned her elbows on the cool stone. The wind promised that warmer days were on their way.

It had been a long, cold winter.

Elodae's gaze shifted back to the Warrior, and she couldn't help but ask him if her true home—her true *family*—waited for her somewhere out there.

CHAPTER ONE

Elodae grunted as her back collided with the ground. "You're lucky this is just training. If we were in a real battle and you were this distracted, I would've killed you five times over now."

Elodae used her wooden practice sword to hoist herself up. She was more drained than usual after her sleepless night. Unable to fall back asleep after her nightmare, she sought comfort in reading, using the books as an escape from reality. Once the darkness had been washed away and the stars had taken their leave, her mind had finally quieted enough for sleep to return. By the time she'd arrived at their training courtyard this morning, she had been exhausted.

Vines grew up the stone walls, and early spring flowers had started to bud along them. Their delicate scent wafted over to her on a gentle breeze. The days had begun to grow longer and warmer, but snow still dusted the ground, soaking into her clothes. Winter in Samarok was beautiful, but the spring and summer months always brought the magic of rebirth.

The courtyard was not supposed to be used for training, but Elodae preferred to train in private.

Using her sword as a crutch, she let her breaths come in heaves and tried to regain her strength.

Elodae shook away the swarming thoughts before they could take root, and pushed herself upright, readying for the next round. She needed physical movement. The only time her mind truly quieted was when she escaped into the worlds of her books, or when it was forced to focus all its energy on her not getting knocked to her ass. This was where the swirling thoughts finally left her alone and Elodae could just . . . be.

A snicker sounded from before her, and she glared at her sparring partner, who was trying, and failing, to hide his amusement. Alden, the head of her personal guard, stood before her with his practice sword still half raised. He hadn't even sprouted a sweat yet. He was a good bit taller than her, and she was by no means short. His normally shoulder-length, ash-blond hair had been tied back with a leather strap to keep it out of his smirking face. He was only two years her senior, and yet he had climbed higher in rank than anyone else his age.

Elodae seethed at the arrogance in his ice-blue eyes.

He cocked his head to the side, his smile blooming in full. Oh, he knew what he was doing. He could see the thoughts running rampant in her mind , and knew she needed the complete exhaustion of a grueling workout.

It angered her even more, that he knew her so well.

He raised an eyebrow at her, waiting for her to bite out a retort, but she was too tired to reach for her usual quiver of sarcastic and rude comments. She instead stuck her middle finger up at him. It conveyed everything she would've said anyhow.

Alden tilted his head back and laughed. A few pieces of his hair fell out of the leather strap as he motioned for her to attack. "Let's see if you can back that up."

"Bite me," Elodae growled through her teeth. She was not in the mood for his wit today.

A wild gleam entered his eyes. "I love that little accent of yours."

Elodae scowled. Her *little accent* had faded over the years, but it was still prominent enough that others could realize she was not from Samarok. The slight elongation of her vowels was hard for most to miss. It only ever served as a reminder that she did not belong here. She knew Alden was egging her on, that he'd only said it to piss her off. So she let her anger take over and lunged toward him.

He easily sidestepped her attack and used his sword to block her. Even though they were using wooden ones, the reverberations still hurt like hel. He counterattacked, but she met him blow for blow. A sweet ache grew in her shoulders as they parried.

Her mind quieted again, and she nearly sighed with relief at the silence, but the peaceful ambiance instantly vanished as Alden made a swing for her side. The attack forced her to leap out of the way, throwing her off balance.

Elodae's breathing grew faster the harder they pushed each other. She spun and came down on him with her sword, but he jumped to avoid her strike, leaving his side open.

Alden knew she could continue like this for hours. That she would push herself to her body's limit, *over* her body's limit, if no one stopped her. So that move he just did; he knew she'd go for the finishing blow, knew she would never pass up the opportunity to be the one to knock him on his ass for a change.

After training with him for nearly two years now, she knew Alden had left himself deliberately open. Still, Elodae quickly cut her sword back and was met with the satisfying crunch of wood on his ribs. He yelled out at the impact, and Elodae spun low, kicking out one of her legs. Air whooshed out of him as he slammed down onto the stone ground. A splatter of snow ricochetted out from around where his body had made impact.

She pointed her sword at his neck, breathing heavily. "Now you're dead, too."

Alden grunted something under his breath, too low for her to hear, and swatted away her sword. He groaned as he picked himself up and wiped his brow with the back of his hand. He dusted the snow from his pants, intentionally flicking some of it at Elodae before he made his way over to the water table. "That was a cheap shot," he muttered, even though they both knew he had let her win.

Elodae scoffed as she followed him. "Cheap doesn't matter on the battlefield, Alden. I won, and you're dead."

Leveling an exasperated look at her, he set his wooden sword on the table, filling one cup and handing it to her, and then filled a second for himself.

Elodae propped her sword up against the table and took a sip, feeling the cold water spread through her insides. "And

I know you kept your left side open for me on purpose," she accused over the brim.

Alden merely shrugged and drank from his own cup. Elodae would never admit it to him, but she appreciated him for stopping her from pushing too hard. For knowing when she was about to do more damage than good. He ignored the look she gave him, as he always did, and they stood in comfortable silence for a moment while they drank their water.

She had always appreciated that about Alden; that the urge to fill the silence around them with constant chatter was not inside him. That they could happily sit in the silence together. She felt at peace around him, which was exactly what she needed after the night she'd had. Though, more often than not, he was a giant pain in her ass.

Alden nudged her with his elbow. "So, where'd you go off to earlier?"

She blinked up at him. "What?"

"Where'd you go off to earlier? During the first few rounds, your mind seemed elsewhere."

"It's nothing. I'm fine."

"I didn't say you weren't. And that's not what I asked." She scowled at him, and he winked back. He took the empty cup out of her hands to refill it, and as he handed it back, he sighed. "Seriously, El. I know you love the stars, but that doesn't mean you can space out on me. Especially in the middle of our training. What were you thinking about?"

Elodae shook her head as she took the cup, "I said it's nothing."

"Don't do that. Everyone knows that when someone says it's nothing, it's obviously something."

"Profound," she grumbled and drained her second water.

"All right," he scoffed. "Well, if it really is nothing, then it shouldn't be such a big deal to tell me."

"Why are you so chatty today?"

"I don't like it when you shut me out."

Elodae fought the urge to shift on her feet as the raw honesty of his confession. Whether he was aware of the heart he laid on the table between them, she didn't know. If he was —then he was a fool.

"Oh." She didn't know what else to say.

"And I had to let you win today." Alden lifted the water to his lips to hide his smile.

"Oh?" she repeated, then grabbed her wooden sword and tried to whack his shin.

Alden dogged her swing, spilling his water down the front of his white tunic.

"Look, I'm just saying." He set down the cup and untied the leather holding back his hair. Putting the strap between his teeth, he raked his fingers through the tangles before tying them away from his face.

Elodae forced her eyes away from the fair skin now showing through his wet shirt and the muscle definition she would surely see if she glanced.

He gave her a pointed look, his icy blue eyes pouring into hers. He looked at her as if he already knew what had her so distracted.

She merely slapped on a smile and asked innocently, "What?"

A crease of concern formed between his brows as he gazed at her. "Did you have another nightmare?"

Elodae clenched her teeth together. "What makes you think that?"

Alden crossed his arms and shrugged. "My mother is your lady's maid. She told me that your bed hadn't been slept in and to go easy on you today."

"Oh."

Only five people knew what had happened to Elodae thirteen years ago. King Vanor, her father, Princess Irelia, her sister, Alden, whom Elodae had told the first night he'd awoken her from a screaming sleep, and Alden's parents. Lillianna Einar and her husband, Charon, had been the ones to find Elodae that fateful day on the beach.

"I thought it had been getting better," he said gently. "That it wasn't as bad as it had been when we were children."

Elodae's arms folded around herself, squeezing her tightly.

They had grown up together in this very castle. With his mother being her lady's maid and his father being the previous head of her personal guard, Alden was around all the time. They would play until the odd hours of the night, falling asleep while telling each other the wildest stories they could conjure. They were inseparable. But then Charon had died, and everything suddenly changed.

Alden had been training to become a royal guard since the day he could walk. So, when he was given his new position after his father's death, he had become too caught up in a life of his own that he had simply grown . . . distant. There had been no more sneaking off into the city that surrounded the castle gates. No more stealing wine from the kitchens. No more wild stories to replace the horrid dreams that plagued her.

Elodae unfurled her arms, taking in a deep, calming breath. "They are getting better."

He tilted his head as though he didn't believe her. She hated that look he gave her. Like he knew her very soul better than she herself did.

Alden had remained her friend these last few years. In some ways, at least. They still trained together every morning, and he even had lunch with her occasionally. They sometimes laughed and joked like they used to, but if things ever got too comfortable, if she ever dared to let him a little too close, he would go distant for a couple of days.

But no matter what, he never missed a training session. Alden had been the one to teach her how to defend herself after—

Elodae locked that thought back to where it had escaped from and eyed Alden, his face so similar to that of his late father, but with a softness from his mother.

Alden snapped his fingers in front of her face. "El?"

Elodae blinked and slapped a smile to her face. "Yes, Alden. I'm all right. Truly."

She tried to swallow, but her mouth had dried out. Alden knew the bare details of what had happened to her—that she had been in a shipwreck and his parents had found her. That she had no memories of her life before Samarok, and that she had occasional nightmares. She had never wanted to go into any more detail, and she wasn't about to start now.

Alden gently took her face in both of his hands, startling her with the softness of the touch. His calluses scraped against her cheeks as he locked his eyes with hers.

"When you are ready, whenever that may be, I will be

there to listen. And if that day never comes, I will still be there. To help in whatever way I can. All right?"

The urge to shoot her words at him bubbled up, but when was the last time someone had comforted her? When was the last time she'd let someone close enough to even try?

"Thank you."

"Only doing my job." He flicked her nose and dodged her retaliating swat. The half smile he gave her was noticeably forced.

With a pained realization, she knew that tomorrow, Alden would pull away again. She made herself roll her eyes, concealing the ache that formed in her chest, as he picked up both of their practice swords and handed hers over. They made their way back into the makeshift training rink.

He nodded toward her sword. "You ready?"

"Are you?"

"Give me your best, Princess." Alden threw her a teasing smile, one that was even more forced than the last.

Elodae stuck her middle finger up at him, and their sparring began once more.

CHAPTER TWO

Elodae's body was tired. Her *mind* was tired. She couldn't wait to crawl into bed and slip into a silent sleep. With a nod to the guards stationed outside her door, she strolled inside.

Peering into the room on her right, she debated whether she wanted to take a bath or sleep. Neither, she decided. Instead, she chose to exhaust her mind further by curling up with the book she had started last night, reading until her eyes couldn't stay open a minute longer.

She found that reading not only cleared her mind but also gave her an escape in a world that offered none of its own.

Elodae padded over to the room on her left, where floor-to-ceiling shelves housed hundreds of books. There she sat down on a pine-green sofa before a fire. She smiled at the roaring flames. She would thank Lillianna for having it ready later. No matter the time of year in Samarok, Elodae always felt a slight chill in the air this far north.

She was just about to pick up the book she had been reading the night before when the door burst open.

"A month!" a voice shrieked.

Princess Irelia stomped into the library a moment later and plopped herself down next to Elodae with such dramatic force that she bounced a little in her seat. The princess' lilac-colored dress fanned out around her with the motion.

Elodae gawked at her sister. "First of all, a month until what? Second, will you keep your voice down? You'll burst my eardrums."

Irelia only lolled her head in Elodae's direction and gave her a vexed expression, her long, peach-blonde hair falling around her pale and freckled shoulders. Elodae leaned her head against the back of the sofa and crossed her arms, one eyebrow raised.

"Well?" She pressed when Irelia stayed silent.

"You need a bath, E. You reek."

Elodae scoffed. "I will in a moment. Don't change the subject. What happens in a month?"

"I'm to meet Prince Fornax." Irelia made a disgusted grimace when she said his name.

"Ah." Elodae watched her sister closely and tried not to laugh at the loathing stark across her face. "So, Prince Fornax of Dolannish is to come and that upsets you, why?"

"Because he's awful, Elodae. Him *and* his people."

"Have you ever actually met him?"

Irelia's cheeks flushed bright pink. "Well . . . no. Not exactly."

"Then how do you know he's awful?"

The princess sighed, shoving to her feet, and started to pace before the small table separating the sofa from the fire. Curled ends of her luscious hair brushed gracefully against her hips when she turned to pace the other direction.

"You've met people from Vastolis before. They think they're above everybody else simply because they live in the capital of Eldonia. They're snobby and stuck-up and . . . and —" Irelia let out a frustrated growl. "I will not be tied to King Malum."

Elodae listened as her sister spewed her thoughts around the room. The King of Dolannish *was* hel-bent on weaseling his way into every other court on the continent.

"And they had all but refused aid to Asiva years ago. Every time I look at Finn, I'm reminded why he's here. Why he can't return home." The princess' voice took on a broken sound when she spoke of her guard. "Forget me not wanting him here. Think about how Finn will feel having to be around him every second of every day."

Elodae offered, "You don't know why they refused aid, Irelia. There could be a number of reasons—"

"None of which are excuses, E," her sister interrupted. "Finn lost his crown, his *kingdom*, because of that coup. And Dolannish just stood there and did nothing."

Elodae's heart weighed heavily in her chest. She still remembered the day the prince and his family had shown up on Castle Cronanth's doorstep, pleading for sanctuary in Samarok.

"Father was kind enough to give them asylum, to give Finn a position that kept his family safe. And now he's just going to invite the people that overthrew him into our home?"

"You don't know if Dolannish was behind it, Irelia. No one does."

Irelia sighed, pinching the bridge of her nose, and finally stopped her pacing. Her sea-green eyes met Elodae's, and after a moment of silence, she asked, "Why were you up so late last night?"

Elodae started. "Excuse me?"

"Warren said you were up all night." Irelia motioned toward the doors and the guard that surely stood just outside them.

Elodae clenched her jaw. *Warren.* Another pain in her ass. "He always weasels his way into things he has no business being a part of."

Irelia laughed lightly. "He'd be a better spy than guard."

"Truly," Elodae mused. "But how did he know?"

Irelia merely shrugged. "All he said was that you had been up all night, were probably exhausted, and for me to not bother you." She gave Elodae an apologetic look at that.

"Hmm." With a loving sigh at her sister, Elodae stood and stretched. Her muscles ached from the grueling training session that morning. She'd never get any reading done with Irelia here, so she might as well change out of her sweaty leathers.

The rustling of Irelia's dress followed her as she made her way out of the library, through the sitting room, and into her bedroom. She pulled out her favorite emerald-colored robe from the armoire and turned in time to see Irelia flopping back down on the bed.

"You're twenty-two," Elodae chided. "When are you going to stop doing that every time you come into my room?"

Irelia brushed away the hair that had fallen across her face and huffed a sigh of contentment. "When it stops being fun."

"I guess the answer is never then," Elodae said under her breath and then walked toward her bathroom to change out of her leathers.

Elodae had always trained in leather clothing to keep her skin safe from being accidentally nicked during practice. They were hot as hel, but after getting so many splinters and cuts throughout the past few years, they made a world of difference.

After shucking off her clothing, she slipped into the robe and tied the sash around her waist. Elodae turned the knob attached to the sink and cupped her hands under the waterfall that sprouted, thanking the gods that, over time, their people had figured out how to create intricate piping systems.

Elodae splashed some water on to her face and placed her hands on the cool, metal basin of the sink, gazing at her reflection in the mirror. Dark marks streaked under her eyes as though a painter had chosen her face as their canvas during sleep. She ran a finger over the shadow as if they could remove the stain from her light-brown skin. Freckles were starting to appear beneath the darkness, her skin already deepening in the early spring days. Another reminder that she didn't belong in Samarok.

With a sigh, she returned to her bedroom, where Irelia was still sprawled out on the mattress.

Elodae crossed her arms, leaning against one of the four bedposts, and carefully examined her sister. The princess' eyes were closed, her head tilted toward the rays of sun trying to break their way through the sheer curtains that draped the glass doors to her balcony. Something was eating at her. Irelia tried to cover her disdain with pretty smiles and flirty words, but Elodae could always see through her masks.

Elodae steeled her face into mild curiosity—almost bored—and said, "Why, may I ask, did you come all the way down here to whine about Fornax again?"

"You mean Forn*ass*," Irelia drawled. She turned toward Elodae, her eyes tired; older somehow. Lifting a hand, the princess reached for her.

Elodae reached for her sister's hand, allowing Irelia to pull her onto the bed beside her. She watched as Irelia burrowed into the wall of pillows against the headboard, fluffing a couple that weren't quite to her liking. She always made herself at home, no matter where they were.

Elodae envied her sister with a smile.

It would be nice to always be comfortable in her surroundings.

"We need to come up with a plan to get me out of this arranged marriage."

"Irelia," Elodae scolded.

"Oh, come on, E. You're the master schemer."

"About small things. Not something like this." Elodae waved her hand to encompass her sister and her impending marriage. Her other hand found its way to the forever-cold metal of her necklace.

Irelia's eyes tracked the movement, watching her twist the circles this way and that. "I feel like I'm getting close to translating that pendant of yours."

Elodae suppressed a groan and laid her head back against the headboard, but allowed the shift in topic. "We've been over this *a hundred* times." The pair of them had repeated this conversation almost every other week since Elodae had first shown Irelia the engravings that adorned each of the three circles. "You always say that, and it's always a dead end. The script is probably just too faded to read properly, so it looks like some ancient text."

Irelia picked at the ends of her wavy hair, letting the subject drop. Guilt consumed Elodae, but she was very protective over her necklace. It was the only thing that tied her to her life before these shores. The princess chewed on her lip, curling the ends of her hair tightly around a finger.

Elodae wanted to help her sister. But to fight Vanor's order . . .

The king so rarely made demands of the two girls. For him to have made this decision and hold firm, even at Irelia's protest, made Elodae wary.

"Are you all right?" she asked softly when her sisters fidgeting didn't subside.

Irelia waved her off and completely ignored the question. "You should come with me to the Magicks tomorrow."

Elodae snorted derisively.

"You know I can't stand that place after what happened last time." Elodae added after a moment, "And I don't believe in magic."

"Well, I do."

"I know."

Irelia sighed and laid her head back against the pillows. Silence stretched between them, and Elodae forced herself to relinquish her necklace and clasp her hands in her lap.

"I know you don't like that place. That you think it's all spell books and fiction. And after last time, you know I wouldn't normally ask this of you, but . . ." Her sister's words flowed off. "I need you, E," Irelia confessed quietly.

Elodae's heart ached in her chest, even as her body threatened to shiver at the thought of going near that place again. It was as though her very being was telling her to stay far, *far* away.

"How can you spend so much time there?"

"Because it brings me joy. Learning about our history and how our world used to be; how it could be again. Does it not bother you that a huge part of it has been erased, and no one knows why or how?"

Elodae had no response for that. With all the holes in her own memory, magic had never been a concern.

Internally kicking herself for the next words out of her mouth, she said, "Very well."

The brightest smile Elodae had seen all day spread across Irelia's face. "Really?" Elodae nodded, and Irelia grabbed her hands, giving them a gentle squeeze. "Thank you."

She smiled, hoping it concealed the nausea that writhed within her.

"Now," Irelia started. "Tell me about last night."

Elodae shrugged. "There's really not much to tell."

Irelia caught her gaze, challenging her to voice the words she knew were buried deep within, but Elodae held her ground.

Waving her off, her sister stood from the bed and made to leave. "Fine, don't talk about it then. I'm starving, though. So, wash up while I go grab us some food." And with that, the door clicked behind her.

Elodae buried her face in her hands for only a moment before she relented and stood. She made her way into the bathroom and turned on the faucet to the stone tub built into the bathroom wall. She stuck a hand under the stream and then closed the drain on the bottom. Deeming the water too cool, she returned to the fire and grabbed a pair of steel tongs kept by the fireplace for this very purpose.

Plucking up a couple of coals, she went back into the bathing chamber and plopped them into the tub. Then she rummaged through the different soothing tonics she kept close by and picked a floral-scented one. Her favorite. She dumped the contents into the rising water, quickly glancing at the label on the bottle.

Floral. Imported from Lunala, was all it read.

She scoffed a laugh. "Stingy bastards."

Lunalians had never set foot on Samarokan soil, or any soil on this side of the Amphian Strait, for that matter. No one left Lunala except to trade in the middle of the Strait. And no one—absolutely no one—went in. If they tried, they never came back.

She put the stopper back in the bottle and then ran her fingers through the water to mix the contents, letting the sweet scent calm her nerves.

Elodae stood and untied her robe, hooking it on the wall next to the tub before sitting down on the lip again, swinging her feet in. Her breathing picked up, and trying to control her rising panic, she closed her eyes.

Elodae stiffened as the water slowly rose, creeping up her legs.

She refused to tell anyone that she still struggled to do even the most basic of things. Bathing. As time had passed after Elodae washed up on shore, and the nightmares had grown few and far between, so had the crushing anxiety of being submerged in a bathtub. She didn't want anyone to pity her. And if she could admit it to herself . . . she was embarrassed that she still wasn't healed after thirteen years.

You are not on a ship. You are in your bathroom. You are safe.

Elodae repeated that until she could lower herself into the water. Her breathing remained steady, though the water level rose when her body submerged, and she squeezed her eyes shut even tighter.

Elodae swallowed hard and tilted her head towards the ceiling, cracking her eyes open. Her heart raced as she took a breath and then shoved herself under the water to wet her hair and face. She gritted her teeth as she surfaced.

Reigning in her anxiety enough to control herself, she picked up a lavender and honey-scented hair soap. She dunked the bar into the already milky water, rubbing it between her hands until gentle suds formed. Setting the bar back down, her fingers started to work the soap onto her scalp and through her hair.

Elodae paused to dunk her head under the water.

You are in your bathtub. You are safe.

She scrubbed the soap out of her hair as quickly as she could without growing frantic and emerged again. Wringing the water from her hair, she took a deep, steady breath. Grabbing a second bar of soap, she scrubbed at her body and face, then went under the water one last time.

Get through this.

When she emerged, Elodae unplugged the drain at the bottom of the tub and stood. She reached for one of the two towels hanging by the tub and wrapped it around her hair, then wrapped the second one around her body.

A knock sounded on her door just as she padded to the armoire, pulling out a pair of dark brown pants and an oversized white top. Irelia's peach-blonde hair appeared through a gap in the doors.

"I've got the goods."

"All right. Give me a moment to get dressed."

The sound of Irelia setting the tray down in the sitting room sounded, followed by the clinking of glass as Irelia made her way into the bathroom and started to put away Elodae's bathing supplies.

Elodae smiled softly to herself.

Irelia, though younger, had always tried to take care of her. Irelia had no mother of her own—not one that she remembered, anyway. The queen had died giving birth to the princess, and the king never remarried. Never even tried to. He still saved a place for her on the dais, at their dining tables, and at every play or performance they attended.

Elodae's fingers brushed the silken, soft fabric of a simple, black gown. She loved the dresses like the ones Irelia wore, but she told herself that pants and a shirt were more practical. But the truth was, deep down, Elodae felt she didn't deserve to wear the exquisite clothing Irelia preferred. The Hailwyns had already given her everything. How could she ask even more of them?

Irelia still bought her nice things now and then, insisting she kept them whenever she denied the gifts. Irelia said buying things for Elodae made her happy, but it didn't stop the guilt that ate away at her insides.

Shaking her head to banish the thoughts, she pulled on her pants first. Elodae had to jump a little to get them over her thighs and backside. Having wet legs didn't help with the struggle. Once they were on, the pants gapped a bit around her waist. She always hated that about pants. Unless they were tailored specifically to her body shape, they never fit quite right. Her thighs were thick with muscle, as was her backside.

She pulled the shirt over the towel still wrapped around her hair, dropped the one around her body, and walked back over to the armoire to retrieve a leather belt. Fastening it around her waist, she then tied the lacing on the V-cut front of her shirt.

"Balcony?" Irelia asked as she came out of the bathroom and walked into the sitting room where she'd left the tray of food. She grabbed it without waiting for Elodae to answer and walked outside. Elodae followed her out beneath the orange and pink sky.

She gazed toward the sunset. Where had her day gone?

Alden must've let them train for far longer than usual if the sun was now setting. She had been so consumed by their workout that she hadn't noticed the clock towers chiming throughout the city.

"I ran into Alden on my way back," Irelia said as she sat in one of the two lounge chairs, rearranging her skirts.

"Oh?" Elodae hated the summersault her stomach did at the mention of her guard's name.

"He genuinely worries for you, E." Irelia sighed contently and closed her eyes, tilting her head toward what little warmth remained from the disappearing sun.

Elodae winced as she sat in her usual chair next to Irelia's. "What makes you say that?"

"Apart from it being his job?" Irelia teased. "He always finds a way to steer any conversation we have toward you."

Heat burned in Elodae's cheeks. She bit down, perhaps too hard, on a piece of meat, shaking her head. She looked skyward, to the stars that were just starting to blink into existence. Finding the Warrior, she let out a long breath.

"Do you worry for him?" her sister asked slowly.

"I don't have feelings for him, if that's what you're insinuating. I don't have feelings for anyone, before you ask," Elodae clarified as Irelia's head snapped her way, mouth open, ready to say something. "Because to let someone in—"

"Opens the door for hurt," Irelia finished for her. "I know. You say that every time." The princess swung her legs off the chair so she was facing Elodae and grabbed a handful of berries. "But it could also open the door for something wonderful. Things may not work out, but maybe seeing if they do will be the best adventure ever."

Elodae snorted. Irelia had always been a hopeless romantic. Elodae herself loved to escape into her romance novels, but they were always the same. Two people met, fell in love, and lived happily ever after. In her world, happily ever after didn't exist. Ever.

Like Vanor saving a spot for his queen, his Auriel, everywhere he went. The pain and longing etched across his face whenever he'd glance to his side where his wife should be, it only served as a reminder to Elodae that pain was a given with love.

Irelia, on the other hand, found it to be a symbol of their love. That it was so true and eternal, it lived on long after her mother had left their plane. That the ache in the king's heart was a reminder that love was there. And it still was, in some ways.

With a soft smile to herself, Elodae glanced over at her sister, and they sat in silence for a while.

She watched the sky grow darker and the stars grow brighter while Irelia watched the sun, which dipped further and further beneath the horizon. Though they had always been close, Irelia was forever in love with the day, waking up when the sun did and spending as much time as she could basking in its warm rays.

Elodae was the opposite. She was in love with the night. The stars and the moon sang to her soul. She found comfort in the darkness, found peace in it—a stillness that only the night could bring. She would much rather sleep the day away and be up with the moon.

Removing the towel wrapped around her hair, she turned, tossed it into her room, and combed her fingers through the tangled strands. They were already starting to create waves and soft curls. Elodae ate the last bit of meat and berries as Irelia stretched and yawned, saying nothing.

Once the sun finally disappeared beneath the horizon, Elodae stood and offered Irelia her hands. Irelia sleepily took them in hers and let Elodae haul her up. She led her sister out into the hallway with a hug goodnight.

"The Magicks tomorrow," Irelia said, squeezing Elodae's hands gently.

"Yes." Elodae forced a smile. "The Magicks tomorrow."

Finn, who had been waiting for the princess, stepped forward with a bow. His onyx eyes held Elodae's for a moment before he turned and followed Irelia down the hall. He had to be well over a foot taller than her sister. Although he was only twenty-five, he was broad, and his deep brown skin stretched over his muscles. His cropped hair put the nasty scar down the left side of his face on display. She had never dared to ask how he received it.

Elodae glared at his back as they left. She never knew why, but Finn had never taken a liking to Elodae, and she was more than inclined to share in his feelings.

Nodding to her own guards, she made her way back into her room and out onto the balcony to bring in the empty food tray. Stopping short, her gaze wandered to the Warrior again. She could have sworn he pulsed slightly brighter than usual as she stared at it. A thrill shot through her chest as the constellation seemed to gaze back down at her.

Her eyes were locked on the light of the stars, watching as they grew brighter and brighter—so bright it was almost painful to look at them. Elodae blinked, seeing spots behind her lids. But when she turned skyward again, the stars had dimmed back to their usual twinkling dots.

A shiver ran down her spine, but she shook her head. Surely, she was seeing things. Grabbing the tray, she retreated into her bedroom but left her balcony doors open to allow in the soft breeze.

Moments later, she crawled under the warm sheets, clothes still on, and settled down into the soft mattress. She drifted off to sleep, gazing out past the softly billowing drapes, thinking of the Warrior.

She couldn't shake the feeling that he was trying to tell her something.

And whatever it was felt like a warning.

CHAPTER THREE

Alden glared across the carriage at Elodae, who was trying—and failing miserably—to hide her laughter.

Irelia and Elodae had climbed in first and sat next to each other on the same bench, leaving the three guards to squeeze onto the other. Alden was stuck between a brooding Finn and a smirking Warren.

"You're all going to get wrinkles if you keep your faces like that." Elodae smiled at the three of them. Irelia elbowed her sister.

"So," Warren drawled. Alden could hear through the forced calm in his brother's voice. "What did Vanor say when you told him where we were taking his daughters today, Finn?"

"The *King*." Finn corrected Warren. Elodae rolled her eyes at Finn's usage of Vanor's title. Finn always addressed everyone by their title, no matter how many times that person opposed. "Was thrilled," Finn went on, "to hear that his daughter would be accompanied by guards this time instead of sneaking off with his niece. Especially after the disappearances."

Elodae was the one who asked, "Disappearances?"

Alden picked at the skin on his thumb. Vanor had briefly mentioned there had been a surplus of people being reported as missing, but he hadn't explained further. The king had sent out a search party or two, but other than that, he knew little to nothing. Alden explained as much to Elodae, but that did little to comfort the duchess, who leaned back in her seat, chewing on the inside of her lip.

Watching the white-haired woman, he couldn't help but remember the first night he'd met her. It had been a cold winter's day, the snow falling heavily outside, when they had arrived at the Grand Hall to offer their welcomes to the king's niece. His father had warned him about the newcomer and told him that if he made a fool of himself or his family, there would be consequences.

Alden had bowed his head, already towering over the other children, and mistakenly said, "Lovely to meet you, princess." To which his father had coughed a laugh and quietly informed him she was not actually of the royal bloodline. He had only been twelve at the time, so even though no one thought his incorrect use of title was to mock her, his father had still made his disappointment very well known when they returned to their rooms.

However, it had become a joke between Alden and Elodae; to call her *Princess*. Ever since then, he only ever called her that when he was trying to make her smile or laugh, which at that age had been a frequent occurrence. Now . . . Now he was lucky if she gave him any sort of smile. The thought caused an ache in his chest.

After all these years, the guilt he'd felt that day with his father was nothing compared to the smile Elodae had given him, and only him, the entire night.

Elodae's eyes, green as the pines in the winter that night they'd met, locked with his. She tilted her head slightly to the side, causing her moon-white hair to fall over her shoulder, and raised her eyebrows at him.

Alden quickly averted his gaze. He feigned interest in whatever Irelia and Warren were discussing. In his periphery, he saw Elodae recoil slightly at his dismissal. His fists clenched in his lap. He was being unfair, and he knew that, but ever since he'd taken over his father's position as not only a member of the royal guard but one of *Elodae's* royal guards, he had to keep his distance. He had taken whatever feelings he'd developed for her as they'd grown up and locked them away—buried deep within his heart.

But now and then, he couldn't help but linger by her side or brush his knee against hers. When she moved, he moved. He was drawn to her, had been since that snowy night long ago when she had mocked him for calling her a princess for the entire evening.

But that little boy within him still craved his father's approval. Even though it had been years since he'd died, Alden still punished himself if he made a mistake. Denied himself things he wanted—people he wanted—because he knew his father would not approve.

Alden couldn't help but glance back over at Elodae, only

to find that she had turned away from him and was looking out the window.

He told himself to look away, but his eyes wouldn't listen. He hated the walls she had put up against him. Even more so, he hated that she felt she needed them. But he was her guard now. He had to make his father proud, even if it meant he had to push away the one person who had ever brought him true happiness. He wouldn't jeopardize his position. Not even for her.

Maybe for her.

Finn pulled back the curtain behind the three guards to inquire about how much further they had until they arrived at the Magicks. The driver informed them they were about to pull up.

The carriage came to a stop moments later, and Elodae made to step out of the door the driver opened, but Finn held up his hand in protest. Alden bit his tongue to keep from barking something he'd surely regret, but calmed when Finn said, "We should do a quick search to make sure the area is safe."

"Give us two minutes. Warren, stay with them," he added, agreeing with Finn's suggestion.

Warren cast Alden a smile and tucked his arms behind his head. He kicked his legs up on the empty bench as Finn and Alden stepped out of the carriage.

Alden rolled his eyes at his brother. The boys had been close when they were young children, and when Warren's parents died in that brutal fire, Warren became his brother in more ways than just name. Alden's father had taken Warren under his wing, spending almost every afternoon training together in an open field by the Tyrian Peaks, and allowing

Warren to listen in on meetings with the king long before Alden was ever permitted. It had grown a sense of jealousy in him as a young boy, to see the man who had sired him be a better father to Warren than he ever was to himself. He'd acted out on purpose, getting into trouble, coming home drunk, and sneaking out to be with Elodae.

But as they grew older, Alden realized it didn't matter. He was just glad Warren had a father figure in his life. And when his father had died, Alden felt compelled to look after Warren a little more closely, trying to teach him right from wrong. Warren was still a loose cannon, but when he had become a royal guard, Alden couldn't help the swell of pride that spread through his chest for his brother.

He shut the carriage door behind him and turned to face Finn. He held out his hand for Finn to walk ahead. Putting a hand on the pommel of his sword, Alden set off to follow him.

ELODAE ROLLED UP THE HEM OF HER PANTS AND then the sleeves of her emerald green tunic. It had turned into one of those rare, hot, first days of spring. Next to her, Irelia's eyes were closed, and her freckled face was tilted toward the sun rays that spilled through the open window.

Warren was still sprawled out on the bench across from them. His short, wavy hair was cast in golden hues from the morning sun. Elodae was always surprised by how beautiful he was. His tanned skin matched his dark blond locks. His soft brown eyes even had a honeyed color to them in the sunlight. He was simply *golden*.

"All clear," came Alden's deep voice, along with a thump on the side of the carriage.

The driver swung open the door once more, and Elodae nudged her sister, who was still lost in her daydreams. Irelia stirred and followed Elodae out of the carriage, Warren trailing right behind them.

Elodae gazed up at the towering building before her. Her mouth dried out as that strange sensation washed over her.

The Magicks.

She'd never forget the unease that consumed her every time she looked at those sun-bleached, grey stones. No windows adorned the three-story building. Not even one. Massive, marble columns held up a balcony that hung over the front steps.

Warren and Alden headed up those very steps in front of Elodae and Irelia while Finn trailed behind them, guarding their backs. A chill snaked down her spine as she made her way up the stairs, closer and closer to the massive, wooden double doors. They were twice as tall as Finn, who normally had to duck under doorways to avoid hitting his head.

Irelia was practically skipping when Warren pulled the rope attached to the doorbell. Nothing happened for a moment, but then both doors slowly creaked open. When they crossed the threshold into the main foyer, Elodae realized no one was there to hold the doors. She ground her teeth, forcing her feet to follow Irelia, who bound into the opening with no hesitation.

The foyer of the Magicks' manor was a half-circle clad in rugs of blues and greens. Dozens of sconces lit the entryway since natural light did not pour inside. A black marble archway stood in front of them, the only way to go that didn't lead back outside.

Irelia shucked off her cloak and threw it down on a dark wooden bench against the wall to their left. It was the only piece of furniture in the room.

It had been nearly five years since she had set foot inside this place, and she had tried to block mostly everything about it from her mind.

"I'm sure they're all in the library," Irelia chirped and headed through the archway.

The nausea in Elodae's gut only worsened as Irelia was devoured whole by the gloom that yawned beyond the arch. She tried to swallow, but her mouth was completely dry. She didn't see Finn hurry after Irelia, or Warren turn to roll his eyes at Alden. Didn't see him then cast worried eyes in her direction. Or the subtle nod Alden gave him before he turned to follow Finn.

Elodae was just staring into the gloom, into the blackness that shrouded her friends as they made their way to the Magicks' library.

A hand softly brushed her hair over a shoulder, making her flinch.

"Are you all right?" Alden asked with a gentleness that had her heart calming ever so slightly.

Elodae nodded. "Fine. I just hate it here."

"Me too." He scanned their surroundings. Always looking out for her. Always protecting. It calmed another small piece of her.

Despite the gnawing sensation that still ate at her insides, a small smile spread across Elodae's face.

"Come on." He jerked his head toward where the others had vanished. "I won't let anything bite you, Princess." He smiled and put a hand on the small of her back.

She couldn't control the blush that heated her cheeks at the feeling of his touch.

Elodae let Alden lead her out of the foyer, through the darkness, and toward the voices that trickled in through the lit archway at the end of the hall.

CHAPTER FOUR

A weight had been lifted from Irelia's chest the moment she'd stepped out of that carriage and seen the towering building she had grown to love so much. The building had become like a second home to her. Irelia knew her sister was wary of this place, but that was only because Elodae did not understand it as she did.

Irelia couldn't hold back the broad smile that spread across her face as she made her way down the long, dimly lit hallway, passing door after door that led to gods only knew where. Heading toward the light of the library tucked far inside the manor, she could hear the others behind her, though Irelia knew Finn was the closest to her without having to look over her shoulder.

She didn't know what to make of him. Although he was her guard, she still obeyed his commands more often than he did hers.

Irelia loathed giving the guards orders. She felt almost guilty about doing so. Not just with them, but with any attendant in the castle. She hated that everyone in her home assumed she was the same as any other royal; like the princesses in the stories Elodae had read to her as a child who only cared about how their hair looked and waited for a prince to come and save them.

Irelia let everyone think of her that way, though. It was easier if they did. People left her alone if she behaved the way they thought she would. Constantly fluffing her dress and curling her hair, she would reapply her cosmetics whenever she so much as took a sip of her drink. Always keeping her face doe-eyed and a soft smile in place. Always the happy one. The together one. The *my-life-is-perfect* one.

Maybe that was why Irelia had grown to love the Magicks so much. Here, she never had to pretend to be anyone but who she truly was. They never walked on eggshells around her, never held their breath if they contradicted something she said or corrected her when she was wrong. They fed her thirst for knowledge. *Folklore,* as Elodae liked to call it. But to Irelia, to the Magicks, this was the truth. Magic was alive, but something had stifled it. And for whatever reason, Irelia wanted to do whatever it took to set it free.

Free.

She didn't know why every time she thought of that word, her heart twisted and lurched. She wasn't trapped here in Cronanth. Her father never pressured her to do anything she didn't want to do. He loved her and Elodae with his whole heart. She never questioned or doubted that. But then the king had arranged Irelia's marriage to Prince Fornax of Dolannish. Even when Irelia begged and begged him not to make her go through with it, her father had put his foot down. Maybe it made her the privileged princess everyone believed her to be, but when did freedom of choice become a rare commodity? When did her desire to choose her own future make her spoiled?

"That's the sad truth of our world," Elodae had said to her the day after their father had told them that Irelia's engagement to the prince was indeed happening. Irelia had burst into her sister's room in tears at the realization that she would be tied to a horrible man for the rest of her life—a man who would likely force Irelia to give up her passions, to give up her research, and make her move to Dolannish with him. Force her to leave her family and everything she cherished in this city by the water.

Irelia sighed, pushing the thoughts that had circled for months to the back of her mind.

"Are you all right, Your Highness?" Finn asked from close beside her.

Irelia stumbled a step, not having noticed his approach. His hand caught her elbow to steady her. The size of it swallowed her small arm whole.

"I'm all right," she said, cursing herself for the words that came out meeker than she intended.

Finn cleared his throat, and Irelia realized she'd been staring at him and that he was still holding her elbow. She let out an embarrassed laugh and stepped out of his grasp, absently toying with the end of a peach-blonde curl.

"What are you two doing just standing in this creepy hallway?" Alden called from behind them.

Irelia turned to see him and Elodae approaching. Alden had a hand on Elodae's back, guiding her. From the tight look on her sister's face, Irelia knew Alden was doing it to keep her moving forward, to keep her from turning and running back out of here. Irelia hated that Elodae disliked this place so much. This place that had saved her in a way she couldn't begin to explain.

She wanted to share this place with her sister.

But Irelia saw the discomfort on Elodae's face and wanted to kick herself for even asking this of her. Yet with the prince coming so soon, she needed Elodae by her side. Irelia had always found comfort in that. Just being near her sister eased her soul. And the fact that Elodae had shelved her disdain of the Magicks for Irelia . . . it meant more than she would ever know.

Irelia smiled at her sister as she and the guard approached. Elodae was more her best friend than anyone else in their kingdom.

She offered Elodae a broad smile, the perfect portrait of the happy, mindless princess everyone believed her to be. It only became more honest when Elodae's shoulders relaxed slightly at the sight of it. "We were waiting for you two."

"Are you all coming or are you just going to stand in the dark the whole time?" Warren called from the library's entrance.

"We're coming," Alden called back and steered Elodae toward the light at the end of the hallway.

When Irelia turned back to Finn, she found him staring at her. Waiting. Heat rose in her cheeks again, and she wanted to kick herself for it.

She steeled her spine and lifted her chin. "Aren't you going to follow them?"

Finn gave her a curt nod and lifted his hand. "After you, Princess. Always."

His onyx eyes bore into hers, and she couldn't help but duck her head. Not wanting to linger a moment longer in the dim hallway with Finn, Irelia practically raced toward where the others awaited.

ELODAE HAD TO BLINK SEVERAL TIMES FOR HER eyes to adjust to the brightness of the library as they entered. She internally thanked Solas, the god of the day and light, that this room was not shrouded in the same ominous darkness of the hallway they had just exited.

When her eyes finally focused, she couldn't help but release a breath of awe. As much as Elodae detested the Magicks, she had to admit their library was extraordinary.

The Round Library, as the Magicks called it, was, well . . . round and at least several hundred feet across, with a spiraling ramp around the perimeter that led up to all six levels of floor-to-ceiling bookshelves. The bottom floor where they stood had twelve archways that led into subsections of the library. Some went far, far beneath the surface. They housed tomes and scrolls that were rumored to simply crumble to dust if one so much as touched them. A thirteenth archway stood on the ground floor, however, directly across from the hallway entrance.

It was also the only one that housed a door.

"It's sealed shut," Irelia said from beside Elodae, following her gaze. "No one knows how to open it."

Elodae gave Irelia a tight-lipped smile and made a mental note to stay far away from that arch.

Rugs of various shades of green and blue were strewn across the center of the room. Plush settees, the same colors as the carpets, were laid randomly throughout the rugged area with low-lying worktables in front of each. Curved, dark wooden desks lined the walls between each section of the library. The walls themselves were a deep red color, offsetting the blues and greens of the furniture. In the very center of the room stood an enormous statue with trickling water that flowed from various places into a shallow pool at its feet.

Elodae cautiously walked toward the statue, keeping a good distance back, leaving the others to chat idly by one of the many settees.

A man was carved into the center of the statue. No. A *fae male*. Elodae saw the gentle point of his ears and the slightly elongated canines in his mischievous smile. His hands were wreathed in a darker stone that looked like water or mist. Irelia had once told Elodae that some fae could possess the powers of shadows and bend them to their will.

She glanced away from the fae male to the woman on his right. The woman's upper half was human, but as Elodae looked toward where her legs and feet should've been, she saw the legs of a doe. A shifter—someone who could transform into any living creature they desired, altering their body entirely to become that being.

On the male's other side was another man. This one appeared human but was holding a book with shapes and runes written over the entire cover. The warlock language, Elodae realized. Irelia loved studying those symbols and runes, staying up until the odd hours of the night translating various texts. Unlike the fairy tales Elodae often read, where witches and warlocks were always old, withered men and women, the Magicks believed true warlocks to be mostly men. Female witches were apparently very rare.

Around the back of the statues, five people—fae—sat around a small fire. One's hands were wreathed in flames, and another had a flower springing from their palm. The one closest to where Elodae stood had water weaving around their arms and crowning their head. The one next to them had leaves flowing around them on a phantom breeze, it seemed. And the one in the middle had a combination of all four elements. An elemental.

A man came out from one of the archways on the right-hand side of the room and held out his hands for Irelia, who skipped over to him, her own hands outstretched. The man looked to be barely into his third decade of life and had the same dirty blond hair and blue eyes that most people in Samarok did.

Alden glanced in Elodae's direction, and she gave him a slight nod, letting him know she was all right and would stay over by the statue. He gave her a soft smile and turned to join the others. Elodae wanted to go to her sister, to be a part of this, but the people who worked here still unnerved her.

Turning back to the statue, she took a step closer to the next figures. A woman bent over a basket, her hands in it, a slight smile on her face. A healer, then. Just behind her was another fae, female this time, with her hands made of the same darker stone as the first male Elodae had seen. Her face was that of pure evil. Elodae remembered Irelia telling her horrifying stories of some fae being able to control death itself. An unsettling feeling nestled in within Elodae, and she had no doubt that most used it to bring death, not to keep it at bay.

Goosebumps pricked her skin as Elodae turned to the last figure. A fae male again, but this one had everything wrapped around him. Water, leaves, and fire encircled him. Spuds were sprouting from the tops of his feet. That same darker stone—shadowstone, Elodae finally recognized—crept over a shoulder. A book of runes in one of his hands, the other was clawed like a beast from one of Elodae's stories.

Raw magic.

To possess it was to be able to control any element, heal anyone, save them from death, or bring it down upon them. To be able to shift into any creature or vanish into shadows.

Elodae sent up a silent prayer to the gods that if magic did exist and ever made its way back, they would spare them from someone so powerful.

She started to walk back around to the front of the statue, toward the others still chatting by one of the plush settees, when she noticed a slight discoloration of an empty section of stone on the statue. She walked over to the lip of the pool and leaned over to get a better look.

Just as she was about to reach out and run a finger over the surface, a chilling voice sounded from behind her, "You noticed the discoloration."

Elodae jumped and spun around. Clutching her necklace, she came face to face with the man who had been talking with the others mere moments ago. She looked over her shoulder to where her sister and the guards sat. Irelia was rambling on about something that had Alden and Warren tilting their heads back in laughter.

The man in front of her cocked his head slightly. "You noticed the discoloration," he said again.

Not a question, but Elodae nodded all the same, not trusting her voice to be steady enough to speak.

The man just continued to stare at her with those blue eyes that were so similar to Alden's. But whereas Alden's were filled with warmth and depth, the orbs of this man were shallow and made her blood ice over.

He finally tore his gaze away from her and stalked over to her side, facing the statue. The air whooshed back into her lungs, and she slowly turned back to the figures before her.

"It is said that there used to be a thirteenth type of magic," he said softly, for only her to hear. Although Elodae was looking at that slightly lighter spot on the stone, she watched him out of the corner of her eye. "Celestials."

Elodae turned to look at him fully again, something writhing deep within at the word.

He continued to stare at that spot. "They were said to manipulate the powers of the universe itself. They could crush someone by controlling gravity. Could emit light as bright as the sun, blinding or scorching their enemies at will." Elodae shivered and took a small step away from him. He looked at her then. "They could make stars rain and conjure the abyss of the void. They could control Starfire."

"Starfire?" Elodae asked, barely more than a whisper.

"Fire that burned so cold it could turn even the most

powerful fae into nothing but a pile of ash in the blink of an eye." The corners of his mouth tipped upward. "There is no defense strong enough to shield one from the wrath of Starfire."

Elodae felt the color drain from her face. The sage blinked, and it was as if life returned to his eyes. The pink came back to his cheeks, and he gave her a smile that actually touched his eyes as looked at her fist clamped over the pendant. "Are you finally ready for us to take a look at that and see if we can translate it?"

"No," was all Elodae said before she turned without another word and rushed over to her sister and the guards.

Irelia stood and hurried to her side, clearly reading her distressed expression. "Are you all right?"

Elodae nodded. She didn't want to make her sister leave. She would not be cowed by these people. "He asked about my necklace."

Irelia let out a soft sigh. "They're interested in it, E. The engravings are written in a lost language—"

"We don't know that. I don't want them touching it."

Irelia chewed on her lip for a moment. "Would you let me look at it, then?" she asked gently.

Elodae mulled over the idea for a moment. "I don't want to take it off."

Irelia was already nodding before Elodae even finished her condition. "That's fine. I'll go find my notebooks and a few tomes that might help with the translation." Her words grew distant as she walked toward the spiraling ramp that led to the upper levels.

Finn was immediately on his feet, following her.

Alden stood and walked over to Elodae's side. "El?"

"I hate this place."

Alden brushed his hand against hers. "Say the word, and we're out of here."

He meant it. She knew he did. He would leave Irelia with Finn and Warren and get Elodae out if that was what she needed.

"I'll be fine." She wrapped her arms tightly around herself despite her words.

Alden looked over her with the frankness of a soldier. Assessing. Making sure she was truly all right.

She tilted her head, her hair falling over a shoulder with the movement. "What?"

"Nothing." He shook his head, putting a hand on the pommel of his sword.

Their eyes held, the icy blue calming her racing heart. Elodae took a deep breath in and out before she tore her gaze away. She ran a hand through the strands of hair that had fallen out of her braid and glanced around.

"I'm going to take a look around while we wait." She made to turn toward the archways on the left side of the room, but Alden's steps followed. Elodae stopped, turning to look at him over her shoulder. "I think I can handle a library," she said with a forced smile.

Alden once more looked her over, making sure she could, in fact, handle a library. She bit her tongue to keep her words retained. He nodded once and sat down on a settee. Turning away from him again, Elodae released a quiet sigh.

Wandering over to the closest archway on her left, she ran a hand over the wooden carvings that adorned it. Flowers and herbs intertwined to weave vines along the curve of the arch. Silvan magic; natural remedies.

Elodae peered through the archway to find an endless greenhouse full of books and caches of all kinds of foliage. Vines grew up the shelves and wound their way across the stone floor.

It was an odd place to keep paper books, yet none of them seemed to be worn down by the constant dampness inside the room. The greenhouse also appeared to be the only place in the Magicks' manor that had any windows. Elodae was half inclined to hide out in here for the rest of their visit.

Soft leather brushed against her fingertips as she ran her hand along one of the many bookshelves. Picking at random, she grabbed a light green tome and flipped to the first page.

Silvan is the only form of magic available to people today, as it takes no magical power to learn. Most people who learn Silvan magic use it for healing purposes. Although, according to some, certain herbs or plants could help aid in spell work, spell working requires the wielder to have magic running through their veins to begin with. Since magic is no more, healing is all anyone can truly do.

Elodae closed the book, returning it to its home amongst the others, and glanced around the stuffy room. She stepped out of the greenhouse and made her way to the next archway.

This archway held cresting waves. Water magic. Elodae carefully treaded into the room and marveled at the deep blue tiles laid around its entirety. She peered into the pointed end of the room hundreds of feet away and noticed it was tear-shaped. A reflection pool lay in the middle of the space, the water gently moving to and fro.

Surprisingly, she liked this room. Calm serenity encompassed the space. The air was cooler here. Crisper, too.

Not humid and stuffy like the greenhouse, but fresh. Like the breeze off a not-yet-frozen lake during wintertime.

Elodae wandered over to one of the blue-marbled shelves and read some of the titles: *Tides of Time*, *Water Healing*, *Rain's Reign*.

Her reading was interrupted by someone calling her name. She tore her eyes away from the books as her name was called again. Irelia.

"Elodae," Irelia called again. She could hear the worry in her voice this time, so she huffed a sigh and walked out.

Elodae found Irelia and the guards hunched over a large table by the statue, tomes, scrolls, and notebooks scattered across its surface. She made to go join them when a hand grabbed her elbow.

Elodae started and whirled around, using a maneuver Alden had taught her to dislodge a person's grip. One of the sages, a short, plump woman with greying hair, stared at Elodae with glazed eyes. It was the same look the man from earlier had before he'd shaken the life back into himself.

Elodae took a careful step back from the woman, who mumbled something under her breath in a voice that was both young and old. Elodae looked around for her sister or the guards but couldn't find them.

The woman grabbed Elodae's elbow again, making her flinch. Those glazed eyes locked onto her necklace. The sage's words became audible as she took a step toward Elodae, her grip like stone on her arm.

"*An eye of pine, an eye of sky—it begins,*" the woman mumbled over and over again.

"I-I don't know what you mean."

"*An eye of pine, an eye of sky—it begins,*" the woman repeated, reaching her other hand toward Elodae's throat.

Elodae slapped the woman's hand away and ripped her arm out of her grasp. The woman blinked at Elodae, and just as the man before, life visibly returned to her eyes, and pink reclaimed her cheeks.

"Elodae," Alden said from beside her.

Elodae jumped and whipped her head in his direction.

"Where did you come from?" she asked, her heart pounding in her ears.

"I've been next to you the whole time," Alden said slowly, his eyes bouncing between Elodae and the woman still in front of her, who was now smiling brightly up at Elodae. "She asked if you needed help with anything."

Elodae didn't realize how cold she was until the warmth radiating from Alden seeped into her. She turned back toward the sage, whose smile hadn't faltered. Her heart still raced as she stared and stared.

"Elodae," Alden said again, worry thick in his voice.

She wouldn't look away from the woman, though. The woman finally shrugged and turned to disappear into one of the dark libraries. Same as the man before her. Elodae watched until she couldn't see her anymore.

"Elodae, please say something. You're scaring me," Alden pressed, reaching for her.

She pulled her eyes from the arch the woman had gone through and looked at Alden. "You really didn't see her grab me? You didn't see her try to grab my necklace?"

Ire flashed in his eyes. "What?"

Elodae gave him an incredulous look. "You really didn't see any of that?"

"I saw her approach you, and you had this blank look on your face. She asked if you were all right or needed help. She reached for your hand, and you slapped it away. That's when I came over."

"That . . ." She didn't know what to say.

Her skin was cold, and her chest tightened further with every passing minute. Elodae clamped her mouth shut, but Alden didn't look away from her eyes.

By the time the clock chimed, signaling their sixth hour of being at the Magicks, Irelia was no closer to deciphering Elodae's necklace than when they had started. Her neck ached with how often she had to crane it for Irelia to get close enough with a magnifying glass to finish copying the script down.

Elodae watched in awe as Irelia transferred the script on her pendant to the piece of paper. She had no idea Irelia was such a talented artist. The foreign language was a combination of symbols and swirls, all of which were very intricate. Irelia had spent the better half of three hours tracing and retracing them onto her paper. The remaining three hours were spent hunched over countless books and scrolls, trying to match the symbols.

When the clock finished chiming, Warren threw down the book he was combing through. "Are you sure those are even the correct symbols? The necklace is so faded. How can we know for sure that's what is truly engraved on it?"

Finn shot Warren a warning look when Irelia stiffened.

"Yes, Warren," Irelia said with exasperation, dismissing his concerns.

Warren threw up his hands and leaned back on his cushion.

Irelia set down the scroll she had been studying and ran a hand over her face. "Maybe we should call it a day and come back tomorrow."

"No," Elodae said, too quickly to be casual. The four of them looked at her. "If we haven't solved even one of those symbols in six hours, then maybe Warren's right."

Alden brushed his knee subtly against hers as if to say, *I know what you're not saying*. That she didn't want to return here in the morning.

But he hadn't been able to see how that woman had grabbed her. Hadn't heard what she had said. The words Elodae had replayed over and over in her mind.

An eye of pine, an eye of sky—it begins.

What the hel was that supposed to mean?

Elodae needed a strong drink, a good book, and to sleep for two days straight.

"I suppose you're right." Irelia sighed after a moment, shoving away the scrolls. "Help me put these back?"

Elodae knew the question was posed to her, but nonetheless, Warren and Finn both scooped up the remaining texts and followed Irelia back up the spiral ramp.

"Are you going to tell me?" Alden asked, watching her warily.

Elodae merely shrugged, and that was that.

The others rejoined them, and they made their way back out of the Magicks' manor, the poor driver and his carriage still waiting for them on the streets below.

The ride back to the castle was quiet, and Elodae bade her sister a quick goodnight before making her way to her room with Warren and Alden. With a goodnight to them thrown over her shoulder, Elodae closed the doors behind her and nearly sagged with exhaustion.

Everything that followed was a blur. Her bath, brushing her hair, eating dinner, and changing into one of the silk nightgowns that clung to her still slightly damp body. She brought a book into bed with her, but Elodae only read the first sentence before she was pulled into a fitful sleep.

That night, she dreamed of a man with sky-blue eyes.

CHAPTER FIVE

Creaking sounded as Elodae reached into her armoire and took out a midnight-black cloak. She wrapped it around herself, pulling up the hood.

Her shoulders barked in pain as she adjusted the hood, her body still sore from her prior training session with Alden. He had gone back to his usual aloof self, which pissed her off to no end. Every time she tried to talk to him, and he gave her a one-word answer, it only made her angrier.

Elodae looked at herself in the full-length mirror, making sure her face was completely concealed beneath the material. Not many of the townsfolk knew who she was, but she had to disguise herself to sneak out of the castle, especially during the day. She wouldn't be allowed to wander about Cronanth alone while the castle filled with people from foreign kingdoms.

And those disappearances Finn had mentioned the

other day . . . She still had no idea what that was about. Her father hadn't said anything to her or Irelia about it. When Elodae had brought it up to Vanor at breakfast before her training that morning, he had simply said, "Disappearances happen, Elodae. Unfortunately, there's not much we can do but send out search parties in hopes our people return safely."

She prayed to Eirene, the goddess of peace, that he was right, especially with Prince Fornax on his way. That was the last thing Samarok needed—to be blamed for any Dolannish people vanishing.

Every time she thought about the Dolannish, unease filled her. She wouldn't put it past them to try something in Samarok. Try to snake their way into her father's ear. It was no surprise King Malum had his sights set on their snowy kingdom. Samarok was the largest realm on the continent. He'd be a fool to not be worried about them turning on him.

Nonetheless, Vanor had brought in some of his armies to serve as extra guards around the castle. The normally empty garden beneath her balcony was now filled with guards strolling through at all hours of the day and night. The only way in and out of her rooms was the front door, which now had four guards permanently stationed outside.

"We're letting strangers into our home," her father had explained at breakfast that morning.

Blindly reaching up to toy with her necklace, she remembered she'd tucked it inside her cloak. It was a telltale sign of who she was. Not being able to feel its comforting touch only made her more anxious.

She could take a guard or two with her, if need be, but the Astronomers was her sanctuary. She liked going there alone, pouring herself into studying the universe and all it offered without someone breathing down her neck.

Elodae's heart strained. She would have to take Irelia to the Astronomers sometime. Her sister would absolutely love it. But right now, after yesterday, she needed some space. Needed to be alone. To get out of her head and away from everything, if only for a little while.

From the table, she plucked up a black mask that would cover everything but her eyes. She hastily wrapped it around her neck, under the hood, and then pulled it up over her mouth and nose. She adjusted it as she cracked open one door and poked her head out. Emptiness greeted her, and she blinked—not a single guard. She slowly crept out and closed the door as softly as she could behind her.

As though she'd summoned one, a guard turned down her hallway, hurrying over to where she stood.

Shit.

But as the guard approached, she recognized him as Warren. Sweaty and out of breath, he skidded to a halt and bent over, hands on his knees. He panted, "I bought . . . you time."

"What?"

Warren stood up and leaned his head back, the ends of his golden hair sticking to his face as he blew out a breath. "Gods, that was fun." He laughed, still panting.

"Care to explain?" Elodae whisper-shouted.

"I saw that look you had when you left the king's room this morning," Warren rasped, looking at her again. "I knew you would go to the Astronomers."

"How—What?" Elodae didn't know what to say. "You're not going to tell me to bring you along?"

Warren waved a hand at her, still not having caught his breath yet. "As long as you swear you'll be safe."

Elodae rose onto her toes, pulling her mask down to smack a kiss on Warren's cheek. She internally cringed at the sweat that still dampened his skin. "I promise."

She hooked her little finger with his, but he batted her away as she repositioned her mask.

With a smile that he couldn't see, she raced down the hall to the hidden door she knew would open to an abandoned attendants' passageway. She pulled back the trick door and slipped inside. Then she was homebound.

She hurried down the stone passageway, having memorized the twists and turns as a young girl wandering the castle alone her first few months in Samarok. She headed toward the door that would lead her to an empty alley on the southwestern side of the castle.

Right now, she needed to empty her mind. Empty it of guards and sages and princes and shipwrecks. Empty it of everything except the moon and the stars.

Pushing open the door, she winced when it groaned loudly, the sound echoing throughout the stone alleyway. She quickly shut it behind her, placing a crate—the one she'd left as a young girl to mark the safe way back into the castle—in front of the door. She adjusted her hood, making sure her hair was concealed beneath it, and turned her head in all directions. The noontime sun straight above didn't so much as caress her face.

Elodae grinned to herself, pulling the mask tightly around the lower half of her face, and made her way down the alley and into the bustling street ahead.

People of Cronanth rushed about along the streets.

Shops were thrown open, the owners leaning out their doors and windows, calling their customers in. A couple walked hand in hand on the sidewalk in front of Elodae as she slid into the flow of foot traffic.

Horses whinnied as they passed by, pulling carriages of all colors. It had been a while since Elodae had been outside the castle walls unaccompanied. Vanor had never kept the girls from the city, but he made it abundantly clear that while Cronanth was safe, bad people resided everywhere, and they could not trust anyone at face value.

If only Elodae had trusted in her father's advice before she'd met the one who had broken her heart.

Pushing the thought from her mind, she crossed the street. The shops that lined the roads had windows above the storefront that led to bedrooms for their owners. Some buildings she passed as she headed toward the eastern side of the city were strictly for housing. Some streets Elodae had learned the hard way to avoid at all costs. Places where the sun never shone, and people snuck around in the shadows. Where drunkards were out at all hours of the day and night, trying to lure women, or anyone really, into their sheets.

Elodae held the side of her hood with a hand as she pushed through a dense crowd of people who were staring into a shop. She looked up at the sign and rolled her eyes.

Magickans.

People from the Magicks had set up shops around Cronanth to show the people how to spell herbs and make things vanish before their very eyes. How to brew healing tonics and remedies for cuts and illnesses.

The actual healers of Cronanth, the ones that studied

under the Head Healer for years and years, hated these kinds of shops. Elodae was inclined to agree.

She hurried past the shop but froze when she walked by two men huddled together, talking in hushed tones.

"They still have no idea what happened to poor Grant?" one whispered, shaking his head.

"Poor lad. He's been missing for nearly a week now. His family must be a wreck," the other said.

She hesitated for a second to listen to the men talk about the missing boy. This must be one of the disappearances Finn had mentioned. Why wasn't her father worried?

She didn't want to believe her father would lie about something so serious, but she couldn't deny that something was clearly happening in Cronanth, and he hadn't told her.

Elodae continued down the street when a towering man plowed into her, practically running her over.

"Watch it!" She caught herself on the brick wall of a nearby shop and glared at the stranger.

He turned toward her, only the bottom half of his face visible beneath his own hood. A scar cut through the right side of his mouth as he flashed her a grin. "Apologies, love. The ice."

With a gloved hand, he pointed to the ice and snow that had only just begun to melt in the early spring days.

The man beside him, not quite as tall as the one who had run into her, grabbed the collar of his companion's cloak and pulled him away from Elodae. The man with the scar watched her for a short while, his smile widening before shrugging his friend's hand off. He playfully shoved the other, and Elodae heard the two of them laugh as they made their way through the wave of people.

Shaking her head, she turned down the next street.

There.

On the far side was the Astronomers.

Her heart leapt in her chest at the sight of the dark stone building.

Elodae rushed toward the towering manor. The front of the building stood only three stories high but jutted up another four in the back. The back tower was domed. A slit in the rounded top could roll backwards so the astronomers could look out above the city. The entire dome itself could turn all the way around so they could see all the stars all the time. They could take their astrolabe up to the top, roll back the dome, and map out the stars and their movements.

The sight of the manor eased some of the weight on Elodae's chest; a weight she hadn't realized was there.

Elodae sped up, walking as fast as she could without running. A smile, more genuine than any she had worn these past few weeks, spread across her face as she neared the arched door that led inside.

Pushing open the heavy, wooden door, the smell of old books and crackling fires hit her as it started to budge.

She threw back her hood and closed her eyes, leaning against the shut door. Elodae pulled her mask down so she could breathe in the comforting scent.

"Elodae," a man called from down the hallway.

She opened her eyes and saw Byron, a large, dark-skinned man in the latter half of his sixth decade of life, approaching with outstretched arms. She beamed at him and hurried over, embracing the old man in a hug. "I've missed you."

"And I, you," Byron said in his rich Samarokan accent.

Elodae released him and gazed around the entryway. The

bottom front half of the Astronomers was laid out like a house, the entire space paneled in dark woods. Curtains on the windows were thrown open, letting the sunlight in. Carpets of blues and purples lay scattered around the floors, worn from the many years of people passing over.

In front of them was a long hallway that led to the library in the back, much like the Magicks. But where the Magicks was dark and ominous, the Astronomers was full of life and warmth.

Byron waved an arm, silently asking Elodae to walk with him. She followed his lead and walked down the long hall, passing by a staircase that led to the rooms above where Byron and three others lived, one of whom was his wife. The others were his two sons, Castor and Pollux. Twins. Castor was around often, in his late twenties himself. He had taken up after his father, studying the universe alongside him. Pollux, however, had opened a small bakery down the street with his husband.

Doors lined the hall. Some were propped open, one showing a kitchen that connected to a dining room, and another showed a bathroom.

Many were filled with floor-to-ceiling shelves that housed centuries-old books. Chairs and settees and tables sat in the centers of the shelved rooms. Elodae would make her way through those one day, but she was always too nervous to touch any of them without Byron or his wife Daphne present.

Elodae wondered aloud where the woman was.

"Where do you think?" Byron said, smiling over his shoulder as they approached the double doors at the end of the hall.

Elodae returned the grin.

Byron pushed open the doors with a grunt. Everything in the Astronomers was wood. It was all very heavy but perfectly made.

Elodae bowed her head slightly in thanks and entered the Astronomers' library. Students were spread out among five long, wooden tables that sat in the center of the rectangular room. Three spiral staircases stood in the middle of each wall of the room, apart from the one Elodae and Byron currently stood against.

The staircases led to the upper six levels. Unlike the Magicks, these levels were only surrounding the perimeter. They did not wind deep into a maze within the manor but always sat open and lit. Welcoming settees sat along the walls, separating the bookshelves. The bottom level's shelves did plunge into the building, however. The further back you went, away from the light, the older the books became. Byron said it was to help preserve the delicate texts.

Throughout the years, planets, constellations, and moon phases had been carved into the wooden panels that lined the walls. Some were made by students, some by the Astronomers themselves. People carved their names under their made-up constellations and planets or named them themselves. Elodae herself had carved the Warrior into a discreet corner in the far back three years ago.

Elodae walked over to the table on the far right, her preferred one, and slipped off her cloak, hanging it on the back of one of the wooden chairs. She unwrapped her mask from around her neck and set it down on the table.

Byron leaned against the back chair opposite hers. "Well, my dear, you know what to do."

And with that, he smiled and walked away.

Elodae let herself take in the library. The sounds of rustling paper as the students poured into their studies. The clank of someone walking up and down the spiral staircase. Idle chatter. The smell of old books being opened and carefully read.

She loved being here. Being surrounded by people who shared her passions. The Royal Library in the castle was extraordinary, having close to half a million books, but it was always full of snuffy lords and ladies preening about this or that.

Was this how Irelia felt about the Magicks?

She wanted to kick herself for how open she had been with her disdain for that place over the years. Something about it just raked at her. And with the strange interactions she'd had both times she went, could Irelia really blame Elodae for feeling that way? She hoped not.

Sighing, Elodae gazed up toward the dome, where she spotted the fiery red curls of Daphne bounding around empty shelves above her.

After a map of the night sky was sketched up top, either Daphne or Byron would check and recheck it to make sure everything was perfect. Then the books were brought down to the bottom level, where they were shelved for students to study in their lessons.

Daphne loved the dome at the top of the library. Even during the day, like now, she would sit up there and wait for the sun to go to sleep so she could throw open the roof and begin studying the stars. Daphne had tattoos of her favorite constellations all over her body. Tattoos of the goddess Rhiannon, ruler of the night, also scattered Daphne's arms and legs. She was even more obsessed than Elodae was, and that was saying something.

Elodae wandered over to a row of shelves that held books with maps of the night skies. If she walked to the very end of this row, the earliest scroll would be dated back ten thousand years.

As Elodae scanned spine after spine, her fingers skimmed a small stamp at the bottom of each book—a tiny shield with a sword on the front, cutting through a crescent moon. Lunala's seal.

The moon-shaped island was home to all the records and origins of not just the stars in their sky, but the universe they belonged to. Its people were very protective of their knowledge.

What she would give to read some of those books. To learn about the vast universe that surrounded them. Maybe the stars held some answers about her past. How they would, she didn't know, but she could hope.

Since Samarok was the northernmost kingdom in Eldonia, they were the ones employed to research the stars. The winters were long, and the very top of their kingdom didn't see sunlight for two full months around the winter solstice. Elodae sometimes snuck off into the Tyrian Peaks to get away from the lights of Cronanth and see the stars come to life during those dark months.

Lost in her thoughts, she didn't hear someone approaching until a man's voice purred, "Well, well, well."

Elodae turned and looked up at Castor, who stood with his arms crossed, his cream-white sweater pulled tight over the muscles in his arms. He smiled down at her, leaning against the shelf across the aisle. His light-brown skin had already begun to deepen in the early spring sun. He pushed the curls of his dark red hair out of his face and fixed his glasses. His light-brown eyes crinkled with his grin.

"Hello, Castor," Elodae said back, not able to fully keep her lips from turning up at the ends. He had one of those smiles that were contagious. It made it hard to dislike him.

"Fancy seeing you here," he teased, picking up a stack of books he'd set down on the workbench that sat halfway up every row of shelves. "Thought you'd be at the castle getting all prettied up for the prince."

Elodae scoffed. "Right. Like I need to get *prettied up*."

He raised an eyebrow at her.

"Shouldn't you be teaching a class, Castor?"

"I've got about ten minutes. Came to collect the books I'll be needing and saw my father leading a certain white-haired beauty into the library."

Elodae felt her cheeks flush. "You're a shameless flirt."

"Only for beautiful women."

"Your students are waiting," she remarked, pushing past him to continue reading the spines of the books.

Elodae found a title she had yet to read and stood on her toes, reaching for it. Even at the height she was, her fingertips barely brushed against the bottom of the spine.

Castor laughed, the sound soft and deep. He set his books back down on the work shelf and stepped close to her. He smelled of parchment as he reached up to grab the book. She looked away from him as he handed her the tome with a half-smile.

Elodae offered him a faint one in return. "Thank you."

Castor dipped his head and picked up his large stack of books before following her out of the shelved hallway. He tapped a knuckle on the cover of her book to get her attention, and she blinked up at him.

"One of these days, I hope you'll reconsider my offer and teach a class with me."

"You know I'm not allowed."

He set his stack of books down on the table and leaned his arms on them so his eyes were level with hers. "Well, as the Heir Astronomer, *I* say what is allowed and what isn't."

He winked and picked up his books again, then walked away without another word.

Elodae's heart fluttered in her chest as she watched Castor leave the library and head back down the hallway she and Byron had entered through. He was headed to one of the smaller libraries where classes were held.

The classes were small, four or five students in each, but the idea of teaching someone astronomy had Elodae's stomach doing flips. She would never do the universe justice if she tried to teach it.

Byron spoke of the universe in a way that captivated people. The love and fascination that radiated from him as he spoke about the birth of stars entranced her. The way light carried on throughout the universe even after its source had died. How their world was gliding through the vastness, racing through the void on a never-ending journey.

It hurt her head to think about it sometimes. How vast the universe was. She'd never even left the rolling hills of Samarok.

Elodae flipped open her book, and as she began to read, her mind went quiet—blissfully quiet. The only thought within was of faraway galaxies.

There Elodae sat, head amongst the stars, until the sun

went down, and Daphne opened the slit in the dome. Until the rest of the students had long since left, and the full moon's light beamed down onto the tables below.

IRELIA'S LADY'S MAID BID HER A GOODNIGHT AND closed the door with a click.

"Are they gone?" a voice whispered from behind the pink settee nearby.

"Yes," the princess said with a smile. Her cheeks instantly reddened as Lady Astrid, a beautiful, fair-skinned woman with straight black hair that hung just below her breasts, stood and walked around the settee. The dark blue dress she wore hugged her curvy figure perfectly. Her sapphire blue eyes darkened as she looked over Irelia, taking her in. Irelia shifted on her feet and toyed with her skirts as the lady neared.

"You're so beautiful," Astrid breathed, stopping a hand's breadth away.

One deep breath from Irelia would have her breasts brushing against Astrid's. The lady ran her fingers up and down her arms, leaving chills in their wake. Irelia tilted her head back, closing her eyes, and Astrid brushed her lips softly against the column of her neck.

Irelia breathed a moan, tangling her fingers in Astrid's midnight hair. The lady pushed her back against the wall by the doorway to her bedroom, sucking and biting on her neck. Irelia fisted Astrid's hair, holding her close to her body.

Their meetings were always like this. Hot and wild. Fast and claiming. They couldn't risk getting caught.

Astrid kissed along her jaw as she began bunching up the skirts of Irelia's dress. She claimed her mouth again, silencing Irelia's moan when she began to move her middle finger against where she was the most sensitive in slow, taunting circles. Irelia bit her lip and leaned her head back against the wall. Astrid always knew exactly what to do.

"Do you like that?" Astrid breathed against Irelia's lips.

Irelia nodded, focusing on not making any noise lest the guards in the hall might hear. They didn't think twice when the lady came and went from her room at the odd hours of the night. They assumed they were simply friends enjoying each other's company.

Well, they were right about one thing at least. Irelia *definitely* enjoyed Astrid's company.

Astrid dragged her finger through Irelia's center and moaned, "Gods, I want you."

Irelia tugged Astrid's lips against hers, kissing her hungrily. "Then take me."

A wicked grin spread across Astrid's face at that. She dropped Irelia's skirt and then grabbed her wrists, pulling her into the bedroom. Astrid stopped by the side of the bed, tugging the princess in for another kiss before shoving her shoulders, sending her flopping back onto the mattress.

Irelia giggled and propped herself up on her elbows in time to see Astrid pull off one of her shoes. Irelia's skin burned where the lady touched her. She couldn't help but squirm when Astrid took off the other one painfully slowly and whined, "Astrid."

Astrid batted her eyes and asked innocently, "What?"

Irelia glared at her, but she knew it had little to no effect. "You said you wanted me. So fucking take me."

"Such filthy words, Your Highness," Astrid purred. She lowered herself to her knees on the floor by Irelia's bed and pushed up her skirts.

Irelia lay back as Astrid kissed her way up Irelia's leg, starting at her ankles and traveling to the bones that stuck out at her hips.

"Take this off," Astrid ordered, tugging at the neckline of Irelia's dress.

Irelia quickly pulled the dress up and over her body. She kept the slip on, though, until asked otherwise. Her heart pounded as Astrid moved over her.

The lady ran her thumb over Irelia's bottom lip. "Good girl."

And then she kissed her.

The next three hours went by in a tangled blur of passion and lust. Astrid finally slipped out of Irelia's room with a kiss long after the sun had gone to rest, leaving her strewn across the bed, breathless and sleepy.

Being with Astrid was freeing. It was an escape. A way for both to get away from their day-to-day lives and find some sort of release. No love stretched between the two of them, only lust. It was fun, though, and it brought her a sense of rightness. Irelia didn't have to hide the deepest part of who she was when she was with the lady.

Samarok claimed to be a tolerant place but being with someone of the same sex—that was where Samarok fell short. Irelia had once been to a tavern years ago and seen two men get beaten within an inch of their lives because of who they'd loved. As though it were something they could control.

Ever since then, Irelia had kept her desires locked deep within. That was until a drunken night two years ago. Irelia, having no one to turn to, had found comfort in the bottom of a bottle, only to discover that Astrid had been seeking a similar distraction. The girls had laughed and cried as they talked. And then they had tumbled on a bag of flour, coating themselves in the white powder. They still joked about that night, and to this day, they had no idea how they hadn't gotten caught. Irelia had been *extremely* loud that first time.

As the princess lay there, staring at her ceiling, a sound came from outside her bedroom door. Her heart jumped in her chest as she sat up straight, pulling her sheets around her still-naked body. Straining her ears for any hint of noise, she found herself hoping it was Elodae returning from wherever she had snuck off to and wanting to fill Irelia in on her adventures.

But when the hall outside remained silent, a pit in Irelia's heart cracked open. Elodae wouldn't come, and the only other person who would had already left. She blinked rapidly, trying to push away the tears that suddenly sprung to her eyes.

Irelia looked around her room. She was alone.

Completely and utterly alone.

CHAPTER SIX

Not quite ready to go home for the night, Elodae meandered through the empty streets.

She'd bid Castor, Byron, and Daphne a farewell after they had practically force-fed her a late dinner, insisting she needed to eat before making the trek back to the castle.

The moment she stepped out of the Astronomers, the thoughts she had shoved away came rushing back. Irelia and pine and sky eyes and princes and Alden. That last one became increasingly difficult to ignore. Nothing could be done do to change anything. She'd tried many times six years ago when he'd taken his father's position to make him open to her, but nothing she did or said had made any difference.

Elodae shook her head and folded her cloak, the hood once again thrown over her head, tighter around her body. Her mask was already wrapped around the lower half of her face. She needed the silence back. She couldn't return to the castle and sit in her room alone only to fall asleep and dream of the horrors that haunted her.

Elodae decided she needed a large glass of wine and made her way to her favorite tavern.

Turning down an empty street, Elodae paused and looked around. Something felt . . . off. A denseness fell over her, snuffing out any sound as she strained her ears. Nothing seemed awry. Tingles shot down her spine the way they did when she knew someone was staring at her. Their gaze scorched her skin, but no one was around. Not a single sound echoed around her.

Something brushed against Elodae's leg, and she shrieked, the sound muffled by her mask. A black cat scurried away, and she breathed a laugh and put a hand to her heaving chest.

Deep inside her, something cracked open an eye and tugged her along, ready to fight any invisible threat.

She forced her feet to move again.

Elodae spotted the tavern up ahead and picked up her pace, practically running toward the faded wooden door. She shoved inside and nearly moaned as the warmth seeped into her skin. Heart still racing, she made sure her hood and mask were still in place and scanned the room, looking for a certain someone in the crowd. The person who had broken her so thoroughly in the past.

Her ears started to ring as her eyes bounced around the room. Nausea fell in her stomach like a stone as the weight of someone's stare grew heavier on her skin. He was nowhere to be seen.

Spying an open seat at the end of the L-shaped bar,

Elodae made her way over and sat on the stool in the corner next to two men. She didn't dare take her hood or mask off in a place like this.

"Drink?" the barkeep asked.

"Mulled wine, please," Elodae said, looking up at him. She had to practically yell over the noise of the games and chatter that echoed around the cramped space.

The man beside her laughed and took a sip from his own ale, accidentally hitting his elbow against her. She glared sidelong at him but kept her mouth shut. This was not the kind of place she wanted to get into a fight.

The barkeep came back with her wine and Elodae handed him a copper coin. The noise in the tiny tavern was ear-shattering, but that was exactly what she needed. Elodae took a deep swig of her drink and let the mind-numbing sounds bounce around her head, shoving her thoughts far down.

She had drunk half of her mug, pulling down her mask every time she wanted to take a slug and then putting it back up over her face and nose when the man next to her elbowed her again.

"Watch it!" she yelled. Her wine sloshed over the sides of her mug and spilled onto her lap.

The man held up his hands. "Apologies, love."

Elodae opened her mouth to bite something else out at him when she stilled. Her hand held the cloth the barkeep had just given her in midair. She blinked at the man next to her. She could only see the bottom half of his face, but a scar ran through the right side of his lip.

Gritting her teeth, Elodae realized it was the same arrogant bastard that had run into her in the streets earlier.

His friend, whose hood was also still up, shook his head and drained his glass to the dregs. He then slid the empty cup toward the barkeep with gloved hands and grabbed the scarred man's glass, taking a deep sip from it as well.

The scarred man flashed Elodae the same crooked smile he had in the streets. "I remember you," he said over the roar of some game in the corner.

"Well, aren't you lucky," she said in a sarcastic voice.

He nodded at her. "The cloak. The mask. They're far too fine to be anyone else's."

"Leave her alone, Ri," his friend grunted.

Elodae looked over Ri's shoulder at his friend. His cloak didn't quite sit right on his back. Two strange lumps sat between his shoulders. A concealed sword, maybe.

Definitely do not pick a fight with them.

Dragging her gaze back to Ri, she said, "Rye, is it? Like the bread?" and slapped the wet cloth down onto the bar in front of them.

Ri's smile broadened. "Ri. Like Orion."

His friend went unnaturally still behind him.

"Hmm," Elodae hummed, thanking the gods her voice was smooth and bored. Something about the two of them scared her. But at the same time, she had trouble turning away.

"And what do they call you, love?" Orion asked, grabbing his glass back from his friend without so much as a glance in his direction. The man shouted his protest.

"Uninterested," Elodae purred and turned back to her own drink.

Orion's friend coughed into the new ale the barkeep slid to him, his shoulders shaking with laughter. Elodae smirked behind her mask and tucked her head down. She pulled her mask away slightly and took a sip of wine.

Orion watched her for a moment longer before he turned back to his friend, who was still laughing. Elodae could've sworn Orion growled something and tried to shove his friend out of his chair, but she didn't dare look over. The two men laughed and talked amongst themselves, leaving her alone.

Elodae couldn't pinpoint their accent. It was rich and deep and rolled off their tongues in a way that had her heart skipping beats in her chest. Without seeing their faces, though, she couldn't determine any distinguishable features to gauge where they were from. She could ask, she supposed. The scar on Orion's lip kept flashing through her mind.

She hadn't realized she'd turned back toward them and was staring until Orion looked over toward her and drawled, "May I help you?"

"Are you a part of the king's army?" She didn't know why the question had bubbled up. Or why she'd let it escape. Something about Orion drew her in. Something about him made her need to know.

Both Orion and his friend went unnaturally still again. Her heart jumped into her throat.

"You're very bold, aren't you?" Orion asked slowly.

"You didn't answer my question."

"You haven't answered any of mine."

Elodae ground her teeth. *Fine.* "My name is Auriel," she lied.

"Like the late queen?" Orion asked, pulling her from her thoughts.

"The very one."

His crooked smile appeared once more and then he

turned back to his friend, dismissing her completely. They didn't look her way again for the rest of the night.

Elodae drank her wine in silence, turning her head toward the wall whenever she pulled her mask down to take a sip. If they were foreigners, they would have no idea who she was. Unless they'd been to court before, but she would have recognized them if they had. It'd be hard not to.

Orion and his companion finished their ales and left a small pile of silvers on the bar as they got up to leave.

"See you soon then, Auriel," Orion called over his shoulder.

His friend once more grabbed the back of his cloak and dragged him out of the tavern.

Elodae looked after them for a second. Then she turned back to her glass of wine and finished it. She left several more coppers on the bar for the tip and looked over at Orion's pile of silvers. That was far more than necessary for three ales.

She left the tavern and stepped into the cold night air, shivering against the brisk breeze that blew by. She made her way back toward the castle, not nearly having had enough wine to quiet her mind tonight. But that odd encounter with Orion had left her reeling.

As she turned down the street that held the alley back to the castle, that same dense air from before washed over her. With each step she took, the weight of the air grew thicker and thicker. The stars dimmed. The black of the sky darkened.

She slowed her pace, controlling her breath so it didn't make a sound. Chills snaked down her spine again. She whirled around, but no one stood behind her.

The oil lamps that lined the street flickered. All of them

did. The shadows seemed to grow darker. She had to be imagining things. She'd blame the wine, but it had been like this before she'd entered the tavern.

A meow shattered through the dead street and Elodae nearly jumped out of her skin as that same damn cat wound its way through her legs. She ground her teeth and glared down at it. "You're lucky you're cute."

It just blinked its big grey eyes up at her and then trotted away.

Shaking her head, Elodae turned down the obscure alley where the door she had come out of earlier sat.

A stone skittered across the alley behind her. She whipped around again and pulled out the dagger she kept attached to her thigh. Ever since she'd asked Alden to train her, he had insisted on her always carrying a weapon. Even in the castle. She'd never had to use it before. Never had she even harmed someone, let alone kill them.

She'd only ever been close to needing to end someone once. But back then, she'd had no weapon to defend herself —to protect herself.

Forcing Alden's lessons on defense into her mind, she slowly backed herself against the wall. The night grew darker still, blinding her almost completely. The shadows seeming to curl themselves around her ankles as the cat had done.

"Strike first. Do not wait for them to get close. You aim to kill, not simply get them down." Alden had said to her in those early days.

"Aim here." He'd taken her wrist, wooden dagger in her hand, and guided her toward his throat, then his heart. The soft spots between the ribs, the eyes, the temples. Showed her where the major arteries were. How to cut someone in such a

way that they would bleed out and the gash wouldn't clot. *"Never let them get their arms around you. Always know what's behind you. Keeping yourself against a solid wall will help at first but could be a problem if there is more than one attacker."*

She'd nodded along, reciting the information over and over and over until it was ingrained in her mind.

*"And never—*never—*let them take you to a different place."* His face had grown lethal. *"Because if they do, your body will be the only thing we recover."*

Elodae tightened her grip on the dagger's hilt, her hand shaking. Could she take another's life? She prayed to Nath that she wouldn't need to, but if it came down to it—she also prayed that she'd be able to.

She stayed like that for a while, back against the wall, begging her eyes to see through the shadows. No other sound came. No scuffs against the stone. Nothing. Not even the cat.

Until suddenly, the cold edge of a blade pressed against her throat.

Elodae sucked in a sharp gasp, blinking, trying to pierce her vision through the shrouded dark. She hastily reached for the dagger strapped to her thigh, but it wasn't in its sheath.

She couldn't see her assailant, couldn't feel them around her. Not even as the blade pressed harder against the soft skin of her neck. Warmth trickled down into the collar of her tunic. They mumbled something under their breath, words she couldn't decipher as she stood motionless, her back to the wall.

Don't freeze. Fight back!

Shoving backwards, she hit the stone wall and turned her head to the side, dropping into a squat. She kicked her leg out, swiping around her in a wide circle, hoping to catch her attacker off guard in the darkness.

Whoever it was landed with a satisfying *oomph* followed by the clattering of metal against stone. She could barely make out the glimmer of the blade in the thick night air, but she made a beeline for it. Managing to grab the hilt, she spun around, scanning the alley for the person who'd attacked her.

Were they responsible for the disappearances of her people?

She would not be one of them.

Elodae had not fought back once, and it had cost her everything. She would never be weak or helpless again.

Gripping the blade tightly in her hand, she heard the scuffs of boots as the person got to their feet, stumbling around the alleyway. They tried to say something, but their words were muffled.

"He needs more," they said louder this time.

Elodae stumbled back a step, hoisting her weapon higher. "*He needs more.*"

She didn't give them the chance to explain before she turned and sprinted out of the alley. Elodae raced and raced for the towering castle gates. She'd explain it later, but for now, she just needed to be safely within the walls of Castle Cronanth.

The guards gave her strange looks as she frantically yanked her hood and mask away from her face, revealing who she was. They immediately let her in, eyeing the small trail of blood winding its way down her neck. The cut was small and would heal over within the hour, but still Elodae ran.

She ran up the sloping lawns, through the towering front doors, past guards and lords and ladies still wandering about the castle. She ran past her own rooms, through the winding halls of the castle until she reached comforting, familiar wooden doors.

Elodae did not stop to knock, or to allow Finn the chance to announce her or open the door, she pushed past him and the other guards, straight into the princess' room.

Irelia was curled up on her bed, her shoulders rising gently with sleep. Elodae's heart immediately slowed at the sight of her sister. A shudder rocked through her body, tears threatening to overflow as the events of the night soaked in. Not wanting to wake her sister just yet, she quietly made her way into her adjoined bathing room to clean herself up.

The cut had already clotted with the beginnings of a scab. Elodae couldn't meet her own eyes in the mirror. So stupid. She had been so stupid to wander outside alone, to stay out as late as she did.

He needs more. The man from the alley's words raked her mind.

Fingers trembling beneath the stream of water, Elodae made quick work washing her hands and face. She flung off her cloak and yanked off her boots, leaving them in a pile on the floor of her sister's bathroom.

Gently, oh so gently, Elodae made her way over to the sleeping princess and climbed into bed. Irelia's sea-green eyes cracked open, a tired hum on her lips.

"I'm sorry I woke you," Elodae breathed. "Is it all right if I stay here tonight?"

Irelia merely nodded, her eyes drooping once more, and reached out a hand.

Elodae shuddered, tears blurring her vision as the comforting warmth from her sister seeped into her skin, her delicate hands clasped safely in hers.

CHAPTER SEVEN

"Explain it to me . . . one more time."

King Vanor paced around his War Room. Elodae and Irelia sat across from him at the round table, Alden and Finn at their backs. On his knees in a bow, Warren hung his head in shame.

"Sire, it was my—" Warren began.

Elodae cut him off. "No, Uncle. It was my fault and I take full responsibility for being outside the castle walls alone last night. Do not blame Warren."

"How could you let this happen?" Vanor asked Warren in a lethally quiet voice despite her protests.

"I have no excuse, Your Majesty."

Elodae made to speak again, but Irelia simply laid a hand atop hers. Silencing her with a single movement.

The sisters had woken that morning, and it took one look at Elodae for Irelia to notice the pink cut on her neck and the disheveled look of her clothes to know something had gone horribly wrong. Elodae had tried to calm her sister down, to explain that she was unharmed and to not mention it to their father. But once she had explained, it had become abundantly clear that Vanor needed to know.

There was someone on the loose in Cronanth, possibly multiple someone's, responsible for the disappearances of their people—and they had almost gotten Elodae.

"How did you even get out of the castle?" Her father turned on her.

Fighting the urge to shrink in on herself, Elodae forcefully met the king's gaze. His sea-green eyes bore into hers. So many questions swirled behind his stoney face; worry and fear and anger.

Elodae steeled her spine as she said, "There is an abandoned attendants' passageway."

Releasing a sigh, Vanor pinched the bridge of his nose. "Dalo, Mac, go find this passage near the Duchess' rooms and have it sealed imminently."

Her heart sank in her chest.

Dalo and Mac bowed low at the waist before they disappeared through the towering oak doors on the far side of the room.

Once the doors had swung shut behind them, the sound reverberating through the cavernous space, Vanor laid his hands on the table, his greying-blond hair falling around his face.

"Elodae." His voice was soft, but the disappointment in it shot across the table with malice, striking her soul.

"Uncle, I—"

"Alden," the king ordered, and the head of her personal

guard stepped forward, his arms tucked behind his back. He hadn't met her gaze this entire meeting. "As the Head of her Personal Guard, I trusted you to be responsible for all of her guards, including your brother."

Warren flinched at the king's words.

"Therefore, I am leaving it up to you to decide a rightful punishment for Warren Torvus' incredible lack of judgement." King Vanor stood up straight once more. The agony swimming in his eyes wasn't missed as he glanced down at the still kneeling Warren. "As for my niece . . ." And then those commanding eyes turned on her.

Elodae braced herself. Irelia's hand still rested atop of hers and the princess gave her a gentle squeeze.

I am here.

"You are not to go to the Astronomer's again until I say otherwise. You are not to exit the walls of this castle unattended. If you are caught doing such . . ." Another bat of agony flashed across his face. "You will be banned from the Astronomer's for life."

It was a miracle the shattering of her heart didn't break every window in this room—in this castle. The Astronomer's was the one place she could escape to, the one place that was *hers* and no one else. Where court and her past did not follow her. No one understood that better than her father. And for him to take that away from her . . .

Numb. That was all she felt. Completely and utterly numb.

"Yes, Your Majesty," was all she managed.

"Irelia," their father said, turning on her next. "The same goes for you with the Magicks."

Irelia's hand tightened on Elodae's. "Yes, Father."

Vanor looked at his guards and the other nobles around the room. "You all are dismissed." Irelia made to stand but the king held up a hand. "All but the five of you," he said with a pointed look at his daughters, their head guards, and Warren. Who, still, was kneeling on the ground.

Frozen to her seat, Elodae could not have moved even if she wanted.

Once they were alone, Vanor heaved a great sigh and fell to his seat, head in his hand.

"I understand that I did not make clear how very serious these disappearances are. For that I take accountability." He lifted his head, meeting all five of their gazes. "But hopefully these punishments will make it abundantly clear from henceforth."

Finn and Alden bowed, acknowledging their king. Warren lowered his head once more and Irelia dipped her chin in understanding. Elodae's eyes were glued to a spot on the map that was forever sprawled across the center of the large round table. Over the tiny dot in Cronanth that was the Astronomer's.

"Elodae." Vanor's voice was gentler this time. She slowly lifted her eyes to his. "I need you to understand how serious this is. You could have died; you could have been taken by whoever attacked you. We could've lost you . . ."

Alden shuffled on his feet at her side and Warren's swallow was audible in the eerily silent room.

The king held her gaze strongly. He was her father in every way that mattered, but he was still the ruler of this kingdom, the ruler of *her*. He expected to be obeyed—and obeyed he shall be.

So, Elodae dipped her head in a nod.

Satisfied, Vanor turned and called toward the closed door, "Radford." It immediately opened and the Captain of the Guard stepped into the War Room.

Radford was a short, burly dark-skinned man whose one good eye instantly met Elodae's gaze. The eyepatch covering his other one was a beautiful glacial blue—Samarok's color.

"Gather whatever guards can be spared," Vanor ordered. "We cannot have someone like this running around Cronanth a moment longer. Especially with the Dolannish Prince arriving in such short time."

Radford bowed low. "Consider it done, my king."

CHAPTER EIGHT

Flowers bloomed along trees and vines, the last of the winter's chill melting away as the sun warmed the earth. Birds began their joyous song, cheering with their loved ones as they return home.

Elodae embraced the spring, but she couldn't deny that she missed the comfort the autumn and winter months brought. Where the moon and stars would shine brighter, the air crisper, the nights longer. The sun lingered too long for her liking in the spring and summer, setting later and later, prolonging her nightly stargazing.

On that particular sunset, Elodae tried to help Irelia pick out the dress she would greet Prince Fornax in. The prince was due to arrive in just a handful of days, and her sister had begun to panic.

Lounging on her sister's bed, Elodae rolled her left shoulder as she finished a chapter in her latest novel. Her training session with Alden that morning had been brutal. He had knocked her on her ass four times before she even got a single blow through his defenses. Her shoulder still ached from the last fall she'd taken.

Irelia emerged from behind the screen and Elodae sat up, gaping at her sister.

Irelia had left her peach-blonde hair down in soft ringlets that brushed her hips. Two golden suns pinned the sides of her hair back in graceful swoops. Her gold gown was immaculate. The neckline cut down to just below her sternum and the sheer straps hung loosely off her freckled shoulders. The bodice was fitted enough that it accentuated her waist and the skirts fell in a puddle at her feet. The outermost layer of the skirts sparkled in various shades of pinks and oranges as Irelia walked past the windows and over to the edge of the bed where Elodae sat gawking.

She looked like the most exquisite sunrise. The sun would be jealous of her sister's beauty.

"Well?" Irelia asked tentatively.

A slow smile spread across Elodae's face. "If that doesn't bring the prince to his knees, I don't know what will."

Irelia blushed bright red and walked over to her full-sized mirror. She smiled at her reflection, spinning this way and that to see all the dress. Her smile became more genuine as she continued to study her reflection. "Oh, yes. This is the one."

Elodae gave her an approving nod and picked up her book, stomach rumbling. "Please tell me we can have dinner now."

Irelia rolled her eyes, even though she was still smiling. "Yes, E. We can have dinner now."

"Fantastic." Elodae jumped from the bed, tossing her book down in the process, and hurried to the front door of her sister's rooms. The simple black dress she wore swayed around her feet as she yanked open the door, mouth open to ask one of the guards to call for dinner. She froze at the sight she was met with.

Alden stood in regular clothes; a hand raised as though he were just about to knock on the door. He lowered his hand and swallowed.

Elodae realized she had been staring when he shifted on his feet, waiting for her to say something. She dragged her eyes from him and looked over his shoulder at one of the guards there. She said as sweetly as she could, "Could you please call for dinner?"

She may have batted her eyelashes a little and delight shot through her when Alden went stiff in front of her. The guard she'd asked bowed his head, blushing slightly, and made his way down the hallway. Only then did Elodae turn back toward Alden.

She slapped on an innocent smile. "Hello, Alden."

"Elodae," Alden said softly and bowed his head. The way he said her name sent a thrill through her, but his eyes were trained on the guard that had gone to retrieve the girl's dinner. A muscle ticked in his jaw.

Elodae hated how much she loved his jealousy. Hated that he even dared to feel such things.

Irelia appeared beside her. "Alden. What are you doing here? Shouldn't you be out with—" She cut herself off when Alden's eyes snapped to hers and flared.

It was Elodae's turn to stiffen. She somehow kept her smile in place as she turned to her sister. "Out with whom?"

Irelia looked between Alden and Elodae too quickly to be casual and then shook her head, laughing nervously. "I'm mistaken. Apologies." The princess turned on her heels and rushed back into her room. Elodae narrowed her eyes at her sister.

"I came by to give these to Irelia."

Elodae faced Alden again and looked down at three small glass vials he held out. She held out her hand for them and he set them gently in her palm. She could've sworn he purposefully brushed his fingers against hers as he pulled his hand back.

Lightning ricocheted through her body.

"She forgot them at the Magicks when we went a few weeks ago, and one of the sages just dropped them off. They've been tested and are good for her to use."

"And you're delivering them on your night off. Why?" Elodae couldn't keep the accusation out of her question.

"I ran into them on my way out and I figured I'd have them tested and then bring them up before I met—" He cut off his sentence and cleared his throat, shifting on his feet again.

Elodae clenched her fist around the vials, careful not to break them, and asked as plainly as she could, "Who are you meeting, Alden?"

His throat bobbed before he finally said, "Astrid."

"Astrid?" Elodae blinked.

"Astrid Marlow."

"I know who she is."

Alden cleared his throat again. "Right. Well, I have to leave, or I'll be late." He leaned forward to peer into the room behind Elodae and called, "Goodbye, Irelia."

His oak and spice scent wrapped around Elodae. She watched as a strand of hair fell forward over his shoulder at the movement.

"Goodbye, Alden," Irelia called from somewhere in her rooms.

Elodae schooled her features in enough time that when Alden righted himself, she had a pleasant smile in place. "Well, you have a nice night, Einar."

Alden winced at the use of his surname but heeded the dismissal. He bowed his head and turned to walk away. Elodae watched him for a moment, and just as she was about to close the door, the guard from earlier turned the corner at the end of the hall, tray in hand.

She probably imagined it, but Elodae could've sworn Alden stiffened and looked a little too long at the guard when they passed each other.

Of course you're imagining it, a snarky voice said in the back of her mind.

The guard approached and handed Elodae the food tray. She smiled and thanked him before turning to kick the door shut behind her.

Stomping her way out onto the terrace where Irelia was setting the table, she slammed the tray down. Irelia jumped and whirled around.

Elodae passed Irelia the vials and then went back inside her sister's rooms, heading straight for the bathroom. She turned on the faucet of the sink and rested her hands on either side of the basin. Leaning on the edge, she watched the water flow for a minute before she finally ran a hand under the stream. The chill of the water felt good as she wiped it across her forehead. She repeated that several times; rubbing it along the back of her neck, her chest, trying to cool down.

She shut off the water and studied herself for a moment; the way her white plait draped over her shoulder. The soft neckline of the black dress she wore. The long sleeves hooked around her middle finger to hold them in place. The slight splatter of freckles across her nose and cheeks from her time spent outside as the days grew warmer and longer.

Astrid Marlow.

Lady Astrid Marlow.

Elodae shook her head and ground her teeth. Astrid was beautiful, to say the least. Apart from Irelia, she was the most stunning woman Elodae had ever seen. Of course, Alden would be taken by her. Nearly every man at court was.

And of course she would be taken by him, said that annoying voice in the back of her mind.

Astrid was perfect in every way Elodae could never be. She grinned when Elodae glared. Astrid pulled people in effortlessly. Yet, one look from Elodae sent whoever had approached sprinting in the opposite direction.

The thought of Astrid sitting across a dark-lit table from Alden made Elodae's stomach turn.

Astrid was a candle flame—and Elodae was a wildfire.

She breathed a sigh and pushed away from the counter. Thinking about Astrid and Alden spending the evening together helped no one and nothing. So Elodae made herself walk back out onto Irelia's terrace.

Her sister sat in the middle of the far side of the table closest to the railing and the sea beyond. Elodae sat diagonally across from her and piled food onto a plate. The sisters ate in silence for a while, watching the sun slowly drift beneath the Tyrian Peaks to the west.

Irelia studied the vegetables she pushed around on her plate while she said, "So . . ."

Elodae clenched her fork tighter, staring down at the food she had barely touched, but kept her face neutral. "I don't want to talk about whatever it is you're about to say."

Irelia set her fork down and grabbed a strand of hair in her hands. She twirled it for a second before she shut her eyes and sighed. Her sister reached a hand across the table, laying it on top of Elodae's. "I see the way you look at him sometimes." Elodae glared at her, but she pushed on, "Would it be so bad to let him in?"

"I have let him in."

"Have you?" Irelia asked sternly, pulling her hand back. "Have you let any of us in? Truly?"

Elodae blinked. Irelia had never spoken to her so harshly before. So bluntly. Elodae was always the one who said whatever was on her mind, nice or not, but Irelia—Irelia was the kind one. The soft to Elodae's sharp. The light to her darkness.

Heat flooded Elodae's cheeks, and she pulled her hand back. It became increasingly difficult to hold her sister's stare, but she weathered it. "Yes." The lie tasted bitter on her tongue. But she couldn't let someone in. Not again.

Irelia tilted her head, seeing right through the lie. As she always did. Irelia was too observant for her own good, and she didn't even realize it. The irony would've made her laugh.

"E."

"What?"

Irelia's gaze turned pleading, but when she saw Elodae

would not be budged, she shook her head. She stretched a hand across the table again, taking hold of Elodae's once more. "You're safe with me. You can talk to me about anything."

Breathing became near impossible. It felt like water was pouring into her mouth, her lungs, her nose. It felt like she was drowning again. "There's nothing to talk about," she said, a forced smile on her face.

Irelia watched her for a moment longer before standing to gather their plates. As she took them out into the hall, a wave crashed beyond the terrace ledge.

Elodae flinched, her eyes shooting toward the black waters just beyond the railing.

She'd survived. She was safe.

You're safe with me, her sister had said.

Elodae looked over her shoulder to where Irelia was smiling, chatting with a guard at her door. Would she ever be able to meet kindness with a true smile instead of teeth and claws?

Meandering through the winding halls of Castle Cronanth, Elodae stopped by a glassless window that overlooked the glimmering port city.

Boots scuffed against the floor next to her and she knew who it was without having to look over as they, too, leaned against the sill. Both stood there in silence for a while, watching the lights shimmer below. The

Astronomers and a paper-thin cut on her neck all that encased her thoughts.

"What's on your mind?" Warren asked, breaking the tranquility of the gentle night breeze.

Elodae took a deep breath, watching the carriages stroll down the streets; taking their owners to dinner, a show, a concert, or to see a lover. Carrying their own burdens as they tried to navigate this thing called life.

I don't know why I am the way I am, she almost said. *I don't even know* who *I truly am.* But Elodae didn't say that—she didn't say anything at all. She just shook her head and continued watching the people below.

Warren nudged her with his elbow. When she finally looked at him, he tilted his head. An unspoken question arose in his golden eyes.

Are you all right?

A weight she may never not know the crushing sensation of fell upon her shoulders. "I'm just tired," she said with a close-lipped smile.

Warren gave her a look that said he didn't believe her, but she didn't have an ounce of arguing or sarcastic quips left inside of her. So, she released a quiet breath and turned away before she asked, "Does it get easier?"

"Does what get easier?"

"Letting people in."

Warren was silent for a long while. Elodae thought he wouldn't reply, but then he murmured, "Yes and no."

"Very wise, Warren."

The right side of his mouth kicked up in a half smile. "I wasn't done, smartass."

Her own lips tugged up at the ends.

"No. It will not get easier."

Although she had been expecting the answer, that didn't stop the sinking of her heart.

"But what will get easier," he continued, "is overcoming that fear. It will never be easy to open yourself up to someone. You are not like others. You don't let everyone see every emotion you feel. You don't wear your heart on your sleeve—you keep it encased in iron."

It took all of her strength not to hang her heads at his words.

"I do, too." He nudged her again with his elbow.

She looked over at him, the boy who had become so much like a brother over the years and took his hand as the sad smile he wore struck her to her very core.; all traces of that sarcastic boy gone.

"But you will find some people are worth giving a key to."

"How do you even decide something like that?" she breathed, turning back to the lights of Cronanth.

"You don't."

Elodae glanced sidelong at him.

"You don't," he repeated, pointing to her forehead. Then he pointed at her heart. "But you do. You must take it out of its cage every once in a while."

Elodae pulled her hand back and reached up to hold her pendant. "I can't do that."

"Not yet, but someday . . . someday you will."

"How do you know?"

"Because you will find that a life without love is not worth living."

She turned to face him fully again, tilting her head to the side. "You say that as though you know the feeling."

"I do."

His confession struck her like a bolt of lightning.

Warren shrugged at her puzzled stare. "I'll give you a key if you give me one."

She considered it for a moment, taking in the man before her. The man that was her mirror in every way she hated. His claws were just as sharp as hers, but not sharper than their bite. Their words the greatest weapon they could ever wield. But perhaps that was why it was so easy for her to hold up her little finger and extend it toward him.

"Promise?"

Warren hooked his little finger with hers. "Promise."

THE STARS FOLLOWED ALDEN WHEREVER HE WENT. Whether it be the middle of the day, or the cloudiest of nights, the stars burned into his skin, marring him, through the pine-green eyes of the woman he was sworn to protect with his life.

Even now with his head down, he could feel their piercing stare scorching into the back of his neck as Alden trekked across Cronanth.

He was torn between lingering in the streets or rushing back to the castle so he could bang on the duchess' door until she agreed to talk with him. He hated lying to her; it ate away at something integral within him. But every time he was about to tell her the truth, about to lay his bloody and bare heart at her feet, he swallowed down his words.

How could he tell her what he felt for her? How could he explain how, even now, his father's voice echoed throughout his head every time he did anything?

He was her guard. And guards did not marry duchess'.

Alden shook his head, running fingers through his hair. He'd seen that look in Elodae's eye when she'd put two and two together earlier. She knew he had gone to spend an evening with Astrid. What it meant. And he hated that. That gleam in her beautiful green eyes. The walls that shot up behind them.

Closing his eyes with a sigh, Alden stopped to lean against a shop's door. Thankfully, the streets were blissfully quiet, leaving him alone with his circling thoughts.

"All right there, lad?"

Alden's heart leapt into his throat, and he whipped his head in the man's direction. His hand instantly went to the dagger at his hip, but the man who'd spoke just propped himself against the door of the next shop over. His hood was up, and Alden could barely make out the bottom half of his face.

"I'm fine," Alden said and leaned back against his own door, his hand still hovering over his blade.

"Fine is a large step from all right," the man said, a rich accent rolling off his tongue.

Alden glanced sidelong at the hooded figure and narrowed his eyes slightly.

The two of them stood there in silence for a while before the hooded man spoke again. "Girl trouble?"

Alden scoffed but didn't deign a response.

"Boy trouble?" the man added at Alden's silence.

"The first one."

The stranger nodded his head. "Does she know?"

"Know what?"

"What you feel for her."

Alden started, but the man's right side of his mouth tilted up in a half-smirk. He titled his head in a way that said he knew better than to believe whatever lie had been about to come out of Alden's mouth.

As the streetlamps illuminated the bottom half of his face, Alden noticed the scar that ran through his lips.

"No," Alden finally replied, shaking his head, and pulled his eyes away from the man's scar. "No, she doesn't."

"Well. That's probably why there's trouble, lad."

Alden snorted. "I reckon you're right."

The hooded man shrugged. "I usually am."

A reluctant smile spread across Alden's face, and he laid his head back against the door, gazing up at the stars. Easily, he found the one Elodae had taught him when they were younger. The Warrior. It was her favorite and sometimes he'd look up at the sky and wonder if she was looking at it too. It brought him a sense of comfort, knowing they were under the same sky, looking at the same stars.

A hand clasped onto his shoulder, startling him. Alden whipped his head down to see that the stranger had stepped around and was standing in front of him.

"Tell her," the stranger commanded. "Or someday you'll lose her, and you'll spend the rest of your life wishing you had just one more minute with her."

Alden tried to ignore the pit that cracked open at the bottom of his stomach. "You know the feeling well?"

The man remained silent for a while and then he removed his hand from Alden's shoulder before saying softly, sadly, "In a way."

And without another word, the man turned and headed down the street. Alden watched after him, but then the stranger paused and looked over his shoulder. "If you do somehow hold on to her . . . love her well."

Something swelled in Alden's chest as the man spun back around, shoving his hands into the pockets of his cloak, and vanished into the shadows. Alden watched him disappear and turned his gaze to the castle. To where a woman with hair white as the moon rested inside. He swallowed hard.

Love her well.

He ran a hand down his face and forced his feet to move again. As he started his trek back to the castle, his thoughts were full of a girl with moon-white hair and one with midnight black. One held his heart, while the other held his mind.

One a wild dream, one a promise.

Sighing, Alden pushed through the front gates of the castle, nodding to the guards on duty by the doors.

Heart or mind.

He wasn't sure which would win. Even more so—he wasn't sure which he *wanted* to win.

CHAPTER NINE

Prince Fornax Branton of Dolannish had just arrived in Cronanth.

Elodae watched from beside her sister, the gathered court members chatting merrily with one another as flutes of sparkling wine passed around.

Thousands of lush green garlands had been hung across the Grand Hall. The chandeliers that hung from the vaulted ceiling had been draped in vines with flowers of every color woven into them. The sills of the arched windows were filled with flowers upon flowers. The carpet that led from the double wooden doors to the dais had been swapped from Samarokan blue to the pale pink of a budding rose.

Various noblemen surrounded King Vanor and his guards, eager to bask in his presence. He'd always been admired by his people. Clad in Samarokan colors, glacial blue and snow white, the king greeted each nobleman and lady by name. The wrinkles in the corners of his sea-green eyes were on display as he beamed at everyone. He was filled with joy today—after all, his beloved daughter's engagement to the wealthiest kingdom in Eldonia would be officially announced soon.

Irelia, on the other hand, clutched her wine glass as though it were a lifeline. Her skin had gone pale, and her eyes were filled with anxiety, though Elodae caught Irelia peering down at the skirts of her immaculate golden dress and fondly running her fingers through the fabric.

The duchess herself was in a beautiful pine-green gown, the same color as her eyes. The dress had intricate silver stitching along the bodice and skirts in the shape of a forest. Trees and stags and various critters and plant life were strewn about on her skirts. Lillianna had curled her hair and pinned it in a half-up fashion. The sides, like Irelia's, had been swooped back from her face. But where Irelia's had golden suns, Elodae's was pinned back with silver leaves.

Elodae took a sip of her sparkling wine, a tight smile on her face, and watched her father weave his way around the Grand Hall to greet every last person. Radford, Finn, and Alden followed him closely. Elodae tried not to look too long at the latter guard. She hadn't seen him, apart from their training, since the night he'd dropped off Irelia's tonics to help with her nerves. The princess had guzzled them down before getting dressed this morning, praying to Silva to let them calm her racing heart.

She looked sidelong at her sister. Irelia had been her usual self the past few days. She'd smiled and laughed like nothing was wrong. And maybe nothing *was* wrong, but guilt took root in Elodae's stomach. Her hand itched to reach out. To offer Irelia a key, as Warren would say.

They had both been stripped of the one place that brought them a sense of comfort in their times of need. And it was entirely *her fault*.

Irelia turned and gave Elodae a closed-lipped smile. The princess then threw back the rest of her sparkling wine and grabbed another glass from a nearby attendant.

Elodae internally winced and stepped closer to her sister. If she couldn't bring herself to reach out with her words, then she would simply be there for her sister. In whatever way she could manage. Even if it was just standing by her side through this day. To let Irelia know that no matter where she stepped—if she fumbled or fell—that Elodae would catch her.

"I think I'm going to be sick," Irelia whimpered.

"You'll be all right," Elodae said, giving her sister a one-armed hug. She took Irelia's empty wine flute and set it on the tray of a passing attendant. "I'm here."

A moment later, a messenger came rushing in and whispered something in Radford's ear. The captain then walked over to Vanor to relay the message.

Their father turned and grinned at where the girls stood atop the dais. He made his way over, flanked by the three guards, one of whom Elodae did her best to avoid eye contact with.

Vanor laid a broad hand on each of his daughter's shoulders. "Prince Fornax's party is approaching." He looked between them both, his gaze settling on Irelia. "Are you ready to meet your fiancé?"

Irelia paled even further and blinked up at her father.

Elodae took her sister's hand in hers. "Lead the way, Uncle," she said to Vanor, making sure to use the title of *Uncle* in front of that many court-goers.

Vanor's smile softened as he looked at Elodae and gave her shoulder a gentle squeeze. He held out his other hand for Irelia and her sister released Elodae's to take it, looking nervously over at her. Elodae nodded reassuringly and followed her father and sister down the dais and across the Grand Hall. Alden, Finn, and Radford fell into step behind them.

Elodae followed behind Vanor and Irelia as they walked down the gravel path to the shining bluestone wall that encircled the castle's grounds. The intricate gate, made of the deepest blue sapphires, had been thrown open in anticipation of the Dolannish Prince's arrival.

Guards holding flags with the Samarokan seal, a sword with a stag's horns as the handle, lined the path from the castle doors to the gate. Excited murmurs sounded from the guests following behind Elodae and the others when the herald atop the bluestone wall sounded his trumpet.

Vanor and Irelia stopped a few yards from the gate to give the prince's carriage enough space to get inside. Elodae stood a step behind them—they were the king and princess, and she was the niece.

Vanor never made her feel or treated her as less than, but on days like today, where it was obvious that she did not truly belong here, with them, or as a part of their family, it made her uneasy in a way she didn't want to unpack. Not here. Not now.

A golden carriage came into view, the same gold as Irelia's dress, and the lawn grew quiet. Four magnificent white horses stopped the carriage just inside the sapphire gates. Alden, Finn, and Radford walked over to the carriage and greeted the Dolannish guards that had already stationed themselves outside the door. The driver, clad in Dolannish gold, hopped down from his seat and opened the carriage door.

Elodae heard, more than saw, Irelia's breath caught as the most handsome man she'd ever seen emerged from the Dolannish carriage.

IRELIA WENT STILL WHEN PRINCE FORNAX STEPPED out of the carriage.

The prince was in simple, yet exquisite clothing. His pants were a light brown with scrolls of gold stitched into the sides of each leg. His tunic the same gold as Irelia's dress—Dolannish gold—and had swirls across his chest and shoulders. The clothing made his brown skin appear almost golden. His dark copper hair even had streaks of gold that shimmered in the midday sun. Fornax's deep brown eyes, slightly upturned, held Irelia's the entire time he approached. A half smile spread across his face, displaying a dimple on his right cheek.

He stopped a step away and bowed low. Vanor bowed his head in return and when Fornax righted himself, his eyes met Irelia's again. She realized then that they were not dark brown, but more of a russet color, almost red in the sunlight.

Elodae cleared her throat softly behind her, and Irelia

blinked. She hadn't realized Fornax had held out his hand for hers. She hadn't even curtsied yet.

No, she was just staring at him like an idiot.

Irelia curtsied and paused a little too long at the bottom to control the blush she was certain showed on her face. When she straightened, she placed her hand in his outstretched palm. She could've sworn his eyes twinkled with amusement. He kept his deep red gaze locked on hers as he kissed her knuckles. Fornax towered over her, so he had to bow quite low to reach her hand with his lips. A smug part of her loved that.

"Princess," he whispered onto her fingers with that half-smile.

His voice was surprisingly gravelly, and Irelia couldn't help but find his thick Dolannish accent beautiful. The courtiers from Dolannish that came and went from court spoke as she did. What would she sound like to him? Would he find her accent beautiful?

Irelia mentally shook her head. What was she thinking? She couldn't find this man attractive, couldn't let a handsome face change her plans. She would not go through with this marriage. "Prince," she said with forced sweetness.

Fornax's smile grew, hinting at a dimple on the other side of his face. He didn't drop her stare, not even as he turned his head toward her father. Only when he was facing the king fully did he finally tear his eyes from hers, leaving Irelia breathless. "My father sends his condolences that he was not able to be present for the announcement."

Again, Irelia furrowed her brows at the roughness of Fornax's voice. He was so soft and *princely* that she'd have expected his voice to be light and musical.

"Not to worry, my boy," her father said, clapping Fornax on the shoulder.

Something flashed in the prince's russet eyes, but it was gone too quickly for Irelia to know for sure.

Vanor turned and held out an arm. The people gathered behind them hurriedly cleared the path, making room for them to return to the castle. The two men walked up the gravel path, leaving Irelia to fall into step next to Elodae.

Irelia heard the Captain of the Guard give Warren orders about leading Fornax's carriage and remaining men to their stations. Two of Fornax's guards were close behind Alden and Finn as they made their way back up the sloped front lawn.

As they passed rows and rows of guests, Irelia caught Lady Astrid's eyes. The woman had a gentle smile on her face, and her sapphire eyes heated when they met Irelia's. Irelia felt her cheeks flush and quickly averted her gaze. She couldn't be thinking of Astrid right now. Or what they'd done last night—and again, this morning.

If Fornax found out, would he still want to marry her?

Her stomach did a flip. That could be a sure way to end this engagement and save her from marrying him, but at what cost? Only Astrid knew she enjoyed the company of women. She'd never even told her sister.

Irelia felt Elodae's eyes on her then and turned to look at her. Elodae raised an eyebrow in question, but Irelia simply shook her head and looked forward again. Her sister shifted closer and brushed her fingers against Irelia's. She smiled softly at the touch and Elodae gave her a reassuring smile, easing some of the weight.

Irelia lifted her skirts in her hands as she climbed the

front steps behind her father and Fornax. The light shining from the Grand Hall made her nauseous.

Elodae brushed her fingers against Irelia's again, and somehow, Irelia felt more at peace with her sister right there beside her.

Elodae entered the Grand Hall after Vanor and Fornax. Irelia, wide-eyed and smiling beside her, kept toying with the skirts of her dress. She wanted to say something to comfort her sister, but it would do no good. Their father was about to announce Irelia and Fornax's engagement, and she hated that there was nothing she could do to stop it.

The four of them walked across the Hall and stepped up onto the dais. Vanor turned and waited for the guests to finish piling back into the room. When the room was full once more, their father lifted a hand toward where Fornax and Irelia stood. The crowd immediately went silent, and Irelia went still as death. Even as her soft smile remained perfectly in place.

"I am overjoyed to announce that my beloved daughter, Princess Irelia Hailwyn of Samarok, will marry Prince Fornax Branton of Dolannish." Their father's voice echoed throughout the cavernous room.

The crowd erupted into cheers. Some cried, some hugged each other, and some simply clapped. Elodae joined in with the latter, plastering a smile onto her face. It had been some time since the kingdoms had married outside of their own people. With the coup that had happened in Asiva two years ago, uniting Samarok and Dolannish was exactly what the people wanted. What they needed.

Peace.

Fornax stiffened slightly, and Elodae's eyes immediately shot to him. He turned to face Irelia and held out his hand, wearing a smile of his own. The perfect portrait of a male satisfied with his bride. Elodae's eyes narrowed slightly as Irelia took his hand and beamed at the crowd. The couple stepped forward, and the crowd grew louder.

Vanor took a glass of sparkling wine from an attendant and raised it into the air. Elodae took hers without taking her eyes off Fornax. Irelia and the prince took their own flutes of sparkling wine and lifted them. Everyone in the room followed suit.

"To our future." Vanor smiled.

"To our future," Elodae and the crowd parroted back.

As one, they all lifted their glasses to their mouths. Irelia and Fornax bowed their heads in thanks as they drank from their own.

Musicians began playing at that moment and before Elodae could take a step toward her sister, Fornax handed both of their flutes to an attendant and swept her into the crowd. Others paired off and the floor quickly became a sea of dancers.

Elodae didn't know whether to be curious or wary. She prayed for the former, but a familiar sensation settled over her. Off, and thick, like that night on her way to the tavern. She sent up a prayer to Eirene that nothing was awry—that her sister would be safe with the Dolannish Prince.

Only time will tell, Irelia would say.

But Elodae didn't intend to wait for time. She had a habit of getting in the middle of things she had no business being a part of.

She watched her sister and the prince dance for a moment before tilting back the rest of her wine and stepping off the dais into the crowd. Alden took a step forward as though he would follow her, but she simply handed him her empty glass and kept walking. She could've sworn a growl of frustration followed her as she wound through the twirling dancers.

Then she spotted her target: a young nobleman who had been in and out of court the past few years, making arrangements for his prince to have everything he needed when he arrived. She'd never learned his name, but that mattered little.

He had the same golden-brown skin as the prince, but instead of Fornax's deep red, his hair was silken black. His eyes, though . . . they were a vibrant yellow. Something off hung around the angles of his features. He was handsome and yet terrifying.

Those golden eyes locked with hers over the rim of his glass and Elodae made sure to slowly look him up and down as she sauntered toward him. Then she brushed her arm against his as she continued past.

"Pardon me," she said softly, forcing her cheeks to redden.

She made her way over to the tables piled with food and plucked up a chocolate-covered strawberry. She hummed quietly to herself along with the music as she moved from tray to tray, pretending to admire the feast before her.

"Your Grace," came a thickly accented voice to her left.

Taking a bite of her strawberry, she batted her eyelashes and looked over her shoulder. She found the nobleman standing there, smiling down at her. His eyes darted to her lips as she finished her bite of the strawberry.

She put a hand over her mouth while she finished chewing and discarded the top of the strawberry. A nervous giggle escaped her lips. "Apologies, Lord . . .?"

"Hadeon," he said, taking her hand in his and bowing to kiss the top of it.

Everyone knew she wasn't the king's true daughter. That meant she was reachable. Obtainable. Men knew they would never stand a chance at gaining Irelia's attention, but Elodae . . . With Elodae, they might. Everyone wanted the king's favor. They wanted to have dinners beside him and go on hunting trips with him. Become a member of his royal family. Even foreigners wanted a seat at Samarok's court. Elodae couldn't count how many times men, and even some women, had tried to court her. To earn a spot by her side at their table.

No one paid her any mind until they realized who she was. Their attention always went immediately to Irelia. Not only for her title, but her beauty. Irelia had beauty women would die for. Beauty that men would start wars for. Like the sun her sister loved so dearly, Irelia's beauty radiated off of her wherever she went, following her into any room she entered, casting those lucky enough in the golden beams of her soul. Elodae had never been jealous of her sister for her looks, though. It meant that she could slip into the shadows unbothered most of the time.

Which explained why, when a young man had seen

Elodae and chosen her without knowing who she truly was, she had given him her love. A love that he had destroyed over and over and over again.

She would sooner die than give her still healing heart to one of these greedy bastards—but that didn't stop her from using their blatant exploitation of her position to her advantage. Like now.

"It's lovely to meet you, Lord Hadeon," Elodae said softly.

He raised his brows at her, waiting for her name, though he was clearly aware of who she was.

"Elodae," she blurted, allowing an embarrassed smile to spread across her face. "My name's Elodae. The king's—"

"Niece," he finished for her, stroking a thumb along the back of her hand. "I know who you are. Would you care to dance, Elodae?"

Elodae nodded, turning her smile more eager as she let him lead her onto the dance floor. She found Irelia's peach-blonde hair immediately and was surprised to see her smiling up at Fornax, who lifted her off the ground and spun them around.

She wanted to know everything she could about the man marrying her sister. He didn't look like the stories she'd heard about him. Stories of a sickly shell of a boy. The man currently dancing with her sister was anything but; he was handsome and rugged and fierce. He stood proudly; his body toned as though he'd been a soldier once. And the way he watched Irelia . . .

Lord Hadeon put a hand on the small of Elodae's back, making her flinch. She'd nearly forgotten he was there. She threw on a pretty smile and rested her hand on his shoulder. He pulled them into the dance, joining the song perfectly.

Elodae was no dancer. She preferred to make music and watch others bask in the sound rather than dance herself. Elodae had been forced to take dancing lessons alongside every eligible lady in Cronanth, but they hadn't improved her pitiful skills much at all.

"A beautiful couple, aren't they?" Lord Hadeon asked, looking over at his prince and the princess.

Elodae beamed over at her sister and future brother-in-law.

She still couldn't place what it was about Fornax that set her off, but something about him made her anxiety ring. "They most certainly are," she lied easily.

The lord spun Elodae perfectly—once, twice—and her smile became more genuine. All right, the poor bastard could dance.

"Are you close with the prince?" she asked, looking up at him through her lashes.

Hadeon puffed his chest out ever so slightly as he said, "Grown up alongside him." His use of the common tongue was a little misshapen. Dolannish was a guttural, harsh language.

"Would you consider him a friend, then? The prince?" Elodae sidled a little closer to the lord as the music changed to something soft and slow.

"You could say that," he said in a low voice, the hand on the small of her back drifting lower. Elodae ducked her head again, feigning embarrassment at his brash touch. Inwardly, she calmed herself so she wouldn't take that hand and twist it until it snapped.

Hadeon pulled her closer, and she gained enough power over herself to blink up at him with wide eyes. "Tell me about him," she whispered.

"What do you want to know, Your Grace?" he asked, brushing his nose against her temple. His scent wrapped around her, and she nearly choked. He smelled of Dolannish spices, but they mingled horribly with whatever skin oil he'd put on that morning.

Elodae ran her hand along his shoulder and over the back of his neck. "I'm surprised he hasn't married yet with how charming he is."

Hadeon barked a laugh that sent an uneasy chill down her spine. "His Highness has had many offers. The new Princess of Asiva, many, *many* noblewomen. Hel, even some noblemen."

The new Princess of Asiva?

Elodae couldn't help but glance over at Finn.

She forced herself to let out a breathy laugh and meet the lord's gaze again. "And none of them caught his eye? Not even the Asivan Princess?"

Hadeon suddenly became very serious. "It is not my place to tell."

Elodae blinked at the harshness in his tone. "I'm sorry. I'm just trying to learn more about my princess's future husband."

And just like that, he smiled again. "Of course."

They danced in silence for a while, and then the music changed again. This was an old piece that caused partners to switch numerous times before it ended. No one knew which kingdom it had come from, but every kingdom in Eldonia knew it.

The piece was one of Elodae's favorites. Even though she had two left feet and usually tripped over her dress while spinning into the arms of her new partner, she didn't care how badly she danced. The music was too beautiful. As a young girl, after she had grown accustomed to her new life, Elodae had begged the musicians to play it over and over during every event. Vanor eventually had to step in, and the only way he could get her to stop was by picking her up into his arms and dancing with her. It was the first piece she had asked her pianoforte instructor to teach her.

Hadeon leaned forward, pulling Elodae from her memories. His fingers brushed gently over the center of her neck. "What happened here?"

Elodae stiffened and pulled back from the lord. He gazed at her, something swirling in the dark depths of his golden eyes. Before she could ask what, he'd meant, Hadeon spun her away, landing her in the strong arms of her new dance partner.

Letting out a frustrated sigh, she looked up at the man that swept her back into the dance with ease.

All the breath rushed from her lungs as Alden's icy blue eyes met hers.

CHAPTER TEN

Elodae froze for all of a second before she put her hand on Alden's shoulder and followed him into the song. "He dances," she grumbled, not making eye contact with him.

"He does."

Elodae looked around the Grand Hall. "No other guards seem to be dancing."

Alden stiffened, and Elodae met his eyes then. He was already looking at her, his eyes instantly holding hers. Her breath betrayed her, escaping her lungs in a subtle whoosh.

She looked over his shoulder, air once again refilling her chest, and saw Lady Astrid and her father, Lord Marlow, speaking with the king. The lady was perfect as always. Her dusky pink gown was simple yet breathtaking, and her long black hair had been left down in soft curls that brushed her waist as she laughed at something Vanor said.

Alden tracked her gaze, landing noting who had made her body language shift.

"You're scowling," he murmured in her ear.

Bumps raised along her body as his breath caressed her skin. "I am not," she said, looking away from Astrid and meeting her guard's gaze again.

A hint of a smile formed. "You most certainly are."

Elodae may have stepped on his foot then. Alden's hand tightened around hers, her fingers splaying across her back. The warmth of him burning a hole through her dress.

The music swelled, almost reaching the next switch of partners, but Alden said, "You've been avoiding me."

He spun her around and caught her with ease. She ignored the way her stomach flipped. "I've been busy."

Alden gave her a look that said he didn't believe her. It was true that she'd been busy helping get the castle ready with Irelia, but the two nights he had come knocking on her door, she had been available. The first time, she had pretended to be asleep, and the second she'd pretended to be getting in the bath. Both times he had cracked open the door, but quietly latched it again a moment later.

Elodae didn't know what to say to him, didn't even know how she felt.

The music continued to build, and she readied herself to be spun into the next partner's awaiting arms, but Alden only pulled her closer. As close as Lord Hadeon had, but this felt different. She didn't have to force the blush to rise to her cheeks. Didn't have to feign nervousness at his closeness.

Alden's eyes burned into hers as his throat bobbed. "Elodae . . ." The way he said her name sent a shiver down her spine. Made her lean a little forward in his hold. "Astrid and I are—"

She never got the chance to hear what he said after, because the next thing she knew, the windows that lined the northern side of the Grand Hall, exploded, and darkness swept in.

ONE MOMENT ALDEN WAS DANCING WITH HIS duchess, about to explain everything to her. The next, the world plunged into darkness. Not the comforting, peaceful darkness that night or sleep brought, but the frigid, endless darkness of death.

Dancing with Elodae, he had tried and failed not to notice how perfectly her hand fit in his. How her other hand rested on his shoulder, searing his skin even through his sleeves. How she had batted her eyes, blushing and smiling at that prick of a Dolannish lord. Alden had been so jealous that he'd left his post on the dais steps and stormed across the dance floor, grabbing the first partner he could and made sure he was the one who caught Elodae as she spun out of the lord's arms.

He had no right to be jealous. Not with what he still had to tell her.

But then the glass shattered, and screams tore through the Grand Hall. Low, vicious growls followed close behind.

Alden instinctively wrapped around Elodae, holding his

arms across her chest, shielding her heart. Panicking screams filled his ears as his people tried to flee from the dark abyss.

Get her out.

That was all that flowed through his mind.

Finn and Radford could get the king out—and Fornax, who had been dancing with Irelia, wouldn't abandon his bride. Alden hoped.

"Where's Irelia?" Elodae asked in a frightened voice, her hands digging into the skin on his arms as he held sturdy against the bustling crowd.

Alden ushered them toward the alcove behind the dais. He knew this hall, this castle, like the back of his hand. One of their training lessons had been to tie black pieces of fabric around their eyes and then be placed in different hallways. Their task had been to make it onto the castle's front lawns within the hour. Alden and Finn had completed the test in twenty minutes.

"Where's Irelia?" Elodae asked again, squeezing his bicep tightly.

He didn't respond; he was too busy fighting to just keep them standing. Panicked partygoers pushed and shoved them in every direction. Their shouts were so loud that he could barely even hear his own thoughts.

The growls from whatever creatures had barreled through the windows grew too close for comfort, and Alden tucked Elodae tighter against his chest and charged through the surging crowd.

He stuck out his hand, knowing they must be close to the wall. Sure enough, his hand pressed into the rough, cold stone. He followed it around to the back of the dais and into the alcove. There he blindly ran his hand along, trying to find the iron door that would lead down to the attendants' corridor. The passageway would take them back to the kitchens, far enough away from the Grand Hall that they would be safe.

As long as the darkness didn't follow them there.

The screams and growls behind them did not stop.

Alden sent up a prayer to Nath, the god of war and strength, their protector, to give his people a fighting chance. They had doubled their security for this event, but none of them could've been prepared for this. Whatever *this* was. His only priority right now was to get Elodae to safety. Then he could go back and try to get more of his people out. The princess was still out there, as was the Dolannish Prince. Astrid Marlow and her father were out there.

You're failing them, son. They're going to die and it's because you didn't save them, his father's voice growled in his head.

Shoving away the voice that did not belong to him, Alden's hand finally hit the cold metal of a handle. He flung open the door and saw light from the sconces that lined the passageway for a moment before darkness swept down the stairs and to the corridor below. He pushed Elodae inside and locked the door behind them. Almost instantly, the darkness vanished.

Alden blinked against the light that flooded the stairwell.

"We need to find Irelia," Elodae cried, trying to push past Alden and back to the door.

Alden opened his mouth to protest when a voice came from below. "Elodae?"

He nearly sagged with relief when he saw King Vanor and

Finn appear in the archway below. He heard the scuff of footsteps behind them. Radford, then.

"Take her," Alden ordered Finn. "I'm going back out there."

A savage growl sounded, too close, behind the door.

"I'm going with you," Elodae said.

Finn was already climbing the stairs, reaching out to grab Elodae's elbow. She whipped her head around when he towed her back down the stairs to where her father waited, safe, at the bottom. She spewed a multitude of impressive curse words at the guard.

"Keep them safe," Alden said.

"With my life," Finn replied.

Alden nodded and turned.

He halted, hand on the handle, as King Vanor added, "Bring my daughter back alive, Alden."

Alden turned in enough time to see Finn haul a bucking Elodae, growling like the creatures beyond the door, into the dimly lit hallway below. Vanor held Alden's gaze for a moment. He could see the battle raging inside the king. His daughter was out there, but he knew he needed to survive this. Knew that Alden would have the best chance at finding the princess.

So, Alden bowed his head to his king. Vanor left then, following Elodae and Finn down the curved passageway.

Alden turned back to the iron door and braced himself for the hel on the other side.

Please let her be safe.

He didn't give himself think about who he meant before he shoved open the door, and the darkness swallowed him whole.

Irelia did not want to die today.

Never having fallen in love. Never seeing the sun again. She did not want to die in this darkness.

The last thing she remembered was being surprised at how much she was enjoying herself with Fornax. The prince was a beautiful dancer and knew all the Samarokan songs. Which made her hate him even more. She hated the way he smirked and smiled. Not just at her, but at any lady that walked by. Hated the hand that constantly grazed up and down her back. Hated how his eyes devoured her as they danced.

But then suddenly, glass rained down on her, cutting her arms and shoulders. A terrible, otherworldly sound came from behind her. It was the sound of a creature from the farthest depths of hel—hel that had been unleashed in Cronanth.

Fornax began to shout for his men in the endless void. He pulled her tightly against him and then threw her to the ground. Glass cut into her back as Fornax covered her body with his.

"What are you doing?" Irelia yelled at him.

But then he screamed.

A horrifying crunch and then warm, sticky wetness dripped onto Irelia's chest. Right above her heart.

He had protected her. How he had known one of those demons was near, she didn't know. She couldn't hear anything over the horrified screams of her people.

People tripped and kicked them as they lay there on the floor. Then all at once, an immense weight was lifted off her and she was hauled into a standing position. She still couldn't see anything. Couldn't see the sun outside, or any of the people that pushed and shoved against her.

A calloused hand grabbed hers, linking their fingers together.

"Hold on to me," Fornax's rough voice commanded.

She could hear the pain in his voice, could still feel the warmth of his blood marring her own skin.

A roar sounded far too close behind her, and the prince broke into a sprint, towing her along behind him. Irelia had to fight just to remain upright as he shoved through the people scrambling to escape. She stumbled over something fleshy and begged the contents of her stomach to remain where they were.

People pulled her this way and that. Her hand started to slip from Fornax's, and Irelia and shouted over the chaos that surrounded them, "Don't let me go!"

The prince stopped immediately and lifted her into his arms. He started to run again, and his breaths heaved against her ear as he barreled through the surging crowd.

"Never."

The noise from the chaos in the Hall was deafening, but Irelia clung to the prince, letting him carry her through the darkness. He yelled for his men again.

A man's voice came from their right. "My prince, is that you?"

"Where the fuck are we?" Fornax shouted to whoever was beside them.

"Near the wall, Your Highness. There must be a door here somewhere, a way we can get out of here."

Something crashed into them, hard as stone, and Fornax lost his grip on Irelia, sending her tumbling to the ground. Pain shot up her leg as the thing they'd run into tore through her dress and skin. Irelia screamed and tried to scramble away. Fornax roared her name with a voice that would make death itself tremble, but it was nearly drowned out by the sound of the demon's claws scraping against the stone floor. Stalking her. Enjoying the hunt.

Pressing a hand to the wound on her thigh, her stomach churned at the agony. This was it. This was indeed how she would die. But then she heard the creature yelp in pain, and strong, sturdy arms lifted her off the ground again.

"We need to get out of here. Right fucking now."

Fornax.

Irelia's eyes drifted shut. Or maybe they had always been shut. She couldn't tell the difference anymore. The wound on her leg throbbed immensely, it was the only thing that fogged her mind.

Pain pain pain . . .

"Get. Us. The. Fuck. Out. Of. Here. *Now.*"

Irelia felt one of his guards put a hand on the shoulder her head rested on. Then they were running. The jostle of Fornax's movements had her leg hurting so badly that she cried out at the pain.

"I . . ." Her voice came out weak. So, so weak. What was happening? "I don't feel well."

Fornax's grip on her tightened. Warm, sticky liquid soaked into her shoulder from his own wounds. How was he holding her?

"She's losing too much blood," the prince growled at one of his men.

"This way, Your Highness!"

They took a sharp turn and then a loud click, the turning of a deadbolt, sounded.

Light pierced Irelia's eyelids. She was dying. She knew she was, but she forced her eyes to open and glanced at her surroundings. They were in a small bedroom. Three of Fornax's guards stood panting by the iron door. The room was cramped, but Irelia didn't care.

It was *light*. There was the sun, peering through the small window in the corner. She could almost weep at the sight of those golden rays.

Just beyond the sunlight, she could barely make out the Grand Hall. Perfect darkness had engulfed it. But the world —the rest of the world was lit. Guards ran around the outside of the Hall, helping people who were jumping from the windows onto the sloped lawn below.

"What is that?" she croaked. Still so very weak. She fought against the nothingness that threatened to swallow her alive. She didn't want to go back into the darkness.

Still, Fornax held her, but his grip loosened as though he too were about to pass out.

Just before Irelia lost her battle, Fornax whispered, "That is the ending."

CHAPTER ELEVEN

Alden's sword was slick in his hand, not from the blood of the demons terrorizing his people, but from the blood of the ones he was desperate to save.

Darkness was all he knew, was the only constant in the chaos this world had become.

Death surrounded him, echoing with every breath he took, mocking every step he made. People cried out, begging their gods for help, but none came. The demons tore through anything in their path. Every time Alden tried to strike one, nothing happened. Their flesh like the steel of his blade.

He had yet to find the princess in the frenzied Hall, had not even found his brother. Warren and Irelia had to be alive. Alden would accept no other alternative. Finn and Radford had gotten the king and duchess to safety, that much he knew for certain. But that did little to ease the tremendous weight from his chest. Every scream he heard sounded like Elodae's. Every ragged breath and trampling footfalls sent his mind racing to the white-haired woman hopefully retreating far from this hel.

Someone screamed near him, followed by that deafening roar of the beasts. Alden raced toward that scream, raced toward death.

"Please gods, someone help!" that voice shouted over and over again.

Tunneling into that dark, calm, place inside of himself, Alden steeled his mind. He followed that voice, found the owner of it, and shoved the stone-like beast off their body. Alden lunged forward with his sword, striking true, but like every time before, nothing happened. The demon simply roared its anger, and the sound of claws raced away. Off to its next victim.

"Help, me," the voice begged again, weaker this time. Too weak.

"I'm here," Alden assured. "I am a member of the royal guard. My name is Alden Einar."

"W-Waylen," the voice shuddered.

"Waylen." Alden dropped to his knees by their side, hauling them toward one of the nearby walls. He had to shove something out of the way, something he wouldn't let himself think about in that moment. "Are you hurt, Waylen? Did one of the beasts injure you?"

Waylen groaned as Alden moved him, but he couldn't risk keeping him out in the open. If he could assess the man's injuries, he could get him to the safety of the passageway Elodae and Vanor had retreated from.

"My—" the man took a shuddering breath. "My leg."

Alden felt over the man's body, finding his legs—

One was missing; torn off just above where the knee should be.

Shit. Shit shit shit.

Ripping off his belt, Alden dropped his sword, fumbling in the darkness for Waylen's leg. Hands slick with the man's blood, Alden strapped his belt around Waylen's leg, tightening it as far as he could.

Waylen screamed out in agony, but Alden had to shove that away. He wouldn't let himself wince at the stark anguish in that scream.

"Talk to me, Waylen," Alden ordered, for the man had gone silent. Even his breaths were so faint that Alden could no longer make out the sound, only knowing he still lived by the irregular rise and fall of his chest.

Yanking off his shirt, Alden bundled it up and shoved it against the open wound.

"I—I wasn't supposed to be here," Waylen croaked. "My parents . . . they told me not to come . . ."

Alden froze. "How old are you?"

"Fifteen."

He thanked the gods for the darkness then, thanked them that Waylen could not see the tears spill out of Alden's eyes. Could not see the number shoot through his body like a jolt of lightning. Young. *Too young.*

"I'm going to die, aren't I?" Waylen asked, his breaths rattling with every intake.

The chaos of the room had not subsided, concealing Alden's choking sob. He pushed his shirt into Waylen's wound. Begging the life-giving substance to stay inside. "No.

You're not going to die. I'm not going to let that happen," Alden promised. "I'm here. I am with you."

Waylen's next words broke Alden's heart completely. "I can feel it, sir. I can feel Hela beckoning me."

No. Hela would not take this boy from him. Not yet. Not before he even had the chance to live.

The boy's silence stretched, but Alden could not let go of the belt or his shirt to check for a pulse. "Talk to me, Waylen," he commanded.

Waylen took a rattling breath, the sound one Alden found himself thanking the gods for.

"I—" Another rattling breath. "I wanted to be a guard. Like you."

"When this is over, I will make it happen." Alden tightened the belt. "I will train you personally. You have my word, Waylen."

"Thank you, sir." Another too short, too shallow breath. "I'm glad I'm not alone right now."

The Hall was still filled with people scrambling to get away, the demons roars sounded few and far between, but Alden knew what the boy meant. Knew that he, too, was glad to not be alone, to be here next to Waylen.

"I don't hurt so much anymore," the boy whispered. Alden's heart sank. "I . . . feel cold, though."

"I'll get you somewhere warm. You just have to stay with me, Waylen. All right? Stay with me." Alden's voice took on a desperate edge.

The boy's hand found Alden's shoulder; his hands coated in a warm, slick liquid. Blood. "I want to go home now, sir," Waylen whispered.

Alden closed his eyes, his heart shattering completely.

"I'll take you home. We'll find your parents and get you home."

Waylen sighed a rattling breath. Alden could practically hear the smile in that release of air. But then the boy went silent, his hand sliding off Alden's shoulder.

"Waylen?"

Nothing.

Alden swore. "No no *no*." He relinquished his hold of the shirt, finding Waylen's throat. There was no pulse. No air escaping his mouth or nose. His chest did not rise or fall. Alden bowed forward, laying his forehead on the young boy's still chest.

Young. *Too young*.

For what felt like hours, but were mere moments, Alden stayed there next to the boy. The screaming subsided, the roars long gone. Pitch darkness faded to a pale, light grey. And then all at once, the sun returned to the world, casting the horrors of the hour in stark daylight.

Alden sat back on his knees, his eyes immediately finding the young boy's.

Waylen's brown eyes were open, staring blankly ahead. Freckles splattered beneath the layer of dirt and blood on his face, a soft smile on his lips. Alden lifted a bloody hand, his fingers shaking as he gently closed the young boy's eyes.

Bowing his head, Alden said a silent prayer. A warrior's prayer. For the young guard who never got his chance to live.

Slowly, Alden got to his feet, his eyes still glued to Waylen. The young boy had dressed in his finest clothes, clothes that looked too big for him. Clothes that perhaps he'd taken from his father's wardrobe.

Pounding footsteps sounded as Samarok and Dolannish

guards alike stormed into the Grand Hall, instantly pulling survivors out and rushing them to the hospital wing

Still, Alden could not leave Waylen's side.

Not even when a gentle hand laid on his shoulder.

"Alden?" his brother's voice said softly.

Alden met Warren's questioning gaze, his brother's brown eyes, so similar to Waylen's, fell to the young boy on the ground at his feet. A pool of his blood surrounding them.

Warren hung his head as he understood. "We'll find his parents. We'll get him home."

Alden nodded. He still didn't want to leave the boy's side.

"Alden."

He looked at his brother.

"There are others that need us right now," he said gently.

Alden's eyes shuttered, and he looked back at Waylen.

You made a promise you did not keep. And now that boy is dead. Because you didn't save him, his father berated in his mind.

Guilt, heavy a pure, consumed Alden, but Warren was right. There were others that he could try and help. Others that could still be saved.

He nodded at Warren, who smiled sadly and turned to leave.

Alone with Waylen again, Alden turned to look at the boy one last time.

"I'm so sorry," he breathed, barely a whisper on the wind.

Finally, Alden turned to follow his brother and help him carry the injured to the hospital wing.

"It's safe to come out. Whatever those creatures were, they're long gone now."

"My people?" Vanor asked as he stood.

Radford's eyes shuttered and his head dipped slightly. "There are . . . many dead, Your Majesty."

Elodae took hold of her father's trembling hand in the middle of the kitchens.

The king nodded, squeezing Elodae's hand. "Take me to the Grand Hall."

Radford seemed inclined to argue, but he bowed his head and nodded toward Finn, who fell into step behind Elodae and Vanor.

The captain wound them back to the Grand Hall and Elodae was not prepared for the sight she saw.

Dozens of people, Samarokan and Dolannish, even a few Callumerans who had been at court, littered the floor of the hallway that led to the Grand Hall, and the Hall itself.

Elodae released her father's hand and pivoted just in time to vomit all over the floor.

Vanor turned toward Finn. "Take her to her rooms and under no circumstances is she allowed to leave. No one you do not know, or trust may enter her rooms. Do you understand?"

Finn gave a curt nod at the king's orders and reached for Elodae. He gripped her elbow, gentler this time.

She shook off his grip. "I'll be fine. I need to know if Irelia is all right."

"We would know if she wasn't," was all her father said before following Radford into the horror of the Hall.

Elodae turned pleading eyes on Finn. She didn't care if it was no use. She *needed* to see her sister. Needed to find her. And Warren. And Alden.

Alden, who had gone back into that hel willingly . . .

"Finn, please." She would get on her knees and beg if she had to.

"The king gave me orders. I will not disobey him." His eyes softened slightly. "If they are safe, I will send them to your rooms. If they are injured, I will inform you."

"And if they're dead?"

His eyes hardened. "As the king said, we would already know."

Elodae stared at him for a moment, trying to decipher whatever it was that swirled around those onyx depths, but he placed an unreadable mask across his features. "Fine," she conceded after a moment.

Finn led her back to her rooms on the western side of the castle, where he went in first to make sure it was truly safe. The two guards that had been stationed outside her doors that morning were still there. They wedged her between them, her back to the wall. And when Finn emerged, they escorted her the ten paces to the open doors.

The guards shut the door behind her with a click and locked it.

Elodae was alone—and she was so tired. But she couldn't sleep. Not after everything she'd seen. Not until she knew everyone was all right.

So, she sat in her foyer until the clock struck nine, the sun having long since set. A knock on the door had her jumping off the plum-colored settee and darting over to open it.

Finn appeared in her doorway, expression grave. Elodae could've sworn she felt her heart splinter before he spoke. "Irelia was injured by one of those creatures. So was Prince Fornax. They are both in the hospital wing. Both are unconscious."

Elodae wasn't sure she was breathing.

Finn continued, "Alden is unharmed. As is Warren."

She closed her eyes, thanking Eirene and Nath for that small blessing. "Where are they? You said you would bring them here if they were all right."

"Alden wished for me to tell you he will come see you after he's finished telling the families of the dead what happened."

Elodae's next words came out far weaker than she intended. "How many?"

Finn stiffened. "Thirty-seven."

Thirty-seven people. Gone. Just like that.

Elodae's stomach turned again. "And Warren?"

"He is helping bury them."

Elodae squeezed her eyes shut and said, "I need to see my cousin."

"No."

Elodae steeled her spine and lifted her chin. "That was not a request, Finn."

"Your orders do not trump the king's." But then he sighed, and said gentler, "When the search party has returned with information, then you will be allowed to see the princess." Without waiting for Elodae to reply, he closed the door in her face.

Her breathing quickened, and she debated slamming her fists against the door again and again until he opened it, but the exhaustion of the day suddenly crushed her.

Elodae shuffled into her bedroom. She didn't even bother to take off her ruined gown before she crawled into bed.

The sounds of screams and terrifying roars chased her to sleep.

CHAPTER TWELVE

Nearly two full days passed before it was deemed safe enough for Elodae to leave. Two days of endless pacing and racing thoughts. It was a miracle there wasn't a worn path in the stone floor of her entry room. Her hands were cracked and dry from the constant wringing they'd endured. Worry had consumed her so greatly that sleep had all but eluded her, leaving dark, heavy circles beneath her green eyes.

Every able-bodied man had gone out hunting for those creatures, but whatever they were, wherever they had come from . . . were nowhere to be found.

Finn led Elodae to the hospital wing with his sword drawn. She fiddled with her necklace as they neared the hospital wing, healers darting through the hallways.

When the entrance to the wing came into view, Elodae closed her eyes and took a deep breath.

White sheets of curtains lined the cavernous room and healers rushed about. The room had been sectioned off to give each patient the privacy of their own room so to speak. Some of the curtains had been pulled back and the injured lay in their beds, surrounded by their loved ones. Some were asleep, some were tended to, and some—some appeared to be clinging to life.

Finn sheathed his sword and led her to a curtained section in the back of the room. He stopped outside the sheet and lifted a hand to knock, but hesitated before he announced, "Finn and Elodae."

"Elodae?" Irelia's broken voice came from behind the curtain.

Elodae didn't think as she threw back the sheet and flung herself onto her sister. She didn't care that she was sobbing, didn't care that Finn stood behind her, seeing it all. She didn't even care that Alden stood on the other side of Irelia's bed. She just clung to her sister.

Irelia's arms wrapped weakly around her, and Elodae felt her shudder as she, too began weeping.

She didn't know how long they stayed like that, holding each other. But at some point, a healer put a hand on Elodae's shoulder and asked if she could move aside so they could tend to Irelia's wound.

Reluctantly, Elodae unwrapped her arms from around her sister but still felt the need to hold her hand. To know for certain that Irelia had made it out; that she was safe.

The healer pulled back the sheets and Elodae was stunned by the sight of the gash on her sister's leg. At some point, Irelia had been removed from her gown and put in a patient's robe. And that cut on her leg . . . she must be in immense pain.

Elodae looked up at her sister, and when Irelia's pain-filled sea-green eyes met hers, she made a silent promise that she would find those demons and whoever had created them and destroy them all.

"It looks worse than it feels," Irelia said with a forced smile. She gently squeezed Elodae's hand in reassurance.

Elodae nodded, watching the healer apply a salve to the wound. Alden stepped around the bed and came up beside her. He touched the small of her back. A silent question.

She turned to look at him. His icy blue eyes looked exhausted. Black and blue smudges lay beneath them. Had he slept at all these past two days?

Alden subtly tilted his head toward the hallway, and Elodae nodded.

She glanced down at Irelia. "I'll be right back. Finn, you'll stay with her, won't you?"

Finn nodded and sat down in a small wooden chair next to Irelia's bed. The chair groaned under his weight.

Irelia put a hand on her forearm, halting her. "Bring me back some food, please?"

Elodae looked at the healer for confirmation. The young woman nodded. "A light stew and bread."

She dipped her head and then followed Alden out into the hall. They walked in silence for a moment as they headed toward the kitchens.

Then Alden stopped, and his arms wrapped around her.

Elodae stood frozen. Stunned. Then, slowly, she lifted her arms and embraced him.

"I was so worried about you," he breathed into her neck.

Elodae ignored the way her heart flipped. "You got me out safely, Alden. It was *you* I was worried about."

He shook his head against her shoulder.

"What happened in there, Alden?" she dared to ask.

Alden took a shuddering breath, but just shook his head again.

Elodae didn't push further, she just let him hold her in the middle of the hall.

IRELIA HAD WOKEN THAT MORNING THINKING THAT she'd died. But when the smell of healing tonics on the table hit her senses, she knew she had survived. Everything came rushing back to her.

And then she had wept.

She had wept like a small child until a healer came through the curtains of her section and sat in the chair by her side and just held her hand. The young woman—Emma, Irelia now knew—had sat in silence while Irelia cried and cried and cried. And once Irelia had finally gained control of herself, only then did the healer ask to see her wound.

Irelia had yelped the first time the healer applied a salve to it, but with how often they had to reapply it, the sting was nothing but a nuisance now.

Irelia had tried to put on a brave face when Elodae showed up, but the moment her sister embraced her, the sobbing had taken over once more. Irelia had truly believed she would die in that darkness and never get to see the sun or her sister again.

When the girls finally let go and Elodae and Alden had disappeared to get her lunch, leaving her alone with Finn, Irelia asked about Fornax.

"He lost a lot of blood," Emma told her, cleaning up the remaining salve on her leg. "He carried you here after it was safe to move about the castle again. The tourniquet he made saved your life. The moment you were in this bed, he collapsed to the floor."

Irelia bolted up, but hot pain shot through her leg. "Where is he now? Is he all right?" She couldn't hide the panic in her voice. She had known the man for barely two hours before all hel broke loose, but he had defended her. Protected her.

Saved her.

She chewed her lip at the uncertainty that swirled through her body.

"He is fine. More than fine, actually." Emma laughed lightly, discarding the bloody rag she'd used to clean Irelia's cut. "He strolls around the hospital wing, flirting and joking with the healers and patients. It brings him joy, making them smile. And he checks in on you frequently."

"He does?"

"You are his betrothed, are you not?" the healer asked bluntly, raising an eyebrow.

Irelia blushed. "Right. Of course."

Thankfully, Elodae and Alden pushed through the curtains then, stew and bread in hand.

Irelia nearly moaned as the smell of spiced stew hit her. She made a grabbing motion at the bowl, and Alden chuckled, handing it over. The warmth from the stew seeped into her hands. She closed her eyes and sighed, breathing in the scent deeply before she took the spoon Elodae held out for her.

As though he'd been summoned, Prince Fornax appeared through the sheet, a smile on his face. Not a full one, Irelia noticed—hated that she noticed—because only one of his dimples could be seen.

When his russet red eyes locked with hers, his smile fumbled slightly. He took one step forward, just one, as if he'd reach for her.

Irelia just sat there, blinking up at him.

Elodae, having noticed the pair's silent interaction, nodded to Alden and Finn. The two guards stepped outside the curtain, and even though two people had left the small space, it still felt crowded.

Irelia froze when Elodae turned to look at Fornax. She did it with a frankness that made Irelia thankful she was not on the receiving end of those green eyes. Fornax weathered it, though, smile in place.

But then Elodae did the unthinkable. She wrapped her arms around the prince, careful of his left arm, which was in a sling, and said, "Thank you for saving my cousin."

Fornax dipped his head as she released him, and with a final glance at Irelia, Elodae left too.

Alone with Fornax, Irelia quickly looked down at her stew and began eating.

Gods, she was starving. She hadn't realized how hungry she'd been until that first bite. She began shoveling the food into her mouth, scalding hot or not, in a very un-princess-like manner.

Fornax sat in the chair Finn had vacated with a quiet groan. He remained silent while Irelia finished her stew, then her bread, and then drank three full glasses of water.

Turning toward the prince, she got her first good look at him since the attack. His left arm was in a sling, his shoulder wrapped in white gauze. Irelia could just make out the hint of red showing through. He was no longer in his golden clothing, but instead wore basic pants and a loosely fitted grey tunic. His hair was no longer in perfectly combed waves, but instead, pieces stood on end around his head. It made him look younger. Boyish, almost. And like the rest of them, he had dark circles under his eyes.

He was alive and healing, though. That lifted a huge weight off her chest.

Once Irelia put the bowl down on the table by her bedside, Fornax finally spoke. "How's your leg?"

"Fine."

The prince leaned forward, resting his good elbow on his knee. "You nearly died, Irelia. Please don't lie to me. If it hurts, tell me and I'll call the healer back."

Irelia looked sidelong at him. "I have a gash on my leg from knee to hip. Of course it hurts."

Fornax pressed his lips into a thin line. The dimple on his right cheek reappeared.

"What is amusing?"

The prince just shook his head, the corner of his mouth tilting upward, and leaned back in his chair. A hint of worry still shone in his eyes, though. "I'm just glad the attack didn't dampen your cool disdain for me."

Irelia blinked. "What? I don't—"

Fornax held up his hand. "Your face says everything your

mouth does not. I'm not a fool, Irelia. I frighten you for some reason—even after having saved your life."

Her nostrils flared.

"And yet you find me handsome," Fornax went on. His rough voice lightened with the laughter that followed his words.

"I do not," Irelia said tersely.

Fornax's smile widened, the left dimple coming into view. "Right."

"I don't like you." She prayed her shock at the words that tumbled off her tongue wasn't written across her face.

His smile faded as he looked her over, his eyes lingering on her forever-ruined thigh. She pulled the sheets up over her legs. Fornax's deep red eyes met hers again, and his voice returned to that gravelly tone as he said, "You don't even know me."

"I don't have to know you to know I don't like you." She was acting unreasonable, but she had grown up hearing horror story after horror story about Dolannish and the hel they had unleashed on the other kingdoms. How they'd been pushing and pushing against Asiva for years and when Asiva needed them most, they looked the other way. Pretended they didn't see. When she looked at Fornax, all she saw was Finn and his family begging her father for sanctuary. Fornax was not his father, was not the one who had made that call, but he had been raised by him. How different could they really be?

After a moment of silence, she said quietly, but not weakly, "I will not marry you." She would not be the Queen of Dolannish. She would not be the queen of anything except her Samarok. He could drag her away from this land if he wanted to, but she would always find her way back home.

He leaned back in his chair. "That's not exactly your decision, sweetheart."

She smiled sweetly as she said, "We'll see about that."

Fornax narrowed his eyes at her, then shoved out of his chair. He stepped close and brushed a strand of her peach-blonde hair out of her face.

Irelia went still.

He leaned forward, resting his hand on the mattress by her hip. His eyes poured into hers, sending her heart fluttering. "You haven't even said thank you yet, princess." A smirk formed on his face. "Manners are important in a marriage."

She glared at him. "Thank you," she said through her teeth with a fake smile.

"You still don't like me, do you?" he asked, his eyes dipping to her lips for the briefest of seconds.

"No. Surprisingly that hasn't changed in the last two minutes."

Something flashed in his eyes as they met hers once more. But again, whatever it was had vanished too quickly for her to decipher. "The feeling is mutual, princess," was all he said. Then he turned and left.

Irelia stared after him for a moment.

The feeling is mutual.

Her hatred for him burned. Why did he make her heart flip in her chest? She had known the man for two hours before hel had been unleashed on the castle, for Amara's sake. If that wasn't an omen, Irelia didn't know what was. The goddess of love was probably looking down at her and laughing.

She had no idea what to think or feel. The events of two days ago still haunted her every thought.

Finn pushed past the curtain a short time later, her father a step behind him.

Irelia smiled up at them, tears once more flooding her eyes, and all thoughts of princes and demons vanished.

CHAPTER THIRTEEN

*G*lass exploded around the Grand Hall of Castle Cronanth.

Growls and roars from the creatures of hel echoed throughout the eerily silent room. Elodae was alone in the Hall, and it was not shrouded in darkness, but light. The sun shone through the arched windows lining the Hall.

But the demon in front of her was a thing of nightmares.

A black, four-legged being stared at her with milky white eyes. It looked almost human—like a human that had transformed into this demon. Its arms had been stretched and used as front legs. Its face had been contorted into a snout. It opened its maw and jagged teeth dripped a milky liquid the same color as its eyes. It scraped long claws on the floor, carving gouges into the stone.

Sharpening them.

Elodae ran then, but she could not run fast enough.

A woman's scream sounded behind her, and Elodae turned in time to see the demon jump on Irelia. Elodae screamed her sister's name, lurching forward. But then the endless darkness swept over the world once more. She fumbled for something to grab, to save Irelia, but then suddenly Elodae was suddenly on a ship.

Irelia's screams turned into the scream of the wind as it tore around the cabin. The shatter of glass morphed into the snapping of wood. The scrape of the demon's claws on the stone shifted to metal singing against metal.

She knew this ship. Knew what was about to happen.

A faceless woman rushed toward where Elodae crouched on the floor. Water lapped at her ankles from the holes in the ship's side. The woman said something, but Elodae couldn't make it out.

The woman hooked something around Elodae's neck. Elodae looked down at the pendant. Her small, childlike hands spun the three different circles. She looked back up at the woman, who tucked a strand of hair behind Elodae's ear.

The woman said something again, but Elodae still couldn't make it out.

Then she vanished and excruciating pain lanced through Elodae's mind.

She screamed.

Darkness swallowed her whole, but not before Elodae heard a gentle voice whisper, "Come back to me, starling."

Elodae gasped and lurched upright in her bed, clutching at her necklace.

Sweat beaded on her forehead as she tried to calm her racing heart. Elodae dragged a hand over her face and kicked off the covers. She stumbled to the bathroom and turned on the faucet, splashing cool water on her face.

Cupping her hands, she waited until the water filled her palms and lifted them to her mouth. She drank two more handfuls before her heart finally calmed enough for her to walk over to her armoire and pull out her green robe and some blankets. Spring had arrived in Samarok, but the nights were still cold and crisp, lingering from their long winter.

She slipped on the robe and tied it around her waist as she walked out onto the balcony. There she sat in her preferred chair, tucking the blankets around her, and looked up at the stars, seeking out the Warrior.

Elodae found him almost instantly. He rarely moved in the night sky, no matter the season. Seeing him eased some of the weight on her heart. She sat out there for a while, content to count the stars until the sun came up and they vanished once again.

"Why am I not surprised to find you out here?"

Jumping in her seat, Elodae whipped her head around to see Alden leaning against the balcony doors, arms crossed. She leveled an unamused glare at him. "Why am I not surprised to find you snooping?"

Alden laughed, and a shiver ran down her spine. He closed the distance between them and took up the lounge chair opposite hers and gestured to the blankets tucked securely around her. "It's not even cold out, El."

"It's *always* cold in Samarok, Alden." Elodae rearranged her blankets. "To what do I owe this pleasure?"

"It's nearly four in the morning. All your guards know you're usually awake at this hour."

"Well, that's a little unsettling," she murmured.

Alden chuckled softly. "It's our job, as your guards, to know your habits. But . . ." he leaned forward so his icy blue eyes were level with her, his arms resting on his knees, "I am the only one who knows why."

Elodae's stomach flipped. "Don't flatter yourself, Alden."

Alden knew she was deflecting. "Do you want to tell me about it?" His voice was soft in a way that caused her heart to strain.

She took a deep breath and tried to coax herself out of the instinct to strike and make a sarcastic comment to push him away. "Not really, no," she admitted, toying with her necklace again.

They sat there in silence for a long time.

Elodae hadn't realized she had started to cry until Alden's thumb brushed away the wetness on her cheek. Their gazes locked and held for what felt like minutes, his thumb making gentle passes on her skin.

"I've been having nightmares, too," he breathed.

Alden's eyes held hers for a moment longer. They were so tired, those icy depths. Tired in a way she understood at her very core. He dropped his hand from her cheek, as if realizing what he had been doing, and stood.

Elodae cursed herself for allowing that touch. For allowing him to be the one to pull away first. But then he reached for her hands. "You've had a long week. Let's get you back to bed."

Despite her better judgment, Elodae allowed him to help her from her seat. She looked up at him and was shocked at the openness of his face. At how much he laid bare for her to see.

Too close. She was too close to the edge again.

He twined their fingers together as he led her through the balcony doors and into her bedroom. It took all her self-control not to pull her hand back from his. She really didn't want to be alone right now.

And as much as she hated to admit it—she missed Alden.

So, she followed him through the doors. His oak and spice scent washed over her, calming the anxiety that lingered from her dream and the attack. The fire roaring in the hearth instantly heated her skin. Had he started it before coming outside? Had she been so lost in the stars that he had not only snuck up on her, but built an entire fire?

Heat rose in her cheeks.

The stone floor had warmed from the flames, and it soothed her chilled feet as they padded to the large four-poster bed against the far wall. Alden released her hand to remove her cocoon of blankets. Elodae shivered against the breeze from the still-open balcony doors while he folded and placed them on the bench at the foot of her bed. She crawled onto the soft mattress and sat cross-legged, watching as he strode back to the balcony doors, and paid no attention to the way the muscles along his back shifted as he moved.

He closed the doors gently and turned to head out of her rooms. "Well, goodnight, El–"

"Wait." The word was out before Elodae realized what she was doing.

He halted in his tracks and turned, slowly lifting his eyes to hers.

She swallowed and tried to gather her emotions, her thoughts. She was stuck between not wanting to let him in and not wanting to be alone. So, she let her mouth decide which path to take.

To let him leave or ask him to—

"Stay."

She held her breath, waiting, while he stood like a statue. His glacier-blue eyes burned into hers. The longer he stood there and looked at her, the more she hated herself for saying anything at all.

Fool. You're a fucking fool.

"Please." Her whisper was barely audible, as though her mouth had a mind of its own.

Alden moved then and kneeled beside her. "Elodae." The way he said her name caressed her exposed skin. "I'm only hesitant because . . ." His eyes closed for a moment as he sucked in a deep breath. "I worry what others may think."

"The horror. A man sleeping in my room. I am twenty-three years old you know. That certain mystery died long ago."

She looked up to find that Alden's face remained serious. "A *guard* sleeping in your room," he clarified.

Understanding dawned on her, and she nodded slowly.

"It is an honor to be a member of the Royal Guard," he went on. "Especially for a king like Vanor. I don't want to mess that up."

She knew he spoke the truth, but still. They had been friends once before things like titles mattered.

"It wouldn't be the first time we've shared a bed." She couldn't meet his eyes as she laid this next part of her out on the line. "I . . . I can't be alone tonight."

Her vulnerable words hung there like the stale spring air outside.

She didn't know why tonight was different. The nightmare had been as usual for the most part, but the one with the demons—that had chilled her to her core. And it was true; they had spent the night together many times in the past. It had never gone beyond sleeping next to one another, though.

She didn't know why this was important to her, for him to lie beside her tonight as he had hundreds of times in the past . . .

But it was.

As children, Alden would make up stories to lull Elodae back to sleep whenever she woke from her nightmares. Elodae knew, deep down, that those nights were the reasons she read books like they were the gasps of air that kept her alive while she drowned. She could never get enough. Those stories had given her the strength to get out of bed each and every day.

Elodae had only ever asked Alden to stay the night one other time since he had become her guard.

She had snuck out to a tavern with Irelia, and they had gotten much too drunk from mulled wine. When they had crept back into the castle, they'd knocked over a suit of armor, causing such a noise that Alden and Warren had come racing toward them, swords drawn. The men had then rushed the giggling girls back to their respective rooms before more guards could show up.

On the way back to her rooms, Elodae had been awestruck at how handsome Alden had become. Her wine-hazed brain had thought a public hallway was the perfect place to push him against the wall and kiss him.

So that was exactly what she'd done.

To her surprise, he hadn't immediately pulled away. In fact, he had done the opposite. One of his hands had gripped her waist while the other plunged into her hair, holding her lips to his. He'd only stopped when her hands had trailed down his uniform. Then he had taken both of her hands in one of his and gently pushed her back. He hadn't said a single word to her the rest of the walk to her room. When they finally made it back unseen, Alden had tucked her into bed.

She had asked him to wait, and then to stay. But that night when she had breathed the word, please, he'd only bowed, then turned and left.

Now, Alden sighed and ran his fingers through his hair. He was staring at her lips as if he also remembered the last time she had spoken those words. "It's different now. You know that," he said quietly.

"I do, but . . ." Elodae tried to find the words to explain how she felt. She had never been good at explaining her feelings. Even simple ones, like when someone angered her or said something that offended her. She had no problem standing up for those she cared for, but when it came to herself, Elodae had no idea where to start.

Strong, callused hands covered hers to stop the wringing she was unconsciously doing to her bed sheets. She shook her head. "Never mind. I understand why you don't want to. Goodnight, Alden."

He opened his mouth. Closed it. And tried again. "It's not that I don't want to. I . . ." He seemed to be struggling to find the right words as well. As though his mind raced just as chaotically as hers did. She had seen the look on his face that day in the hospital wing after the attack. And the way he had held her in the hall—she knew he had witnessed horrors no one ever deserved to see.

"Don't be alone tonight either, Alden." She lifted her hand, brushing a strand of hair out of his face.

Frozen to his spot on the floor, his eyes wide as they held hers, he sucked in a shuttering breath. They bounced between hers for a beat before his lips curved into a soft smile. "Very well, *princess*. I shall keep you company tonight."

She felt her cheeks redden at the nickname.

Alden stood and started to remove his uniform. The guards wore basic tunics and pants underneath, but Elodae still looked away to give him a sense of privacy.

He placed his sword atop his folded uniform, next to where the blankets had been laid earlier. The bed shifted, and a hand played with the end of the wavy hair that almost reached her waist now. A slight tug on the back of her robe had her lying next to him. Instead of the soft goose-feather pillow, her head hit the firmness of his arm. She peered through her lashes and blinked at the closeness of his face.

Neither of them said anything for quite some time.

"Do you want to tell me about it?" She asked, breaking the silence.

Alden's eyes shuddered and he shook his head.

Silence filled the room once more and the pair of them simply lay there, watching each other.

"You are safe now. They can't reach you here," Alden whispered. The same words he had said as a young boy, rocking her back to sleep after she'd wake, screaming, from the nightmares. Now, instead of comforting her, she knew he said it more to himself in that moment. She wondered how often over the past agonizingly long hours he'd reminded himself that he, too, was safe.

Silver threatened to line her eyes, and Alden's thumb was instantly there, ready to catch the tears before they could leave her lashes. He rested his hand on her cheek, as if just in case he needed to catch more.

She . . . liked not being alone. Although she found comfort in the silence, after the deafening darkness two days ago and the dream she had woken from, she didn't find it peaceful tonight.

Elodae had almost forgotten how it felt to be cared for. How it felt for someone to know her so well that a single movement could tell them about the thoughts behind her eyes.

Releasing a deep breath, Elodae whispered back, "You're safe now, too, Alden."

A stroke of his thumb against her cheek was the only response he gave.

Eventually, his eyes drifted shut and his breathing evened out, but Elodae was too unnerved to fall asleep. At some point, her traitorous fingers lifted to finally tuck a strand of hair behind one of his ears. The sleepy sound of contentment he made had her blushing like a fool.

No matter how hard she tried to push him away, or how hard he pushed her away, he was always there in the end.

And though she would deny it to her grave, she would always be there for him, too.

Elodae couldn't remember when, but at some point, the soft strokes of Alden's thumb against her cheek and his oak and spice scent lulled her to sleep.

No dreams haunted her as she slept safely in his arms.

CHAPTER FOURTEEN

Elodae tried to roll over but was met with a low groan of protest from behind her. She smiled into her pillow as Alden's arm tightened around her stomach. She didn't plan on leaving the warmth of this bed anytime soon.

She had just drifted back to sleep when Alden bolted upright and jumped out of bed. Sitting up, she twisted to gawk at him, her hair spilling over her shoulder.

He stared at her as though he had just seen one of those demons.

"What's wrong?"

Alden began putting his uniform on, not answering her question.

"Alden?"

He continued to ignore her, shoving his boots on. Her

mind began to race, every imaginable thought bombarding her.

Her spine straightened and her chin lifted. "Guard Einar."

He flinched as though she had struck him. She had never used his official title to address him before, but he had never made her feel so exposed, either. Elodae shoved from the bed.

"I'm sorry, Elodae. I'm late for a meeting with the king and the nobleman to discuss the attack and how to move forward."

"Is that all?"

He froze, stopping the tying of his boots to look at her. She crossed her arms tightly across her chest. More so to make sure she wouldn't fidget than anything else.

"Yes, but . . . when I woke up and saw I was holding you . . ."

She nodded, stepping away from him.

He sheathed his sword and walked around the bed to stand in front of her. "We—we can't. We can't ever go there, El." He pinched the bridge of his nose, shaking his head. "I know I agreed to stay the night. And we are friends. But—"

"If you're trying to explain or justify what just happened, don't."

Alden's jaw clenched. "I am your *guard*, Elodae. We would do well to remember that. You cannot ask that of me again."

"And *we* would do well to remember, *Guard Einar*, that you do not give me commands." She straightened her spine and managed to look down her nose at him even though he towered over her.

"Actually, I serve the king." His nostrils flared, and he

opened his mouth to say more, but stopped. Instead, he sucked in a deep breath and slowly blew it out. "This sort of thing cannot happen. It's not appropriate."

Elodae scoffed and pushed past him, heading toward her bathing room.

"I'm to be engaged, Elodae."

She stopped dead in her tracks.

Alden's pain-filled eyes met hers as she turned to face him. He held out his palms as if confessing to a crime. "Gods above, El. This is not how I wanted to tell you, but you need to understand why that can't happen with us again."

Every wall she had ever taken down around him shot back up with enforced steel.

"I've been meaning to tell you. Lord Marlow has been discussing my potentially being wed to Lady Astrid and—"

"Lady Astrid?"

Alden went stiff-backed at her shocked tone. "I am a lord, Elodae."

"I thought you planned on never using that title. Unless, apparently, to find yourself a wife. It's only beneficial to use it to get your way, right?" She hated the accusation of her words, but she couldn't stop them once they had started.

"I made a promise, Elodae." His eyes shuttered, and a muscle ticked in his jaw.

"And a promise you shall keep."

Alden took a step forward at the coldness of her voice, his hand outstretched toward her. Elodae took a step backward.

"You may leave now Lord Einar. You should not keep the king waiting on your presence." Her arms remained tightly wrapped around her body.

Hand still in the air, her guard stared at her, but she held firm. Cold and still.

Slowly, Alden let his hand drop to his side and dipped his head in a bow. "As you wish, Your Grace."

Elodae watched him leave, and with the click of the door behind him, she locked her heart securely in its cage and threw away the key.

ALDEN NEVER MEANT FOR THE CONFESSION TO escape his lips. Not in that way, not in that manner. He had regretted it the moment he'd uttered them, the moment he'd seen the words strike her like a physical blow.

His hand against the cold wood of her door, Alden took several deep breaths before he pushed away and turned to make his way to the War Room. Boots clomped down the hall and Alden looked up to find Warren racing toward him.

"You're late, you idiot. The king is holding the meeting but *hurry*."

"Fuck," Alden grumbled and broke into a run alongside his brother.

Warren looked sidelong at him as they ran through the winding halls of Castle Cronanth. "What were you and Elodae doing?" When Alden didn't answer, Warren smirked. "*Oh?*"

"Shut up," Alden growled at his brother. "Nothing remotely of the sort happened."

"Excuse me."

They rounded a corner and Alden found himself admitting something to his brother that he'd never even admitted to himself. "I can't stay away from her, Warren. Everything in me leads back to her. Every path I take, she's always at the end. No matter how far I run or how hard I pull away, she's there."

Warren was silent for a long moment before he suddenly stopped, halting Alden with a hand on his forearm. His brown eyes met Alden's, a silent question swirling within.

Alden shook his head and ran his fingers through the mess of his hair. "I panicked, Warren. I woke up with her in my arms, and everything I've worked toward these last six years, everything I promised Father—I was ready to throw it all away. And that terrified me." Alden shook his head. "Charon was always a wonderful father to you. He cherished you. You could do no wrong in his eyes."

Warren's brows furrowed.

Alden continued, "He would constantly remind me you were what a son should be. That he wished you were his *true* son, his heir. He once told me he wished I had died in that fire with your parents." His brother gaped at him; shock written across his face. "He made me promise to marry Lady Astrid. I don't know why. I didn't ask—*couldn't* ask. But he did. And I *hate* that a big part of me is still scared to let him down."

A joyless laugh escaped Alden. "And I just told Elodae in the worst possible way."

"It'll be all right, brother." Warren laid a hand on Alden's shoulder. "You will make it right; I know you will. You always do." He flashed Alden a bright smile. "But just remember . . . don't hurt her now because of your hurt from the past."

His brother's words struck true and deep. Alden nodded and the brothers began their walk to the War Room once more. They turned the corner, the towering red double doors coming into view.

"I had no idea Caron was so cruel to you," Warren said softly as they approached. "I'm sorry for not noticing it."

Alden merely shrugged. It wasn't his brother's fault, wasn't his issue to fix.

A warm hand clasped Alden's shoulder, halting him just before he lifted a hand to open the door. Turning toward Warren, misplaced guilt swam in his brother's brown eyes. Nothing would've prepared him for Warren's next words.

"You were and *are* an amazing son."

Alden reined in his flinch and was only able to give his brother a tight-lipped smile before he shoved open the doors and stepped into the crowded War Room.

Dolannish and Samarokan guards and noblemen alike stood huddled around the large circular table in the middle of the room. Their voices mixed together as they pointed to places across the map of Eldonia, spread over its center.

"My men say they saw the darkness come from the north," one Dolannish lord said.

A Samarokan cut him contradicted, "My men told me it came from the west, from the Tyrian Peaks themselves."

"Could it be the gods? Has Samarok earned their wrath somehow?"

"Samarok has done nothing of the sort," King Vanor said with a slam of his fist.

The room went silent.

Warren and Alden approached the mass, but Alden spotted Prince Fornax and the lord that had danced with Elodae huddled together on the outskirts of the group, whispering in hushed tones. He watched them out of the corner of his eye.

"Ah, Alden, my boy," Vanor said, waving a hand for Alden to come to his side. Alden approached his king. "You were there during the attack," Vanor went on, "and you managed to not only leave the darkness but also return to it. Something our men could not do. Once they were outside of that black wall, they could not re-enter."

Alden blinked. "How is that possible?"

"That's what we would like to know," the lord at Fornax's side said, stepping forward with his prince. "We fear this may be the beginning of something similar to the events that happened in Asiva two years past."

Alden saw Finn stiffen out of the corner of his eye.

"Does Dolannish plan on aiding Samarok if such a thing occurs?" A Samarokan lord asked. "Since your prince is now officially engaged to the Princess of Samarok. Surely, Your Highness, would not leave his bride's kingdom to fate."

Prince Fornax opened his mouth, but his lord answered first, "Dolannish will do what is best for *Dolannish*."

"Hadeon, that is enough," Fornax snapped.

Hadeon dipped his head in a bow, heading his prince's words. There was no small part of Alden that burned with fury as he looked at the black-haired lordling. The image of his hand sliding further down Elodae's back scorched through his mind every time he looked at him.

"The Dolannish army that journeyed here with me will help in whatever way they can. That you can be assure of,

King Vanor. They are at your disposal." Prince Fornax bowed his head to the Samarokan King. A muscle ticked in Lord Hadeon's jaw, but he kept his mouth shut.

Vanor dipped his head in a nod and turned back to Alden. "Since you were the only one that could penetrate the darkness, you will be heading a company of men set out to leave with the dawn tomorrow."

Alden couldn't feign the surprise stark across his face. "But, Sire, I do not know how I was able to get through the darkness. I have no idea where to lead a company of men to even begin searching—"

"I believe I can help with that," Prince Fornax interjected.

All eyes in the room turned toward the Dolannish Prince.

"Some of my men saw the darkness retreating to the west, into the mountains that border your city. They will accompany and lead you in that direction." Several Dolannish guards nodded around the War Room.

"Fantastic," Alden bit out, unable to keep the sarcasm from dripping from his words. "That only helps with one part of the problem. Say we trek out west, the Tyrian Peaks are still blanketed with snow. We don't know what we're searching for, or what to do once we find it. We don't even know what we're truly up against—"

"Again," Fornax interrupted, holding up a hand to silence Alden. Alden had to control himself as to not rip that princely hand from his very body. "There is an old prophecy in Dolannish, an old warning: of the birth of our ruination, destroying all things good in our world, and leaving the land riddled with scars. I would like access to the Samarokan

Royal Library to do research to see if anything similar comes to light."

"Of course," Vanor said. "Captain Radford will see that you have everything you need. I would personally help you research, Prince Fornax, but I am set to leave for a couple of weeks."

Alden blinked. That was the first he was hearing of the king leaving.

"And you believe that this . . . child has been born?" A Samarokan lord asked, stepping forward, pulling Alden's eyes from his king.

Lord Hadeon broke his silence then. "We do. There is no denying that there has been a shift in the world. This winter was long and harsh, even in Dolannish. The spring is already angry with storms." Murmurs broke out amongst the lords, both Samarokan and Dolannish alike. "Something has disturbed the balance," the lord carried on. "It started in Asiva, and a radical group saw that as an opportunity to overthrow their kingdom during their time of fragility. We fear the same may be starting in Samarok."

Again, Finn went utterly still behind Alden.

"Why Samarok?" The king inquired.

Prince Fornax let Hadeon respond. "It took Asiva, our southernmost kingdom. And now it seeks out Samarok, the northernmost. Whatever it is, whatever this ruination has awoken, will suffocate us from the outside in." An eerie chill settled over the space. "So that there's nowhere left to run."

CHAPTER FIFETEEN

Alden raised a hand and knocked twice on the wooden door.

"You may enter," Elodae called.

Alden's heart slammed in his chest as he eased open the door and shut it softly behind him once he stepped into her chambers. He knew where she'd be without having to look, so he padded over to the room on the left, where floor-to-ceiling shelves were filled with all her favorite books.

There, he found Elodae curled on the emerald green sofa, a book in hand, before a roaring fire. He chose one of the matching soft chairs and sat, propping his feet on the arm roll of the sofa.

"You know, it's probably not wise to have a fire going in a room full of paper books," he teased. A pathetic attempt at normalcy.

"Do you know other kinds of books besides paper ones?" she asked without looking up.

Elodae: one. Alden: zero.

He forced out a chuckle. "Fair enough."

Pretending to scan the room, he watched her out of the corner of his eye. He tapped his fingers on the sides of the chair and whistled quietly to himself.

Elodae huffed a sigh and closed her book. "May I help you?"

"I'm just doing my job."

She scowled at him and opened her book once more.

"What book are you reading this time?" Get her to talk to him. About anything.

"I don't know," she said, turning a page.

"You don't know?"

"Nope," she chirped without so much as glancing in his direction.

"How do you not know what book you're reading?"

Elodae simply flipped to the next page, ignoring him.

Alden narrowed his eyes and stood, snatching the book too quickly for her to do anything but stare at where it had been between her hands.

"Wait!" She was immediately on her feet, jumping to steal the book back from him.

He held it above his head, too high for her to reach, and read aloud, "Fingers fisted in my hair as he held my head down on his—" Alden choked on the last word.

His stunned hesitation was long enough for Elodae to yank his arm down and grab the book out of his hands. She retreated, clutching it to her chest.

They blinked at each other for a long moment, and then Alden threw his head back and burst into laughter.

Elodae pressed her lips into a thin line. When he doubled over, a hand on his knee, the other on his chest, she joined in.

Damn him if her laugh wasn't the sound of angels.

It took them quite some time to calm down. They sat next to each other on the sofa and Alden rubbed at the stitch in his side while Elodae wiped her eyes. The sight of her tears, even though they were joyous ones, brought him back to reality as though a bucket of ice watered poured over his senses.

He turned toward her and gripped her hands in his. "I'm sorry. About earlier."

The smile still playing on her lips faded.

"It should've never come out that way. I'm sorry," he repeated, running his thumb along the back of her hand.

Elodae pulled her hands from his and tucked her moon-white hair behind an ear. She looked down at the book in her lap and was silent for so long that Alden squirmed where he sat. He didn't know which scared him more: the words she liked to wield or her unending silence.

Slowly, she blinked down at her book and ran a hand over the cover. "You're engaged."

It wasn't a question, but he knew she wanted an answer.

"Not yet," Alden said softly. "Lord Marlow and I have been discussing marriage to his daughter. He and my father had been contemplating it for years. I don't know why, but . . ." He shook his head, trying to gather his thoughts. "I am a lord, but you're right. I do not wish to use the title. I don't like to. My mother insisted I hear Marlow out because—" He stopped himself before he revealed too much.

"Because?" Elodae faced him fully, her pine-green eyes boring into his.

"Because my mother thinks Astrid will make me happy," he lied. He still couldn't tell her the real reason. Not yet.

Her face became unreadable as she nodded.

"I only told you earlier to explain why we shouldn't be as we once were. I'm sorry if my reaction made you feel as though I regret things. I don't. But that doesn't mean this sort of thing can happen again."

Alden reached for her hands again, but she moved out of reach. His hands hovered there for a moment before he whispered, "Elodae."

"Don't," Elodae said, standing. Her arms wrapped around herself.

Alden stood, the coffee table between the sofa and the hearth now separating them. It felt like a vast distance. "You are brave and kind. You deserve the world, Elodae. You deserve everything . . ."

Everything I cannot give you, he nearly said.

Elodae's arms only tightened around herself. "Thank you. And congratulations." She smiled at him then, but it didn't reach her eyes.

He understood the dismissal.

Elodae turned and walked out onto the balcony. He couldn't help but watch her for a moment. The sun shone down on her as if its sole purpose was to do so. She glowed in its rays like a newborn star.

"I will not see you tomorrow," he blurted, desperate for something to say in the silence.

Elodae turned, her hair flowing behind her like liquid starlight. Manicured brows raised on her face.

"I'm set to leave with the dawn with a company of Samarokan and Dolannish men to try and find the source of that darkness and whatever attacked our people."

Elodae blinked, turning to face him fully. "Oh?"

"I just thought I should let you know." Alden bowed low. "Your Grace."

With that, he turned and strode out of her room, the click of the closing door shooting through him like an arrow.

Many years ago, Alden had built a wall as strong as this castle around his heart. But last night—last night, Elodae had found a crack, and he wasn't sure whether that'd be his saving grace or his damnation.

CHAPTER SIXTEEN

"What makes you think the Silver Lake will hold any answers?" Finn asked beside Alden.

Clad in thick, warm clothes and boots, the company of men trudged forward through the snow that still dusted the land surrounding the Tyrian Peaks. Cronanth sat behind them, growing ever smaller as Alden marched them further and further west. The two men, one Dolannish, one Samarokan, that claimed to have seen the darkness retreat, strolled a few steps ahead of them.

"I don't think it will," Alden admitted. "But its directly west of Cronanth, tucked amongst the mountains. It's the only lead we have." He shrugged, adjusting the sword at his hip.

Squinting against the reflection of the sun on the snow, Finn shook his head. "This will either be a fool's mission or suicide."

"No one said you had to come," Warren offered with a broad grin from the royal-turned-guard's other side.

Finn ignored his brother as he always did, and asked Alden, "How did you get inside that darkness?"

Memories came rushing back; the unending void, the screams of his people, the roar of monsters, a young boy dying in his arms. Alden cleared his throat, forcing the thoughts out of his mind before he deigned to respond. "I truly don't know. I . . . I just did."

"The lake approaches," the Dolannish man, Maloc, called from ahead, silencing whatever Finn had been about to say.

Alden rushed forward, to the hill the man stood atop, and peered down the snowy cliffside. At the bottom of the valley sat the Silver Lake. Most of its water still frozen in the center.

Nothing seemed amiss as Alden scanned the area. A gentle breeze drifted by, swaying the tips of the green blades that dared to peek through their snowy beds.

Two stags stood on either side of the lake, both of their heads bowed to the crystal clear water, pausing for a drink. Their horns engraved onto the plate of his chest.

"It seems peaceful out here," Warren said from Alden's side.

Alden was inclined to agree, but that's what unnerved him the most. The stillness of it all.

"I don't—"

"Sir!" Dalo, the Samarokan guard that had helped lead their company called, interrupting Alden. "Over there."

Alden followed the man's outstretched finger, pointing

to the far side of the lake, directly in the middle between the two stags.

There, on the far side of the Silver Lake, sat something so dark, so completely black that it seemed to soak up every ounce of sunlight that dared to touch it.

"What in Hela's name is that?" Finn breathed.

Those were the last words Alden heard before that sickening darkness swallowed the company alive.

IRELIA WAS TIRED OF SITTING IN THAT damned bed.

Her back ached. Her leg ached. She wanted to bathe, to walk, and stretch. Wanted to curl up on her terrace with a book from the Magicks and research the darkness.

But she couldn't do any of that.

Glaring at Emma, who was applying a salve to her wound for the hundredth time today, she said, "When can I leave?"

The healer sighed and looked up at the princess. "Once this heals, Your Highness."

Irelia groaned and threw herself back against the pillows. She was losing her mind. Not to mention that the prince insisted on visiting her once a day to 'get to know' her.

Speaking of the demon himself, his fiery red hair poked through the curtains of her pathetic 'room'. He smirked when his russet eyes met her glare. She was becoming unspeakably grumpy being cooped up like this.

"Ah, sweetheart. You're awake," he drawled and stepped through the sheets. He nodded at the healer. "Emma."

The healer blushed and curtsied before leaving.

Fornax walked around the bed and settled himself into the same chair he did. Every. Single. Time.

"You don't have to do this, you know."

He rolled his shoulder, wincing slightly. "I do, actually."

"And why is that?"

"You'll be my wife someday. I think we should at least learn to like each other."

Irelia ground her teeth. "As I've already told you; I have no intentions of marrying you."

"I don't particularly enjoy your company," he said quietly. All amusement had disappeared from his eyes.

"The feeling is mutual, prince."

"Hmm." He gave her a tight-lipped smile. "But unlike you, I will do whatever I need to for my kingdom."

Irelia whipped her head in his direction. "I will do what needs to be done for Samarok."

"Doesn't seem like it."

"I was nearly killed," she seethed.

"So was I," he snapped. "But you weren't. Because I saved you. And yet you still hate me."

"Just because you saved my life does not entitle you to have any sort of claim on me."

His eyebrows shot up. "*Claim on you?*"

"Yes."

"We were given an order—by our kings—to marry one another. I don't like it either, but I *will* do it. For Dolannish."

Irelia ground her teeth so hard she thought she'd chip

one. "Right. Because Dolannish hasn't already gotten everything it's ever wanted."

Fornax watched her for a moment before he stood and walked over to her bed. Her heart pounded in her chest at his closeness. He placed his hands on either side of her hips and leaned forward so their faces were mere inches apart. "Why?"

"Why what?" She thanked the gods her voice came out bored and steady even as her body trembled.

"Why do you hate me so much?" he asked, his gaze dipping to her lips and then lifting to her eyes once more.

"Other than the fact that you flirt with literally anyone who looks in your direction?"

He let out a single laugh. "Is the princess jealous?"

"What? No, I—"

Fornax leaned even further forward. One slight move and their lips would brush. "Tell me, sweetheart. Why do you hate me?"

The words were out of her mouth before she could think twice. "Because if I marry you, I'll be trapped."

He cocked his head and furrowed his brows. "How would you be trapped?"

She wet her lips, her mouth suddenly going completely dry.

His dark gaze watched her tongue dart over them. "If you're going to hate me, you should at least know who you're hating."

"I've heard stories of you," Irelia whispered. "Your kingdom. Stories of a prince who rode into battle and killed innocent men."

"And you believe them? These stories?"

"What's not to believe? I've seen the pain inflicted from your kingdom firsthand."

Fornax went completely still. "Your guard?"

Irelia said nothing.

"Hmm." He dragged a finger up her arm, leaving chills in its wake.

Irelia sucked in a shaky breath.

"Do I scare you, princess?"

Despite herself, she nodded.

"A lot?" He tilted his head the other way and ran that finger back down her arm.

Words were lost to her, so she shook her head.

His finger ran up her arm once more, and then he cupped her jaw in his hand. Brushing his thumb over her bottom lip, he breathed, "You scare me, too."

Irelia swallowed hard.

"Am I interrupting something?"

Irelia squeaked, pulling away from the prince, who stood stiff backed, and looked over at the 'door'. Elodae stood there, arms crossed, an unreadable look on her face as she stared at the prince.

"No," Irelia said, flustered. Her cheeks burnt.

"Good," Elodae replied, still staring at the prince, even as she made her way over to Irelia's bed.

The prince and duchess glared at one another, neither one daring to look away. Challenge laced their eyes, threatening the other to bow first. Neither did, of course.

"Can you both stop that now?"

Fornax was the first to relinquish his hold and looked at Irelia, his russet eyes immediately softening when they met hers. She hated that. Hated that she even noticed. The gentle touch from his fingers moments earlier still burned into her skin.

"I came because I heard you were going to be doing research in the Royal Library." Her sister continued to warily watch the prince, who froze for all of a second, before looking back at the duchess.

"And how did you hear that?"

Elodae merely shrugged. "I want to help you research."

Prince Fornax scoffed. "No offense, duchess, but I don't need help."

"I wasn't asking." Her sister had a deadly smile of her lips.

"Enough," Irelia sighed, holding up her hands. "We will help you, Fornax. If it's the Veiling you are researching, then it is to help our people as well."

"What did you call it?" Elodae asked, her brows furrowing.

"The Veiling. That's what everyone in here has been calling it. A veil of darkness just draped over the Grand Hall." Irelia shivered as she remembered what it felt like to be in that darkness. The total loss of her sight, the heaviness of the air on her skin.

Irelia looked at Prince Fornax. "Find me a wheelchair, and we will be on our way."

He hesitated. "Your healer said you weren't ready to leave yet—"

"I'm fine." If it would get her out of this bed, out of this room, she would suffer being by Fornax's side to do it.

Elodae emerged once more from behind the white sheets hanging around Irelia's bed, wheelchair before her.

Fornax, despite his protests, rushed to Irelia's bedside to

help her. Lifting her into his arms, he gently set her down in the chair. Her cheeks burned at the warmth of his touch, searing through her dress.

She managed to control her face enough by the time he released her, his calloused fingers brushing against her exposed skin, and his eyes met hers for a brief moment.

Without asking, Elodae grabbed the handles on the back of Irelia's wheelchair and strolled out of the hospital wing. The wooden wheels clanked over the stone floors of the castle, but Irelia didn't care. The sound echoed within her. Freedom.

She was finally free from that bed, free to roam her home once more.

Irelia tilted her head back, listening to the sound of her wheels on the stone, the sound of her sister and the prince's shoes shuffling behind her. People rushed about, their murmurs floating to her ears, sobering her immediately.

Her people were in danger, and she needed to find a way to save them. And fast.

Towering doors to the library came into view as Elodae pushed her around a corner and it took all of Irelia's restraint to not leap from her chair and rush into its familiar space. Even stationary, her leg yelled at her in pain, but she shoved it to the back of her mind.

"What exactly are we looking for?" Elodae asked, pushing Irelia up to the end of a long table in the far back of the spacious room.

Prince Fornax told them of the Dolannish prophecy: or the child of ruin born to destroy their world. Irelia couldn't help but shiver as the prince's words settled into her.

"I'm hoping there's something in this library that might help better understand that prophecy," Fornax mused.

"Why would Samarok have something like that?" Irelia asked.

Fornax shrugged, running his fingers through his wavy hair, the strands immediately falling in front of his face again. Their tips brushed the brown skin of his cheeks. Irelia mentally kicked herself for noticing.

"Our prophecy was tucked far within the Dolannish library, kept hidden and safe. It's the only lead I have that something similar may be here, as well."

Elodae took off down one of the corridors lined with books. "Let's begin then, shall we?"

HOURS OF RESEARCH AND NOTHING. ABSOLUTELY nothing.

Elodae had found several books about the history of Samarok and Eldonia as whole, but it led nowhere. The closest thing they found to something relating the Veiling, as Irelia had called it, was a scroll tucked far within the confines of the library, out of reach from the damaging lights that shone around the cavernous room. The scroll was in some ancient text none of them could translate.

Irelia had mentioned perhaps taking it to the Magicks to be translated, but Elodae had reminded her sister of their father's threat. She wanted to help the Samarokans, help their people and help protect those in the future, but to be banned from the Astronomers for life? To risk going out into Cronanth alone, since she knew damn well none of the guards would agree to accompany her after the king's decrement, and potentially run into the one who had scared her throat?

"We can keep looking, Irelia," Elodae offered, placing a gentle hand on top of Irelia's. Her sister's fingers were red and blistered after a long day of using the wheelchair.

Her sister smiled sadly but nodded in agreement. Prince Fornax, whose fingers were gripped tightly in his hair as he poured over his hundredth book of the evening, said nothing.

The sister's eyed each other, and Elodae nodded, understanding. She stood and began to take her sister back to the hospital wing.

"What are we going to do, E?" Irelia asked tiredly as they approached her bed.

The duchess helped her sister into the soft sheets, tucking her in. "I don't know, Irelia. But I do know we'll find something."

"How do you know that?" Irelia's sea-green eyes looked so tired, so helpless.

Elodae brushed her fingers over her sisters. "Because we have to."

CHAPTER SEVENTEEN

Elodae was sat on the pine-green sofa in her library, book in hand, when a voice drawled from behind her, "Another dirty book, Your Grace?"

She slammed her book closed and tucked it behind the pillow she leaned against. "What is it with my guards and sneaking up on me?" she spat as Warren walked around the sofa.

"How's Alden?" She asked calmer when he sat down across from her.

It had been two weeks since the morning they had departed, searching for the source of the Veiling. The company of men had returned, but not whole. Dozens upon dozens of soldiers had died, the ones that remained not fairing much better. Alden had made it out with only a gash on his arm. She had rarely seen him since; the guard having taken time to decompress. Elodae didn't let her mind wander toward what he witnessed out there. Finn had returned unscathed, somehow. Only a mere scrape on his shin as proof of his endeavor.

Elodae had still trained every morning, Warren taking up Alden's place to work with her.

Warren picked up her legs and draped them across his lap, then leaned back and closed his eyes, his honey-brown hair falling away from his face. "The king wishes for your presence in the Grand Hall." He yawned, picking up a pillow and lying it on his face to block out the sunbeam Elodae had followed around the room, trying to get as much warmth as she could.

"He's home?"

"Returned this morning."

"Then why aren't we going?"

"We are." Warren didn't move.

Elodae kicked his hip.

Warren yelped. The pillow fell from his face as he sat upright and glared at her. "What was that for?"

"You are terrible at your job," Elodae scoffed and stood. She set her book down on the coffee table and went into her bedroom to change into something suitable to wear for an audience with the king. Since Warren had addressed him as such, and not as Vanor, she knew it must be important.

Lady Lillianna appeared a moment later. "Oh, good. You're getting ready. Here, let me help you. I've just come from the princess's room and we're already behind schedule, so we must hurry."

Irelia had finally left the hospital wing only a handful of

days earlier. The princess finally healing enough, and badgering her healers enough, to be released.

Lillianna tugged at her robe. Elodae slipped out of it and eased into the slit her lady's maid held open for her. She then stepped into the blue fabric and pulled it up her body. It hung off her shoulders and had intricate designs in a shimmering silver glitter that reminded her of moonlight. She picked up the corset that went with the dress and held it in place for Lillianna to lace up her back.

Once Lillianna had finished lacing up the corset, Elodae stepped into matching silver slippers and sat down at the vanity to let the lady work on her hair.

Thirty minutes later, Elodae's hair was half up, her natural soft curls falling over her shoulders. Random braids were threaded through her hair.

Elodae smiled and stood to walk to the full-length mirror in her bathroom. She admired the image reflected there. The dress hugged her figure perfectly, accentuating her hips and softening her slightly broad shoulders. The corset didn't lift her breasts as most did but displayed them in a soft and subtle way. This gown was long enough to cover her feet the way it was supposed to.

Her smile faded as she continued to gaze at herself. The dress was immaculate, but that little voice in the back of her mind told her she didn't deserve any of this.

A knock sounded, pulling her back to reality, and Elodae gathered her skirts in her hands and walked over to the doors. She opened them and blinked at who stood before her.

Alden.

He was not in his guard uniform, but rather in regal-looking clothes, black slacks, and a matching tunic embroidered with Samarok's seal in a vibrant blue. Despite the formal attire, though, his sword still hung from a belt at his hips. Elodae looked down at the celestite crystal embedded in the pommel. It was the same beautiful glacial blue as the eyes that now raked over her. His ashen hair had been cut to the nape of his neck and combed back out of his face.

Pressing his lips into a tight line, he cleared his throat. "You look beautiful."

Elodae opened her mouth to say thank you, but nothing came out. She clasped her hands together and tried again. "Where's Warren?"

Lillianna came up behind Elodae. "Why are you escorting her and not Lady Astrid?"

Elodae turned to her lady's maid and raised a brow, but not before she saw Alden glare at his mother. Interesting. She turned back to Alden and asked nonchalantly, "Lady Astrid was invited?"

"I've brought Lady Astrid to the Grand Hall already," he answered his mother. His voice softened as he said to Elodae, "All the lords and ladies have been asked to attend for some sort of announcement. It was last minute as the king only just returned earlier today. I was asked to retrieve Your Grace. Warren is already on duty waiting for us there."

Such formal words.

Alden held out his arm. Elodae looked up at him, trying to catch his eye. Her heart strained in her chest when he refused to meet her stare. Alden stood proud, a soft splatter of rubble littering his jaw and cheeks. He did not appear to be in much pain anymore, and she couldn't see a sling on either of his arms. So, she hesitantly took the one he offered her, and let him lead her to the Grand Hall.

ALDEN HAD BEEN STRUCK STUPID WHEN ELODAE opened the door and he'd seen that gown on her. She had stood there, looking like night sky personified, like the most beautiful constellation he had ever seen, and he had just gawked. He wanted to kick himself for it. Lady Astrid was waiting for him in the Grand Hall. That was the woman he should be admiring.

Ignoring the fact that every time he blinked, every time his eyes were forced to be in darkness, the sounds of those demons roaring, the pain of his arm getting sliced open, the soft brown eyes of a boy who died too young, flashed across his mind. He had spent the better part of the last two weeks practicing, begging, himself to remain calm in the dark.

Not all of them had made it out alive, but he had. Which meant he had to fight until the next day, for those who were taken from him.

Alden shook his head and turned a corner, leading Elodae toward the Hall. In truth, he had no idea why all the lords and ladies had been invited to hear the king's announcement. The king had seemed excited, though, about whatever it was he had to share.

Elodae's hand burned his skin through his tunic as they made their way to through the castle. He breathed in her sweet floral scent, and it calmed some piece of him deep within. Chasing the darkness from his thoughts.

"So," Elodae mused. "Lady Astrid is formally attending this event with you, then?"

It took all his willpower not to turn to face her. If he did, he'd lose what small control he'd gained over his heart. "She is."

Elodae's grip tightened on his forearm, but he refused to meet her stare. They rounded a corner and the hallway opened before them. The ceiling jutted toward the sky and paintings were scattered on the walls of the castle's main entrance.

Alden made to steer them to the Hall's entrance on their left, but Elodae pulled lightly on his arm. "Alden."

His entire body tensed at the sound of his name on her lips. He turned slowly, forcing a smile. "Yes?"

Her green eyes locked with his and he held his breath, worried that any movement would reopen that crack he'd repaired in his defenses.

Her eyes bounced between his, looking for something. Their pine-green depths danced with something he couldn't read. He wanted to swim in those eyes, to study them, tracing every brown fleck that scattered amongst them.

Alden fought the urge to squirm under her gaze, but he refused to let her see how much she affected him. He was her guard. He knew better.

"Never mind." Elodae's voice seemed to come out weaker than she'd intended because she immediately straightened her spine and lifted her chin. She released his arm and walked herself the rest of the way to the Hall.

He wanted to reach for her, to follow her, but he saw his

mother approaching out of the corner of his eye. So, he turned away from Elodae and smiled at his mother.

"Mother," he said, bowing his head.

She gave him a condescending stare. "Whatever you're thinking about the duchess, stop now. Before you mess things up with Lord Marlow entirely."

"I don't know what you're talking about," he responded simply.

"Do not play coy with me, boy."

His leash snapped. "Why do you push me so hard to marry Astrid? Why her out of all the available ladies? Why did *Father* push so hard for this?"

She struck him.

Alden's head snapped to the right. He bit his tongue and slowly turned back to face her.

Lillianna shoved a finger in his face. "You do *not* question your father."

"Father is dead," he snarled back. His mother raised her hand again, but he moved out of the way.

She shook her head in disgust. "You never could do anything right, could you?"

Alden's heart splintered.

"Your father died ashamed of you and yet you still disobey him."

And with that, she turned and made her way into the Grand Hall.

Alden sucked in a shaky breath and shoved his breaking heart down until he felt nothing at all.

Irelia sat on the left-hand side of the dais, smiling at the gathered crowd.

The Grand Hall had been cleaned, the windows miraculously repaired in the time since the darkness had swarmed through the castle and its demons had given her the gash on her leg. She tried not to look at the archway where she'd been told her people had made their last stand. She had wept and wept when her father had brought her the news.

Irelia had asked Alden and Warren for a list of the names of the deceased so she could pray at the temples of Hela, the goddess of death, and Eirene, the goddess of peace, that those who were lost would find rest in the Afterworld.

The princess had held on to Finn the entire walk from the hospital wing to her rooms to get ready. And then the entire walk to the Grand Hall. She'd never admit it to the healer, but her leg hurt like hel.

The sun was setting, casting the ocean out the windows to Irelia's left in oranges and pinks.

She was gazing out those very windows when a rough voice said from close by, "Princess."

Irelia knew that voice. Hated how, after such a short while, that voice had been imprinted in her mind. They had spent most of their recent days inside the books of the Samarokan Library, searching for something, anything, that would help their people. She hated to admit it, but those hours spent in his presence weren't . . . horrible.

She turned and smiled up at Prince Fornax. The prince

bowed, gently lifting her hand to kiss her knuckles. She felt her cheeks redden as he released her and stood straight again. Fornax flashed her a smile. Only the right dimple showed.

"Prince," Irelia said softly, looking up at him through her lashes. Always the innocent princess everyone wanted to see. Always the shy, gentle girl.

Fornax's right dimple disappeared, even though his smile remained in place.

Irelia tilted her head slightly, studying him.

"May I bring you anything?" he asked after a beat of silence.

"No, I'm all right. Thank you."

Why wouldn't he leave? His cronies were waiting for him, casually talking amongst themselves at the bottom of the dais.

She looked at his group of friends and then back to the prince who still stood before her. His eyes were no longer on her face but on her right thigh, where a vicious-looking scar had formed beneath her dress. Irelia had to fight the urge to shift in her seat.

Fornax's russet eyes slowly raised back to hers. "No fight today?"

Irelia felt her smile tighten. "No, Prince. No fight today."

Wicked delight flamed his eyes. "Shame."

Without another word, he turned on his heels and walked down the dais steps toward his awaiting noblemen.

Irelia stared after him for a moment before movement in the entrance caught her eye. Elodae emerged a step before Alden. Irelia internally winced at the sight of the pair entering the Hall. Astrid stood on the right side, surrounded by noblemen and women alike. Alden headed in their direction while Elodae continued straight, heading for the dais.

The princess hadn't seen Astrid in a couple of days. The lady had visited her those first few days, but something between them felt off. Astrid had behaved differently—strange. Irelia didn't know what had changed, but it had been so uncomfortable between the two of them that she'd told her not to come back and that she was fine.

Warren came up on Irelia's right and said out the corner of his mouth, "Do you have any idea what's going on with those two?"

She sighed, "No. You?"

"Not a damn clue. She looks *happy*." He gave the princess a look and went to check on the other guards around the Hall.

As her sister neared and Irelia couldn't contain the smile that broke across her face. "You look beautiful, E."

Elodae gave her a soft smile of her own. "Thank you."

Her sister looked so tired. Too inside her own head.

"Any clue what Father's big announcement is?" Irelia asked her sister quietly, hoping to keep both her and Elodae out of their own thoughts. If only for a little while.

"I didn't even know he had an announcement to make," Elodae said. "All *that* idiot told me," she ground out, even though a smile still sat on her lips, as she nodded in Warren's direction, "was that the king requested my presence."

Irelia tried not to blink at Elodae's use of their father's title. Even now, thirteen years later, her sister still called their father the king every now and then. It continued to strike her as odd, but deep down she knew Elodae still felt displaced within Samarok's court.

Their father entered a moment later, and Elodae helped Irelia stand. The crowd grew silent as Vanor walked across the hall, a grin on his face. He climbed the steps of the dais, bowing his head slightly to his daughters and mouthing the words, "I missed you." The girls smiled at him, and then he turned to face the crowd.

His voice boomed throughout the silent room as he said, "People of Samarok; in just five months, the Prince of Lunala will visit our court."

Murmurs broke out amongst the guests, and Irelia's mouth dropped open.

Lunala.

No one had housed a member of Lunala at their court, let alone a royal, in centuries. Millennium.

Elodae was ramrod straight on her left. Her arm was still wrapped around Irelia, helping her stay upright.

"He believes his people may have an answer to the darkness that attacked our castle nearly two weeks ago," Vanor continued.

The crowd silenced once more.

"Nothing is more important than my people's safety. I am willing to do anything and everything I can to ensure that as long as you are in Samarok, you will be protected."

Irelia smiled at her father as the gathered guests clapped and cheered.

Elodae hesitantly clapped along with them, and Irelia looked over at her sister. Her face was unsurprisingly blank. She was about to ask her if she was all right when their father spoke again.

"And if all goes according to plan, in exchange for their

aid. . ." Vanor turned toward them, holding out a hand for Irelia.

No. For Elodae.

Elodae froze for a split second and then looked at Irelia. She nodded, shuffling to hold onto the side of her chair as her sister slowly walked over to their father and took his outstretched hand.

And with his next words, she saw her sister shatter inside.

"The Crown Prince of Lunala will marry my niece, Elodae."

CHAPTER EIGHTEEN

"*Come back to me, starling,*" a woman's voice whispered.

Elodae swayed on her feet. She blinked and looked around, searching for where the eerie voice had come from. Then she turned back to look at her father, who was staring down at her with worry in his eyes, looked out at the sea of people gathered before her. All staring at her, waiting for her to say something. Ringing sounded in her ears.

"Elodae," her father said gently.

"Yes. Sorry." Elodae flushed with embarrassment. She cleared her throat and then addressed the room. "I am overjoyed with this news. To unite another kingdom with Samarok is an honor."

The guests cheered once more and then music began to play. Elodae walked back to her seat beside Irelia. She couldn't help but glance over her shoulder every now and then. To the west. Waiting for that darkness to return.

It felt like it already had. When Vanor had announced Elodae's marriage, she could've sworn a light inside her went out.

"Elodae?" Irelia whispered.

Elodae just stared at the table. Silent.

She would marry a Lunalian. A Lunalian Prince. The *Crown* Prince. She wasn't even a princess. Wasn't even Vanor's true daughter. Why hadn't he arranged this marriage for Irelia?

She must've asked the question out loud, because the king leaned forward from his seat on Irelia's other side and said, "Irelia has been promised to Prince Fornax since she was nine years old."

Irelia went tense.

The prince in question was currently chatting with a hoard of noblemen. He glanced in their direction, as though he felt their eyes on him, and Irelia quickly ducked her head.

"The . . ." Elodae's voice came out far too weak. She cleared her throat and tried again. "The wedding will take place in five months?"

"No, my child." The king laughed, taking a sip of his wine. "The wedding will take place on the winter solstice."

Eight months from now.

Elodae had eight months to find a way to get out of this marriage.

The attendants brought out the feast. Roasted chicken, stews, vegetables, fruits, cheese, and meats, all Elodae's favorites, but her appetite was nowhere to be found.

"But I am not . . ." Elodae's throat dried up. She tried to

smother her rising anxiety as she whispered, only loud enough for him to hear, "I am not your actual daughter. Or niece. Or a part of your family in any legitimate way." She reached for her necklace. "How can I, someone who is *not a princess*, marry a prince?"

Vanor's sea-green eyes softened. "He does not care about titles. I have offered him a substantial amount of money and goods. And you *are* my daughter. In every way that truly matters."

Elodae tried not to flinch at the words. *I have offered him a substantial amount of money and goods.*

Irelia, who was sitting between the two of them, cut into the meat on her plate. At the beat of silence, she glanced up and met Elodae's stare.

Do not push this, her expression said.

Like you're one to talk, Elodae shot back.

Irelia glared at her and turned back to her food.

The king had turned to some noble on his right and Elodae stood, excusing herself in need of the bathroom. The king waved a hand in her direction, continuing his conversation.

Warren stepped forward, ready to escort her, but Elodae shook her head. She needed a moment alone.

"You know better than to wander about the castle alone after what happened. I'm coming with you," Warren said, no wavering in his voice.

Elodae bit her tongue to stop herself from snapping at him. "All right," she bit out.

Warren helped her step down from the dais and they made their way out of the Hall. After they cleared the corner and were no longer in view, she increased her pace. When she saw a hallway that was deserted, Elodae turned down it and *ran.* She ran and ran, as though she could outrun everything that had just happened.

She only stopped and leaned her forehead against the cold stone wall when her feet began to ache in her slippers. Her breaths came in sharp pants and sweat beaded down her back and along her brow.

"Elodae?" Warren asked, his own breathing ragged from keeping pace with her.

She turned so the calming cold stone was pressed into her back. "Marriage. Me. Lunala."

Water flooded into her mouth, into her nose. She couldn't breathe.

Warren leaned against the wall next to her. He ran a hand through his slightly damp hair. But he said nothing, just stood there beside her.

Elodae slowed her breathing, forcing deep breaths into her lungs. "Of all the eligible men for me to marry. Why did Vanor pick one from a land notorious for killing outsiders?" She turned her face up toward the ceiling, a humorless laugh escaping her lips. This had to be some sick joke.

"How did he even get an audience with their queen?"

Warren shrugged, still not speaking.

"I'm overreacting," Elodae babbled, pushing off the wall. She paced in front of Warren, fiddling with her necklace. "Our people are going to be joined for the first time in— ever? This is historic. And look at Fornax. All those stories about a sickly child who didn't look as though he could make it past the age of twelve were obviously false. And we've never met a Lunalian, so he can't be that horrible. Right?"

Elodae dropped her necklace and chewed on the end of a

nail. She continued her pacing. "We don't know anything about them. Or their *prince*." She said his title as though it tasted like acid. "All we've heard are rumors. And if he is as horrible as they say, he might just have to accidentally fall off the roof."

Warren coughed a laugh at that.

"It's going to be fine." She stopped her pacing and faced Warren again. "Right?"

"Right."

"Are you just agreeing with me so I'll shut up?"

"Right," he repeated, smiling.

Elodae rolled her eyes, letting herself smile a little, too. "You're very helpful. Thank you."

"Elodae." Warren shoved off the wall and clasped her shoulder. "You will be fine. I, and everyone else who cares for you, won't let anything happen to you. Hopefully, you won't need protection, but if you do, we're there." He nodded toward the way they had come. Back to the Grand Hall.

"Plus," he continued, "you've been training for nearly two years now. You could just kick his ass yourself."

Elodae chuckled softly. She wanted to believe him, but she couldn't help but think of the woman who had given her the necklace. Had that woman loved her? Had she, too, once promised to protect Elodae no matter what?

Her thoughts shifted from the woman in her dreams to a man who had once held her heart. Marrying the Crown Prince of Lunala would mean that one day she would have to give him heirs. That she would have to . . . *be* with him.

Elodae's stomach churned.

Marrying the prince, marrying anyone, would also mean that Alden—

She shook her head, banishing the thoughts from her mind.

Warren smiled reassuringly at her and swept out an arm. Sighing in resignation, Elodae allowed him to lead her back toward the Hall.

Alden's leg bounced underneath the table.

He could've sworn his heart had fallen out of his ass when the king announced Elodae would marry the Crown Prince of Lunala. The king had never mentioned negotiating with them in the past. That had to be where the king had gone off to these last two weeks. The foreign negotiations he'd mentioned. Alden had just assumed he'd meant Callumere or Dolannish. Not meeting with a Lunalian dignitary off the coast somewhere.

It had taken all of Alden's willpower not to follow Elodae and Warren out of the Grand Hall minutes ago.

Astrid laid a hand on top of his right knee. "Are you all right, Alden?"

Alden loosened his white-knuckled grip on his silverware and stilled his leg. "Yes. Sorry. My mind is elsewhere." He gave Astrid an apologetic smile, and her cheeks turned a rosy color.

Astrid truly was beautiful, but he couldn't help comparing her midnight black hair to Elodae's moon-white. Her pale white skin to Elodae's soft tan. Her bright blue eyes to Elodae's deep green ones.

Astrid lifted a hand and rested it on his cheek. "Are you sure you're all right? You have a distant look in your eyes."

It took all his control not to flinch, and he gently grabbed her wrist and lowered it. "I'm fine. I promise."

Astrid gave him a slight nod and then leaned forward, brushing her lips against his. He went completely still.

Elodae and Warren walked back into the Hall at that moment.

Alden's eyes locked with Elodae's as Astrid pulled back to press a second kiss to his cheek. He saw the muscle tick in Elodae's jaw as she tore her gaze from his.

Astrid turned. "Oh, we must go congratulate Elodae," she said excitedly and pulled Alden from his seat. She rushed them over to where Elodae had stopped by one of the long tables.

Alden scanned the crowd, making sure his mother was not near to witness what she surely would claim was a mistake on his part. Several lords and ladies, including his mother, were gathered around the dais talking with the king, and Alden quietly sighed with relief.

His relief was short-lived, however, when he noticed Irelia was no longer on the dais. He searched the room, but no one seemed to be concerned. Warren left Elodae's side to return to his position on the dais. The king was laughing at something some Dolannish lord said. Finn was also nowhere to be seen, which brought a sense of calm to Alden. If Finn was with Irelia, she would be safe.

He let Astrid lead him over to Elodae, who filled a glass of wine. When she turned, her green eyes immediately locked with his.

His heart lurched when he could still see those walls behind her eyes.

Astrid beamed, her hand in Alden's, as they stopped in front of Elodae.

Elodae's heart dropped into her stomach at the intimacy between the two, but she put on a pretty smile, making sure it reached her eyes, and turned toward Alden. "Your fiancée looks lovely."

She looked at Astrid, who was still beaming up at her. Elodae was a good few inches taller than the lady, even with Astrid in heels and Elodae in her slippers. She hated to admit it, but Astrid did indeed look beautiful. Her long black hair cascaded in soft curls that reached her waist. Her sapphire eyes shone with her smile, and her blush stood out starkly against the paleness of her skin.

The lady curtsied deeply; her pale lilac dress brushed against the stone floor as she said, "Your Grace. You look stunning yourself." Her smile did not falter as she straightened.

"Your Grace," a Samarokan lord called boisterously. Elodae turned to face the balding dark-skinned man as he lifted his glass toward her. "I must offer you, my congratulations."

"Thank you," she said with a dip of her head.

"Lady Astrid. Lord Einar," he said, turning toward the couple, "I don't believe I've offered my congratulations to you two yet." He clasped Alden on the shoulder and he could've sworn she saw him flinch.

"Congratulations for what?" Elodae asked innocently to the lord, taking a sip of her wine. She'd regret this later, but all sense had fled from her mind from the moment her father announced her betrothal.

The lord froze, his wineglass halfway to his mouth, and shot Elodae a confused look. She was pleased to see Alden's nostrils flare and Astrid's smile fumble the tiniest bit. If Elodae hadn't been looking for a hiccup in the perfect lady, she would've missed it.

Astrid recovered herself and looked up at Alden. "You have not told her yet, my dear?"

The lord's eyes bounced between the three of them and cleared his throat. "Ah, my wife has finally arrived." And with that, he hurried away.

Alden turned to Astrid, but his eyes remained on Elodae for a moment longer. When his eyes met Astrid's, he said in a hushed voice, "I'm not sure I know what you mean, my lady."

"That we are to be married." Astrid laughed, putting her hand on his chest and turning back toward Elodae.

Alden went entirely still. He turned to face Elodae fully again, and something akin to sorrow swirled through his icy blue eyes.

Elodae was torn between acting like the respectable woman she was or pissing them off. She narrowed her eyes at him and when his sorrow changed to frustration, she chose the latter.

Elodae tilted the rest of her wine back. She grabbed another glass from a passing attendant, replaced it with her empty one, and took a long sip. "Well, congratulations." She swept her arms out wide to encompass them both, her wine sloshing in its glass. "You two make the most *beautiful* couple. Maybe one day I'll find someone as wonderful as you, Alden."

Alden shot daggers at her with his eyes.

Elodae smiled and took another sip of her wine. "Oh, wait." She giggled, lowering her glass, and pressed her fingers to her lips. "I'm now engaged to the Crown Prince of Lunala."

She lifted her glass toward the gaping Alden and turned without another word. Spotting Warren on the dais, she headed in that direction.

Elodae took another giant gulp of wine before walking up the steps to return to her seat. She blinked at the empty seat beside hers and then around the room. Her sister had gotten out of this whirlwind of a mess.

"That was . . ." Warren blew out a long breath. "Hard to watch."

"Shut up," Elodae hissed through her teeth. She finished her glass and set it on a passing attendant's tray, then grabbed another. Out of the corner of her eye, she saw Warren's shoulders shaking with silent laughter. She growled at him, which only made the guard laugh harder.

If she had to be stuck in a room with all these nobles, with Alden and Astrid, and Warren's laughing ass—she was going to need a lot more wine.

CHAPTER NINETEEN

Irelia had tried to wait for Elodae to return, but her leg ached so badly that she nearly begged Finn to carry her back to her rooms so she could rest.

The guard currently had a hand around her right elbow, his other wrapped around her back as he helped her walk. Each step sent burning jolts of pain up and down her right leg, and a whimper escaped her clenched lips with her next step.

Finn stopped. "Princess?"

Irelia sagged against him and shook her head. She was afraid if she said even a single word, the tears she was keeping at bay would break free.

Before she could give in and ask Finn to carry her the rest of the way, footsteps sounded behind them.

Finn looked over his shoulder and Irelia felt him tense.

She tried to look over her shoulder, but the twisting movement sent another shot of pain down her leg.

A familiar voice brushed down her spine. "Princess."

Fornax.

He walked around where the two of them had halted, one of those dimples already appearing with his sly smile. Irelia could still see a hint of a bandage under his tunic spotted with red.

"Why are you here?"

Fornax's eyes flamed at her tone. "I can't walk down a hallway?"

Irelia managed to look around. No one was with the prince. Not even a guard.

"By yourself?" Finn asked. His thoughts had clearly gone in the same direction.

The amusement faded from the prince's russet eyes as he turned them on Finn. "I am more than capable of handling things on my own."

Finn straightened, standing taller, if that were even possible. "Your men let you walk around this castle alone after what happened?"

"They are *my* men. They do what I tell them to."

Finn grunted.

The three of them stood in silence for a beat. Neither Finn nor Fornax moved.

Irelia's leg ached. She tried to take a step out of Finn's arms to brush past them and continue to her rooms, but she barely lifted her right leg before she cried out in pain. Two sets of strong arms caught her before she collapsed to the ground.

"You shouldn't be walking on that leg," Fornax said roughly.

Irelia looked up to find the prince glaring not at her, but down his nose at Finn. The same way Elodae did whenever the two got into an argument.

"The healer said it was fine for her to walk on it. The princess would let me know if it pained her too much," Finn growled.

Both men still had one arm around Irelia.

"She nearly fell to the floor just now. Of course it pains her," Fornax shot back.

"I'm all right," Irelia said tiredly.

Fornax and Finn just continued to glare at each other.

"I am the head of her personal guard. I have known the princess for over a year. I think I understand her better than you, *prince*."

Irelia stared at Finn in shock. Never had she heard him use such a tone. Not even at Elodae. And never—*never*—to a royal. What did Finn, the former Prince of Asiva, see when he looked upon the Prince of Dolannish?

Fornax stepped closer to Finn, still not removing his arm from around her. "Let the princess go, *guard*."

"Stop talking about me as if I'm not right here," Irelia barked at the men.

Both finally tore their gazes away from each other and looked down at her. Finn released Irelia's arm, forcing her to lean into Fornax for support.

Finn bowed low to them both. "Apologies. That was inappropriate of me. I still wish to accompany you both back to the princess's room to ensure your safety."

Formal words. She had never seen his temper snap so

easily, let alone at all, in the year she'd known the guard. Prince, she supposed. In his own right.

To go from being the crown prince of a kingdom like Asiva to a guard for the royal family of Samarok . . . Irelia couldn't imagine what it must be like for him. He'd had to flee his country just to keep his life and save his family.

Asiva was ruled by vicious people now. Their daughter, the princess, soon to be queen once the old crone in power finally died, was even more so. Anyone who so much as spoke out against them was publicly slaughtered. Irelia's father had tried to talk with them once, a few months ago. His accompanying party had returned with half its number.

No one knew why the coup had happened. Or why none of the other kingdoms had tried to stop them. Asiva had called for aid, but by the time Samarok had gathered their troops, it had been too late. Irelia still felt the shame of it every time she saw Finn's family. Thankfully, they had not been at the castle during the attack two weeks ago. But Finn —oh, gods. Finn had been.

Irelia looked up at him, and for the first time in a long time, she saw a man before her. Not her guard. Not a prince. But a man. A man who had risked everything to save his family. Who was now risking everything to protect her. "I would appreciate that very much, Finn. Thank you."

"It is my job and my honor." Finn bowed his head, placing a hand over his heart, but Irelia didn't miss the twitch in his jaw. He then motioned for them to walk ahead.

Fornax looked between Irelia and Finn, then gently adjusted his arm around her back and took hold of her left hand with his other.

Irelia mumbled her thanks.

"Are you sure you can walk?" Fornax whispered in her ear. Irelia merely scowled at him, so he relented and led them down the hall.

After what felt like forever, they finally reached Irelia's rooms. She could have cried with relief. Fornax helped her into her bed and told her he was going to send for a healer. Before he left, he bowed and kissed the knuckles on her hand. She didn't need to fake the blush that rose in her cheeks this time. Having him in her room was . . . intimate.

Fornax's eyes were lit with an invisible fire when they met hers again. A smile formed on his handsome face, both dimples appearing. "See you tomorrow, sweetheart," he said. Then he turned, leaving her breathless for some reason, and clasped Finn on the shoulder with a nod before he left.

Finn watched the prince walk back down the hall before turning to look at Irelia. And for the first time since she'd met him, Finn looked tired. Utterly exhausted.

"Get some rest tonight, Finn. Go see your family or something. All right?"

Finn stared at her for a moment. Then he bowed and took his leave, shutting the door with a click behind him.

Irelia released a long breath.

A healer arrived a short while later. After she'd tended to Irelia's wound, helped her bathe, and then dressed her for bed, Irelia slipped into a deep, undisturbed sleep.

CHAPTER TWENTY

Elodae sat with her head in her hands at one of the five long wooden tables that lined the Grand Hall. The decorations from last night's celebration had long since been taken down. Or Elodae had drunk them all away. The last thing she remembered was sitting on the dais, nursing her fourth glass of wine and glaring at the dancing crowd. Alden and Astrid had danced song after song after song together. Warren had asked her numerous times if she wanted to leave, but it was her party, for the gods' sake. She wasn't going anywhere.

She'd said as much to Warren, who held up his hands in defeat and let the subject drop.

Then Elodae remembered nothing.

She'd woken up in her bed that next morning wrapped in her green robe. The curtains had thankfully been drawn shut. Her dress from the previous night had been hung back in the armoire, her slippers neatly tucked away.

Sitting up to rub her eyes, Elodae had glimpsed a folded piece of paper on her bedside table. Familiar handwriting had welcomed her as she unfolded the note.

> *I helped you back to your rooms and you practically bit my head off for it. But don't worry, my mother was there and got you undressed and into bed.*
> *I think we should talk, though. About everything.*
> *Meet at our spot when the clock chimes 8 this evening?*
> *– Alden*

Elodae had read and reread the note. Not once, not twice, but three times.

Talk. He wanted to *talk.*

People moved about the Hall. Some were eating breakfast, and some merely chatted with friends or read a book over their food. Others talked in hushed tones about the darkness and its demons.

The Veiling, they all had started to call it. The sheet of darkness that had fallen onto the castle.

Someone from Elodae's left whispered, "My nephew was in the city that day and he said it looked like the Goddess Rhiannon dropped a blanket over the castle. No one could see past it."

Someone else whispered back, "My son said the guards tried to get inside the darkness to help, but it was like an invisible shield had been placed around the castle. But not all of it. My son was up past the northern wall hunting and he said the western side of the castle wasn't in shadows. Only the Grand Hall and the eastern side."

Elodae lifted her head and looked over at the two men. "And did either of your boys see anything?"

The two men went quiet. The one across the table's cheeks turned a bright red. "No, Your Grace. They said that they could hear the velarum's roars, but—"

"Velarum?" she asked, sitting up straighter.

"The demons that attacked," the other one replied for his friend.

"Did they say what happened once the darkness vanished?"

"No, Your Grace," the first man said. Elodae tried not to wince at the title. "My nephew said everyone had taken shelter in their homes. That the Veiling suddenly just . . . vanished. And the guards along the gates could finally get inside to help."

Elodae could hear her heart pounding in her head. Dipping her chin in thanks, she turned back to her food and poked at it with her fork.

"We must go to Rhiannon's temple tonight to pray for her mercy from the darkness and then to Solas's temple to pray for the sun to always remain," the nervous one whispered once she'd turned away.

"Should we bring an offering?" his friend asked.

Elodae tuned them out. She highly doubted it was the Night Goddess's fault the Veiling had happened. And the sun had been shining when darkness fell over the castle, so if Solas couldn't keep the velarum at bay, then she doubted their praying to him would do much good.

The fact that the people of Cronanth had named these

demons made her uneasy. It made it real. Which was foolish, because every time Elodae saw her sister, she knew it was very, *very* real.

Thoughts of the attack plagued her mind when boots scuffed across the table. Elodae swallowed her groan and looked up to find the prince standing across from her.

Fornax swung a leg over the bench opposite hers and sat, straddling the seat. He rested his elbow on the table. "Rough night, Duchess? Or should I be calling you princess now?"

Elodae rubbed her temples. She had woken that morning praying that her father's announcement had been a dream. But then she'd read Alden's note, which was currently tucked in the pocket of her black pants, and people had congratulated her the entire walk from her room.

"The wine was not my friend last night," Elodae grumbled and picked up her glass of water.

She had chosen to eat breakfast in the Hall with everyone else today, thinking the constant noise would help her not to be alone with her thoughts for too long. It was not proving helpful in the slightest.

Fornax chuckled.

Elodae set her glass back down and looked around the room for Hadeon and the other Dolannish lords, but she couldn't see any. In fact, she didn't see any of his guards either. Not even one. "Where's your lord that follows you like a pup and the rest of your men?"

The prince snorted. "I can take care of myself, princess."

"You're a fool if you think you don't need at least some protection after what happened," she chided the prince.

Fornax smirked. "And do you?"

"Do I what?"

"Need protection?"

Elodae eyed the prince.

"Surely a princess should not be wandering the castle by her lonesome," Fornax continued, tilting his head to the side.

"One: my guards are with me—as this is my castle." She waved a hand toward the guards that stood around the Hall. "Two: I'm not a princess."

Amusement flamed in his deep red eyes. "Yet."

Elodae ground her teeth. He was the Prince of Dolannish. Biting his head off this early in the morning would not do her any good.

Fornax looked away from Elodae then and around the cavernous room.

She watched the prince for a moment. She hadn't been able to gather any more information on him since she'd danced with Hadeon after they arrived. The nobles and guards he had come with had been scarce these last few days.

"Where's your cousin?" Fornax asked, looking back to Elodae. He reached across the table and plucked up a potato from the pile on her plate.

Elodae picked up her fork to shoo away his hand. He flashed her a grin as he popped it into his mouth.

"Her rooms, I suppose."

"Hmm." His eyebrows furrowed as he looked around the room once more.

When his gaze landed on Elodae again, she cocked her head in silent question.

Fornax's eyes narrowed. Then he roamed those eyes over her face—really looking at her. Elodae was tempted to throw her fork at him for the frankness of that stare. His gaze lingered on her neck and then he nodded toward it. "That's pretty. What does the star and the moon mean?"

Elodae's blood stopped cold. "What?"

He raised a manicured brow at her. "The star and the moon? I feel like I've seen them before."

She did her best to school her face into remaining neutral. Unreadable. "I don't know."

Fornax stared at her necklace for a moment longer before he lifted his eyes back to hers. "Where are you from?"

She blinked, her grip tightening on her silverware. She was not having this conversation. Especially with Fornax. People asked about her necklace all the time; where she had gotten it, who had given it to her. So on and so on. But no one—not ever—had asked about the star and moon. Everyone had always assumed it was because of her love for astronomy. Or that it was simply a beautiful necklace.

For Fornax to insinuate that it symbolized something . . . Elodae didn't like it. Not one bit.

"Samarok," Elodae lied, answering the prince's question. "My parents died when I was very young. I don't remember much about them."

At least the last bit was true.

"Hmm."

"Did you need something, Your Highness?" Elodae asked, forcing a smile onto her face. She couldn't keep the bite out of her next words. "Or were you just pining for my cousin? Your next conquest."

She knew it was the wrong thing to say when the prince's usual smile fell away and his eyes hardened, making her spine lock into place. He swung his other leg over the bench and rested both elbows on the table, leveling his gaze with hers.

Elodae's heart raced under his stare, and she forced her body not to shift. Forced herself to weather his gaze.

"I don't know what you think you know . . ."

Elodae's body itched to bow under the dominance radiating from his eyes.

Fornax cocked his head, as though he knew exactly how he made her heart flutter. "But you know nothing of who I am."

"I know you're the heir of the kingdom that was set to take over our continent not a few years ago," she replied with the same lethal calm. "I know who your father is—what he's done. What *you've* done."

Fornax went completely still, his dark red eyes flaming with barely contained rage.

"I know you're the man set to marry my princess because of some agreement between our kings. I know she deserves to be married to someone who loves her and will cherish her. Someone who will take care of her and her people. And I know that someone is *not* you."

Fornax's jaw clenched. He leaned back, sitting up straight. "You know nothing, duchess." He pushed away from the table and turned to leave but stopped and looked over his shoulder at Elodae. "Do I not deserve the same?"

And with that, he strolled out of the Grand Hall, hands shoved into his pockets.

Elodae watched until he disappeared through the towering doors of the Hall. She didn't trust him. Didn't like him. Part of her still felt like his marriage to Irelia was just another ploy for King Malum to wedge his way into the other courts.

She stabbed at her now-cold potatoes and finished the

rest of her food in silence. The men to her left continued whispering about the Veiling, seemingly oblivious to the conversation she'd just had with the Dolannish Prince.

Princes and guards and demons and darkness and nightmares.

When had the world become so uneasy? When had her lazy days with Irelia in the garden turned into flinching at every noise that came from behind her? When had her love for the night turned into terror of the void? Since the Veiling, all darkness seemed to hold that unnatural sense of emptiness. Inescapable. Unsavable.

Elodae's thoughts chased her in circles as she left the Hall and made her way back to her room. She needed to get out of this castle. More so, she needed to get out of her head.

ALDEN HAD JUST FINISHED A GRUELING TRAINING session with Warren when Dalo, another of Elodae's guards, walked into the barracks with a letter in hand.

Alden's heart gave a jolt when he recognized the seal. Elodae.

Nodding his thanks to Dalo, he walked over to the benches that lined the room. Warren plopped down next to him, pulling his shirt off and using it as a rag to clean off his face.

"What's that?" he asked, running the shirt through his hair.

Alden sucked in a deep breath and let it out slowly before he replied, "A letter from Elodae."

His brother draped his shirt over his shoulder and reached for a glass of water. "And you're not opening it because . . .?"

He just shrugged. The truth was, he wasn't sure why he was hesitating. He was the one who had written to her first. He was the one who had asked her to meet him later that day.

Warren snatched the letter from Alden's hands. "Need me to read it for you?"

Alden grabbed at it, but his brother stood, moving out of the way. Before Alden could tackle him, he ripped it open and unfolded the note.

"Alden," Warren read, a broad smile on his face as he continued to back away from him. "I'll see you then. Elodae." His brother flipped the note over and scanned the back, then looked inside the sealed envelope. "That's it? That's what you were scared to read?"

Alden snatched the letter back. "Give me that, you prick."

Warren threw up his hands and turned to head back toward the training ground.

He glared at his brother's back, then sat on the bench and reread her note.

> *Alden,*
> *I'll see you then.*
> *– Elodae*

That truly was it. That was all she'd written.

What had he been expecting her to say, though?

Alden laughed humorlessly to himself. He had no idea what he would say to her tonight.

"You coming, Einar?" Radford barked from the center of the training ring.

"Yes, sir," he called back and folded up the note, tucking it into the pocket of his pants.

ELODAE WANDERED THROUGH THE CASTLE LAWNS. Birds soared overhead. The sun shone down on her. The trees rustled in the soft spring breeze.

Each passing day grew longer, which meant she had plenty of daylight to kill before meeting Alden later.

Four guards trailed behind her as she meandered through a grove of trees. She kicked at small rocks that lined her path, sending them skittering ahead of her, and headed toward the spot where she would meet Alden.

Our spot, he'd called it.

She smiled quietly to herself, looking down at her feet. They'd come out here as children so frequently that a path had been worn in the grass. To this day, it'd never quite grown back over.

Two swings hung from a tall branch on a red oak tree. How they had managed to climb the behemoth of a tree and tie the swings up there, she had no idea. As children, they had thought themselves invincible. She walked over to where they swayed gently in the spring breeze. She'd marked one with an E at thirteen years old because Alden kept switching which one he wanted and it had annoyed her to no end. The one next to it had an A on it. Brushing her fingers over the splintery A, she closed her eyes and sighed.

"El?"

Elodae whirled around and was met with Alden walking over to her. He was visibly sweaty. He wiped a hand across his forehead, which made his shirt raise slightly, displaying the rough surface of his stomach. The light trail of hair there.

Her cheeks heated, and she forced her eyes to meet his. She should not notice such things. So, she gave him a smile and hoped her blush came across as though she'd spent a little too long in the sun today. "What're you doing here?"

"I could ask you the same thing." He walked over to his swing and took a seat. It groaned under his weight.

"I'm not sure these are fit to hold us anymore."

"You may be right, but there's only one way to find out." He patted the seat next to his and grinned up at her.

When was the last time he'd looked at her like that? Open and carefree.

Hesitantly, Elodae sat in her own swing and pushed herself back and forth with the toe of her boots.

"So," Alden said slowly.

Elodae leaned back in her chair, swinging it higher and higher. Her feet left the ground. "So," she said back mockingly.

Alden watched her for a moment, and then he pushed himself as far back as the swing would go. He lifted his legs, sending him flying forward. The branch their swings were attached to swayed with him.

"Alden," Elodae shrieked as her swing bounced.

Alden tilted his head back and laughed. The sound was

full of pure joy, and Elodae couldn't help but stare at him. He stuck his legs out, skidding to a stop, and looked over at her.

She met his gaze, and something in his eyes made her stand and move toward a pair of benches.

"El." He jogged after her and grabbed her elbow.

Elodae stopped and turned to purse her lips at him. She blinked at his closeness, his chest rising and falling in an uneven pattern.

An urge she had not felt in a long time washed over her. Yearning to reach out and brush the hair from his eyes, to feel the callouses of his fingers over her skin.

She *wanted*.

The thought sent a bolt of lightning through her body, and an unknowing smile spread across her face.

Alden blinked, his eyes shooting down to her mouth. Her heart pounded as he slowly dragged his gaze back to hers. He was engaged. So was she, she supposed. She could not be feeling those things around him.

He reached up, tucking a strand of hair behind her ear, and said softly, "Live a little with me, El." He motioned back toward the swings.

Elodae wanted to, wanted to live a little with him. The yearning grew within her, so she forced herself to ignore his unspoken question and walk over to the benches. The crunch of twigs told her he followed.

They remained there in silence for a moment, letting the breeze stir around them. Elodae closed her eyes and sighed. The air had turned warmer, heating her skin even in the shade.

Alden cleared his throat.

She glanced at him, but he was toying with a stick on the ground with his boot. When he finally looked up, he offered her a nervous smile, and she raised her brows in question.

"You said you wanted to talk," she said carefully when he remained silent.

He nodded, lifting a leg and swinging it over the other side of the bench so he was straddling it.

"So, talk."

He sucked on his teeth and looked down at the bench. "I just . . ." He cleared his throat. "With everything that's happened, I—I don't really know what I'm doing. It's like the better I try to be . . . the worse I become."

Elodae's heart strained in her chest. She wanted to reach out a hand and offer comfort, but she couldn't.

Alden sighed and shook his head. "The truth is, I . . ."

Elodae kept perfectly still. She was afraid to move, as if it might break this spell and he wouldn't say whatever he needed to. She bit her tongue and tried to keep her face as open as possible.

"I've missed you, Elodae," he said quietly. "I've missed being able to talk to you and laugh with you. I miss calling you my friend. I—I wish I had never made that promise to my father. That I would marry Lady Astrid and get away from all of this. Get away from court. Because if I hadn't, then I could . . ." His eyes shuttered, and he sucked in a shaky breath.

"Then you could what?" Elodae asked quietly.

His glacial-blue eyes locked with hers. "Then I could be with who I truly want to."

Despite her better judgment, she felt those inner walls coming down. Felt herself unlock her heart, readying to hand over the key. And that—that terrified her. Her heart raced inside her chest and her palms grew sweaty. Her vision blurred around the edges and all she could hear was glass shattering and screams upon screams.

Worry fell over Alden's features. He reached a hand for her, but she pulled back and offered him a tight-lipped smile.

"I truly wish for you to be happy. I understand you made a promise to your father. And I'll always be your friend, Alden." Her heart lurched, so she shoved to her feet. She had to go. Had to get away. "I must get back. Was that all?"

Alden swung his leg back over the bench and stood. He opened his mouth, then closed it again. His face became unreadable, and he nodded. "That was all."

"All right." She tucked a piece of hair behind her ear and took a step back. "Well . . ."

She turned to head back to the castle before he could say anything more. Before he could voice the words she could've sworn he'd been about to say. She couldn't hear them. Not now. Because those words . . . they were a trap. They were used to lure someone in. To bend them. Break them. To use them for your own will.

Alden seemed to take a step toward her. As though he'd reach for her again. Stop her. But he didn't, so she just kept walking away.

CHAPTER TWENTY ONE

Cross-legged on a reclined chair under the shade of a willow tree, Elodae flipped to the next chapter in her book, pretending to read, but her mind truly raced full of a guard with ashen-blond hair and icy-blue eyes.

Irelia slowly paced in front of her, wincing now and then as she continued to put weight on her leg.

Elodae set down her book at last and watched her sister limp back and forth in front of her chair. "Please rest."

"I've rested for too long."

Elodae sighed and opened her book once more, letting her sister continue her painful walk.

Another party of soldiers had been sent off that morning, to return to the Silver Lake and try to find more about the demons and the Veiling.

Irelia finally relinquished her incessant pacing and plopped onto the chair beside Elodae's. She squeezed her eyes shut as she scooted back, massaging her right thigh. "Did you bring the salve down with you?"

"Of course." Elodae closed her book and pulled the tiny tin of salve out of her pants pocket.

"Thank you." Irelia uncorked the glass and pulled out the small wooden wand used to apply the salve. She handed it over to her sister.

Her sister flushed as she bunched the skirts of her light-green dress up around her right hip. Elodae looked away, and the guards that had accompanied them outside did too. The princess massaged the balm into her still-healing wound.

Finn appeared around a bend at that moment, Fornax beside him.

Irelia squeaked, nearly dropping the salve, and hastily pushed her skirts back down. She slapped a smile on her face as the two men approached, and Elodae bit her lip to hold in her snort.

"Princess." Finn bowed. "Duchess," he said to Elodae, bowing too, but not quite as deep as he had for Irelia. Still, Elodae was shocked that he had even used her title at all.

"Finn," Irelia said softly, dipping her head slightly.

Elodae looked sidelong at her sister. The way she had said the guard's name—Elodae didn't know what to make of it.

Fornax bowed low, taking Irelia's left hand in his and kissed her knuckles. "Princess," he whispered with a half grin.

Irelia blushed and dipped her head. "Prince," she said, not nearly as kindly as she'd said Finn's name.

Fornax's eyes held Irelia's as he straightened. He pulled his gaze away from the princess long enough to bow his head to Elodae. His deep red eyes moved back to her sister a second later.

Elodae knew she should stand, that she should curtsy and address Fornax properly, but she simply smiled up at both men and said, "Prince Fornax. Finn. To what do we owe this pleasure?"

Fornax's eyes shot to Elodae's, a slow smile appearing on his face. "I heard Irelia was here and thought I'd join her."

Irelia played with the ends of her hair, looking anywhere but at the prince and her guard.

Fornax raised a brow at Elodae. He was dismissing her, she realized.

She smiled at him and stood, picking up her book. The prince cocked his head, watching her as Elodae brushed past him.

"I'll be up there when you're done," Elodae told Irelia, pointing to her balcony that overlooked the garden.

"All right." Irelia looked inclined to follow her, but she remained seated, her light-green dress rustling in the soft spring breeze.

Elodae glanced over her shoulder once more before entering the open door that would lead to the stairs up to her rooms.

Fornax sat on the chair she had vacated, then just looked at the princess.

And Irelia—Irelia, who normally hated people staring at her—stared right back at the prince.

Elodae couldn't read their faces from this far away, but Finn bowed to the pair of them and turned to take up position amongst the other guards in the garden.

Something shifted in the air. The breeze turned colder, the sun beat down a little harder, and that thing deep inside Elodae tugged again.

Irelia stared at the prince. She didn't know what to say. So, she idly twirled a strand of her peach-blonde hair around a finger and chewed on her lip.

Fornax's russet eyes broke away from hers and slid down to her lips. She hated how it made her heart skip a beat. She knew little to nothing about this man. Her enemy. Her fiancé. Her future king.

A shiver snaked down her back.

Bandages still peeked out through the top of his white shirt. The shirt that clung to his shoulders and arms but gaped open at the unbuttoned neckline. The skin on his chest looked smooth and yet hard. Fornax clearly trained, and often, for him to be as muscular as he was.

Irelia couldn't help but think of how his calloused hands had scraped against her arms and hands while they'd danced, and while he'd helped her to bed the previous night.

She took in his clothes, the way his white shirt billowed softly in the breeze, and how his brown pants were cuffed at the bottom.

"Enjoying what you see?" Fornax asked, amusement thick in his voice.

Irelia's cheeks warmed as she lifted her eyes back to his. "Why are you out here?"

She internally winced at the question. She didn't know why Fornax made her bolder, angrier. More nervous. She would normally smile and bat her eyelashes at a man's attention, letting them see what they wanted to see.

But with him—with him, she found herself slipping. Slipping into who she truly was.

A moody, not-so-perfect princess. One who liked to study folklore and magic. One who rolled her eyes and threw sarcastic comments around.

Fornax shrugged. "I told you, princess. I heard you were out here and thought I'd come say hello."

"Oh."

"Is that a problem?"

Yes. "No."

A slow smile spread across the prince's mouth. "Is that a problem?"

Yes. "No," she repeated.

Fornax shook his head and leaned back on his palms, looking up at the tree above them. Irelia narrowed her eyes, not quite sure what to do.

A guard drifted past, checking in on them, and continued on.

"Why don't you like me?"

This again. "I don't know you."

"Then why haven't you gotten to know me?" he asked, swinging his legs off the chair to face her fully.

"Because I don't care."

She knew she was being a bitch, but something about him raked at her.

Fornax leaned forward, so his elbows rested on his knees, and locked his eyes with hers. "I'll tell you what I think, princess," he said quietly but not weakly. "I think you decided you didn't like me before I ever set foot on Samarokan soil. I think you hate the idea of being promised to someone, anyone, let alone a prince. *Especially* the prince of the kingdom the world hates so very much."

His dark red eyes held hers as he continued, "I think you've heard stories of how spoiled and wretched the people of Dolannish are. Heard about what we had to do in the war. Heard the worst things possible about my father and my kingdom. And so, you assumed the worst of *me* in turn. But worst of all, princess, I think you don't *want* to get to know me because you're afraid it's all a lie. That you *will* actually like me. Hel, maybe you'll even fall in love with me *and* my people. And all of that terrifies you."

Irelia's mouth had fallen open as she stared at the man in front of her. "I . . . That—"

"Am I wrong?" Fornax asked, his gaze so intense that Irelia had to look away. When she didn't say anything, he went on, "I don't like the idea of being *promised* to someone either. Especially to someone so open about her hatred of me and my kingdom. Dolannish is not perfect, nor is Samarok. But it's home. And unfortunately, I have no say in the matter of our marriage. And you don't either, I'm afraid." He looked down at his hands. "But I was at least hoping . . ."

For the first time since she'd met him, the prince seemed to be at a loss for words.

Then he shook his head and let out a single laugh. "I was hoping we could at least become friends. Or learn to enjoy one another's company. But I've been here three weeks and you practically run from me every time I come near. I . . . I just wish you would see me for *me*. Not for who you think I should be."

Shame washed over Irelia. How often did she pray people would see her for who she truly was and not for who they wanted to see? Who they thought she should or would be solely because she was a princess.

"I'm sorry," she whispered.

Fornax looked up from his hands. The shock written across his face made her shoulders heavy with guilt.

Irelia sighed, sliding herself up against the back of the lounge chair, wincing at the hot flash of pain that shot up her leg. She saw his hand twitch but ignored it.

"You're right," Irelia said after she had adjusted her dress and hair. A force of habit. "I've been unfair. You've been nothing but kind to me since you arrived. You saved my life, and all I've done is shut you out."

"Why?" Fornax asked softly.

Irelia chewed on her lip, thinking. "I am afraid, as you said."

He waited for her to say more, but when she didn't, he just nodded. "I'm afraid, too," he admitted with a breathy laugh.

She looked over at the prince, and he smiled at her. Both dimples appeared on his cheeks, but this wasn't the same flashy smile he'd worn before.

No. This was one softer. More genuine.

True.

So, Irelia offered him one in return.

SHE'D SMILED AT HIM.

Fornax stared at the princess, praying his shock wasn't

written across his face. And the way she looked at him now—it was more open than before. He'd meant everything he'd said, and he knew everything had struck true. He wanted her to let him in. Needed her to.

He couldn't fail his father again. Not in this.

Leaning back in his chair, he brushed a hand against his pocket, making sure the ring box was still there. Irelia's cheeks were stained red as she looked away, toward the blooming flowers surrounding them.

Gods, she was beautiful.

Fornax begged his heart to stop skipping a beat every time she looked in his direction and leaned his head back, closing his eyes. He let the sun's warmth sink into him as he lay there, next to the princess.

Next to his queen.

Elodae bolted upright, having fallen asleep reading a book on the sofa in her library, when Irelia flung open her bedroom door.

"I need to get away from the castle," Irelia begged, limping over to her.

Elodae stood, setting her book down on the table before her, and hurried over to help her sister sit. "And where would you go?"

"The Magicks." Irelia squeezed her eyes shut in pain as she lowered herself into the chair.

Elodae froze. "You heard what the king said. We aren't

allowed out of the castle unattended and we cannot go to the Magicks or Astronomers."

"I know," Irelia sighed. "But . . . I will ask him. I need to get away, E. Find Alden and Warren, I'll find Finn and we can go." She didn't give Elodae a chance to respond before she shoved back out of the chair and walked out of the room.

Elodae stood stunned in the doorway of her library for a moment, blinking at the closed door.

All right then.

She scrambled around her room, grabbing cloaks for her and her sister.

What felt like hours but Elodae knew were mere moments later, Irelia burst back into her room, Finn on her heels.

"Father agreed."

Elodae froze once more. "What?"

Irelia did not reply as she rushed over and grabbed the cloak in Elodae's outstretched hand.

"Why the sudden need for distance?" Elodae asked, slinging on her own cloak and pulling it up over her head.

"Fornax," Irelia grumbled. Her sister's gaze went to the door that led from Elodae's bedroom to the balcony. And the prince beyond.

Elodae looked out the windows and saw the sun beginning to set over the horizon. The prince and princess had been outside for quite some time. "What did he want?"

"To get to know me." Irelia let out a lifeless laugh.

Elodae raised an eyebrow at her sister.

"Oh, don't look at me like that." Irelia pulled her curling hair out from the neckline of the cloak. "How can I show him who I truly am when I don't even know myself?" Irelia whispered. Elodae understood what her sister meant all too well. "I mean, he's Dolannish, for the gods' sake. He's Father's enemy. *Eldonia's* enemy."

Elodae couldn't help but glance over her sister's shoulder at the towering guard behind.

"And yet Father just welcomed him into our court, our *home*, without so much as batting an eye. Fornax is . . ." Irelia made a frustrated sound. "He's forward and blunt. He flirts with everything that walks and he's always got that stupid smile on his face. It bugs me to no end. *Get to know me*," she mocked. "Like I would want to do that. And gods—he thinks I'm going to fall in love with him."

"Oh, my gods," Elodae said slowly. "You're falling for him."

Irelia whirled on her. "Excuse me? I am not."

Elodae laughed and ran a finger through the strands of hair that had fallen out of her braid. "Oh, you most certainly are."

Irelia's cheeks reddened. "E, that's not funny."

Elodae gave her a knowing look, but Irelia only crossed her arms and glared.

"Fine," Elodae conceded. "But your solution is to go off to the Magicks and avoid him?"

"No," she said slowly. "I just need space to think and continue researching the Veiling without the prince."

Elodae nodded. "All right."

"I—I need to get out of the castle. Ever since the attack, I haven't been able to think straight."

Elodae remained silent. It was a feeling she knew all too well.

"When I close my eyes," Irelia said quietly, "all I hear is

my people dying. All I feel is that thing tearing through my leg. I feel Fornax's blood soaking my dress. I hear him say it was *The Ending*." She looked down and toyed with the ends of her hair. "I *need* to get away from here. If only for a while."

The Ending? What the hel did that mean?

Elodae shoved down the thought. Fear can cause people to do and say the most outlandish things.

"All right. I'll go find Warren and Alden."

ELODAE DIDN'T LET GO OF IRELIA UNTIL THEY WERE in the Round Library. Even then, she didn't remove her hood. Irelia, however, threw her own back and plopped down on a settee near the statue in the middle of the space. The two had exchanged comforting words on the walk over to the Magicks. Although it was a seemingly simple question, when Irelia had asked Elodae if she was alright, it was meant to acknowledge Elodae's complicated history with this place.

Now standing in the space, Elodae placed her hands on her hip, catching her breath after the rush of them getting here.

Alden and Warren did a quick sweep of the space, Finn standing guard beside the princess. The two brothers returned moments later stating that everything was safe. Alden pointedly ignored Elodae's asking looks. He hadn't said a single word to her the entire time. Not even when she told them that the king had agreed to let them go to the Magicks accompanied.

"My child," a short plump woman cooed, entering the main space from one of the six archways on the right side of the room. It was the same woman who had talked about someone with blue and green eyes the last time they were here.

Elodae clenched her teeth at the memory. The woman was a fraud. There had been no eye of sky or eye of pine, nothing of the sort. And yet the Veiling had still happened, had still terrorized their people.

Still, she slowly backed away from that woman, feigning interest in a book that was lying on a nearby table.

The Moon Kingdom.

Strange symbols had been etched beneath the words written in their common tongue.

Elodae blinked.

They looked like the symbols on her necklace.

She was about to reach for it when a hooded figure emerged from the Shadow Library's archway, a stack of books in their hands.

The figure made a beeline for the sisters.

Elodae hurried to Irelia's side, heart racing, but the man was only heading for the Magick, probably eager to ask her some ridiculous question about shadows and death.

Shaking her head, Elodae opened her mouth to ask her sister if she needed her to get anything when the figure, an old man it seemed, croaked, "Where did you get that necklace?"

Elodae went still and looked down at her cloak. She'd left her necklace out.

Fuck.

Alden, despite blatantly ignoring her, stepped up to her side. A comforting presence.

Slowly, she turned to look at the man. She looked him up and down, taking in every detail. His size, his stance, his voice, even his smell. Even the books he was carrying. The top one read *The Veiling*. And again, beneath the words, were those same symbols.

Elodae's eyes shot back up to the man. His face was mostly concealed beneath his hood, but she could just make out weathered skin and dulling grey-blue eyes.

Irelia was trying to push herself up, but Elodae held out a hand, halting her sister from rising.

"What do you know—"

"Why do you ask?" Elodae asked, cutting her sister off with a glance.

The old man tilted his head. She fought the urge to shift on her feet as his phantom stare raked over her. Like he could see right through her. She wanted to run away from here and never come back. Gods, she hated this place.

She really fucking hated it.

Warren stepped up beside Alden.

"How long have you been in possession of it?"

"For as long as I can remember," Elodae said stiffly.

The old man went still. Unnaturally still. And then, faster than he should've been able to, the man grabbed hold of her necklace.

Irelia screamed. Alden and Warren, even Finn, lunged for Elodae. She reached for his wrist to push him away, but the man yelped, dropping his stack of books and yanking back his hand.

Irelia was yelling at him, shouting something, but Elodae couldn't hear it.

Her heart pounded in her ears as she clenched a fist around her necklace, staring at the man's hand.

He'd been burned.

Her necklace had burned him.

Elodae could just make out an eight-pointed star resting atop a crescent moon. Scorched onto his palm, just below his thumb.

"Do not touch her," Alden growled in the man's face.

Warren and Finn coming up on either side of Elodae.

A preternatural growl came from the hooded man, and then a heavy darkness fell on the Magicks.

CHAPTER TWENTY TWO

Elodae had the horrible sensation of falling.

She tried to reach out and grab something—anything. An endless void that smelled slightly like salt-kissed winds wrapped around her. Her heart was pounding too hard, ears ringing too loud, to hear anything else.

The sea's scent grew stronger and stronger, encircling all of her, all her senses.

Elodae searched and searched in the void but found nothing.

No light. No sound. Only that ocean smell.

Had the velarum returned? Were they at the Magicks right now? This darkness felt different. The other one had been bone-chilling, as though all the joy and light in the world had been snuffed out, but this one was heavy. Thick. Like the night she'd gone to the Astronomers.

She had to find Irelia. She couldn't let anything happen to her again.

Elodae tried to scream her sister's name, but no sound came out.

She tried again. Nothing.

Again and again and again she tried to scream for her sister. For Finn and Warren, for Alden.

She couldn't go through this darkness again. The sea salt smell sent her back to the ocean, tumbling through that endless black sea, trying to cling to something, anything, that would keep her afloat. She didn't know which way was up or down.

As though a fire had been ignited, her senses came rushing back. The salt-kissed wind vanished along with the darkness.

Heart still racing, she scanned her surroundings once her vision finally refocused.

Her friends. Where were her friends?

But Elodae was no longer in the Magicks.

No, she was in a dark, damp stone room. Thirteen candles scattered about, casting flickering shadows across the wet floor. Water dripped from the ceiling and seeped through her pants.

Elodae tried to stand, but a clattering noise sounded along with a sharp pinch. She looked down to see her ankles and wrists encased in shackles.

She was chained to the stone floor.

Her mind raced. The books. That man. Her necklace.

It'd burned him.

That wasn't possible. But she'd seen it with her own eyes.

Elodae began to panic. She had to get back to Irelia, had

to know her sister was safe and not chained as she was in another room.

Elodae yanked against the chains, but the more she pulled, the tighter they got. She cursed under her breath and looked around the room—cell—and tried to find anything she could use to pick the locks.

Nothing.

Absolutely nothing adorned this space besides her, these chains, and the candles high on the walls.

"Gods," she growled. She bent her head down, reaching for a pin in her hair, but it was as though the chains knew. They shortened and squeezed so tightly on her wrists that she was certain they would bruise.

She had to be going crazy. Chains couldn't do that on their own.

"This isn't funny anymore," she called out toward the door in front of her. The only way in and out.

Water dripped from the ceiling and splashed on Elodae's face. She made to wipe away the droplet, but the chains bit into her skin even harder.

"Oh, fuck off," she snarled at the shackles.

"Talking to inanimate objects now, love?" a man's voice drawled from the now open doorway.

The salt-kissed wind wrapped around her once more. Her heart thundered as she looked up to see a hooded figure leaning against the doorframe. The light from the candles danced across his body as though their flames longed to reach for him. His face remained veiled in shadows so she couldn't make out his features. The fine black mist swirling around his head and shoulders, beckoning to his call.

Veiled in shadows.

This must be who controlled the demons. Must be who was responsible for the Veiling and the attack on the castle. Her sister's injury.

Elodae's body trembled.

The man looked down at his hands. He ran a finger over the palm of his left one and a low growl came from deep inside him, making Elodae's spine lock up.

The man's head turned toward her again.

Elodae forced herself to keep her composure, to still her body. She wouldn't let him sense the unease that shot through her every time she saw the endless void beneath his hood.

She had the unsettling sensation that he was staring at her. Assessing her. Sizing her up.

He glanced down at his hand again, and Elodae caught a glimmer of the eight-pointed star that had been scorched into his palm.

Good.

If he truly was behind the Veiling and the velarum attack, then she was glad to have branded him. Once she got out of these chains, she'd burn the rest of him to ash.

"Care to enlighten me on what you find so amusing?"

She blinked again and her eyes shot to the man's face, or where his face should have been, and found him facing her again. She wiped away the smirk she hadn't realized had formed on her face.

"I'll ask again," the man said, enunciating each word carefully. Like he was unsure if she was smart enough to understand him. He pointed to her necklace. "Where did you get that?"

The man's voice had changed. It was now dark and

husky, yet soft somehow. Like the strumming of a contrabass's chord.

But this new voice . . . the accent that graced it.

Elodae sucked in a breath and composed herself, shoving the realization and fear deep down within her. She said with a fake sense of calm, "First, don't call me love. And second, as I said before, *Orion*, I've had it for as long as I can remember. Would you like me to write it down so you don't forget?"

The man froze. It terrified her a little, how still he had become.

Then he tipped his head back and roared a laugh.

Elodae flinched at the noise. At how genuine it sounded.

He leaned forward again, still laughing, and she could've sworn she saw his face for a fleeting moment.

His eyes . . .

She shook her head, convinced her mind was playing tricks on her.

"You've got an awfully smart mouth for someone who is currently chained to the floor, love." Laughter still echoed in his words as he stepped forward a few paces.

"You've got an awfully stupid mouth for someone who is holding me captive." She picked at her nails, the perfect picture of arrogance. The movement, however, caused the shackles to pinch into her wrists again. She held in her hiss. "And don't call me that."

"I'll call you whatever I damn well please. *Uninterested*," he added after a beat of silence. Elodae could practically hear the smile in his voice.

And he had just confirmed who he was.

"And please explain to me how I am . . ." He paused, and

Elodae could've sworn she saw his shoulders shake slightly with laughter. He had to be insane. "*Stupid.*"

"I now know what you sound like. Smell like. Your *name*. I'd know you blind." Elodae looked up from her nails at him. She meant it. She was committing his smell, his voice, to memory. And those eyes—she wasn't sure she had seen them correctly, but nonetheless, they were imprinted in her mind.

He went still again. "My scent?"

"Yes." She hoped the tremble in her voice came across as annoyed and not terrified. She hated how it made some primal part of her both want to bow under it but also crack open an eye and challenge it.

"You can smell my scent?" the man asked, still unearthly still.

"Yes," Elodae repeated. "That is what a person's scent is, is it not? A smell?"

Clearly insane.

He stared in her direction for a moment and then slowly stalked toward her, not saying another word. He didn't stop until he stood directly between her bent knees, and then gradually lowered into a crouch before her.

Orion still said nothing, didn't even move, for what felt like ages.

Elodae fought the urge to shift. The void beneath his hood was becoming more and more terrifying. She had to get out of here. She *had* to find Irelia. Had to know that her friends were safe. She prayed to Eirene that they weren't here, that they had made it out.

"Who's to say this is my true form?" he drawled.

Elodae snorted.

"What's funny?" When Elodae didn't reply, he pushed, "Do you not believe in magic?"

She gazed into those swirling depths under his hood. "You don't seriously think that I'd believe you can *shapeshift*."

He didn't say anything, just crouched there, facing her. The instinct to cower under that void overwhelmed Elodae again.

"What?" she demanded, trying to cover her discomfort. "You're saying that you have magical powers? Are you truly mad, then?"

"Careful, princess," he said slowly.

"I'm not—" she cut herself off.

The name she had given him the other day. Auriel. It was close enough to Irelia that if he truly was new to Samarok, he could genuinely think she was the princess.

"You were accompanied by royal guards. Do not play me for a fool."

Elodae kept her mouth shut. She would much rather be here, in this cell, chained to this floor, than be safe while Irelia was stuck in here instead.

Orion motioned for her to say something and Elodae made a show of sighing and rolling her eyes again.

"*Magic...*" She made air quotes with her chained hands. The metal dug deeper, and she could've sworn the scent of her blood filled the air as the shackles cut into her skin. Bastards. "Has and never will be real. So, you don't fool me, Orion."

He tensed at her use of his name. Interesting.

"Unless you're one of those," she hummed to herself,

trying to think of the right word, "confused people who believe magic is sleeping."

"If you don't believe in magic, Auriel, then what were you and your little friend doing at the *Magicks*?" He slipped out an onyx dagger and began toying with it.

"Research."

The truth—just not the whole truth.

"You're a terrible liar," he purred, twirling the dagger in his hands.

"As are you."

She didn't know why she was egging him on. He had her chained. He had a dagger out. And here her dumbass was baiting him. Pissing him off. She clearly had a death wish, but she couldn't help herself.

Orion paused his fidgeting.

"Ah, love." His voice dropped an octave as he placed his left hand on the wall by her head, leaning closer. His scent grew stronger, and she noticed another scent mingled in, barely potent.

Crackling embers.

Like the fires Elodae loved to build in the wintertime when the snow was too heavy and full to leave her rooms, let alone the castle. Like the fires of an autumn festival where people danced and sang and played music. Like the flames that still fought to be the one to cast their light on his body. It reminded her of the Astronomers, somehow.

Even this close, she could see no trace of the face beneath that hood.

"I'm becoming bored with this." He suddenly sighed, pulling her from her thoughts. "Either you remove the necklace, or I will cut off your head and take it myself. Lady's choice."

"I don't know who designed these sadistic restraints, but I can't lift my arms any farther than this." She made a show of lifting her arms a couple of inches off the ground and didn't hold back her hiss this time when they clenched.

"Hmm." He considered the chains for a second and then shrugged. "Head it is."

She felt the coldness of his blade against her throat. It happened so fast that she didn't even see him move.

"If you were going to kill me, you would've done so by now." The movement Elodae's throat made while she spoke caused the dagger to nick her skin slightly. She felt the warmth of her blood bead beneath the blade.

"I thought you'd be more useful to me alive. That maybe you'd give me some information about the necklace, but I've grown tired of your rambling."

"Is that so?" She pressed forward into the blade, causing the cut to deepen. Taunting him to do it.

A low growl came from him.

"If you're going to kill me, the least you could do is show me your face." She batted her eyelashes at him, and this time he was the one who pressed the dagger further into her neck. Warm liquid dripped onto the collar of her shirt, splitting open her scar from weeks earlier.

"There is so much you don't know, princess," he said, his voice hoarse.

"At least tell me this." The pressure on the blade eased slightly as her throat moved again. "Why do you want it?"

Orion tilted his head and she could've sworn the temperature plummeted, the flames flickering high above.

"Why now?" She pushed at his silence. "Why didn't you do this when you had me at the tavern? Or in the alley?"

"I wasn't the one in that alley that night," was all he said. Elodae blinked.

"We have the same agenda, Auriel," Orion continued. "We want the same things. Now give me the necklace."

"Show your face," Elodae demanded. She didn't know why, but it was important. For she knew when someone was trying to hide something.

That preternatural stillness settled over him, waking that thing deep within her once more.

Orion removed his dagger from her neck and pulled back his hood. He leaned in, so close that their breaths mingled. His scent encircled her once more. Her heart pounded uncontrollably. With his face now being lit by the flames, she realized she *had* seen his eyes clearly before.

His left eye was the richest sapphire blue, whereas the right one was a deep forest green. Both eyes were golden yellow around his pupils. A scar cut through his left eyebrow, narrowly missing the striking blue eye. And the one she had seen twice before that cut through the right side of both his top and bottom lip. His face was rough-hewn, as though he'd been carved from the Tyrian Peaks themselves. His hair was a dark brown and fell in soft waves that brushed against his shoulders. A hint of a tattoo peeked out from the neckline of his cloak, painting his brown skin with their symbols and swirls.

He was . . . beautiful.

His different-colored eyes bounced between hers, and Elodae fought the urge to squirm under his stare. It felt like he was seeing straight into her soul.

An eerie voice echoed in her mind.

An eye of pine, an eye of sky—it begins.

Oh, gods.

Elodae's breathing came faster, her mind reeling.

The Veiling, the demons, her necklace burning him.

Oh, gods.

It had all begun after that night in the tavern.

"Satisfied?" Orion whispered.

Elodae sat there in stunned silence, staring at him.

Orion peered down at her necklace and reached for it, then hesitated. Probably remembering that it would burn him. "How did the king's daughter get a hold of this?" He seemed to ask it more to himself than to her. His eyes crawled back up her neck, lingering briefly on the cut that had started to clot, and then his stare met hers once more. "Who are you?"

She didn't dare answer. Didn't know if she could.

"You're not really the king's daughter, are you?"

Shit. Shit shit shit.

Elodae forced her face to remain unreadable, to give nothing away to this demon of a man.

"The queen died giving birth to their daughter. And this," he pointed to the pendant, "is not from these lands."

"How do you know that?"

"How did you get it?"

"You didn't answer my question."

Orion smirked. "You haven't answered any of mine."

They stared at each other for what felt like minutes.

"Who'd you steal it from?"

Elodae lifted her chin. She'd die before telling this man anything.

He pushed up and started to pace, throwing angry glances her way and rubbing at his sharp jaw. Then he stopped, and a slow smile spread across his face. "Atlas," he called out.

"Yes?" another male's voice, Atlas, answered from the hallway.

"Bring me the other girl."

Ringing began in Elodae's ears.

"Sorry?" Atlas replied.

"Bring me the other girl." The blue- and green-eyed man met her stare. "This one is not the king's daughter and doesn't seem inclined to be useful. Perhaps she needs a little . . . persuasion." He started walking toward the door.

The man in question, Atlas appeared then, but the hallway was too dark to see anything more than a black shape.

Orion drew his hood back over his head and smiled over his shoulder at Elodae. "We'll be back soon, love. Maybe then you'll want to cooperate."

He turned to leave again.

"Wait," Elodae called after him. She couldn't let him take Irelia.

He paused. "Yes?"

"It washed up on the shore when I was ten. That's where I found it. I don't know where it came from." A half-lie, half-truth.

"So, you've had the necklace for thirteen years?" Orion asked, surprise flickering across his face.

"Yes." She didn't want to think about how he that.

He considered her for a moment and then started walking away again. "Bring me the other girl."

The iron door swung shut on a salt-kissed wind.

CHAPTER TWENTY THREE

No thoughts entered Alden's mind as Elodae vanished into nothing but a swirl of smoke in the Magicks. No sounds reached his ears, the pull of his brother was never felt across his skin. Nothing.

Nothing *nothing nothing*.

Elodae was gone.

She had been taken before his very eyes and there was . . . nothing he could do. He was helpless. Useless.

Alden stumbled forward, as if pulled by an invisible thread. He didn't know where he was going, didn't know where to start searching. He would tear the very fabric of the universe apart to find Elodae if that's what it took. Someone stepped in front of him, trying to halt him as he followed that invisible string, but he shoved past them.

They said something. Or maybe they didn't. He didn't

care, he didn't hear anything, felt nothing but an open maw of emptiness.

"*Alden*," a stern voice broke through his haze.

Alden turned to see Finn standing behind him, Irelia embraced in Warren's arms.

"We need to go back to the castle for reinforcements." When Alden didn't move, Finn commanded. "*Now*."

Alden was just about to follow him, to allow Finn to pull him away from the Magicks, when he heard it. Faint and light, but there it was. A voice screaming.

He froze, rooted to the spot on the ground next to the giant statue in the center of the Round Library. Straining his ears, he listened again.

Muffled screams, so silent he would've missed it had he not been listening.

Without saying a word, he turned and rushed toward one of the dark libraries on the far side of the room. He didn't think twice before he plunged into its freezing depths.

"Wait!" Someone called from behind him, but Alden ignored them. He just kept walking until a hand grasped his elbow, pulling him to a halt.

"Wait," a short, lithe woman panted.

Alden turned glaring eyes on her and she flinched at the intensity of his stare. He was too far gone into that dark and quiet place to care.

"The other guards left to get reinforcements," the woman said. "But I heard it, too. The screams."

"Where?" was all he managed to growl out.

"Come."

The lady turned and rushed from the library. Alden raced

to keep up with her as she wove them up the ramp surrounding the library to the highest level.

"There used to be a passageway from the Magicks to Castle Cronanth," she explained. "It was sealed off decades ago, for it was said to be the home of a monster."

The sage rushed them through curving halls, past books hundreds of years old. Dust clinging to them as desperately as Alden wanted to cling to hope in that moment.

Suddenly, she stopped by a solid wall.

"It's beyond there." She lifted a shaking finger, pointing at the stones.

Alden furrowed his brows, not understanding. He didn't have time for this. He needed to find Elodae and *fast*.

The sage pushed her hands against the wall and murmured something soft and low, too low for Alden to make out. When suddenly, a door appeared as if from nowhere. He lurched backwards, eyes bulging from his head. The sage turned toward him, as if the gentle glow of blue that outlined the door was normal.

"How did you—"

"Tell no one," the sage whispered, shushing him with a lifted hand. "We're not supposed to show normals."

Alden was about to push further, to ask what in the gods name she was talking about, when he heard it again, slightly louder now that the door appeared. A scream from far within.

Without thinking, he shoved past the stone and broke into a sprint.

Elodae screamed and screamed and screamed

"HELP."

"IS ANYONE THERE?"

"CAN ANYONE HEAR ME?"

"ALDEN."

That last one was the one she screamed the most. Just his name. Over and over and over again.

Once Orion and Atlas had left, her cell had been plunged into that heavy darkness. Her anxiety swelled inside of her. Threatening to consume her like the ocean all those years ago.

She tried to breath. Tried to keep it at bay, but the longer she sat in that darkness, the longer that cold water plinked away as it dripped from the ceiling around her, the more and more she fell into that well inside.

"Alden," she croaked, her voice having given out after her shouting. A sob worked its way up her throat.

She was going to die here.

That was when shouting echoed beyond the confines of her darkness. Elodae went still, slowing her breathing so she could hear even the slightest movement.

Yelling and the singing of metal against metal grew louder and louder.

"Where is she?" She heard a voice roar—a voice that had a sob breaking its way out of her chest.

"Alden!" She yelled, her voice cracking as she strained it beyond its breaking point.

Singing of swords reverberated along her body, sending shivers down her spine. Alden would find her; he would save her. She knew it in her soul.

"Elodae," Alden called.

"I'm here! I'm here."

Tiny rocks tumbled from the door before her. Still shrouded in darkness, she couldn't see anything, but she could hear Alden grunting as he tried to shove open the door.

"I'm coming, Elodae. I'm coming," he swore.

Another sob escaped her lips.

"I'm coming," he vowed again.

More rocks clattered to the ground as he shoved and shoved. Elodae struggled against her restraints, but the more she pulled, the tighter they got. Warm liquid trickled down her wrists and she cried out.

Blinding light hit her eyes, a cry escaping her lips as she turned her head away, squeezing her eyes closed.

Pounding footsteps approached her and then gentle, calloused hands cupped her cheeks.

Elodae turned toward him, and she had never seen anything so beautiful as those icy-blue eyes burning into hers. She sobbed, reaching for him, but her shackles dug even further into her skin.

"Elodae," Alden breathed.

"Take them off," she pleaded, shaking the chains.

His eyes instantly landed on her shackles and a muscle tensed in his jaw as he saw her blood coating her hands and wrists. Shoving from the ground, he found a large rock out in the hall that had fallen off the door to her cell and walked back over.

It took several hits against the bolts attaching her to the

floor before they finally released her. Shackles still stuck to Elodae's wrists; Alden helped her to her feet.

"How did you find me?" she asked, a sudden wave of nausea washing over her.

"I followed your voice."

Elodae blinked up at him, at the closeness of his face to hers. Their breaths mingled between them, her heart pounding in her ears.

"We have to get out of here." Alden shoved a blade into her hand, pulling out his own sword, and darted out of the room.

Three bodies littered the floor of the hall and Elodae swallowed the bile that threatened to escape her stomach at the sight of them, cut open and bleeding.

Alden gripped her hand in his and raced forward. Elodae had to fight to remain upright over the loose rocks along the floor.

"Well, well, well," a lilting voice drawled from up ahead.

Alden went utterly still, tucking Elodae behind him, and lifted his sword.

A woman clad in entirely black, a mask covering the bottom half of her face, her brown curls tied into a braid down her back, stood before them as they rounded the corner.

"That wasn't very nice of you," she purred, motioning to the dead monsters behind them.

Elodae lifted her short sword and tried to move around Alden, but he forced her behind him again.

Dual blades sung as the woman pulled them out of her belt and flipped them in her hands.

Not realizing how soaked her clothes had become,

Elodae began to shiver in the depths of the passageway. But still she held her blade firm. The way Alden had taught her.

Alden didn't give the woman a chance to attack first. He lunged at her, sword lifted, and slashed. She moved with a preternatural swiftness, faster than anyone had the right to be. She kicked off the wall, flipping over Alden and landed between Elodae and him.

"You're a hard one to keep," the woman purred, her grey eyes burning into Elodae's as she stalked toward her.

Alden swung at the woman's head, but she dropped low, swinging out a foot and sending Alden flopping onto his back. Elodae lurched forward with her blade, her chains rattling in the stone hall, but then the woman vanished, causing Elodae to tumble forward, landing on top of Alden with a grunt.

Their eyes locked for a split second before he helped lift her up and grabbed her hand, breaking into a sprint once more.

They couldn't pause to think about what was happening, about these people and the darkness, about her being chained up and Alden finding her, about how that woman had just let them escape.

No, they couldn't think about anything but running as far away from here as possible.

Alden hauled her up step after step after step, the air warming the further up they went. And then finally, they broke through; out into a book-lined hallway.

Elodae nearly collapsed with exhaustion, but Alden held fast to her, keeping her upright. He did not let up as they raced down the shelved hall and down the spiral ramp to the center of the Round Library. Dozens of Samarokan guards swarmed the library as they descended.

But Alden did not stop. He did not stop his pace, pausing only to scoop Elodae into his arms when her legs finally gave out.

Only once they reached the safety of the Sapphire Gates did he slow his pace, his chest heaving against Elodae. She urged him to put her down, but his fingers just dug deeper into her skin. His eyes were wild as they scanned every single person they passed as he took her straight to the hospital wing.

Growling something at a healer who tried to take Elodae from his arms, he gently set her down into a bed himself. Relinquishing his grip on her for just a moment before his hand found hers. As though he was terrified of letting her go for even a second. That if he did, she may vanish all over again.

Elodae stared at Alden until she couldn't fight her exhaustion any longer, until a healer tipped a wooden bowl to her lips, telling her to drink. The moment that cold liquid hit her tongue, Elodae's eyes fluttered shut, and fear washed over her.

She didn't want to go back to the darkness.

"I'm here. I'm here," Alden's voice assured her, his warm hand clenched tightly around hers. "I'm here."

And it was those words that lulled her to sleep.

When Elodae's eyes opened next, the sky outside was dark. Silence met her ears as she glanced around the hospital wing, her memories a wild blur in her mind.

Alden sat in a chair to her right, his chest slowly rising

and falling as he slept. A sense of peace washed over her at the sight of him by her bedside.

Elodae didn't know why the thought of him not wanting to leave her side, even for sleep, made her heart clench. She watched him rest for a moment longer, then gently squeezed the hand still wrapped around her own.

Alden's eyes instantly flew open and found hers, as if he'd known where she was, even in his sleep.

"Are you all right?" He asked, his voice rough with sleep.

Elodae nodded, too tired for words.

He gave her a sleepy, crooked smile and brushed his thumb over the back of her hand.

"You should get into your own bed, Alden," she whispered, then blinked at the rawness of her own voice.

Alden shook his head and continued making soft passes on her hand with his thumb. "I'm where I belong."

They watched each other for a while longer, until exhaustion claimed Elodae once more.

CHAPTER TWENTY FOUR

Alden picked at the skin around his thumb as he listened to his king and Samarokan and Dolannish noblemen discuss what action to take to find Elodae's kidnapper. With every click of the large clock on the opposite side of the room, Elodae's absence from his side grew stronger and stronger. He ached to return to the hospital wing, yearned to see her again. He could barely stand to be aware from her for this long.

Radford said something from across the large round table, pulling Alden back to reality.

Finn stood on the captain's other side, and Warren was amongst the guards that lined the walls of the round room. His brother raised an eyebrow when Alden met his stare. Alden just shook his head and looked away again.

One of the Dolannish generals said something too low

for Alden to hear and pointed to the map of Samarok that lay between them all.

Prince Fornax leaned one hand against the edge of the table, the other rubbing his chin while he pondered the information. Vanor talked in hushed tones to Radford about assembling another party to go on another wild hunt for the velarum.

Alden mindlessly rubbed at the raised skin, which was still stitching itself back together after the velarum attack he'd endured mere days earlier.

"Are we even safe here?" Hadeon grumbled into Fornax's ear, pulling Alden's attention.

Alden lifted his eyes from the map to glare at the lord who stood on his right-hand side.

Ever since the night of the ball when they'd first arrived, Alden had hated Hadeon. He tried to convince himself it wasn't because of that dance he'd shared with Elodae, but he was failing miserably.

The other lords had started weighing in on Vanor's suggestions for how to move forward.

"Have we found the man who kidnapped the king's niece yet?" a lord was saying.

"He must be responsible for these attacks, as well," another said.

More and more lords chimed in until the noise reached a roar in Alden's ears. They had told the king this morning that they had yet to find the kidnapper, and his anger had been palpable.

Alden's own blood boiled with rage every time he remembered what had happened to her. That someone had taken her. Harmed her. He caught himself staring at that slightly raised line on her neck occasionally and making promises to all the gods that he would find whoever had done that to her and kill them.

"Easy now," Fornax said in a low voice in Alden's ear.

Alden glared at the prince, loosening his iron grip on the pommel of his sword. Fornax wasn't even looking at him, but nodding along with whatever lord was saying this or that.

Vanor raised a single hand, and the room fell silent. "My niece is still recovering. I will not hammer her with questions about what happened until I know she is well enough. My daughter, who was attacked during Prince Fornax's arrival just over a month ago, is also still on the mend." Alden saw Fornax stiffen out of the corner of his eye. "Forgive a father—and uncle—if his mind is elsewhere right now."

Lord Marlow, Astrid's father, placed a hand on Vanor's shoulder and smiled. "I think we all can understand the burden of seeing our loved ones hurt, Your Majesty."

"We have our men searching the tunnels Alden found beneath the Magicks, but they are an intricate, winding, system," Dalo, another Samarokan guard, one under Alden's command, said to the king. "Between the tunnels and searching for the velarum . . . our men are stretched thin, sire."

"I can spare some men," Prince Fornax announced.

Hadeon tensed at the prince's side, the muscles in his jaw clenching as though internally fighting to keep his damned mouth shut.

"They can search for the velarum while your men hunt the monster that took your niece."

"My Lord," Hadeon started. "We did not bring enough

men to be able to send out full search parties while also keeping you safe."

Fornax growled at his lord, "I can manage by myself, Hadeon. And I did not ask for your input."

The lord's eyes narrowed at his prince, but he nodded and stepped back.

"Alden," Vanor said gently.

Alden's eyes immediately found the kings. "Yes, sire?"

"You were in those tunnels. You found my niece. Correct?"

Alden nodded.

"Do you think you can do so once more?"

Alden paused. That would require leaving the castle, leaving Elodae's side again, leaving her alone. "I did not navigate the tunnels alone, Your Majesty." His next words burned as they left his throat. "I followed Elodae's screams."

Frost settled over his heart as he admitted the words. The air in the room paused for a beat before the king's head hung slightly, sorrow filling his eyes. Guilt was palpable around Vanor.

"But you got her out," the king said, with the heartbroken voice of a father. "For her, can you do it again?"

Could he?

For her, he would try.

So, Alden stood up a little straighter, held his chin high, and nodded. "Yes."

Radford and several of the army generals launched into their plans for who and what would go with him on this next mission.

It took all of Alden's self-control not to dismiss himself

and run back to the woman he knew was still asleep in the hospital wing.

Fornax could practically see the guard to his left trembling with anticipation. His hand continuously tightened and released the celestine pommel of his sword. His eyes roamed around the room as if he were half expecting someone to waltz through the doors at any given moment.

"I'm sure she'll still be there when you get back, Alden," Fornax mused while his own lords and military generals discussed which of their men they would send to the Silver Lake in search of the Veiling and demons.

A muscle ticked in the guard's jaw as he turned to face him.

Fornax offered him a smile he knew would make most people swoon, but Alden just continued to throw daggers in his direction. Bold man.

"Your Grace," Hadeon said over Fornax's left shoulder.

He reined in his eye roll and turned away from Alden and toward the men surrounding the table.

"We will send half of our company for this mission. We will leave our other half here at the castle to help protect it and your people," the lord said for him.

The prince clenched his jaw, his nostrils flaring slightly. He hated how people continuously hovered over him.

He had trained alongside his men, fought in wars with them, for gods' sake. Three years ago, Dolannish had marched on Asiva for the second time. Half of their men had died during that war. A war that had only taken place because of his king's eager need. Only a year later would another army—from where, no one quite knew—do just that. And despite their differences, Asiva had still begged Dolannish for aid.

Fornax clenched his fist at his side so as not to touch the scar that sliced across his stomach. He had begged and begged his father to send men. Any they could spare. His father had given him the scar in retaliation.

The prince looked around at his men. He had bled next to them. Killed next to them. His brothers in arms. And yet here they were, scared of the dark.

His father was the reason behind their changed behavior around the prince.

Ever since the prince's older brother, Nath, named after the God of War, had been killed in that battle between Dolannish and Asiva, Fornax hadn't been allowed to go anywhere without being watched. Hadn't been allowed to fight alongside his men anymore. It had taken the better half of a year before his father even let him train again. The only time he'd ever called Fornax his son was when they were lowering his brother's body into the crypt and the king had named him his new successor.

It raked at something within him, that he wasn't allowed to do the things he used to. He loved the physical labor of training, of going on trips with his men into the Moon Rainforest and Western Marshes to learn how to fight as a unit.

Groups in the western half of their continent threatened the livelihood of their bordering kingdoms. They often raided the eastern cities, setting fire to homes and stealing everything imaginable. So Dolannish and Callumere, and even Asiva at one point, sent a regiment into the untamed lands. Samarok never seemed interested in anything outside their borders. Why the sudden change of heart, he had no idea. It made him cautious, skeptical; of the king, of the people . . . of the princess he was supposed to make fall in love with him.

Fornax loved those missions. He loved the wildness of the western lands. He loved seeing the exotic plants and animals their terrain offered. And more importantly, he loved the fight.

After getting pummeled by Nath his entire life, Fornax had learned that physical labor was an outlet for his rage, one that he loved exerting. He constantly lost himself in the training. His body fell into a kind of trance and his muscles moved of their own accord. The pain he felt during a fight overtook his mind—silenced it, almost—until no other thoughts circled except one.

To push harder.

But then his brother had died, and Fornax had ascended to inherit the throne of Dolannish. And with that title, everything he had grown to cherish had been stripped away. The men he'd fought alongside, trained with since they were boys, no longer sparred with him for fear of injuring the heir. Love interests no longer cared about Fornax the man but sought to get closer to Fornax the prince—the future king. He couldn't so much as blow his own nose without someone needing to look over his shoulder. It had grown a sort of resentment within him, a slight hatred for the roll he was forced to play, the one he never wanted.

"Your Grace?" Hadeon asked wearily.

Fornax blinked, realizing he hadn't given his approval yet. "That sounds fine, Hadeon."

Hadeon bowed his head and turned back to the war generals.

The prince stared blankly at a spot on the map within the castle of Cronanth, where he caught himself wishing a certain princess waited for him as the duchess did for the guard to his left. He needed the princess to let him in. He didn't know what his father would do if she fought this marriage and won.

The thought of tricking her into loving him tightened his stomach, but he would do it if needed. Or else he'd face the wrath of his father's blade yet again.

The clock in the room chimed one in the afternoon before the king called the meeting to a close and took his leave.

One and a half companies of men would go out at dawn in a weeks' time. The Samarokan Captain of the Guard and Finn, the Asivan that watched over Irelia, would leave with Alden to search the tunnels below the Magicks. Alden would stay behind due to his injuries.

Fornax had seen the discomfort in the guard's eyes at that order. He was a warrior to his very core; the same way Fornax was, but he hated leaving the duchess behind.

He was growing fond of the guard, Fornax realized, as Alden bowed and practically sprinted toward the doors toward the woman beyond.

The prince himself was about to turn to leave, to make his way toward the library to continue researching. Hopefully next to a peach-blonde princess. But something out of the corner of his eye caught his attention. Hadeon had stepped over to the King of Samarok.

Whispering something in the king's ear, Vanor nodded and escorted the lord into a small back room on the opposite end of the War Room. Prince Fornax balked as the door shut behind them.

He stepped around the table and marched over to the shut door, leaning forward, eye closed, and strained his ears to listen.

"He says you are doing well, King Vanor," Hadeon's muffled voice said.

"I am merely doing as told," the king responded in a voice that sounded eerily unlike himself.

Hadeon's chilled chuckle scattered across Fornax's skin. "He appreciates your cooperation."

"Prince?"

Fornax jumped, not having heard Captain Radford approach.

"Is everything all right?"

"Yes, Captain. Thank you." Fornax dipped his head and turned to leave. His heart pounded in his ears as he glanced over his shoulder at the shut door.

Something was indeed not all right.

CHAPTER TWENTY FIVE

Surrounded by tome after tome, Irelia hunched over scrawling words in a language she barely understood. The curves and twists of the letters jumbling together in her sleep deprived mind.

Worry for her sister chased after each and every thought Irelia conjured. Guilt consumed her.

It was her fault they had gone to the Magicks. It was her fault that Elodae had accompanied her. It was all her fault.

Her fault. Her fault. Her fault.

The library had become packed with researchers; both Samarokan and Dolannish alike. Everyone with a studious mind was searching for answers for the Veiling and the demons that came with it. There had not been an attack in some time and people were starting to panic. To brace themselves for the impending doom.

"May I join you?" A husky voice asked from across the table.

Irelia didn't need to look up from her book to know who stood before her. She reined in her sigh and nodded once, flipping to the next dusty page.

Prince Fornax sat in the chair diagonally from her and grabbed a book from the stack to her left. Wordlessly, he flipped it open and began to read.

They sat like that, together in silence, for what felt like hours. Combing through page after page in various languages on various topics. Nothing revealed even the slightest of clues. Nothing even remotely similar to the prophecy Fornax claimed to have found back in Dolannish.

Frustrated, Irelia slammed her book closed when the towering grandfather clock chimed its eighth hour.

"We've been searching for days and nothing has proven useful." Irelia ran her fingers through her slightly tangled curls.

Prince Fornax closed his own book, keeping his page with a finger, and leaned back to look at her. His russet eyes had shadows beneath them, as though he too hadn't been able to sleep much.

"I didn't expect to find something immediately, princess."

Irelia's voice was harsher than she intended. "We don't have time to waste, Fornax."

The prince titled his head to the side, his deep red hair falling gracefully against his cheek. She hated the way he looked at her.

"How's the duchess?"

Irelia went ramrod straight and refused to meet his questioning gaze.

Elodae had been unconscious—*asleep* the healers had corrected her—each time Irelia had gone to visit her. The healers had promised that Elodae was all right and that she would be completely, and totally fine.

But if Irelia were to be honest with herself, it wasn't her sister that haunted her at night. It was her people. Every time she blinked; she saw their frightened faces. Every time she looked at them, she saw them on their knees, bent over their loved one's bodies. Weeping and screaming, begging the gods to help them. Begging *her* to help them.

When Irelia didn't reply, Fornax's voice shifted into something gentle. "How are *you*, Irelia?"

Her shoulders sagged slightly, the weight of everything crushing down onto her. Her thigh ached constantly, despite the wound having stitched itself mostly back together. When she managed to sleep, nightmares chased her awake shortly after. And now the one thing she used to seek comfort in, magic and folklore, reminded her of what happened to Elodae. What happened because a selfish princess wanted an escape from the idea of marrying a prince.

Irelia lifted her eyes, vision blurry with unshed tears, and looked at Fornax. He leaned forward, his free hand twitching as though he wanted to reach across the table and comfort her. But he didn't.

His gaze bounced between hers, reading the swirling depths of every emotion she knew was stark across her face.

"We will find a way to save our people," he vowed in a hushed voice.

"How are you so sure?" The words escaped her lips before she could contain them.

Fornax shook his head and shrugged. "Because we have to."

And that was that.

Their gaze remained locked for a fleeting moment before Fornax opened his book and began to read once more. Irelia couldn't help but watch him, blinking away the tears she didn't dare to release. He flipped page after page, a furrow forming between his brows, before his eyes bulged and he nearly dropped the book. Irelia jumped at the sudden sound.

"This references an ancient Samarokan text about an ominous darkness that plagued the Tyrian Peaks nearly five hundred years ago."

Irelia's heart skipped a beat. "Let me see." She reached for the book and he handed it over.

Her eyes flew across the page, deciphering the scribbled words that were written upside down on the very last page. So small, she had to strain her eyes to read.

The sun hid behind the moon today. It read.

The darkness was absolute and terrifying. Animals retreated to their dens, birds singing their nightly tunes, and flowers curling their colored buds. It had only been six decades since the darkness that destroyed the town of Halun had descended upon the land. There are few alive that witnessed that dark blanket first-hand, but we all remember. For one could not forget the eerie chill, the complete and total night the darkness had brought. And the monsters and scars it left upon our world.

I remember reading the Night of Day as a young boy, passed down from my grandfather. In it, it explained there were three books that aided our people in destroying the darkness and banishing it from our lands. Unfortunately, my grandfather gifted the Night of Day to King Belarn and I fear I will never see it again.

If the darkness ever returns and there are those searching for a way to banish it, find my grandfather's book. It will guide you.

Irelia slowly set the book down, her mind reeling.

"If this book truly exists and it was gifted to the ancient Samarokan King Belarn then it must be somewhere in this library," she spoke mostly to herself, but Fornax nodded all the same. "Why did this man write it so secretly though? Why did he feel the need to hide this information that could save countless people?"

Fornax shifted uncomfortably in his seat. "Maybe there was someone that didn't want people to be able to save themselves from it."

Looking around the library, dozens of people bustled about, pulling books down from shelves, talking in hushed tones, and reading under dimly lit lanterns. Irelia wanted to believe that every one of them were searching for a way to save their people as desperately as she was.

"We have to find it," she decided.

Fornax gave her a single nod, their eyes locking over their own lantern. The yellow hue of the flame flickering across his brown skin, painting him in its golden light. It brought out specks of deep honeyed browns in his eyes that she had never noticed before. That she hated she noticed now.

Fornax offered her a smirk. "And so, we shall."

CHAPTER TWENTY

SIX

Darkness stole and relinquished Elodae time and time again over the next forty-eight hours. Alden had only left her side for the meeting with the king. Tomorrow, he would leave at dawn to hunt for the one who had taken her from him. Alden wasn't ready to leave her side so now, not yet.

The healer, Emma, had finally given up trying to get him to rest in his own bed a full day prior.

Elodae's hand grasped firmly in his, Alden's eyes remained locked on the lightly tanned skin of her face. Freckles just only starting to appear, splattered across the bridge of her nose and brushing beneath her closed lashes. Her lips parted in a peaceful sigh as she slept. He couldn't rein in the urge to reach across the bed and brush a moon-white strand of hair from her cheek. He also could've sworn she leaned into his touch, even in her sleep.

Small groups of men had been sent to the Magicks in random spurts to try and find her captor until Alden and his party departed. They hadn't found anything of value on whoever had taken Elodae. The people at the Magicks had no memory of the man the sisters had described. No memory of someone taking Elodae at all.

Finn had doubled the security on Irelia. Alden doing the same for Elodae. Even though the duchess was still recovering in the hospital wing, he wanted her rooms guarded day and night in case her captor tried to break into the castle. It didn't matter that Alden wasn't Captain of the Guard—the orders he gave were obeyed. He'd marvel over that fact later. And the fact that Radford had allowed him to make such demands of their men.

"Either go take a few minutes and bathe or I am going to have someone haul you out of here so I can tend to her in peace," Emma scolded as she pushed through the drapes surrounding Elodae's bed.

Alden grunted. The only response he'd deign to give her.

A flurry of peach-blonde hair flitted across his vision as Irelia burst into the already small space. Elodae stirred at the presence of her sister, her pine-green eyes fluttering open, but they did not look immediately to the princess at her side. No. They landed right on Alden.

His breath caught in his chest as her eyes bore into his.

"The extra guards have been doing their work diligently, Alden," Irelia said from her seat next to Elodae. It took all his self-control to pull his eyes from Elodae's to frown at the princess. "You think I can't read that look on your face?"

"What look?" He asked, adjusting in his seat, his hand remaining in Elodae's.

The duchess blushed softly as she looked down at their joined hands. When her eyes met his, he saw something he'd never seen there before. His heart lurched in his chest.

"Are you ready for tomorrow?" Irelia asked quietly.

"Tomorrow?" Elodae turned toward Alden, her voice still raw.

The healer handed a steaming cup of tea to Elodae, giving Alden a brief moment to control his swirling thoughts.

"Thank you." Elodae smiled at her and released Alden's hand to take the cup.

The emptiness that yawned open at the absence of her touch scared him.

Elodae moaned softly as the warm cup settled in her hands and rubbed the cup between them, heating them.

Alden made to pull the blankets farther up her body but stopped when Irelia snorted. "What?"

"Nothing." She batted her eyelashes and leaned back in her chair.

He glared at her and continued pulling the blankets further up Elodae's body. "Are you comfortable?" he asked her.

"More or less," Elodae said between sips. "Don't change the subject though, Alden. What happens tomorrow?"

After his second deep breath, Alden explained, "A handful of men and I are going to search the tunnels beneath the Magicks. We're going to try and find the cell you were kept in and hopefully any hints as to who took you and where they went."

The color drained from Elodae's face.

"I know who took me," she admitted, so quiet Alden had to strain his ears to pick up the words.

"What?" Irelia gasped, sitting forward.

Elodae stared down at the cup of tea in her hands. "His name is Orion. I—I've actually met him once before."

Alden wasn't sure he'd heard her correctly.

His confusion must've shown on his face because Elodae hurriedly explained, "It was the night I got attacked. I had left the Astronomers and wanted a drink so I stopped by a tavern and . . . he was there."

Irelia had to be the one to take down written notes of Orion's description for Alden was too consumed by his rage and worry to do anything but stare at the duchess before him. He felt her words, each one pelting his skin.

He should've protected her. He should've saved her. He was her guard. Her protector. And he had failed.

"We'll find him," Alden vowed once she was done explaining everything.

Elodae chewed on her lip. "That's not all."

Alden braced himself for whatever she was about to say next. For whatever it would unleash.

"They're after Irelia, too. They left to retrieve her. That's why they weren't there when you came for me." Her green eyes were soft as they met him on that last statement.

Finn, who had been standing guard outside of the drapes pushed through them at that.

"We will inform the king and proceed with caution." His onyx eyes landed on the princess, who, to Alden's surprise, nodded in agreement instead of pushing back as she normally did.

The four of them come to an agreement that the two

girls would not travel anywhere, within the castle walls or outside of them, without at least two guards. Satisfied, Finn left to update the king, Irelia's note of Orion's description in hand.

With that settled, Elodae set down her empty cup. "I think I'm ready to go back to my rooms."

"No," Alden said too quickly. Both girls blinked at him. "You need to be near a healer right now."

"No, she doesn't," Emma called from somewhere else in the wing. Irelia snickered, trying, and failing, to stifle the noise.

He scowled at her. "Fine," he relented. "I will take you back to your rooms."

"I'll help." Irelia made to stand.

Alden held up a hand. "You should get some rest, Your Highness. You've had a long several days, as well. Sleep and know that Elodae is safe."

The princess narrowed her eyes at him for a moment, but then she nodded and kissed her sister's cheek goodbye with the promise to check in on her soon.

"Any more word on the velarum?" Elodae asked, pushing herself further up in her bed while Alden collected salves and tonics from her bedside table to bring with them.

His shoulders slumped slightly. "No. Prince Fornax has offered up his men to aid the next hunt, though. They leave at dawn as I do."

Elodae sighed, running her fingers through her slightly tangled hair. "Demons and darkness and people hunting us . . ." She shook her head. "When did life become so complicated?"

Alden sat on the edge of her bed, it groaned under his

weight. He laid a hand softly atop hers, pulling her eyes to his.

"You're safe with me, Elodae. They cannot reach you here." He brushed a thumb along her skin. "I will protect you with my life."

Elodae took a shuddering breath, her lips parting and closing several times, but she said nothing. He wanted to kick himself for the words he'd laid bare between them, but another part of him, one he kept locked deep within, reveled at them.

See me. It begged. *See me, princess.*

A moment passed and Elodae pulled her hand from his, clearing her throat. "I should change." She nodded toward a pile of clean clothes the princess had brought with her.

Alden ignored the chill in his heart and nodded, standing and leaving the space.

A moment later, Elodae stepped out. "Ready."

He motioned for her to lead the way and they made their way back to her rooms.

Elodae seemed to be all right. She walked proudly as she always did, her back straight and chin held high. Her eyes were clear, her face less gaunt, her movements fluid and not stiff like the day he'd found her in that cell. He'd never forget how pale she'd been then. Like she'd had the life sucked from her very bones.

Alden shook the terrifying image from his head.

"You're thinking too hard." Elodae nudged him with an elbow.

He glanced sidelong at her. "I have a lot to think about."

She sighed and looked away from him. "I'm fine, Alden. Truly, I am."

"Now, perhaps. But you weren't before."

"Alden . . ."

"Why didn't you mention Orion earlier?" The harshness of his voice startled him, but he didn't let it show.

Elodae paused. "What?"

"Orion," he said, stopping to look at her. "Why didn't you mention knowing him earlier? He could be anywhere in Cronanth by now, El. Could be anywhere in *Samarok*."

She shook her head. "I didn't remember then."

"Didn't remember?" Alden blinked at her. "El, he could be in this very castle right now—"

"Let it go, Alden," Elodae cut him off. She turned and started down the hallway again.

He stood rooted in his spot and stared at her in disbelief. "Let it go?"

Elodae clenched her jaw as she stopped once more. Her eyes were filled with thinly veiled ire when they met his.

"Let it go?" he asked again, taking a step toward her.

"Yes, Alden. Let it go." She crossed her arms and glared right back at him. "I'm fine now. I appreciate your worry over me, but I'm not the one the man wanted. If you want to fuss over someone, it should be Irelia." She turned away from him again.

"And you don't think I am?" He snapped.

Elodae halted, keeping her back to him.

Alden choked out a harsh laugh. "You don't think I'm worried about Irelia? You don't think I haven't been sleeping, eating, *anything*, because of the threat to *both* of your lives? And all you can say is *let it go?* That you didn't *remember?*"

Elodae was so still he couldn't even tell if she were still breathing.

Let it go.

How could he possibly let go of what happened?

His thoughts were still racing when Elodae suddenly whirled on him, a small streak of silver lining her lower lashes. "Why did you hover over me these past two days?"

Alden scoffed. "Nice change of subject."

"Why?" She pushed, her voice hardening.

He gave her an incredulous look. "Do I need a reason?"

"Yes," she shot back. "You are the Captain of my Guard, not my *only* guard. So, if you were truly so worried about both my and Irelia's life, why were you at my bedside and not conjuring a plan with Finn and let someone else watch over me?"

Why was she so angry? Because it had been *him* to sit by her bed these last two days? The thought cracked something deep inside.

"Why?" she asked again, softer this time.

Alden threw his arms in the air. "Oh, I don't know, Elodae. Maybe because you were *taken* before my very eyes and I thought I'd never see you again. Or maybe because you were kept in a cell beneath the Magicks for hours and when I found you, you had and cuts and bruises on your body." He stomped over to where she stood and glared down at her. "Why do you question that I care for you?"

"Because you haven't cared much these past few years. So why now?"

Alden balked. She thought he didn't care for her? "You were taken," he said again, his voice shaking. He tried to ignore the emotions that he could've sworn flicked across Elodae's eyes.

"I'm fine, Alden. Perhaps you should check in on your fiancée. Or the princess."

He slowly shook his head at her. He didn't want to have this conversation in an open hallway where anyone could hear, with the guards he was sure were listening at his back. Not trusting himself to speak, he stormed toward Elodae's room. He didn't bother checking to see if she followed. From the clipped steps behind him, he knew she did.

Alden braced himself for what was surely to come out once they reached the privacy of her room. What he had dreaded her finding out for years now.

As he shoved the doors open, he prepared his heart for the worst.

"I'm all right, Alden. I'm safe now." Elodae raced to keep up with Alden's strides.

Alden threw open the door to her rooms and charged for her bedroom.

She made quick work of closing the door behind her and then ran after him. "Seriously, Alden. What is your problem? Why are you acting this way?"

He said nothing, just paced in front of her bed.

She stood in the doorway and crossed her arms, watching him. "What is going on with you? I'm perfectly fine."

"Perfectly fine?" Alden stopped in his tracks and finally turned to face her. He grabbed both of her arms, gently despite his anger, and lifted them so she could see. "You were *taken*, Elodae. *Taken*. I found you in a cell, chained to the floor like an animal. You were bleeding and so scared," his voice cracked. "I will never forget the sounds of your screams." Pain flickered across his eyes but vanished almost as suddenly as it had appeared.

She pulled her arms out of his grasp and was surprised when he let go. "I'm fine"

"Stop. Saying. That." He seemed to struggle to keep his voice down as his gaze remained on her wrists.

She tucked them behind her back. "Why are you acting like this?"

Alden looked away, dragging a hand over his face.

"Why?" she pushed when he didn't answer her.

He let out a bitter laugh, still saying nothing.

Frustration swelled inside her. "Why, Alden?" Her own voice rose and she stepped toward him. She grabbed his forearm, halting his incessant pacing. "Why do you care so much?"

He made to pull his arm out of her grasp, but she held fast to him. His hardened gaze finally met hers.

"Why?"

"Because I'm in love with you!"

Elodae staggered back a step, bumping into her vanity.

Alden blinked. As if surprised he'd admitted it.

They stared at each other for a long moment. Their uneven breathing the only sound in the room. She was surprised he couldn't hear the heart pounding inside her chest.

Alden took a careful step toward her.

Elodae shrunk back into herself, leaning on the vanity. A hand clenched around her necklace, and her breaths came in sharp pants.

Alden's throat bobbed. His agony-filled eyes held hers. "I'm in love with you, Elodae." His voice wavered as he said her name. "I have been for . . . for a very long time. And when you vanished before my very eyes . . ." He shook his head, jaw clenched, and looked away from her again.

Elodae was too stunned to say anything—to even move. They remained there in silence for another long moment.

"I thought you were dead," Alden finally said, his words a broken whisper, his cheeks wet with tears.

She reached for him then and put a hand on the side of his face, brushing them away. He was not the same as the man who had broken her. This was Alden. *Her* Alden. She tried to focus on that. On him.

Alden leaned into her touch, closing his eyes, and whispered again, "I thought you were dead. And that you had died never knowing that I loved you." He took her wrist with a gentleness that cracked her heart wide open and placed a soft kiss on her palm. Just below her thumb.

Elodae just stared at him in shock. "Why didn't you ever tell me?" She breathed.

"You're the king's daughter. You could have any man you want. Claim any title. I'm—" Elodae continued to make soft strokes with her thumb on his cheek. His eyes opened, the blue standing out starkly against the redness of his tears. "I'm just a guard. I have nothing to offer you." He lowered her hand from his face and turned his back to her.

Her hand remained in the air between them for a brief moment. Then she slowly lowered it and closed her eyes, losing a breath. "But you can offer it to Astrid," she said quietly, wrapping her arms around herself.

Alden spun back around. "Astrid means nothing to me. She was a promise kept for the sake of my father, nothing more. She's kind and we're friendly, but . . . she is *nothing* compared to you, Elodae."

Tears built in her eyes, but she shoved them down.

"It's always been you," he whispered and gently ran his thumb over her cheek. "But you'll soon be officially engaged to a prince of your own, and . . ." He gave her a sad, defeated smile. "And you should choose him."

He dropped his hand and made to walk away.

"You're a fool," she breathed. Alden tensed, and she grabbed his shirt in her fists, turning him to face her fully again. She shook him. "You're a fucking fool."

He flinched. "I thought you were dead," his voice broke with the surging tears in his eyes.

"I'm here," she said, fists still grasping his shirt. "I'm right here."

He shook his head as if not truly believing his eyes, not truly believing her words. "You need to know that my heart belongs to you. It's covered in scars and I know it's not enough, but . . . it is yours."

"You say you have nothing to offer me, but you can offer me *you*."

"That is not enough," he whispered.

"You are *always* enough."

Elodae forced herself to stay still, to not push him away or cut him with her words. To not take back what she'd just laid bare.

His icy blue eyes jumped between hers, as if searching for a lie. Then they dropped to her lips.

She didn't dare move. Waited for him to say something. Do something.

Anything.

As his eyes met hers again, she shivered at the intensity of his stare. His hand went to the nape of her neck, tangling in her hair, and tilted her head back.

Then his lips crashed down onto hers.

The kiss stole her breath. Knocked the world out from under her feet.

She wrapped her arms around his neck, pulling their bodies closer together. His free hand went to her waist, holding her to him.

A soft moan escaped her when his tongue brushed across the seam of her lips. A silent plea. She parted for him, and a deep groan rumbled in Alden's chest when their tongues met.

Elodae tangled her fingers in his hair and tugged him closer. It wasn't enough. She needed more. Needed all of him. The thought both terrified and excited her.

He broke away far too soon, leaving her breathless. She reached for him, needing his lips on hers again, but he released her hair and moved to cup her cheek. The hand still on her hip clenched and unclenched, as though he were restraining himself from pulling her against him again.

Elodae couldn't look away from his lips. Need overwhelmed her.

Noticing her stare, Alden's tongue flicked out, wetting them, and heat flooded her body. She looked up and found his eyes burning with his own need. She squirmed under his stare, fighting with all her will not to reach for him again, but he looked conflicted enough to make her pause. To let him sort out his thoughts. To clear some of the lust-filled fog from his brain.

"Elodae," he ground out. The barely restrained desire in

his voice had a soft whimper escaping her lips again. His fingers dug into her waist, but he made no move to continue.

She couldn't help herself. Now that he had laid his heart out for her—now that she had a taste of him—she never wanted to stop.

Elodae rose on her toes and tried to kiss him again, tightening the fingers that were still in his hair. He pulled back again, and she frowned. "What is it?"

Alden closed his eyes and laid his forehead against hers. "I need to make sure this is all right."

That gave her pause. Was he asking her, or saying he needed to gain permission from her father? The king. Or perhaps he wanted to stop to break things off with Astrid. She didn't know why the idea of that annoyed her.

"I need to make sure," he continued, drawing Elodae from her storming thoughts, "that this is what you want. Because once I start . . ." His hand moved from her cheek to the nape of her neck again. "I won't be able to stop."

He had voiced the words in Elodae's own head. She bit her lip, nodding, and the wave of rising panic washed away. She brushed her lips against his, but he pulled away again, causing her to make a noise of frustration.

Alden's eyes burned into hers. "I need to hear you say it."

A flicker of worry lay in his eyes, and the crack in her chest yielded completely to him.

Alden was the only other person who knew about what had happened two years ago. How she had been forced to give herself to someone. How that person had broken her in the worst way.

Elodae couldn't fight the tears that flooded her eyes. She nodded again and opened her mouth, but nothing came out.

Alden's hands immediately released her at the hesitation. She grabbed a fist full of his shirt again. "Wait."

He froze, letting her sort out her thoughts as she had done for him. His hands remained at his side.

"I . . ." Elodae closed her eyes and steeled her mind. "I want this."

She opened her eyes, and the love she saw in his face threatened to bring her to her knees. How had she never seen it before? Seen *him* before.

Alden.

It made so much sense. He had always been there. Had loved her in silence for so many years because he was worried that she wouldn't want someone like him. He had ripped his heart from his chest and held it out before her. Without hesitation.

She could offer him the same in return. "I want you," she said. Her voice did not waver. "I want *you*, Alden. In every way."

A soft smile spread across Alden's face—one she had never seen before. He brushed his knuckles against her cheek. Wonder shone in his eyes, as though he couldn't believe she *actually* wanted him.

Did he know his heart was always displayed for everyone to see? It softened some crucial piece of her.

"You're the only one who truly sees my soul," she whispered. "The only one who sees it and doesn't run away in fear."

"I do fear your soul," he confessed.

Elodae flinched away from him.

Calloused fingers cupped her chin, pulling her gaze back to his. The openness of Alden's eyes nearly took her breath away. "I do not fear your soul because of its truth," he amended. "I fear it because it has captured mine entirely."

She didn't know what to say, didn't know if there were words to encapsulate what she felt.

"Your soul is my home, princess," he breathed, brushing a piece of hair away from her face. "I am sworn by oath to protect it, but . . . I never would've imagined it to consume me so."

His name was a whisper on her lips.

"You are my moon," he confessed, learning closer. His voice caressed her with his next words. "My soul belongs to you."

"And mine you," she admitted before she could think twice, just before his lips grazed hers, sparking something to life she long thought burnt out within.

Her warrior with a lover's soul.

His eyes did not, would not break from hers. "I love you, Elodae."

Elodae placed both hands on either of his cheeks. "Kiss me," she said, barely more than a whisper.

For she couldn't say the words he offered so freely. Not yet. So, she tried to convey everything she felt for him in her eyes, in the soft smile she gave him, a mirror to his own. She had only ever said those words to one person. And although she wanted to be with Alden, and she'd meant every word she'd said, she still couldn't say *that*. Not yet.

Because to let someone in . . .

No.

She would not shy away from him. Alden would never lay a hand on her without her consent, never hurt her. He would never disappear. She would never forget him.

Elodae would say those words to him one day. She knew it in her soul.

The crooked smile he gave her at the request eased her mind.

Yes. She would say those words to him one day.

Alden brushed his lips to one corner of hers. Then the other. He pulled back slightly to look into her eyes again, and whatever he saw was answer enough.

He kissed her again. This was not the eager, claiming kiss as the first one had been. No, this kiss was deep and slow, as though he wanted to savor the taste of her. Something deep within her stirred awake as Alden's mouth moved against hers.

He wrapped his arms around her waist and lifted her off the ground. She released a muffled squeal, and he laughed as he walked to her bed.

Earlier thoughts of demons and darkness and hunters fled from her mind at the feel of his lips against hers. She could forget about all of that for one night. They would have this one night together, and then he would leave at dawn to search for Orion. But for now . . . for now it was only them.

Alden sat on the edge of the mattress, his mouth never once leaving hers. His kisses were lazy, like he wanted to take his time learning Elodae's likes and dislikes. What made her moan, like when he tightened his fingers in her hair and kissed her roughly. Which ones made her giggle or squeal, like when he playfully nipped at her bottom lip. Which ones had her melting in his arms, like when he cupped her cheek and kissed her deeply.

Those were her favorite, Elodae decided. The ones where Alden didn't need to use his words for her to know he loved her. When his actions spoke so loudly and clearly that doubt had no room to grow in her heart.

He scooted up the bed until he was resting against her headboard, Elodae still straddling his lap. He made no move to take things further. His desire was apparent beneath her, but that could come later. She had not lain with a man since that night, and she was in no mood to rush things now.

Alden seemed perfectly content just to hold her. To kiss her. To feel her skin beneath his fingers.

Elodae didn't know how long they stayed like that, their hands roaming over each other, careful of the other's wounds.

Learning. Teasing. Taunting.

Their kisses were sometimes lazy and soft, other times heated and rough. By the time the clock sounded seven and they finally broke apart, her lips were swollen.

Elodae made to crawl off Alden's lap and laughed at his sound of protest. "I'm just lying down next to you."

He grunted his approval and kicked off his boots. A moment later, she was wrapped in his arms, his fingers tracing idle circles along her spine, leaving chills in their wake. She could lay like this for the rest of her life and be completely content.

She said as much aloud to which Alden mumbled, "Then let's never leave."

Elodae tucked her head into the crook of his neck and breathed in his scent. Thoughts of Astrid and princes flashed through her mind. Demons swallowed by darkness followed. Tumbling through an endless void with no beginning and no end. She had no idea what would happen once they left this room. She didn't want to think about it, but her mind would not be silenced.

"You're thinking too hard," Alden murmured.

Elodae propped herself up on her elbow and looked down at him. He tucked a strand of hair behind her ear, and she felt her cheeks warm.

"What're you thinking about, princess?" he whispered, blinking sleepily up at her.

Elodae's heart fluttered. He'd never said it like that before. It'd always been taunting, playful, but this time—this time it had meant something. Her chest ached. "What are we going to do about Astrid and Lunala? Or about the Veiling and the velarum? What about—"

Alden sat up and pressed his lips to hers. Her heart pounded so hard she could hear it in her ears. When he pulled away, she found it difficult to catch her breath.

"That's tomorrow's problem," he whispered against her lips.

"But—"

"Let tomorrow's problems stay in tomorrow," Alden said, cupping her cheek. "The world could go up in flames tomorrow and I wouldn't care." Elodae shoved his shoulder, and he chuckled. "I mean it."

She couldn't contain her own smile even as she rolled her eyes. When she looked back at him, his expression had turned serious. Her breath caught in her throat at the intensity of his stare.

"If tonight is all we get, and I get to lay here holding you. Telling you that I love you . . ." He shook his head and sighed. "And get to have you look at me like that."

Elodae blinked, confused, but his next words ignited a small flame at the bottom of her soul.

"If tonight is all we get," he repeated softly, "then I will welcome the darkness with open arms and a smile on my face."

"Alden," she breathed, tears threatening to form in her eyes. Elodae looked at the man before her. He stroked his thumb along her cheek and gazed into her eyes. Into her soul. She nodded and let him wrap her in his arms once more.

Soon enough, his breathing evened out. Alden stirred slightly, tucking her closer to his side, and she couldn't help but smile.

Elodae fell asleep listening to the sound of Alden's heart beating in time with hers.

FLICKERING CANDLELIGHT PIERCED ELODAE'S slumber, rosing her. She cracked open an eye to find the sky still alight with stars, the moon cresting toward the peaks of the mountains far in the distance.

Air brushed her cheek, and she stiffened for a second before she recognized the warmth at her back, the chest that brushed against her shoulders as it inhaled and exhaled. The arm that was a steady and comforting weight around her waist.

Elodae slowly placed her hand over the one that rested on her stomach and marveled at the peace in her heart. At how safe she felt in his arms. She felt more rested than she had in years. And the urge to push him away, to kick him out and mock him for his confessions earlier, was nowhere to be found.

It's because you feel the same, her heart whispered.

She rolled over, needing to see his face, and a groan of protest at her rousing him rumbled from Alden's chest. He tucked her under his chin, and she smiled against his chest, wrapping her arms around him to stroke idle passes along his spine.

Alden sighed contently, his breath rustling her hair. Elodae's smile grew at the sound. She supposed she could let him sleep for a while longer.

At some point, though, he must've woken because his fingers started to trail up and down her back as well.

They lay there, holding one another, for as long as time would allow.

Slowly, the moon crept closer to the horizon, the stars growing dimmer as the sky shifted from midnight blue to an early dawn.

"I have to go," Alden whispered into her hair, his arms tightening around her. Unwilling to let her go just yet.

Elodae buried her face in his chest, breathing in his scent, committing it to memory.

"You'll come back." She didn't pose it as a question, but a command. He would come back to her. There was no other way.

A calloused finger hooked beneath her chin, gently tugging it upward. Eyes of ice met hers and Alden brushed a strand of hair away from her face. His eyes held hers and she could've sworn they saw right to her very soul.

"I'll come back."

And then he kissed her like she was air and he was drowning.

Dawn arrived far too soon. The rhythmic breathing of the woman in Alden's arms begged him not to leave that bed. To remain until the end of his days. But then he remembered where he was to go, and who he was to hunt, and his rage boiled inside him once more.

Elodae stirred in his arms when he tried to untangle himself from her, her fists curling into gentle fists in his shirt. As though she too were unwilling to relinquish him just yet. He still couldn't believe it. Couldn't believe that she wanted him.

More so, he couldn't believe that he'd admitted his love for her. She was promised to a faraway prince and he himself was promised to a noble lady here at their very court. Promises neither one of them had made for themselves.

That thought alone had his blood boiling just as much as the thought of that dark, damp cell he'd found Elodae in.

Pressing a gentle kiss to the top of her head, he breathed in her floral scent one more time before he carefully pulled away from her. She groaned in protest but did not wake. His heart ached at seeing her so content, so at peace in her sleep. No nightmares chasing her, nothing plaguing that beautiful mind of hers. Just complete bliss. He envied her dreams. Being able to whisk her away into far off places where nothing but her mattered.

A gentle breeze found its way through the sheer curtains against her open balcony doors, lifting Elodae's moonlight hair from her face. He committed her in this moment to memory. For he did not know when they would have another quiet, calming morning like this one.

"I love you," he breathed. "I'll come back."

With a final look in the duchess' direction, Alden slipped into his armor, sheathed his sword, and made his way out into the hallway.

Warren was already waiting outside, a quiet smirk on his face.

Alden ignored his brother's question gaze and set off down the hall, winding their way through the castle to the front gates where a small group of men stood waiting.

Surprisingly, Finn stood at the front of the small crowd, his back straight and chin held high. When his onyx eyes met Alden's, he gave a shallow dip of his head. One which Alden returned in kind.

"Ready to hunt men?" Alden asked, his mind slipping into someplace dark and quiet.

It was Finn who replied, "Ready when you are."

Two black shadows huddled in the dark depths of the cells below Castle Cronanth. The frost that coated the stones at their feet was not from the winter chill that lingered in the air, but from the lack of life in their very souls.

"What have you learned, Dark Soldier?" a crackling, aged voice breathed from one of the shadows, the darker of the two. The one that if anyone dared approach, all warmth would be sucked from their body.

The Dark Soldier's shadow pulsed with unease, but still they answered. "The Lunalian prince is set to marry the moonlit duchess, my Dark One." Their voice polished where the other's voice was broken.

"Good," the Dark One's voice the sound of nails against stone, sending even the rats scurrying away. "We need their union to find the starborn child. Before they grow strong and bring about our ruin."

"Yes, my Dark One." The Dark Soldier's shadows swirled with constant movement while their counterpart remained a solid black sheet of icy death. "The sunkissed princess will be an easy mind to takeover, but the moonlit duchess . . . I fear she will not be as easy to break."

"That is what you said of the red rulers of the south," the Dark One growled. "And did I not break them? Did they not bend beneath my will?"

If shadows could cower, the Dark Soldier's did just then. "They did, my Dark One. They did. But—" The Dark Soldier's words cut off before they could finish. The air in the cell plummeted, icicles forming from the ceiling.

"Do you want eternal life, Dark Soldier?" The Dark One's voice had gone terrifyingly calm. "Do you want power beyond your comprehension? To rule worlds like this one and many others?"

"Yes," the Dark Soldier croaked out. "Yes, my Dark One."

The ice continued to grow, coating every inch of the cell.

"Then you *will* find a way to break her. My minions have returned, demons they call them," the Dark One's voice hinted at pleasure at the thought. "I already have their king in the palm of my hand, the sun and moon are the ones I am worried about. If you cannot prove to best them," the Dark One's shadow grew. So large it encompassed the entire space of the cell, "then I will find someone who can."

CHAPTER THIRTY

A hand softly shook Elodae's shoulder, rousing her from her sleep. She groaned and pulled her sheets up over her face.

A husky laugh sounded, and the mattress sank slightly. She knew that laugh, had committed it to memory. It was her new favorite sound.

"Hello, princess," Alden said softly.

Elodae was wrong. His voice was her favorite sound.

Without a second thought, she pushed the covers back and leapt into his waiting arms. He wrapped her in a hug, cradling her against his chest. Sweat soaked his clothes, but she didn't care. He had come back. He had kept his promise.

"Did you find anything?" She asked into the crook of his neck.

Alden shook his head, his fingers tracing lines up and down her back, leaving tiny bumps in their wake.

"No," he sighed. "Nothing. We couldn't even find the cell."

The defeat in his voice had her tightening her hold around him, holding him closer to her. They stayed like that a moment, letting the birds chirping out beyond the open balcony doors be the only sound for a while.

Now that he was hers, she never wanted to let him go.

After a while, Alden pulled back, his icy blue eyes pouring into hers. Elodae's heart jolted in her chest, but she held his gaze.

"I have something for you." Alden brushed a strand of hair away from her face. The tenderness in his touch almost made her eyes water.

She remained silent as his gaze deepened and he leaned forward.

Elodae went completely still as he brushed his lips against hers. Then she melted against him, her hand tangling in his hair. She tugged him further onto the bed until his weight was over her. He groaned against her lips. She couldn't help but deepen the kiss, wanting to swallow the sound. Wanting to imprint him on her body.

They broke apart minutes later, breathless and smiling, and Alden rested his forehead against hers.

"You said you brought me something," Elodae whispered, clenching a fist in his hair.

"Hmm?" He hummed, pressing soft kisses to her mouth, her cheek, her jaw, and down to her neck.

"Alden," she breathed, tilting her head back to give him better access.

He moaned against her throat, softly biting above her collarbone.

Elodae forgot about whatever he'd brought as they tangled in her sheets. They didn't pull apart again until her lips were swollen and raw, the straps of her nightgown having fallen down her shoulders. She ran her hand up and down the hard muscles of his chest.

"I love you," Alden whispered as he placed a kiss on her bare shoulder.

Elodae stiffened.

She wanted to say it—the words were right there, on the tip of her tongue. But she just whispered, "You make my life brighter, Alden."

He smiled against her skin, placing another soft kiss on her shoulder before he pulled back and got off the bed.

Elodae fixed the straps of her nightgown and then followed him into the foyer of her rooms where Alden stopped before a small bag.

Wrapping her arms around his middle, she pressed her cheek against his spine. She needed to be near him. To hold him. To know that he was here, that he wasn't going anywhere, and that he was hers.

Alden rubbed a hand over hers and continued to rummage through the bag with the other. Then he took her hand off his stomach and pressed a small box into it.

Though tiny, the weight of that box was enormous. Elodae relinquished her hold on Alden to gaze at the gift in her hands.

It was a deep red, like the trees that grew along the Tyrian Peaks, and it fit perfectly in her palm. She looked up at him, and the nervousness that shone in his eyes made her heart strain.

Gently, Elodae pulled open the box and gasped at what

lay inside. A star-shaped necklace made of the same blue stone that was embedded in the pommel of Alden's sword.

"It's beautiful," she breathed, carefully pulling it out of the box.

Alden held out a hand. "May I?"

Elodae looked up at the man before her and nodded. She carefully handed him the necklace and turned her back toward him.

Cool hands brushed her hair over a shoulder, leaving chills in their wake. He grazed her skin as he slipped the chain around her neck, and she closed her eyes, leaning into the touch.

He secured the clasp and turned her around to face him.

Staring into his eyes, Elodae couldn't help but think of how she'd gotten so very lucky.

"What do you think?" Uncertainty laced his voice.

Elodae's cheeks warmed, and she peered down at her chest. The necklace lay perfectly above her other one. The blue and gold of the two matching wonderfully. Tears rushed to her eyes when she saw them together.

"It's beautiful," she breathed, smiling up at him. "Thank you."

Placing one hand on his chest, right above his heart, and the other on his cheek, she rose on her toes and kissed him.

Alden's arms wrapped around her waist, pulling her against him.

She leaned back before she got lost in him again. "When did you buy it?"

"I, um . . ." Alden cleared his throat and rubbed a hand along the back of his neck. "I've had it for a while."

Elodae blinked up at him. "How long is a while?"

He cleared his throat again, red staining his cheeks. "A couple of years."

Biting her lip to contain her smile, Elodae shook her head.

"What?"

"Nothing." She smiled and kissed him again.

WALKING THROUGH THE FRONT LAWNS OF THE castle, Irelia tilted her head back toward the sun and sighed. With the weight of everything that had happened since the Dolannish prince arrived, it was rare to have a moment of solitude and peace.

Someone released a breathy laugh beside her. "You and your sunlight."

Irelia startled, twirling around only to catch the sapphire eyes of Lady Astrid. The princess's cheeks immediately heated at the sight of the beautiful woman.

Astrid curtsied, a gentle smile lighting her dark red lips. There were dark circles beneath her eyes, as though she hadn't been sleeping lately. Her skin seemed paler too, making her black hair appear even darker against it.

"Lady Astrid." Irelia pushed her worry to the back of her mind, clasping her hands before her. "To what do I owe the pleasure?"

Together, the two women started a slow walk again. Irelia still had a slight limp from the wound in her thigh, but she managed. A large willow tree with beautiful blossoms and a bench beneath the draping branches appeared ahead and the princess and lady headed in that direction.

Astrid looked over her shoulder toward the four guards that had been following Irelia at a distance through the castle's lawns. The lady must've decided the guards were too far away to notice, or that the shade from the tree was dark enough, because she suddenly pulled Irelia in for a kiss.

Irelia gasped at the unexpectedness of the kiss but couldn't fight the moan escaped her as her lips met Astrid's. A wave of exhilaration washed over her when she remembered where they were, and that her guards stood just out of sight.

Irelia needed the distraction—needed to empty her mind of everything that had happened. The attack, the demons, the darkness, Fornax, all of it.

Especially that last one.

The prince who filled her thoughts more often than she wanted to admit. The prince who interrupted her thoughts at the most inappropriate times.

Like now, when Astrid was moving her lips against hers.

Irelia shook her head and placed a hand on Astrid's shoulder. "We can't."

"What do you mean we can't?" The lady whispered, grabbing Irelia's waist to pull her in for another kiss.

The princess was instantly filled with need. This thing between them, this secret, hidden thing, brought a rush every time they snuck out to meet somewhere. But there, at the back of her mind, a red-haired prince beckoned.

A promise she had never made herself.

"Astrid," Irelia breathed, once more pushing at the lady's shoulder. "We can't."

Astrid's grip tightened on Irelia's hips. "We can."

The lady's mouth trailed down her jaw and along her neck, and Irelia tilted her head slightly to the side, losing herself in the moment once again. Astrid ran her fingers over Irelia's arms. The coldness of the lady's skin was an awakening jolt to Irelia's senses.

"Astrid," Irelia said, shaking her head and doing her best to pull out of the lady's grip. "Are you well? You're freezing."

"I'm no longer engaged to Lord Alden. He broke things off with my father this very afternoon."

That pulled Irelia from her thoughts. "He—he what?" She stuttered.

"He told my father he could not marry me. I'm no longer promised to anyone." Astrid tangled her fingers in Irelia's peach-blonde hair and kissed her again. Her lips were ice against Irelia's at this point.

Something was not right here.

The princess fought against the lady's hold, but she wouldn't let go.

"Astrid. Astrid, you're hurting me."

"I suggest you let go of my queen," a low voice growled from behind them.

Astrid's grip loosened, and Irelia pulled back, gaping in confusion and hurt at the forcefulness of her advances. Astrid's sapphire eyes seemed sunken; the color far duller than before. Her lips, no longer a deep red, but more of a sickly grey.

"Astrid," Irelia breathed, reaching for the lady, but Astrid stepped back, turning toward their interrupter.

A strong hand touched Irelia's back, startling her.

"I suggest you leave," the voice growled again and took a

step toward the lady. Irelia didn't need to see his light-brown skin and dark red hair to know who it was.

Astrid's dark eyes narrowed at the prince before she bowed her head and walked away without another word.

The prince grunted something to his guards. Two of them broke off and followed the lady out of the gardens.

"Are you all right?" Fornax asked gently, removing his hand from Irelia's back.

She turned toward him, ears ringing, the weight of the situation settling onto her shoulders like a thousand stones.

He'd *seen* her.

His guards had *seen* her.

Not only with someone else—but with a woman.

"FORNAX," THE PRINCESS SAID, ALMOST accusingly.

Fornax blinked at her.

The audacity of this woman.

"Princess."

He turned to make sure his guards had followed Lady Astrid back inside when he saw Hadeon spinning around in circles, looking for where the prince had gone. He'd managed to sneak away from his preening lord when he'd spotted the peach-blonde princess under the willow tree. His excitement about the news he had to share consumed him as he rushed over to her side. Only to find her in the arms of another.

"What are you doing here?" Irelia demanded.

"Am I not allowed to walk around outside now?" Fornax raised an eyebrow.

The princess looked away.

"Mind if we talk?" he asked, trying his best to keep his voice calm. She seemed shaken up; he didn't want to send her over the edge.

"Yes, actually. I do mind," she said, raking her fingers through her hair.

Fornax ground his teeth together and prayed to Nath to give him the strength to keep his mouth shut.

"I have nothing to say to you." She crossed her arms.

"So, you didn't just have Lady Astrid, your friend's fiancée, on your lips in the middle of the front lawn?" He swept out a hand to encompass the surrounding garden.

Irelia's mouth parted, and he couldn't help but glance down at them. The princess's chest rose and fell in an uneven pattern. Her voice wavered slightly as she murmured, "I don't know what to say."

"Do you love her?" was all he thought to ask.

She blinked at his question but said nothing. He wasn't sure what he was hoping her answer would be.

"Why does that matter?"

Fornax slid his hands into his pocket, his right one clenching around the ring box he kept in it and shrugged. "I'd feel a little better about this if it was done out of love."

Irelia stepped forward, glaring at him. "No one would think twice if they caught you with someone—in love or not. So why does it matter if I've been seeing someone as well?"

Fornax cocked his head. He couldn't tell if he loved or hated the fire he saw burning inside the princess.

"Well," he said in a low voice, "for starters, no one has

caught me with anyone because I don't have my rendezvous out in the open."

Irelia's cheeks blazed red.

He pushed on, "Second of all, you and I are engaged. And we're royals. And sadly, you're the princess. Which means what you do, and who you do it with, is frowned upon. Regardless of your intentions."

She stiffened and said through her teeth, "It's not like I could even get pregnant from sleeping with her, so it's not an issue of an heir. And you just said—"

"It doesn't *matter* what I think. If anyone found out you were with someone else—*anyone else*—it could mean that we wouldn't be allowed to marry."

Irelia wouldn't meet his eyes.

"Unless . . . Unless that's what you wanted. To ruin any chances of us marrying."

The damn thing inside his chest ached at the thought. But no more than the slash across his stomach. If he failed his father, a twin to the one he already bore would probably be the result.

"That's not why," she said weakly, still not meeting his gaze.

His anger dissipated as tears lined her eyes. He shifted uncomfortably before her.

"Please don't tell anyone," she whispered after a while, a single tear slipping down her cheek as she peered up at him.

Fornax's nostrils flared at the sight of her tears. He would never tell anyone. It was no one's business but theirs. And Alden's, he supposed.

"I wasn't planning to," he said gently. "I just . . ." He looked around the lawn. "For the gods' sakes, Irelia. There are guards everywhere. And I saw you. My guards saw you. They won't say anything—and if they do, I'll have their heads. But if I could see you . . . who else might've?"

Tears streamed down her face as she looked around.

Something in his chest strained at her panic. He took hold of her hand. "But that's of little importance to me right now. Are you all right? Did she hurt you? It looked like things were about to get out of hand."

"If anyone finds out," Irelia's voice broke, not answering his questions, "they'd kill me."

He sighed. "It wouldn't be *that* bad, but—"

"I was with a woman."

"So?"

"So? What do you mean, *so*?"

He gaped at her for a moment, not comprehending. But the terror in her eyes was real. And then it dawned on him, and he couldn't help but breathe a laugh.

Irelia shoved his shoulder. "Why are you laughing?"

"Samarok is so backwards sometimes." He shook his head. "In Dolannish, women preferring women is not frowned upon. It's not even uncommon."

"Well, I enjoy men, too. I've just never—" she cut herself off, her cheeks blazing red.

Fornax watched her for a moment, felt himself softening toward her. He hated it. It meant she had a way in. But he couldn't keep his hand from reaching up to wipe away a tear that lingered on her cheek. She didn't flinch back this time.

"I won't tell anyone."

"Why?" she asked, wrapping her arms around herself. "We're engaged, and you just caught me with someone else . . ." She froze for a moment before slowly lifting her sea-green eyes to meet his. A wisp of a laugh escaped her soft red lips. "Is it only because it would ruin our chances of marriage? And you need this that badly?"

"Do you truly think so little of me?" Fornax dared ask.

Irelia opened her mouth, then closed it. Her shoulders curved inward, an invisible weight crushing down on her. Her head hung low.

He wanted to reach out. Wanted to comfort her. But then she looked at him, and he realized the terror was not truly for others having seen. It was because of him. Because she didn't trust him. Because she *did* think that little of him.

"You're never going to trust me, are you?"

Irelia shook her head and whispered, barely loud enough for him to hear, "I want to."

"But you can't."

His future queen opened her mouth, closed it, and then only tightened her arms around herself.

The ring box in his pocket was a heavy weight as he nodded.

"Can you at least trust me enough to track down some books?"

Irelia's brows furrowed as she looked up at him. "What?"

Forcing a reluctant smile to his lips, Fornax crossed his arms, feigning nonchalance despite everything that just happened. "I may have found the *Night of Day*."

CHAPTER THIRTY
ONE

"Take a walk with me."

Alden leaned against the doorframe to Elodae's bedroom to find her sitting up against the headboard, book in hand, a soft smile on her face.

When she didn't respond, he stepped over to the bed and gentle took the book from her hands. A sound of disapproval left her lips, but he quickly drowned it out with a kiss. She immediately melted against him and he couldn't help but smile against her mouth.

"Take a walk with me," he repeated.

"Where?"

Alden shrugged, marking her page with a scrap piece of paper on her bedside table and laid the book down. "Anywhere. I just want to take a walk with you."

A blush crept over Elodae's cheeks. Alden reached out

with gentle fingers and brushed the tips of them over the pink there.

"Beautiful," he breathed.

Elodae sucked in a shaky breath before clearing her throat.

Alden blinked, coming back to reality, and extended a hand toward the duchess. Slowly, she placed her hand in his, the callouses scrapping against his own, sending chills down his spine. Without thinking, he bowed forward and pressed his lips lightly to her fingers, his eyes never once leaving her face.

Elodae's lashes fluttered against her cheeks, her lips parting slightly. Everything inside of him screamed at him, begged him to do more, to touch her, feel her, memorize every inch of her body. But he made himself stand upright once more and help Elodae stand.

The depths of those pine green eyes held his for a long moment, bouncing between his and his lips. As though her thoughts had gone the same direction as his. If they had though, she never let on.

Before they reached the doors that led to the hallway, Alden stopped Elodae with a hand on her chin, turning her to face him. He pressed his lips to hers, drinking in her scent, her taste, the way she felt against him.

With the Lunalian prince coming in just a few short months, he didn't know how much time they had like this together, and he would not waste a single moment. They would find a way to get her out of that marriage even if it cost him everything.

Alden had already spoken to Lord Marlow before returning

to Elodae's side that morning to tell him he could not marry his daughter. Now the only person left to tell was his mother. He didn't care what promises were made on his behalf, or what his father would think of him now. Elodae was all that mattered.

And they would find a way to release her from the same unmade promise.

Elodae's lips moved eagerly against his, her arms wrapping around his neck. Alden tangled his fingers in her long braid, tugging her closer to him.

When they finally broke apart, all ragged breaths and raw lips, Elodae asked, "What was that for?"

"I don't know how long we'll have private moments like this." Alden tucked a loose strand of hair behind her ear. "And I don't want to waste a single one. Especially if Vanor confirms another hunt tomorrow."

"Another hunt?" Worry furrowed her brow.

"Vanor is desperate to find the source of these demons and the veiling. I can't blame him for it, either. They killed his people . . . my brothers."

Elodae nodded, leaning her forehead against his, and closed her eyes. "Just promise me you'll come back," she whispered.

"There isn't a corner of this world that I would not follow you to, princess. I will always come back to you."

Irelia's hands were growing numb with how

aggressively she wrung them as she hurried down the corridor.

Fornax was at her side, his guards and hers practically running to keep up with them. The constant ache in her leg a secondary thought to the news the prince had given her.

I've found the Night of Day.

Castle Cronanth's library easily housed close to a million books from all over their world. Fornax must've spent every waking moment in that library to find it so quickly.

"What does it say so far?" She found herself asking as they turned a corner, continuing their brisk pace.

Fornax's brows furrowed. "That's the thing . . . I can't read it. It's in a language I've never seen before. I was hoping maybe it was Ancient Samarokan and you could tell me."

Irelia couldn't fight the grin that spread across her face. It had been so long since she'd been allowed to go to the Magicks and lose herself in a folktale or some ancient text. And now she could put that skill to good use? To save her people? There was nothing greater she could ask for. It felt like piece of her was returning home.

Until Elodae and Alden turned the corner at the end of the hall and Irelia practically ran into her sister's arms.

"Irelia," Elodae laughed. "What's got the two of you in such a hurry?"

"We think our research has finally paid off and we can find a way to get rid of this darkness." Irelia's words were rushed as she tried to get everything out.

"Come," Fornax ushered. "They wouldn't let me leave the library with the book so I left it in one of my guard's care, but I don't want to put anything to chance." He grabbed Irelia's hand and started to tow her away again.

Elodae and Alden glanced at each other and then followed suit.

A short moment later, the towering doors to the castle's library dawned into view and Irelia practically skipped the remaining steps. Fornax was close behind.

The moment they stepped into the dimly lit space, a Dolannish guard rushed over to his prince.

"Your Highness." He shoved the book into Fornax's hand with an abruptness. "Someone is asking about this book, seeking it out."

"Who?" Fornax asked, voice stern and commanding.

"I don't know, Your Highness. They're cloaked, searching through the ancient scrolls." The guard's voice was kept hushed, but there was a strange panic in his gaze. One that had Irelia sidling closer to Fornax.

"Thank you, Paf. Keep an eye for them."

Paf nodded and took up stance at the end of the long table the four of them chose. The rest of the Dolannish guards and Irelia's falling into step beside him. All with their hands on the pommels of their swords.

"Who else knows about this book?" Irelia murmured to Fornax as she slid the book toward her.

She ran her fingers over the cover, the leather coating its pages so dark of a blue they almost appeared to be black. In small indentations in the leather, she could make out the words *Night of Day* with her fingers, but they were not visible to her eyes.

Flipping open the first page, she read:

Night of Day. If you've found this tome, then there is fear in your heart. I wish to help, but in case this falls into the wrong hands, I must scribe it in my mother tongue.

And then the words shifted into curling symbols Irelia could not make out. She turned the book this way and that to see if there were any hidden messages, it wasn't until she turned the book to try and read the symbols upside down that Elodae let out a choked sound from across the table.

Irelia looked up at her sister, who's face had gone completely pale, a hand clutching her necklace.

"El?" Alden placed a hand on Elodae's shoulder and she flinched. Quickly, he removed his hand. "What is it?"

With shaking limbs, Elodae lifted her free hand and traced her fingers over the symbols inked onto the worn pages.

With a bob of her throat, Elodae breathed, "These are the same symbols that are on my necklace."

Irelia's mouth fell open slightly in shock. She pulled the book back, flipping it around so she could study the symbols closer. They were indeed familiar to the ones she had spent hours tracing and trying to translate at the Magicks all those weeks ago.

Fornax was watching the three of them with hesitant eyes. "Your necklace?"

"Am I a key to this?" Elodae breathed, barely audible.

The prince at Irelia's side cleared his throat, pulling the book in front of himself. "The only symbols I've ever seen like these were in some old Lunalian astronomy books that were kept in the library back home." He flipped to a random page in the middle with a sketch of some mechanism Irelia had never seen before.

"The . . . astronomy books. Lunala."

Fornax and Irelia both looked up at Elodae, whose eyes

had gone distant and blank, her hand still clenched around her necklace.

"Those are not Lunalian symbols."

Irelia practically jumped out of her seat at the sudden deep voice. She turned to find a large man with a cloak pulled up over his head. Only the bottom half of his face was visible, as was the scar that cut through his lip.

"I'll be taking that now, Princess." The stranger held out a gloved hand for the book.

Instantly, the Samarokan and Dolannish guards crowded behind the stranger, all drawing their swords. The onlookers in the library rushed out of the room, some going to hide in the safety of the dark shelves that lined the lower floor of the library.

"Orion," Elodae breathed.

The hooded man turned his head in Elodae's direction. "Hello, love."

CHAPTER THIRTY
TWO

O*rion.*

That name reverberated through Alden's mind. This was the man that had taken Elodae. This was the man that had chained her up and shackled her in that cell beneath the Magicks. This was the man she had stumbled upon in that bar all those weeks ago, the one who had given her the scar on her throat.

This was the man Alden was going to kill.

"Easy, lad," Orion said to Alden, as though reading his thoughts, and held up his hands slowly as the guards all lifted their swords at him. "I only want what was promised."

"Guards, arrest him," Fornax commanded at the same time that Elodae asked, "What were you promised?"

Fornax was tucking Irelia behind him, the guards creeping forward, when Orion replied, "I will get that book eventually. Along with your necklace." He added the last bit directly toward Elodae.

Alden's rage was white hot as he pushed from his chair, unsheathing his own sword and pointing it directly at Orion's throat.

Orion chuckled low. "I see you've told her. Remember what I said, lad."

Alden blinked. It was *him*. He was the one from the streets. The one that had given him advice on what to do about his situation with Elodae and Astrid. He was the one who had told him to *love her well*.

Words Alden had replayed in his mind over and over in the weeks since.

Surprisingly, Orion lowered his hands, putting them behind his back, just in time for a Samarokan guard to pounce on him, tackling him to the ground and planting shackles over his wrists.

Orion's chuckle wafted over to them as he let the guards haul him away to the dungeon.

Elodae was trembling behind Alden when he turned to look at her, his own eyes wild with fear and uncertainty.

That man had been able to get inside the castle. Had snuck past all the guards without a single question. Gods knows how long he's been in these very walls. What he's seen or overheard. What he knows. What he will report back to whoever his superior is.

Alden crouched before Elodae, shaking his head as her hands found his. Neither one said a word. Fornax and Irelia, however, were sprouting all their ideas as to who Orion was and what he was *promised*. And how now that he was their prisoner, they could question him and gain more information about the symbols since he seemed to recognize them enough to know they were not Lunalian.

"Alden—" Elodae started.

A shout from behind them cut her off. "Brother!"

Alden turned to find Warren, sweat coating his brow, and panting slightly. "Brother. The king demands our presence. *All* our presence."

CHAPTER THIRTY THREE

Words were being said all around her, but Elodae could not hear a single one over the thoughts in her mind.

Eye of pine, eye of sky.

The book with the strange symbols like the ones on my necklace.

Lunalian Astronomers.

Orion.

Orion.

Orion.

At that very moment, the man that had captured her, had chained her up and threatened to kill her, threatened her sister, her family, was imprisoned below her very feet.

Water rushed into her mouth, her nose, her lungs. She could not breath. She was going to drown at sea.

"El," Alden murmured with a gentle stroke along her spine.

Elodae flinched, being pulled back to reality and out of the water in her mind.

"You're safe." Alden sidled closer to her, letting his warmth consume her.

Elodae leaned into that warmth, grasped onto it. Let it ground her.

King Vanor's voice finally pierced her ears. "You are certain this is the man that captured my niece?"

"Positive," Alden responded with a glance at Elodae who nodded in return.

"Sentence him to death."

A choked sound cut through the tension filled room. Elodae felt his eerie presence before she saw him step forward into view.

Hadeon placed a hand over his heart and bowed slightly at the waist. "If I may, Your Majesty. I would suggest keeping the man alive in order to find out his motives, who or what sent him here, and any other information on these . . . Veilings that he might have."

Prince Fornax bit out something harsh and low at the lord, but Hadeon ignored his prince entirely and kept his gaze on the King of Samarok.

Vanor pondered this for a moment, his sea-green eyes meeting Elodae's for a moment.

She gazed at her father, unsure how to feel. Did she want Orion to die? Did she want to know the information he had? He clearly knew Lunalian, and possibly whatever language was on her necklace and in that book. Could he have answers about where she came from?

That last thought is the one that had her dipping her chin in a shallow nod to the king.

Vanor quietly sighed, closing his eyes for a brief second before turning to Lord Hadeon and nodding. "Very well. He may keep his head so long as he proves useful."

"My men will start interrogating him right away." Hadeon bowed and stepped back.

It was Alden who spoke next. "If I may, sire, I would like to accompany Prince Fornax's men in the questioning of the prisoner."

Vanor eyed Alden, taking in the closeness between Elodae and him. The king's eyes narrowed slightly before nodding his agreement.

With that matter decided, the King of Samarok and his advisors started discussing the possible hunt party leaving at dawn the next morning to continue the search for the demons they called velarum.

Irelia slid closer to Elodae, grasping her hand with hers. The warmth of Irelia's skin against her own was a comforting distraction to everything that had just happened.

"We have to learn more about these symbols, E."

"I know." Elodae closed her eyes, willing her breath to remain steady.

Irelia turned to whisper in Elodae's ear. "How are we going to get out of the castle to go to the Astronomers or Magicks? We need answers, E, but . . . I don't see how father will let us leave now."

Trapped. That's what they were. That's the word Irelia refused to use.

Trapped.

Water threatened to consume Elodae once more, but she

forced it away. She could not fall apart in front of this room full of people.

"It is decided then," Vanor said, clasping his hands together. My guards Warren and Finn will head a hunting party to leave at first light. Along with two companies of men. One Samarokan and one Dolannish."

All the lords, both Dolannish and Samarokan alike bowed in agreement and dispersed.

Elodae made to leave but hesitated when Alden lingered by the large table in the center of the room.

"Go," he said with a smile, noticing her waiting for him. "I'll stop by your rooms when I'm finished her. I just need to discuss something with the king first."

Narrowing her eyes at him in question, she surveyed the guard before her. The strong set to his jaw, the determination in his icy blue eyes. She didn't know what he could possibly have to discuss with her father, but she nodded all the same and hesitantly left the room with her sister still in hand, mumbling inaudible words about her various theories.

THE ECHO OF THE TOWERING DOUBLE DOORS TO the War Room reverberated through Alden's body as the last of the remaining people left the large space. Leaving Alden alone with King Vanor.

"My boy," the king inquired, not looking up from the map and his many pieces scattered across the table. "What's on your mind?"

Before his nerves could stop him, Alden blurted, "Elodae should not marry the Prince of Lunala."

Vanor paused, hand in the middle of rearranging a group of black pieces on the map. Slowly, his eyes rose to meet Alden's.

"Oh." Was all the king said.

Alden nodded, clasping his hands behind his back and raising his chin. "Yes, sire. The man that has been captured is Lunalian. And it is not a hard thing to guess that he was sent here to spy on the Samarokan court before the prince arrived later this year."

Vanor's gaze narrowed, a slight tick in his jaw, but Alden continued, "I do not trust them. We know nothing about them or their people. I would not trust Elodae's life in their hands for even a second."

The soft clink of the metal piece being put back down on the table ricochetted around the empty room. Vanor stood at his full height, tilting his head as he took in Alden. His eyes roamed over his entire being, as though he were eyeing an opponent, not a boy he'd known since birth.

"What is the real reason behind this concern, Alden?"

"Your Majesty, I—"

"I am aware of your feelings for my niece. So, it would be wise to not lie to your king."

Alden blinked at the harshness of Vanor's voice. "I care for Elodae, it is true."

"Hmm."

Vanor turned away from Alden and strolled over to one of the floor-to-ceiling windows that lined the eastern side of the War Room. He gazed down upon the city of Cronanth and his subjects bustling about in the light of day.

"What do you know of politics, my boy?"

"Sire?" Alden asked, walking over to the king's side.

"Are you aware of what it takes to run a kingdom? To secure the safety for hundreds, thousands, of people?"

Alden shifted uncomfortably where he stood. "No, Your Majesty."

Vanor nodded. "Are you aware of the promises, the horrid promises, you need to make in order to save your kingdom, your people, your *family* from destruction?"

"No . . . Your Majesty." Alden glanced sidelong at the king. Unsure of what kind of horrid promises Vanor has had to make.

The king turned to face Alden fully, his normally vibrant sea-green eyes darker somehow, even in the light of the sun shining through the windows. "Are you aware of the sacrifices I've had to make? What I've had to give up to *you* and everyone else out of danger?"

"No, Your Majesty. But we are not out of danger." Alden summoned all the courage he had in his body and turned toward the King of Samarok. "Demons terrorize our city, our people. *Killed* them; mauled your daughter. A Lunalian spy has managed to infiltrate your castle walls. Kidnapped the duchess, threatened her and the princess." Alden took a deep breath. "We are not out of danger, sire."

"The prisoner was a minor hiccup in the plan," Vanor growled, his eye growing darker still.

Alden blinked, his brows furrowing. "What plan, Vanor?"

The king took a menacing step toward the guard. "One you will not get in the way of."

"Sire, I—"

"Lunala is coming. Their prince will marry Elodae. There is nothing you can do or say to change my mind on the topic, *boy*." Alden flinched. The king advanced, his voice growing rougher and deeper. "I suggest you remember your place in this court. Put your feelings aside and do as you are *told*. You will never have her."

Never had the king spoken to Alden in that way. Never had he sounded so much like his father . . .

"Yes, Your Majesty."

Alden bowed low at the waist and made his exit. His heart splintering in his chest.

CHAPTER THIRTY FOUR

"What's happening?"

A man ran from the cabin as metal rang on metal above. Elodae looked around the small room. Water leaked in through the cracks in the ship's side.

A man roared something from far away, but she couldn't make out what.

The woman in front of her—her hands glowed silver as she closed her eyes, sucked in a shaky breath, and turned toward Elodae. Her face came in and out of focus.

Elodae sat on the floor next to the bed, watching with wide, confused eyes.

"Okay, my Starling, you need to stay here." The woman kept glancing over her shoulder as if waiting for someone to burst through the door. She unclasped the chain and pendant hanging from her neck and hooked it around Elodae's, softly brushing her hair out of the way.

The woman grasped both of her cheeks in her hands and poured her silver eyes into Elodae's.

"This," she pointed to the necklace now hanging above Elodae's heart, "will bring you home."

"What?" Elodae began to panic.

"Listen to me. You must be brave, my child." The woman looked over her shoulder at the door again. "They found us." Her hands glowed brighter and the sea outside became wilder. "I'm so sorry, Elodae."

And with that, she turned and ran from the room. The door shimmered, then went dark.

Elodae sat there, stunned and silently crying.

She gripped the necklace as the ship rocked harder and the sea outside grew angrier. She had to wrap one arm around the nearest bedpost to keep from sliding across the floor with the tilt of the ship.

The shouting from above continued, and then more voices joined in. The singing of swords grew louder the more violent the sea became.

Footsteps sounded outside her cabin door. Shouting soon followed. Someone yelled at them to stop, but the word was cut off with a wet slash of metal.

The knob on the door rattled as whoever was in the hall tried to enter.

Elodae clutched the necklace tighter, praying to the gods that someone would come back for her.

The rattling of the door became more aggressive, and then a female voice yelled, "Stay the fuck away from her!"

"She needs to be stopped," a man's voice said. Something about it was familiar, but she couldn't quite remember.

"She's only ten. You would kill a child?"

Elodae crawled toward the door. The water that had leaked into the cabin sloshed around her hands and knees.

"Step out of my way, witch," the man said with unsettling calm.

"Over my dead body."

"Well, that makes my job easier."

Then the door to her cabin suddenly burst apart and a hooded man appeared, dragging the woman by her hair. Elodae covered her head as she backed away to protect herself from the wood shards that shot around the room. None hit her, though.

Elodae uncovered her head and saw that her hands were glowing a soft silver. Just as the door had. As the woman's hands had. She looked down at her body, and it also had a soft sheen to it.

The man dropped the woman, who landed on her hands and knees, splashing into the water that still rushed in through the cracks on the side of the ship. The woman winced and got to her feet, a thin stream of blood running from her nose.

The man stormed around the room, looking for something. His hood concealed his face, almost like the light could not touch him. Like he was veiled in shadows.

He was looking for her, *Elodae realized.*

The woman's features finally swam into view and Elodae met her stare.

"I love you," the woman mouthed, a single tear escaping her silver eyes. Her eyes roamed over Elodae's face, as if memorizing it.

She . . . she looked exactly like Elodae. The shape of her eyes, the tilt of her nose, the soft waves and curl of her hair. It was all Elodae. Or who Elodae would become one day. Everything except the color of her hair and eyes.

This woman—her mother.

The man turned on Elodae's mother. "Where. Is. She?" He glanced down at her mother's still glowing hands, then back up to her face.

Elodae's mother stood perfectly still, lifting her chin, not saying a word. Defiance written in her eyes.

"You." His hand was instantly around her mother's neck, lifting her off the ground.

Elodae clamped a hand over her mouth to keep her scream from escaping. She had to force herself to stay still, to not charge at the man, to not make him let her go.

"You will not win," her mother spat. A smile bloomed on her face. "You will never break her."

The last words were muffled as the man's grip tightened around her neck.

"No." A smile echoed in the man's voice. "But this will."

He unsheathed his sword and made to plunge it through her mother's chest.

Elodae screamed then, a world-shattering sound. The ship around her fractured. The sea joined in on the destruction, pouring in through the cracks she had made bigger.

Excruciating pain lanced through her mind.

Her mother and the man disappeared.

Elodae was going to die. She was going to die, and she didn't care.

She couldn't think about anything except the pain in her head. Her mind.

A man's voice roared from above, "Where is Elodae?"

A pause.

"What have you done?"

Elodae knew that voice, felt safe in it, but couldn't recall to whom it belonged.

None of that mattered, though.

Elodae gripped the necklace as she wept. When had she gotten it? Nothing made sense, and she grew more and more terrified.

Another shot of pain through her mind.

"Make it stop!" She sobbed with such force her chest felt like it was going to cave in on itself.

The ship around her did just that.

Imploded.

The last thing she remembered before the world went dark, before the sea finally won its battle against the ship, was a soft voice she couldn't recognize, whispering, "Come home to me, Starling."

ELODAE MADE HER WAY TO THE TRAINING courtyard early that morning. Her eyes burned each time she blinked, her feet shuffling across the stone hallways.

After she had returned to her rooms post meeting with her father, she stayed in her library, reading a new book, waiting for Alden. But he never came. It had been three in the morning before Elodae finally made her way to bed. She had tossed and turned for an hour before sleep had finally claimed her.

And when it did, it had not been kind.

There had to be dark bags under her eyes, but she didn't care. Her mind was racing.

The necklace. The woman. The ship. Glowing hands.

Her mother.

She had been right all this time. And now she knew—her mother was dead.

A broken sob escaped her lips, and she had to stop to lean against the wall in the empty hallway. She clamped a hand over her mouth.

Her mother.

Elodae swallowed the next sob when she heard footsteps scuff along the stone floor. She wiped her eyes and fixed her leather armor as Alden appeared around the corner. She could just barely make out the bags under his eyes as well.

"You didn't come back last night," she said, quieter than she'd intended.

"I know. I'm sorry." He wouldn't meet her questioning gaze.

She stepped toward him, but he pulled back before her fingers could brush his cheek. He nodded down the hall, toward the archway at the end that would lead to their training courtyard.

Elodae schooled her face, not letting the hurt show. Trying—and failing—to convince herself she'd imagined it; she followed Alden down the hall.

They walked down the steps and into the courtyard in silence. The clouds hung low, the air cold and wet around them. The first of the spring storms was coming. The flowers along the vines were in full bloom now. Their colors a stark contrast against the grey sky.

Alden made his way over to the rack of training swords and began fixing them. He was avoiding her. What had happened between the moment they had parted ways and this morning?

"Is everything all right?" She thanked the gods that her voice came out strong and aloof, concealing the pit that yawned in her stomach.

Her mind was still reeling from everything that unfolded the day prior. Orion and his capture and the book they had found with matching symbols to her necklace. None of it added up.

Alden grunted in response.

Clenching her hands into fists, Elodae begged the sharp words that sprang to the tip of her tongue to stay down. She didn't want to lash out at him.

"Why didn't you come back?"

Alden chose two swords and made his way over to her. Handing Elodae one, he turned and stepped into the training circle, still ignoring her question.

Elodae bit her tongue.

Don't lash out. Don't use your words to hurt him. He's just in a bad mood. It's fine. You're fine.

Slowly, she approached him. He still wouldn't meet her gaze. "Alden. Please," she whispered as the first drops of rain fell onto her cheeks.

His eyes shuttered, but he shook his head, his grip tightening on his sword.

Elodae's heart cracked slightly. Why was he shutting her out?

You already know, a voice said in the back of her mind. *You're broken and vile. You're ruined. Why would he want you when he could have someone who is whole?*

She shoved back the thoughts and gripped her sword tighter. As she opened her mouth to say something she'd surely regret, Alden launched into his attack.

Elodae barely had time to lift her sword before his crushed down onto it. She grunted under the weight, her sword becoming slick with the rain poured around them.

Spinning away, Elodae swung out her sword, hard and fast, hoping to land her normal winning blow on his ribs. She would get her fight one way or another.

Alden gripped his sword in both hands and blocked her advance. In retaliation, he swung low at her legs, causing her to jump over his swiping sword and kicking his wrist. He yelped in pain but didn't drop his sword. He shot daggers at her with his eyes, his wet hair sticking to his face as thunder boomed loudly high above.

Elodae just gave him a savage grin.

She dropped low, swiping her leg out, and was satisfied when he toppled over into a large puddle. He growled and immediately got back to his feet.

She opened her mouth to say something, but another bolt of lightning flashed and thunder followed in its wake, drowning her out.

Alden lunged for her again, but she blocked him with her sword.

Swinging high, she brought it down onto him, using all her strength in the blow. He used both hands to brace himself and stopped her sword. The impact reverberated down her arm.

They glared at each other; swords still raised above their heads.

"What is going on with you?" Elodae demanded, blinking the rain out of her eyes. Her arms shook with the extra strain to not lose her grip on her slick sword.

Still, they pushed at each other.

"Nothing."

"Don't lie." She grunted and shoved away from him. They began circling each other as the rain beat down against them. The world mirroring whatever disaster swirled deep inside each of their souls.

Breathing hard, Elodae called over the roar of the storm, "Why are you shutting me out?"

"I'm not."

Her vision blurred red. "I said, *don't lie*!" She lifted her sword and charged at him.

They continued to spar, a blur of strikes and blocks. Lightning flashed and the thunder seemed to never end. Every time she thought she was about to land the winning blow, Alden moved just out of reach.

She was nearing her breaking point when Alden finally jumped back, forcing distance between them. They circled each other once more.

Elodae's breaths were coming in short bursts, and she didn't have the energy to argue with him. She could barely see through the rain at this point.

By the way Alden's chest rose and fell in fast, uneven spurts, she knew he was pushing himself too hard. Like he was trying to outrun his mind.

"Alden," Elodae said between gulps of air.

His eyes shuttered, and he launched into action again.

She fought a groan. Elodae knew how to end this. It would be a cheap shot, but she couldn't think of anything else.

Holding her ground, she waited as he charged at her. Inches before his sword hit her side, she jumped out of the way and stomped down—maybe a little too hard—on the inside of his foot. He roared in pain and hissed a string of curses. Her nostrils flared, but she dropped low once more and this time, when he fell to the ground, she jumped on top of him. Straddling him and pinning him beneath her. The water soaked into her knees as she pressed her wooden sword into his neck.

Elodae leaned forward, her hair dripping water onto his face, and growled, "Next time you lie to me, make sure you at least win the damn fight."

She pushed the sword harder against his throat for emphasis.

Alden glared at her but said nothing. They stayed like that, him on his back and her on top of him, breathing roughly in each other's faces, until finally, he tapped her leg twice.

She pulled her sword away and stood. Not bothering to offer him a hand, she walked over to the water table under cover from the rain. She filled a glass and drained it, then another, before she turned back toward him. Vicious words ready to be wielded.

But Alden was not standing there, ready for another fight.

No. He had gotten himself into a sitting position, his head bowed between his knees, resting in his hands. The rain pelted him so hard she could see the reverberations in his shirt.

Her heart ached at the painting of him in the rain. A sullen warrior with a heavy heart.

Leaving her sword behind, Elodae returned to his side and sat cross-legged on the wet stone. They sat there in silence, the rain plastering her hair to her face and neck.

"Vanor will never let us be together," Alden said, his voice low and broken.

Elodae's heart fell into her stomach as she looked at him. "Why do you say that?"

Alden lifted his head, his eyes red with tears. Her heart strained again. She wanted to reach out, to comfort him, but he'd pushed her away and . . . and those walls had gone back up.

"I spoke with him," he admitted.

"And what happened to make you think my father won't let us be together?"

Alden pushed to his feet, running his hands through his soaking wet hair. He paced in front of her for a while before he finally said, "He wants Lunala. He won't let us be together because . . . because he will make you marry their prince. Regardless of what happens. Regardless of if things don't *go according to plan*," he made quotation marks in the air as he repeated what her father had said all those weeks ago, "you will marry that prince."

Elodae froze, and the rain seemed to freeze with her.

Alden barked a harsh laugh. "Apparently, he's been negotiating with the king of Lunala for *years* about this. Making promises to protect Cronanth, to protect Samarok."

"Protect us?" Elodae breathed. Her mind went wild and she shot to her feet. "But he only said they were coming to help us defeat this darkness and the velarum."

Alden gave her a pointed look.

"He wouldn't lie," she said, her voice wavering.

He wouldn't lie to Elodae. To Irelia. Her father wouldn't sell her off to the highest bidder just because he *wanted* Lunala. Whatever that meant. Even if it was to protect their kingdom. But . . . the Lunalian Prince *was* coming to Samarok in a few short months. The Moon Kingdom was coming. The kingdom that kept their island so veiled that no one could get in.

A cavern cracked open in her chest.

More secrets and lies. So many lies. Alden had lied. Vanor had lied. Her own mind lied to her time and time again. And after her dream last night—she couldn't do this.

Elodae ground her teeth. Harsh, sharp words rose to her tongue. And this time, she did not hold them back. "So instead of coming and talking to me like an adult, you hid from me with your mother like a child?"

Alden stopped his pacing and turned to glare at her, his wet hair swinging around with the motion. He opened his mouth to shoot something back, but she cut him off.

"You—someone who begged me to let him in—shut me out because you're afraid to lose me. Do you understand how fucking idiotic that is?"

Alden flinched. Elodae hated herself for it, but he'd hurt her, too. He took a step forward, but she moved before he could touch her.

"I chose you," she said. Angry tears rushed to her eyes. She was so angry. And tired. So very tired. "I picked *you*," she said again, her voice wobbling.

His throat bobbed.

"And one word—*one word*—from my father and you're

shoving me away again." Elodae took a step toward him, so close now they shared breath, and snarled in his face, "Don't worry about the king not *approving* of us being together."

Alden's eyes shuttered. "El."

But she'd already turned, letting her silent tears fall, and walked toward the steps that led out of the courtyard.

"No," Alden said, and rushed forward to grab her elbow. He wouldn't let her walk away. Not again. It rained harder, the water cooling him down.

Elodae whirled, her nose scrunched in anger. "Let me go."

"No. You don't get to walk away again."

She yanked her arm out of his grasp and shoved a finger into his chest. "*You* were the one to walk away. *You* were the one to push me out."

"Because I'm fucking terrified!" he yelled over a roar of thunder. "I'm absolutely terrified, Elodae."

"Of what?" she yelled back, throwing her arms out wide. Her moonlight hair was rain-soaked, and the falling droplets looked like shooting stars in the grey world.

"I love you so much that *it hurts*. I love you so much that the thought of losing you is like a *knife in my heart*."

Elodae's anger visibly stumbled a bit as lightning flashed overhead.

"And knowing that everyone is against us being together kills me, Elodae. Knowing that they will never approve of you being with a common guard. I know I'm a lord, but I only have the title. My father, he—" His voice broke, but he made himself continue, "He was not always the nice man you knew him to be."

Elodae lifted a hand to cup his cheek, and he couldn't help but flinch away. She blinked and then horror filled her eyes as realization dawned on her. She opened her mouth, but Alden just shook his head and took a step away from her.

"When I disobeyed, he was—he was not a forgiving man. So, when I caught myself falling for you, I was terrified. I was directly disobeying his last request: to marry Lady Astrid. And then your father made it abundantly clear that I could never have someone like you."

Elodae wrapped her arms around herself as though to keep herself from reaching toward him again. She tilted her head to the side in sympathy, a wet strand of hair falling over her shoulder. His heart ached for her so badly he thought it would shatter in his chest.

"But that's why I pulled back all those years every time we got too close," he made himself say. "It wasn't because I didn't care for you or stopped thinking of you or wanting to be near you. It was because I knew if I let myself love you—I would one day lose you."

He couldn't see the tears streaming down her face, but her chin trembled.

"Because I *am* a guard. I know you say it doesn't matter to you, but to the rest of the world, it does. And when I thought you died," he shook his head, words failing him as he took a step forward and gently cupped her face in his hands. "It didn't matter to me anymore. Whatever you offered me, I decided I would gladly take it."

"Alden," Elodae breathed, her voice breaking.

"And I know it's foolish," he said, closing his eyes. "But some part of me truly believed we could be together. That Vanor was getting Dolannish and it would be enough. That if we told him, I loved you and you loved me, that he would honor it and let us be together."

Elodae rested her forehead on his chest.

He wrapped his arms around her, holding her close, and whispered into her hair, "It was a fool's dream, Elodae. He is our king and we must do as we're told."

Elodae shook her head and said between sniffles, "I'll speak with him. I'll make him understand."

Alden's chest ached at the tearing of his heart. "He *needs* Lunala, Elodae. You are going to marry that prince."

She pulled back and stared up at him with those beautiful green eyes. "A lot can change in four months."

"Elodae—"

"And if nothing does," she balled her fists into his shirt, shaking her head, "then just love me while you can."

Reluctantly, he met her gaze again. Her eyes poured into his. Into his very heart. Lightning flashed again, quickly followed by a rumble of thunder. Illuminating her face in silver.

He lifted a hand and brushed a wet strand of hair out of her face. "And when the prince comes?"

"Love me while you can," she repeated, and cupped his cheek in her hand.

He did not pull back this time.

Love her well. Words a stranger—a stranger no longer he supposed—had spoken to him long ago. His hatred for the demon that was Orion would never go away, but he could not deny that those words rang true.

Alden looked at Elodae—truly looked at her.

Four months with her would be better than a lifetime without her. And when the day came for her to walk away, he would leave her with a smile on his face and no regrets in his heart.

He pressed his lips against hers as thunder boomed once more. Her arms went around his neck and his hands tangled in her hair as she melted against him.

He would take anything she'd give him.

So, Alden whispered, "I promise to love you while I can."

CHAPTER THIRTY FIVE

Fornax sat on the sofa in his sitting room, watching the rain fall against his windows. He couldn't get his queen out of his mind. Couldn't get what they'd discovered out of his mind, either.

He knew perfectly well why Irelia didn't trust him. It was why everyone didn't trust someone from Dolannish. They were the kingdom trying to take over the entire continent. All Eldonia. They all but had control over Callumere, and Asiva was controlled by those wretched people. He still didn't know where they had come from. None of the kingdoms had claimed them as their own. Perhaps a tribe that had been gathering forces in one of the kingdom-less lands.

As the prince got himself dressed for an audience with the king that evening, he decided a brief detour to Irelia's room wouldn't be the worst idea.

Snatching the Night of Day, the book he'd managed to slip into the pocket inside his jacket when the guard were distracted with that Lunalian, he meandered out of his rooms and headed for his queen.

AFTER A GRUELING SESSION AT THE TRAINING ROOM by the barracks to blow off some steam, Alden stopped by Elodae's room. It was a worthy detour on his way to the War Room, where he would stand guard while the king held council.

Turning the corner to the hallway that led to her room, Alden's steps quickened.

Love me while you can.

He would. The gods themselves would have to pry him away from her before their time was up.

Alden smiled at Dalo and the others as he approached her door. And just when he lifted his hand to knock, darkness fell over Cronanth.

Only one thought entered his mind the moment that blanket touched his skin.

Elodae.

He had to find her before the demons began their attack.

Alden burst through her doors, not caring if he tore them off their hinges. Frenzied footsteps told him the other guards had followed.

"Elodae!" he yelled through the void.

Shouts sounded throughout the castle, metal singing as it

was released from its confined sheaths. A demonic roar answered somewhere outside.

Alden had to find her. He wouldn't lose her. Not like this.

"*Elodae!*"

"Alden," she called from his right.

He stuck out a hand, blindly feeling his way through the darkness, and stumbled into her room. "Keep talking so I can find you."

Another growl sounded. Close, much too close.

"I'm by my armoire." Her voice shook. "Alden, I can't see anything."

"I know." His mind slipped into a killing calm at the fear he heard in her words. He followed the sound of her voice, her ragged breathing.

"Alden . . ."

He stretched out a hand, blindly reaching for her. A moment later, he locked his fingers with hers and pulled her into his chest. Her body shook violently. "I've got you," he whispered. "I've got you. You're safe now."

Her fingers dug into his back, balling his shirt into her fists, and she buried her face in his chest. He put a hand on the back of her head, holding her to him. But they couldn't linger. He had to get her someplace safe. Had to get her out of imminent danger.

"Light the torches," someone yelled from the other room.

Flint catching fire sounded, but no light followed. The darkness could not be penetrated.

Then a blood curdling scream sounded from one of the guards, the sound one of pure terror. A preternatural growl followed, and his scream was cut short. More shouts sounded. The singing of swords rang in Alden's ears as he backed Elodae against the wall.

They both froze as nails scraped against the stone from several feet away. Alden had no idea how good these demons' sight was in the dark, and he didn't particularly want to find out.

He pulled out one of his daggers, pushing the cold hilt into Elodae's hand.

"Do you have any other weapons?" he breathed, barely more than a whisper on the wind. He tucked her behind him and unsheathed his sword.

"Under the bed. A sword and a dagger," she whispered, her voice still shaking. Her fingers dug into his bicep.

A low growl rattled from somewhere to their right. The velarum was in the foyer now.

Elodae's bed was at least ten paces away. Too far for him to protect her if that demon came in here. Did they rely on scent, or could they see? How good was their hearing? Alden hated that he didn't know. That he was so limited in his ability to protect her at that moment. He couldn't leave Elodae alone in this void, but they needed those weapons.

"Do not make a sound and stay here so I can find you again," he whispered over his shoulder.

She whimpered her agreement.

Claws scraped along the stone again. It sounded far away, like it was prowling back out into the hallway.

Alden didn't think twice before he lunged forward, running to her bed. He hit one of the posts with his shoulder and grunted in pain, but quickly dropped to his knees and stretched an arm out. He fumbled around for a few seconds, but it was still too long.

Those nails scraped again. Closer this time.

Shit. *Shit shit shit shit shit.*

Something punctured the palm of his hand and he hissed at the sharp sting of the blade.

"Alden," Elodae's voice breathed from behind him.

He shot to his feet, his hands slicing open as he clenched the blades in his palms and rushed back toward her voice as the battle continued to rage through the castle.

Horrifying sounds of tearing flesh sent chills down his spine, but he couldn't think of his men right now. Of the brothers he knew were dying. He would see them again in the Afterlife.

But he'd be damned if he met them having let his duchess down.

Reaching out his free hand, he found Elodae's fingers once more. He pushed the hilt of the sword into her trembling hand and sheathed the dagger in a loop on his belt.

Then a blinding pain shot through his leg as the demon's teeth clamped down.

ELODAE HEARD ALDEN'S BONES CRUNCH.

She couldn't contain the scream that tore from her throat as his hand was ripped from hers. She lurched forward, falling to her knees, and tried to find him in the blackness, but the velarum must've dragged him away.

Alden's warning from her first days of training shot through her mind.

Never let them move you to a different location. Because if they do, all we'll be able to recover is your body.

She would *not* let Alden die. Not at the hands of those demonic creatures. If he died today, she would drag his ass back from the Afterlife and kill him herself.

Footsteps pounded through the hallway, through her rooms, but she couldn't think about anything except Alden. One second, he'd been there, pushing a sword into her hands. The next, he had roared in pain.

Elodae heard Alden's sword crash to the floor. Heard the demon's growls as it pulled him away from her. Separating them.

Guards shouted for her. Someone rushed into the room and she heard them trip over him, or the demon, and land with a grunt on the floor.

Alden yelled out in pain, and the gruesome sound of ripping skin filled the room.

She didn't let herself think before she got to her feet and launched into a blind sprint. She held out a hand, feeling around the room.

"Alden!" she yelled over the ear-shattering noises coming from the fight in her foyer, in the hallway, in all Cronanth itself. Gods knew how far and wide the Veiling went.

She didn't want to know what she'd find when the light came back to the world, when the sun finally returned. But she wouldn't accept Alden's body being among the others she knew littered the floors.

The thought stopped her dead in her tracks. The bodies. Warren and Finn were out there somewhere. Her *sister* was out there somewhere. So was her father. Were they safe? Were they still alive?

"Elodae," she heard Alden rasp.

His voice was far away, like the demon was trying to drag him back to wherever it had come from. The sound snapped her from her worries. Fearing the worst would not keep them alive. She needed to keep moving forward.

Following the sound of his voice, Elodae bumped into something soft. She shoved the bile down her throat. She couldn't think about who or what it was.

Elodae continued her advance toward Alden's voice. It had sounded like it was coming from the hallway. The fighting grew louder as she managed to stumble through the doors. Swords clashed against stone as the guards and soldiers aimlessly slashed through the air. How many wounds and deaths would they inflict upon their own men due to their lack of sight?

She had to find a shield.

"Elodae," Alden rasped again. His voice sounded so weak.

Growls came from her left. Elodae turned, hefted her sword in one hand, and palmed the dagger with her other. She sent up a prayer to Nath to guide her through this. To get both her and Alden—and however many of their people —out alive.

Please don't let me hurt anyone, she begged.

Elodae shot forward, sword and dagger swiping through the air. She hit something, and it cried out in pain. It wasn't Alden, thank the gods. It wasn't another of the guards, either. But whatever it was sounded almost—human.

Elodae sheathed her dagger into the waistband of her

leather pants and then stuck out her hand. She was met with the rock-solid flesh of the demon's hide. It was cold as ice and hard as the stone walls. Her hand came away covered in a sticky residue, and she tried not to vomit. The stench of its breath from this close was vile.

Her other senses must have heightened with the loss of her vision, because she could hear the agonizingly slow sound of Alden crawling away from the demon.

Teeth snapped near her face.

She lurched backwards, falling onto her ass. She shoved her sword forward, sinking it into some part of the demon. Or so she thought.

The blade suddenly snapped in two.

The velarum had bitten clean through it.

Pain shot through her shoulder as the demon's claws shredded straight through her top and into the skin underneath.

"Elodae!" Alden roared from behind her as her screams of agony shattered the darkness.

WARREN AND THE OTHER SOLDIERS THAT HAD LEFT the safety of the castle's walls to hunt for the source of the veiling, had barely made it out of the last stretch of houses that lined Cronanth's limits when a black veil had been draped over the world.

Chaos immediately broke out. Men began shouting and running around. Running away, or running to fight off a velarum, Warren didn't know. Every thought emptied except one.

His family was still in the castle.

It didn't matter how many guards they'd left behind or how many soldiers the king had called in to aid in their defenses—Warren was not there. He was not there to protect the people he loved.

Again.

Warren unsheathed his sword and hefted his shield. He spun the sword in his hand, readying for the battle to begin. The rain pelted his face, making his grip on his sword and shield slick. But the sounds of the demons didn't sound around them. They came from behind them. From the city.

He heard the men around him lighting matches, trying to ignite the torches and arrows and whatever else they'd brought with them, but nothing penetrated the endless black.

Either they were immediately snuffed out, or the darkness was so heavy—so final—nothing could be done but pray that the gods would get them out alive.

With a warrior's roar, Warren slammed his sword against his shield in summoning and ran toward the cries of his people.

IRELIA WAS TUCKED BEHIND FORNAX'S BACK IN A corner of her room.

He had knocked on her door only minutes before. "I'm

here to—" was all he had managed to say before the world went dark.

Fornax had immediately pulled her into his arms. The guards instantly pushed inside and barricaded her door. The screams started soon after.

Irelia clung to Fornax as though he was her only tether to reality. Memories of the last attack raced through her mind. The pain, the sounds, the aftermath. She tried to tune out the sounds of her people dying, but they raged in her head.

Clenching her eyes shut, even though it made no difference at all, she buried her face in the back of the prince's shirt. One of his hands was on her thigh, his fingers digging into her skin. Grounding her to this realm.

Tears threatened to spill as her heart pounded in her chest, in her ears. Her leg throbbed. It had been bothering her all day, but the moment the world had plunged into darkness, the pain had become unbearable.

A crushing weight slammed into her chest as Fornax was thrown back against her.

"What was that?" Irelia shrieked over the raging battle.

Fornax didn't reply. His body continued to pin her against the wall.

"Fornax?" she whispered, voice breaking.

He didn't answer. Didn't even move.

Snarling sounded in front of them. Her heart leapt to her throat and she began shaking him, trying to rouse him.

Still, he did not move.

She shook him harder, screaming his name.

Nothing.

She reached around his body, feeling his chest, his arms, his stomach. No blood. Nothing was wrong. But then she felt his head. Warmth soaked her fingers as she pressed them to his forehead. Two deep gouges had been slashed across his face. Across his right eye.

Irelia choked on a sob. "Fornax!"

Men shouted their names.

"In here!" she yelled back.

The snarl sounded again. Closer this time.

Irelia heaved Fornax's limp body from hers, tucking him against the wall behind her. Reaching out a hand, she ran her fingers over his body until she found his neck and felt for his pulse.

She found it. That faint, thumping heartbeat.

Alive. He was still alive.

She choked on a sob of relief and sightlessly fumbled for his hands, seeking the sword he'd drawn only minutes ago when the veil had fallen over their world.

Guards rushed into her room then, or at least someone did, because the growling sound moved from her left to her far right. Someone roared in pain.

"Princess where are you?" someone yelled over the singing of swords.

She recognized that voice. Radford.

"Corner," Irelia choked out, clinging to Fornax's limp body.

Footsteps stumbled over toward them, and Irelia yelped when callused hands wrapped around her bicep. "It's me, princess," Radford said.

Irelia let loose a breath, tears rushing down her face.

He pulled her to her feet and started tugging her through the blackness.

She fought against his hold. "Wait, Fornax is here. He's hurt. We need to help him."

"He is not my priority, Your Highness. You are."

Irelia clawed at Radford's hand, but his grip would not be dislodged. "We can't just leave him," she shouted, yanking and twisting against his hold.

"Irelia, please," Radford bit out, towing her along.

Where they were going, she didn't know. She wasn't even sure a safe place existed for them to go to anymore. "I will not leave him!"

Radford snapped, "He's already gone."

"No," she snarled, and slammed down on the instep of his foot. The way Elodae had taught her.

Radford released her then, spewing a string of curses.

She'd apologize later. Fornax wasn't gone; he couldn't be.

Irelia owed him a debt for saving her life. She told herself that was the only reason she turned around and stumbled back to where she just had been. Now it was her turn to save him.

She tripped over something hard, landing on her hands and knees. A growl echoed throughout the room.

Oh, gods. She stuck out a hand and felt a boot.

Please be Fornax.

Crawling her way up the body, she felt for the man's face. Two deep gouges ran across the right side.

Her knee landed on something cold and sharp. Reaching down, she felt his sword and hauled it up in her hands. Her arms nearly buckled under the weight, but she weathered it as she turned her back to the prince. She cursed herself for every time she'd turned down Elodae's offer for Irelia to train with her and Alden. If Fornax died because of her lack of muscle and skill, she'd never forgive herself. She tried to ignore the slight ache in her chest at the thought of the prince dying.

Aimlessly, she waved the sword in front of her. The sword collided with something as hard as stone, and a human-like yelp followed. And yet the sound was not human at all.

An angry growl followed the cry of pain.

The velarum.

Nails scratched against the floor as it stalked closer.

Then Radford yelled something. She heard things being thrown. Something hard hit her right leg, sending shooting pain down it.

The velarum roared so loud her teeth clacked together. She threw her hands over her ears, dropping the sword.

Armor clambered and the horrible sound of nails against stone chased after it. Men and women shouted out in the hallway.

Irelia's breathing was ragged, and a sob wrenched from her throat. She laid herself over Fornax and listened for his heartbeat. Once she found it, Irelia then used his sword to cut a strip from the hem of her dress. Fumbling in the dark, she tried to bandage his face. The blood had slowed, but with the world still in darkness and the stench of blood surrounding her, she didn't know how long they'd be here before help came.

Or if they'd ever see sunlight again.

So, she laid her head back on his chest, praying that the heartbeat echoing within would not stop, and waited for the sun to return. Or the velarum.

Whichever came for them first.

Irelia lay there, covering Fornax's body with hers, and counted his heartbeats.

The battle raged around them, but no velarum came for her or the prince. The sounds coming from outside her rooms were . . . horrifying. Her people's screams as they died would forever be ingrained in her mind. The first Veiling, the one that had earned her the scar on her thigh, had not been this brutal. Had not gone on this long, either.

The clock in her room boomed one hour, and then another, and then another.

Five hours passed and still, Irelia clung to the prince. His breathing grew shallower with every chime.

Irelia prayed to Silva to save him and then she prayed to Hela to spare him. Prayed to Eirene for peace, to Solas for the sun to return. Then to Rhiannon to send away the darkness.

None of them listened.

Her people continued to die around her, and she felt the man in her arms slip further and further away.

But finally, as the clock chimed its sixth hour, the sky outside shifted from the impenetrable black to a heavy grey.

Holding her breath, Irelia watched as the sky gradually grew brighter and brighter.

And as the first rays of the sun broke through the darkness, the princess wept.

CHAPTER THIRTY
SIX

Elodae was only certain of four things.

One: light had returned to the world.

Two: her arm ached like Hel.

Three: she was lying on a bed, not on the floor of a hallway.

And four: a hand was clenched in hers.

The last thing she remembered was going in and out of consciousness from the pain that radiated from her right shoulder, Alden pulling her against him and then covering her body with his.

She didn't know what day it was, what time, or how long she'd been out, but at some point, the screams stopped, as did the demonic roars. Cries of agony and pain took their place. People sobbed and asked the gods why.

Elodae cracked open one eye and saw light.

Beautiful, shining light.

A sob broke free, and she could not stop the tears that poured down her face. The hand in hers disappeared, and a steady arm draped around her, pulling her against a warm body. She covered her face with her hands and turned into that chest.

Oak and spice scents wrapped around her, embraced her. Alden.

The force of her sobs threatened to split her chest clean open. Her shoulder burned with pain as she rolled onto it so she could tuck herself farther into Alden's arms. She didn't care.

"I'm sorry," she wept.

"Shh," he breathed and stroked a hand over the back of her head.

Elodae just repeated those words over and over and over. *I'm sorry I'm sorry I'm sorry.*

"You have nothing to be sorry for," Alden whispered.

She shook her head, hands still covering her face, and whispered between sobs, "I'm sorry for what I said to you in the courtyard. I'm sorry for all the times I shoved you away. I'm sorry that I'm broken and don't know how to be fixed. I'm so sorry."

Alden drew in a shaky breath, and she felt his own tears fall onto her hair. "We all speak in anger. We all respond to things differently."

Elodae's tears continued to stain her cheeks. Alden's arms tightened around her, tucking her under his chin, and she breathed in his scent. Took comfort from it.

"You are not broken, Elodae," he whispered after a moment, still running his hand over her hair.

"But I am," she breathed. "My heart is covered in scars."

Alden put one hand on the nape of her neck. The other one gently removed her hands from her face.

Elodae let him lift her chin.

He brushed his knuckles against her cheek. "Even the moon has scars," he whispered, his blue eyes never once leaving hers. "And yet, it still glows. Every night. Even if you can't see it, it's there. Is it any less enchanting because of its scars? Does it not still command the waters? Does it not still light up the black of the night?"

Despite herself, despite all that had happened—not just today, or the last couple of months, but the last thirteen years, and the ten before that. Despite all of it, Elodae smiled. A true, genuine smile.

"I love you," Alden whispered.

Elodae tilted her head back and let him kiss her. She didn't care who saw, didn't care how many people were around. Didn't care that they'd almost died. An ember inside her flickered to life when she kissed him back.

Let the darkness come and wash over the world. Let it reign for a thousand years.

As long as she had Alden, there would always be light in her life.

CHAPTER THIRTY
SEVEN

Warren and the other surviving soldiers limped back into the castle, a combination of mud and blood left in their wake.

The storm had finally dissipated along with the Veiling. The sun now shone brightly outside.

Legs feeling like a thousand stones, Warren helped carry one of his brothers up the castle's entrance stairs. All around him men lay dying or having already passed on to the Afterlife.

Less than half of their numbers were returning with the sun.

The Veiling had lasted for nearly seven hours, whereas the first had lasted barely two. In those two hours, with the demons contained to the Grand Hall, too many people had died. The second one Alden and his men had stumbled into by the Silver Lake had lasted barely three hours. Good men had died during that attack, too.

This one, though . . .

Three hundred men had left. Fifty had returned.

Somehow, Warren, Finn, and the rest of the companies managed to make their way back into the city during the attack. It hadn't been too difficult, Warren supposed. He'd just followed the sounds of his people screaming.

He had blood, both red and a blackish blue, covering his entire body, along with mud from the plains that surrounded their city. The storm had continued to rage for the better half of the attack.

Luckily, the demons could also bleed, he'd found out. They had a soft spot under their ribcage, much like humans did. Their eyes and mouth, as well. Warren had been trampled by one of the velarum. Having knocked his sword out of his hand, he had drawn the dagger he kept in his boots and blindly hacked away.

Warren had hit its eye and it had immediately dropped dead, pinning him to the ground. Its blood had reeked like a thousand rotting corpses, soaking into his clothes. His hair. His skin.

It had smelled so horrible he'd nearly gotten sick multiple times after he finally pushed its dead body from him and began stumbling through the black.

No other demons had attacked him, though. Perhaps because he had been covered in velarum blood? Maybe it had made them believe he was one of them. Like when he'd sometimes go on a hunting trip with the castle lords alongside Alden and they'd cover themselves in mud to mask their scent.

Warren's thoughts circled his mind like vultures as he and Finn, along with the three generals who had survived, one Samarokan and two Dolannish, made their way into the War Room. Before he crossed the threshold of the towering double doors, he handed the wounded man he carried to a healer who rushed up to his side.

When the light had returned to their world and they'd seen the destruction the Veiling and demons had brought upon Cronanth, Warren had fallen to his knees.

People—men, women, children—had littered the streets of Cronanth.

But not a single demon's body. Whether no one had killed one as he had, or if the velarum took their dead back with them, he didn't know.

Steps dragging, Warren followed Finn into the round room.

The king, some creepy-looking lord Warren recognized as Prince Fornax's righthand man, and two of Vanor's advisors stood around the table in the center of the room, expressions grim.

Warren nearly collapsed into his seat at the table when Vanor motioned for them to sit. He was still covered in the demon's blood. Gods, he needed a bath. Or six.

No one said anything for a while.

The sounds of people crying out in pain as their wounds and injuries were tended to, echoed throughout the stone room until a guard by the heavy double doors closed it with a bang.

"How many are dead?" Vanor asked after several minutes, his voice low and devastated.

One of his advisors answered, "We are unsure at the moment, Your Majesty. The . . . number keeps climbing."

Vanor closed his eyes for a brief moment before turning to one of the guards at the edge of the room. "And your report states that the prisoner by the name, Orion, escaped during this attack?"

The guard in question stepped forward. "Yes, Your Majesty. In the midst of the chaos, it seems he found a way to break out of his cell and escape."

"Gods save us all," Vanor murmured.

No one said anything for a long while after that.

The king sighed quietly before finally asking, "What happened?"

Warren lifted his eyes when no one responded only to realize the king had directed the question to *him.* He was covered in velarum blood. The only one who had, as far as they knew, managed to kill one of the beasts.

Warren was too tired to care how the king had already heard. It was apparent on his body, he supposed. The blackish-blue smudges across his skin and clothes.

"I . . ." Warren cleared his throat when his voice came out rough and gravely. He tried again, but his voice was still raw. "I don't know, Your Majesty."

Vanor looked at him with sad eyes and then turned to Finn.

The guard straightened his back at the attention of the king. "I saw one of the demons . . . change, Your Majesty."

Hushed murmurs broke out around the table.

Warren gaped at Finn, who sat on his left-hand side.

The room quieted immediately as Vanor asked Finn, "What do you mean, *change*, Finn?"

Finn shifted slightly in his seat. *Finn*. The man who was always composed. Who always had the answers. The man who had been a prince nearly two years ago.

"When the light returned, not—not all of the velarum had left yet."

Vanor leaned forward and rested his arms on the table. "What did you see, Finn?"

Finn's swallow was audible.

The room had gone completely silent. Still.

Warren could practically hear the air drifting around them.

"I saw . . ." Finn cleared his throat, shifting again in his seat. "I saw one stand on its back legs and . . . and it turned into a man."

Warren's mouth dropped open as the men around the table began hammering Finn with questions. Something in the back of his mind yelled at him, but Warren couldn't quite remember.

"That's not possible," Fornax's lord said, leaning back in his seat.

"A man?"

"What does this mean?"

"Did you recognize who?"

"It saw me," Finn said quietly. The room went silent once more. "The man. It—*he*—looked right at me."

Warren felt his blood stop cold. The disappearances. Several weeks earlier, Vanor had mentioned in passing that some people had started to go missing without a trace. No evidence ever turned up as to where they went or how they disappeared. It was as though they'd just gotten up and walked away from Cronanth. The king had deemed them coincidental, but if these *things* were people wearing a demon's skin . . .

Warren couldn't help but ask, "What did you do?"

They all turned to look at him. He was still covered in blood, knew he smelled horrid, but his eyes were locked on Finn's.

"I killed him," Finn whispered, his eyes shuttering.

The room became an uproar again, but Warren didn't look away as he asked, "Why?"

"You killed our only chance at finding out who or what's behind this!" A lord yelled.

"Why?" Vanor repeated.

Finn turned from Warren then. He looked at their king, the yelling stopping once more, and said, "Because he begged me to."

I relia woke up curled next to Fornax on a bed in the hospital wing.

She'd already checked in on Elodae and Alden, both of whom would wear scars like hers soon. Alden's would be on his shin and Elodae's on her shoulder. They, too, were clinging to each other the same as Irelia clung to Fornax now.

He still hadn't woken.

She had kicked and screamed when they found her in her room and tried to haul her off his body. The only way Irelia had known he lived was by the slow, shallow beats of his heart. If they pried her away, she was terrified she wouldn't hear his last heartbeats.

They'd sewn up the gauges on Fornax's face, and she'd been assured that the velarum had not gotten his eye. The demon's claws had missed it by the smallest measure.

He had bandages wrapped all around the right side of his face.

Irelia wanted nothing more than to see those russet eyes. To see him glare at her. Smirk at her. Fight with her.

Every time his body moved, even the slightest bit, she sat up straight and stared down at him, silently begging him to open his eyes. But he didn't.

Fornax continued to sleep.

He was fine. Or would be fine. But it did little to ease her anxiety.

So, when Irelia was not curled next to him, she wandered around the hospital wing, needing to stretch her legs. To regain strength in her right thigh from the last Veiling that had left *her* bedridden.

She helped the healers tend to lesser wounds. Helped mix and brew salves. Applied them to people's injuries. They even let her make some of her own. Make some of the remedies she'd read about in the Silvan library at the Magicks.

The healers were skeptical at first, understandably so, but after they watched her make the salves, saw the ingredients she put in the tonic, they had beamed at her.

That had been five days ago.

For five days, Fornax had laid on that bed. For five days, Irelia had wandered around this hospital wing, tending to people's wounds. For five days, she hadn't known if she'd get to argue him again. To research about the Veilings and the demons that attacked them again.

The healers had removed Fornax's clothing to check for any hidden injuries. Irelia had blazed a vibrant red and turned her back when they undressed him. But then a healer handed her a tiny blue leather book.

The Night of Day.

Irelia had gaped at the tome in her hands. Had immediately hidden it beneath the folds of her skirts. How he had managed to sneak it away, she had no idea.

But after hearing the news of the prisoner that had approached them in the library escaping, Irelia was on edge constantly.

She chewed on her lip and lay back down on the pillow next to Fornax's when he sighed in his sleep. The princess watched the healers stroll around the room and listened to her fiancé's steady breathing. Listened to his heartbeat growing stronger every day.

She'd forever be grateful for the healers and their talent.

"Hmm," Fornax groaned.

She whipped her head toward him, propping herself up on her elbow. She opened her mouth, about to call for a healer, when he breathed her name.

"Irelia."

The way he said it had her heart melting. Had tears rushing to her eyes. "Fornax," she said softly, lifting a hand to place it on his left cheek. "Fornax, I'm here."

His head rolled in her direction and his left eye cracked open a bit before closing again. A groan of pain sounded from his throat. Irelia, not wanting to leave his side, looked over her shoulder for the closest healer.

There.

"Emma," she called.

The healer immediately turned and rushed over to them. "He's awake."

Not a question, but Irelia nodded all the same. She slid

out of the bed and raked her fingers through her hair to detangle it. "He just woke up."

"How is he feeling?" the healer asked her, pulling out a tin of salve and beginning to unravel the bandages around his face.

Irelia couldn't help the sob that broke free. "He's in pain. And he's still weak."

Fornax's left eye cracked open again and immediately met hers. Her heart skipped a beat.

"You don't have to talk for me, princess."

Irelia was torn between throwing her arms around him and punching him. "Only you could be such an ass after what happened."

A faint hint of amusement lighted his eye and the healer shot a look in her direction.

Irelia crossed her arms and glared at him, though it had no bite. She turned back to Emma. "Is he all right?"

A hint of a smile on Emma's lips, she said, "He'll be all right, Your Highness."

Irelia chewed on her lip again.

"Careful, princess. You almost look like you care."

Irelia shot daggers at him with her eyes.

"She's been by your side the whole time," the healer offered.

"Emma," Irelia said through her teeth.

Emma gave her a bashful smile and carefully took the bandage off Fornax's face. The prince winced in pain as she pulled it off completely, and Irelia's heart dropped into her stomach.

With the bandages gone, she got her first good look at the two gashes that now rested on his face.

They both began at the temple on the right side of his face. One ran over his right eye, arching across his nose, and ended just below his left eye on his cheek. The other one ran under his right eye and cut diagonally through his lips, ending on his chin.

She reined in her sob when Fornax gave her a pointed look. "Am I that hideous?" he asked, genuine worry in his voice.

"Absolutely stunning." She laughed, choking back her tears.

"Oh, gods. I'm hideous," he groaned. Emma reached over for her healing tonics and salves as Fornax's deep red eyes focused in on Irelia once more.

The princess shifted on her feet, then realized she was staring at his scars. She slapped a tight-lipped smile onto her face and said, "Well, you're awake now. I must get going."

"Princess," Fornax said when she turned. Irelia halted and closed her eyes, taking a deep breath before she turned back to face him. His eyes flamed once more. "Thank you."

Irelia waved him off. "The debt has been paid."

"What debt?"

"You saved my life and now I've saved yours."

His eyes roamed over her face. "I didn't realize we were keeping score."

"Well, we are now. And you're losing."

"But you just said—"

"You're losing," she called over her shoulder as she walked out of the hospital wing.

As Irelia strolled away from the prince, she knew for a fact that it was her who was losing.

Losing the battle with her heart.

CHAPTER THIRTY
NINE

Elodae and Alden were eating breakfast in the Grand Hall when a large, dusty tome landed next to their plates. The impact caused the water in their glasses to slosh over the sides.

They had just been discussing Finn's promotion to Captain of the Guard. Radford had lost his life saving Irelia and Fornax the day of the Veiling. The funeral for all the lives lost had been held the previous night. Elodae had clung to Alden as they gazed upon the bodies. Some had been his friends. Brothers.

Silent tears had streamed down Alden's face as they left the temple of Hela and Eirene, the goddesses of death and peace.

Irelia plopped down by the book she'd just dropped but said nothing.

"Hello," Elodae mused, using a napkin to clean the mess on the table.

Her sister had been sort of—unsteady—the past several days.

In truth, everyone had.

The number of deaths continued to grow as more people died from their injuries. Elodae wasn't even sure what the number was up to now.

She fidgeted with the strap of her sling, but winced when she moved her shoulder.

"Stop playing with it," Alden chided her with a piece of toast.

"What is that?" Elodae asked, nodding at the book and ignoring Alden.

"The answer," Irelia breathed.

"What do you mean, *the answer?*" Alden asked.

"The answer," was all Irelia repeated.

Elodae and Alden exchanged a look. She turned toward Irelia and placed her good hand on top of her sister's, pulling her sea-green eyes to hers. "Irelia, darling, is Fornax well?"

Irelia seemed to be more on edge whenever the Dolannish Prince was having a bad day. When his wounds wouldn't stop bleeding, or he woke from nightmares, or cried out in pain as the healers tried to mend him.

Her sister's eyes shuttered, but she slapped on a smile. "What does he have to do with anything?"

Bad was the answer, then.

Elodae had checked in on the prince several times herself over the last week and they had started to ... bond. She still didn't trust him, not fully. The prince had a humorous side when he wasn't being a giant pain in her ass, and she had to admit he was nothing like the rumors they'd grown up hearing. He was still Dolannish, so she never let herself be truly unguarded around him.

Whenever Irelia had come by to check in on him and seen Elodae there, she'd slapped on a smile, like she did now, and walked away.

Fornax had asked how she was doing, but with the Veiling and him getting hurt protecting her . . . *Not well* was always the answer.

"Have you been sleeping at all since the attack and finding that book?" Alden asked Irelia gently.

"Yes," the princess said through her teeth, her smile wavering.

Irelia, and many people of Cronanth, were terrified of the night now. The minute the sun dipped out of the sky, people rushed into their homes, boarded up their shops and windows, and lit all the lights in their houses.

Cronanth, a once beautiful and lively city, had become a ghost town at night.

Some people went as far as forcing themselves to stay awake at night and sleep during the day when they could still see the light shining through their eyelids.

Irelia blew out a long breath, shoulders slumping, and her head hung slightly. "I'm sorry. With everything that happened, I just don't feel like myself."

Elodae wrapped her good arm around her sister, rubbing her back. "I know, Irelia. It's all right."

She leaned on Elodae for a moment and then wiped at her eyes. "Now," she said, sniffling, "what I meant was, I believe this book contains how the Veiling is possible."

Alden raised a brow at the princess, and Elodae tilted her head to read the spine of the tome.

The Veiling.

Her heart leapt into her throat, and her ears started ringing. "Irelia, where did you get that?"

"The library."

"Which one."

"The castle's one?" Irelia glanced at Alden, clearly confused.

"Why, El?" Alden asked, his brows furrowed.

"This . . ." Elodae cleared her throat. "This is the book that Orion was carrying in the Magicks the day that I . . ."

Alden went completely still.

Irelia gave her an incredulous look. "That's impossible."

Elodae nodded. "It should be."

Alden grabbed the book and pulled it toward him.

"Wait!" Irelia shrieked.

He ignored her and flipped it open to a random page in the middle. The three of them coughed, waving their hands in front of their faces to disperse the cloud of dust that flew off the tome.

Elodae craned her neck to see what was written in the book as the dust finally cleared. Everything inside of her went completely silent when she saw what was on those pages. "It's the symbols."

Irelia nodded and snatched the book back from Alden. "Yes. But more interestingly . . ." She flipped to the very last page, where in tiny blue ink, there were four words scratched onto the dull paper.

Property of Byron Gemine

IRELIA HURRIED DOWN THE HALL, LEADING ELODAE and Alden to the library. Her mind raced too fast for her to keep up.

She'd been wandering around the library, looking for new salve and tonic recipes to help the wounded. Every time they cried out in agony, her heart shattered even more. She couldn't bear the sight of her people in pain, so Emma had ordered her to go researching.

So, that's what she had done.

But then she'd stumbled across *The Veiling*. It was too much of a coincidence for her to not pick it up. And then she'd seen the text inside, the language in which it was written, despite the title being in their common tongue. She'd run to the Hall, nearly trampling some poor advisor on her way out of the library's doors.

Elodae and Alden murmured quietly to each other behind her.

Irelia checked her pace, remembering Alden had an injured leg, too, and was probably in immense pain. She took a deep breath; she needed to calm down. Her hair looked a mess, she had bags under her eyes, her dress was rumpled, but she couldn't stand seeing her people hurt.

The velarum wounds didn't heal as easily as normal ones did. The scar on Irelia's thigh should not cause her so much pain after two months of healing.

The idea of her people suffering that same pain . . . She couldn't handle it.

Irelia didn't know what she'd do if another Veiling happened. Which was why when she had stumbled upon that book, she hadn't given it a second thought before she grabbed it and went to find her sister.

Entering the castle's library, Irelia heard Elodae's hum of contentment. As a young girl, Elodae had spent hours on top of hours in this room. Irelia had whined and complained, but she had always accompanied her sister. Finally, Vanor had built Elodae her own library in her room so Irelia could dance around in privacy while Elodae combed through book after book.

Irelia made a beeline for the underside of the stairs, where the shelves sat in almost constant shadow. She grabbed an oil lamp on a nearby table as she passed. Alden and Elodae's footfalls followed her as she darted ahead and they limped behind.

They ventured into the depths of the library, and the light grew dimmer and dimmer until Irelia came to an abrupt stop. They had reached the end of the row, tucked completely under the second floor. Nowhere else to go but back from which they came.

"Ow. That was my foot," Elodae bit out at Alden.

"Sorry," he grumbled.

Irelia lifted her lamp, searching the spines.

There.

She set her lamp on a worktable nearby and turned the dial so the flame grew brighter.

Irelia grabbed the book next to where she'd pulled *The Veiling* only moments earlier. And the one after that.

"These," Irelia said, piling them onto the desk next to the lamp, "are all in the same language. The language your necklace is written in." She pulled out one of the chairs and sat, flipping open *The Veiling* and then the book next to it, *The Ancient Kingdoms.*

Elodae read the titles aloud, leaning over the table to get closer to the light.

"Do we have to do this back here?" Alden asked. "Why don't we take the books back out to the main area. Where it's light?"

"Shh," both sisters hissed at once.

He grumbled but kept silent.

They scanned the texts, looking for any symbols they recognized from Elodae's necklace. Irelia pulled out a crumpled piece of paper and flattened it on the desk. It was her sketches from their trip to the Magicks all those months back. Next to the sheet of paper, she laid down *The Night of Day.*

Alden mumbled something about finding another lamp and limped back down the dark, shelved hallway.

"Does it say where the rest of the books are from?" Elodae asked, flipping to the back page in *The Ancient Kingdoms.*

"No." Irelia sighed. "Only *The Veiling*. It doesn't make any sense. We have *four* books in this language, and yet no one has ever seen them before. How is that possible?"

Elodae shook her head, the flames flickering across her face as she chewed her lip, scanning the text. "I don't know. And what's more concerning is this," Elodae tapped *The Veiling*, "was the book Orion was holding. That book and . . ." she trailed off as she looked at the third book's title.

The Moon Kingdom.

The color drained from Elodae's face.

Alden returned then, two more lamps in his hands, and set them on the table. "Elodae?" he asked, concern filling his voice.

Irelia's sister had clenched a fist around her necklace and stumbled back a step. "How is this possible?" she breathed; terror written across her face. "How—how did these books get here?"

"I don't know," Irelia said quietly.

"Elodae?" Alden asked, stepping cautiously toward her.

Irelia's sister finally looked away from the books and over to the guard. He wrapped his arms around her, and she leaned into him. "I can't believe I'm about to say this, but . . ."

She took a deep breath and squeezed her eyes shut.

Somehow, Irelia knew the words she would say next.

"We have to sneak out and get to the Astronomers. Now."

"No."

Elodae's heart still pounded as she turned her stare on Alden. They needed to leave, he had to understand that. She was tied to all of this somehow and so was Byron now. The man she had trusted like a second father all these years. Who had seen her necklace countless of times and never said a single word about the text on it.

She needed answers. And she needed them *now*.

"You—*we*—can't leave the castle. Not after what happened," Alden said, shaking his head.

Irelia stood up straight. "But—"

"No."

"Alden," Elodae said gently.

He just shook his head and tucked Elodae closer into him, careful of her shoulder.

Elodae pushed back slightly so she could look at his face. "Alden, just listen to me. The velarum will attack us whether we're in the castle, in the city streets, or at the Astronomers. Come with us. Bring Warren. Bring Finn. Bring whoever you want, but we need to go."

"Why?" Alden asked, leaning back to look at her. "Why do you have to be the one to figure this out?"

"Because I'm clearly connected to all of this somehow."

"I don't care. We're not going."

Elodae steeled her spine and glowered at him. "I was not asking permission. You can either come with us or stay behind. Either way, I *am* going."

Irelia busied herself with closing the books and stacking them on top of each other.

Alden glared down at Elodae. The orange glow from the lamps set his blue eyes shining, but she tried not to let that distract her.

"This . . ." Elodae grabbed *The Veiling* with her good arm. She let out an *oomph* when she nearly dropped it.

Damn, the thing's heavy.

Elodae got a good grip on the book and then shoved it in Alden's hands. "This is why I need to go. It's titled the same thing we've named the attacks. *The Veiling*. It was the book Orion was holding. It's written in the same text as my necklace. It literally says *property of Byron Gemine.* Tell me those are just coincidences. Tell me none of it means anything."

Alden turned the book over in his hands, jaw clenched.

"*The Moon Kingdom,*" Elodae said, nodding toward one of the two books left on the table. "Lunala is shaped like a crescent moon. It even has the damn word *Luna* in it. *The Veiling.* The velarum attacks. *The Night of Day* specifically telling us to seek these books out. *Tell me it's not connected.*"

Alden held her gaze before turning to Irelia. "And the last one?"

"*The Ancient Kingdom,*" her sister said, picking up the third book.

"Wait." Elodae peered down at the title. "*Kingdom.* Singular. I thought it said *Kingdoms.* Plural."

"No." Irelia turned the book over to get a better look at the spine. "Just *Kingdom.* No *s.*"

Something embedded in the leather caught Elodae's eye, and she took the book from her sister and set it on the table. "What was that?"

"What was what?" Alden asked at her side.

Elodae lined up the three lamps and brushed her finger over the delicate leather of the back of the book. She couldn't feel it, but she could've sworn she'd seen something.

"Elodae, what did you see?" Alden asked.

"I thought I saw a symbol in the corner there." She pointed to the top right corner. "But it's gone now."

"What did it look like?" Irelia asked, turning over *The Moon Kingdom* and looking at its back.

Elodae met Alden's hard gaze. "It looked like my necklace."

"I really don't like this," Alden said, and began pacing.

"I know you don't, but we need to know." Elodae sighed. "*I* need to know."

He hobbled over to her and wrapped her in his arms. "I, too, can't believe what I'm about to say, but . . . very well." He pressed a kiss to the top of her head.

"You're so smitten," Irelia mumbled.

Elodae laughed into Alden's chest.

Irelia just rolled her eyes.

Alden released Elodae, and the three of them each grabbed a book and a lamp. They started to head out of the dark hallway when Elodae gasped.

He whirled around, reaching for his dagger. "Are you all right?" he asked.

"My necklace," Elodae said, gaping down at her chest. "It just—burned me."

"What?" Irelia asked, coming up on Alden's right.

"It burned me," Elodae repeated, her voice distant. Then her head shot up and she turned in a slow circle, looking around the hallway.

"Elodae?" Alden asked.

She didn't answer. Her eyes were wide in the flickering lamplight. Looking for something. A wave of salt-kissed wind washed over her. And she knew exactly who was nearby.

"Elodae, you're making me nervous," Irelia whispered.

"Something is wrong," she breathed.

Alden immediately grabbed Irelia and Elodae's arms and began hauling them out of the dark hallway.

"What're you doing?" Elodae growled, trying to tug her arm out of his grip.

"Alden, you're hurting me," Irelia whimpered.

Alden loosened his grip but did not let them go. Not until they were back in the light of the main room. He made them sit down and pointed at Elodae. "Stay here. I mean it. Please."

"We need to go the Astronomers, Alden."

"I need to *think*," he snipped back.

"E . . ." Irelia whispered.

Elodae looked over at her sister and raised a brow. Her anxiety built and built in her gut the longer they sat here in the library.

Irelia chewed on her lip with unease.

"We need to leave for the Astronomers straight away."

"You're not going," Alden said without looking up.

"Excuse me?"

Irelia made herself busy again.

Alden met her gaze. "You're not going."

She clenched her jaw. Memories of the man she had once loved saying the same thing to her about the Astronomers or something as simple as dinner with Irelia tore through her mind. "I wasn't asking permission. And regardless, you said—"

"I know what I said," he bit out. "But . . . but Elodae you cannot. There is too much risk and I will not lose you."

Her breathing quickened. "You cannot trap me here, Alden. I need to go."

"I'm not trapping you, but you cannot leave."

"That sounds like trapping to me."

She knew he was telling her to stay out of fear and worry for her safety, for her life. Not because he wanted to control her. Not because he wanted to be the only thing left in her life so she had nowhere else to run. In her heart, she knew that.

But her mind wouldn't stop slamming memories of a too similar instance into her.

Glass thrown against the wall. Elodae crying on the floor in a corner, covering her left cheek where he'd struck her.

"I told you not to go," he roared.

Elodae flinched, tears rushing down her face. "I know. I'm sorry."

He got down onto his knees in front of her and she flinched again as he grabbed her wrist, pulling her hand away from her face. "This wouldn't have happened if you didn't do the one thing I asked you not to do," he said in a sad voice.

Her fault. Always her fault.

"It was just dinner with my sister. I . . . I'm sorry."

He sighed and shook his head. Always disappointed. She was always messing things up.

"You're not going again. Understand?" He tightened his hold on her wrist to the point of pain.

Elodae nodded, whimpering.

He released her and stood, leaving her there on the floor. "Clean this up before you come to bed," he said over his shoulder before disappearing through the doorway.

Sitting in the corner, surrounded by broken glass, Elodae wept.

Her vision focused on Alden again. His eyes were filled with concern.

"El," he was saying in a soft voice. "El, what is it?"

Elodae just stared at him, eyes wide. She felt the tears falling down her face but couldn't remember when she had started to cry.

"El?" Alden asked again gently, reaching to wipe her tears away. She flinched back, and his brows bunched. "I'm sorry I was stern—"

But Elodae was already out of her seat. Already rushing out of the library. She didn't know where she was going. All she knew was that she needed to get away.

She couldn't be trapped again. She couldn't.

Elodae ran from the library. From the man she'd left in that chair.

She knew Alden was different from *him,* but she couldn't stand the thoughts swarming in her head.

So, Elodae ran.

She ran from Alden. Ran from Irelia, though she knew the princess was running after her, the pounding footsteps following her gave it away. Elodae ran from the knowledge that she was linked to all of this somehow.

Most importantly, she ran from herself.

She needed to get out. She needed to get answers. She needed to get air, for she was starting to drown again.

Elodae did not stop until she reached the back steps of the castle, the ones leading to a garden overlooking the Tyrian Peaks. Irelia's ragged breathing sounded behind her.

Elodae wanted to stop, knew her sister's thigh must be in pain, but she couldn't. She started walking again, slower this time.

She left the garden and headed toward the towering red oak trees that hugged the base of the mountains. Their peaks were still softened with snow, but down here, the trees were blooming in full. She had often escaped here as a young child when she needed to get away from the castle. To get away from the new faces. The people who bombarded her with questions about who she was. Where she'd come from. Where her family was.

It was eating away at her, bit by bit. If she kept it inside, tried to suffocate it like it suffocated her, would she be lost to it completely? Lost to the darkness that dwelled inside her—that had always been inside her.

Who was she?

She was angry. Anger and rage and sorrow and longing to understand.

And tired. Gods, she was tired. Not just in her body, but in her heart. In her soul.

Everyone looked at her with confusion and outrage whenever she lashed out, but how could she not? She'd given her heart to someone she thought she could trust and he'd destroyed it.

She was lost. So fucking lost. Nothing could bring back her memories. Nothing.

She would never be whole.

Have you let any of us in?

Her sister's words from months ago echoed in her head.

The one time she'd done it, she'd been left broken on the floor.

Could she do it again? Let someone in?

She thought of her sister, following her into the mountains despite the pain in her leg. Irelia was the one constant Elodae had every day since arriving in Cronanth all those years ago.

Maybe . . .

Elodae halted her steps as she neared a babbling creek and fell to her knees on the bank.

CHAPTER FOURTY

Irelia stumbled through the brush and found Elodae kneeling by a flowing creek. She made her way over to her sister and, despite wearing one of her favorite dresses, sat on the muddy bank next to her.

And there she waited while Elodae sorted out her thoughts.

Tears rushed down her sister's face, and Irelia grabbed her bandaged hand.

Irelia kept her gaze on the flowing water and waited, brushing her thumb along the back of Elodae's hand. She would wait by this creek all day if it meant her sister would talk to her when the moon rose in the night.

A clock chimed distantly in the city behind them, ringing two times before going quiet once more.

Still, Irelia sat.

She tried not to think about the prince who would probably be awake. Her sister was her focus right now.

Being out in the woods made her slightly nervous, though. What if the velarum showed up and no one was around to help them? Elodae had been training, but she only had a dagger.

Elodae took her hand from Irelia's and spun the circles on her necklace.

Irelia knew whatever was about to come out would be difficult for Elodae to say, and she was grateful her sister was trying to let her in. It pained her to be constantly shut out. Elodae let her closer than most, but whenever she got *too* close, her sister put those walls right back up.

Long minutes passed as Irelia studied the surrounding greenery, reciting the names she remembered from her lessons with the Magicks about which herbs healed and which were poison, before Elodae finally spoke.

"I . . . I don't know where to start."

She gave her sister a soft smile. "At the beginning. Or wherever you're the most comfortable."

"None of this is comfortable."

"Then don't say anything."

Her sister closed her eyes for a moment and continued playing with her necklace. "I . . . have a hard time letting people in."

Irelia knew that already, had known that since they were small children. But she wanted to let Elodae voice what she needed to say. What she needed Irelia to know.

"I gave my heart away once before."

Irelia prayed her shock wasn't written on her face, but from Elodae's cringe, she knew it was. "When?"

"Two years ago."

She saw the internal battle her sister was having with herself about sharing even that much information. She wanted to throw her arms around her sister and hold her and never let go. But she was afraid that if she moved, if she so much as breathed wrong, Elodae would retreat and those walls would go back up and never come down again.

"I met him while I was out shopping alone one day. He was handsome and charming and he had no idea who I was. He didn't know I lived at the castle, let alone that I was the king's *niece*." She made air quotes. "I wanted to keep it that way, because, well, you know how most men are with us."

Irelia understood perfectly. When men found out she was a Hailwyn, or found out Elodae was *Elodae Kenton*, they changed. They became greedy. Hungry in a way that made her skin crawl.

They always changed. Every time.

Except—except for Fornax. He'd stayed his annoying, asshole self the entire time.

"So, I hid who I was," Elodae went on. "And after a while, he . . . he wasn't very kind. He made fun of my fears when I found the courage to share them with him. He forced me into situations I was not comfortable in. He isolated me from the friends I'd made and pushed me away from my passions." She sucked in a shaky breath. "He didn't like it when I went to the Astronomers or when I had dinner and drinks with a friend—*you*. Not that I ever told him who I was meeting or where I was going, which of course made him even angrier."

Elodae wouldn't meet Irelia's eyes as she said, "Which is why for several months that year . . . you and I didn't see each other." Her cheeks turned red as though she were embarrassed.

Irelia remembered that year. She had always wondered what had caused the rift between the two of them. She had missed her sister like crazy.

"I tried to leave him several times, I really did." Elodae let out a pained laugh. "But he did such a good job isolating me that it never stuck for long. He would constantly push me away and then suck me back in, and—" Elodae shook her head, still refusing to meet Irelia's eyes.

Her voice became a weak, broken thing. "He and I had been intimate before, but one night I went back to his house after sneaking off to the Astronomers and he'd been drinking . . ."

Irelia was practically vibrating with rage. "Did he hurt you?"

Elodae's green eyes finally met hers, and her tears had Irelia clenching her fists.

She didn't care that she had no idea how to use a sword or dagger—she would find him. She would find whoever had hurt Elodae and she would end him. Slowly.

Her sister's lip trembled, and she opened her mouth, but no words came out. Tears rushed down her face with renewed force.

Irelia didn't stop herself from reaching out this time. She slid closer and wrapped her arms around her sister, holding her tight.

Elodae didn't say anything else for a while. The only sound was her poorly contained sobs.

Irelia didn't need her to go on.

To have given her heart completely to someone only to

have them destroy it time and time again, and in the most *fucked up* ways . . . it made her sick to think about.

Irelia didn't trust her voice, didn't trust that she wouldn't pry the bastard's name out of Elodae and then send someone to kill the man, so she just held her sister. For as long as she needed.

When Elodae's tears slowed and her body no longer shook, only then did Irelia pull back. Elodae's green eyes stood out against the redness of her tears, and Irelia gently wiped the wetness from her cheeks.

Her sister closed her eyes and took a deep breath. Then another. And another. And to Irelia's surprise, she continued her story in a broken whisper. "He took from me."

Irelia couldn't stop her own tears then. "I know."

"I loved him, Irelia. And he . . ."

"I know." She didn't know what else to say.

Elodae shook her head. "The thought of giving my soiled heart to someone again, after having everything broken . . . I was so shattered that it took a long time to piece myself back together."

Her next words came out in barely more than a whisper. "It was the hardest thing I've ever had to do. I don't know if I could go through that again. I feel like . . . my heart is like a broken bottle, shattered and then put back together. If someone comes along and barely even touches it . . ." Elodae shrugged. "One wrong move and I'm worried I'll be broken on the floor again."

Irelia shook her head and gripped her sister's hands tight.

Elodae took a shuddering breath. "I'm so scared to take that leap of faith."

"You don't need to explain yourself."

"But I do."

Irelia's shoulders curved inward. She was a terrible sister. It hurt that Elodae had shut her out so forcefully, but now that she knew why . . . Gods, she was horrible. She had made her talk about something so painful.

"No," Elodae said harshly.

Irelia blinked up at her sister.

"Do not think that way. I can read that look on your face. You didn't ask me to talk. I chose to. If I had gotten up and walked away, you would have let me. If I had just cried and cried, never saying a word, you would have let me. I . . . I'm safe with you. As you said. And I have been unfair in how I've treated you. How I've shoved you away. All of you. And I'm *sorry*."

Irelia marveled at the woman before her. The woman who was so much like the girl she had known when they were younger. Open and free and strong. Elodae had still been those things these past years, but there had been something sharper about her.

But right now . . .

"I love you, Elodae." Elodae shrunk away, but Irelia held tight to her hands. "You don't have to say it back. You don't have to say anything, but I just wanted you to know— wanted you to hear it." She gave her sister's hands a small squeeze. "I love you."

Elodae's green eyes bounced between hers, searching. For what, Irelia didn't know. Whatever it was, though, she must've found it, because she threw her arms around Irelia and pulled her close.

They held each other for a moment, then Elodae began

shaking with the force of her tears again. "Who could possibly love a broken soul?"

"No," Irelia whispered, holding Elodae tighter. "Don't say things like that."

Elodae pulled back to look into her eyes. "But I am broken."

"It's all right to be broken. You experienced a horrible thing, E. There is no time frame for healing. You cannot base your healing off others, either. One day, you will heal. Maybe not completely, but you will. And someday, someone will love you exactly as you are. Broken pieces and all." She added after a beat, "And I think someone already does."

Elodae released a shuddering breath, but a gentle smile bloomed on her lips. "You always were a hopeless romantic."

"I'm surprised you're not with all those books you read." Irelia's smile faded. "But I know it to be true, because *I* love you. As you are right now. I loved you when we were children. I've loved you these past two years. And I love you today. And every day that comes after."

Elodae nodded, tears falling once more, and took another deep breath. "And I love you, Irelia."

Irelia blinked at her sister, hearing the words she never thought she would. With tears in her eyes, she wrapped her sister back in her arms.

They held each other under the rustling red oak trees until a clock in the distance chimed its song.

Elodae and Irelia made their way back to the castle arm in arm. As they stepped back through the gate that led to the garden, Elodae saw him.

Alden sat on a stone bench surrounded by blooming lilies, and when his icy blue eyes met hers, he stood.

Irelia squeezed her gently and kissed her cheek, then left her standing a few feet from Alden. She watched her sister enter the castle doors before turning back to Alden.

They stood in silence for a moment, and then her shoulders sagged. Though her conversation with her sister had left her chest lighter than it'd been in years, it had also left her exhausted.

Fiddling with the strap of her sling, Elodae crossed the remaining distance to Alden, who was still standing despite the bandage bulging beneath his pant leg.

She sat on the stone bench, and he sat down beside her. After a few minutes, Elodae slid closer to him and laid her head on his shoulder. She heard the air whoosh out of his chest as he laid his head gently on top of hers.

Elodae reached out her hand, a silent offer.

Alden took it.

And there they sat for a while longer, only the sounds of birds breaking the garden's silence.

Taking a deep breath, Elodae closed her eyes. The same conversation she'd just had with Irelia was coming with Alden, but the thought of taking down another part of her wall, letting another person in, was too much. She had only ever told him the barest of details in the past, but she knew that in this moment, this conversation, she'd have to let him in completely.

So, she sat in silence, leaning into Alden and letting him lean against her, too.

He kissed the top of her head. "What happened back there, El?"

She squeezed her eyes shut and held tight to his hand. He wasn't the same as the boy before. This was Alden. He would never hurt her.

Elodae pulled back and looked up at him. His eyes were open and full of love. Love for her. Something she had never seen in the other boy's eyes.

So, she told him. She told him everything.

About the boy with the heart of a coward whom she had loved. About how he had controlled her and how he'd gotten mad when she had disobeyed him. How she had given up friends, passions, even reading, to please him.

How, the last time she'd ever been near him, he had taken from her.

She talked until her tears fell and her voice grew hoarse. She talked until even Alden began to cry. He never said anything, though. He just held her hand and listened.

Elodae then told him about her dream several nights back. About the shipwreck and how she'd found out the woman in her dreams was her mother. How she believed her mother had died that night, killed before her very eyes. How her mother had given her the necklace she never took off. And now she knew why. Why the necklace meant everything to her.

She talked about how she was terrified her memories would never fully return. How the more information she learned from her dreams, the more confused she became. How she was terrified that her mind was lying to her, only showing her things she wanted to see. How she was afraid everything she knew was a lie. That it would all disappear someday. And how she couldn't even trust herself.

Elodae talked until the sky turned pink and orange above them. Sometimes she didn't talk at all. Sometimes she just cried and Alden held her until she found her voice again.

But he stayed with her. Silent. Listening.

Stayed as the sun went to rest and the stars flickered to life overhead.

And only once she was done—only once she had said everything that weighed on her heart—did Alden speak.

"I love you," was all he said.

It was all she'd ever needed to hear.

CHAPTER FOURTY ONE

Warren stepped out of the bath and wrapped a towel around his waist. It was his third bath of the day, and last week had been the same. It had taken two baths to get the blood fully off his body and then a third to give him some sense of cleanliness. He still felt the phantom coating of blood on his skin.

He shivered.

Making his way over to the sink, he turned on the water and cupped his hands under it. Despite having just washed his entire body, he lifted the water to his face and began scrubbing.

With his eyes closed, he saw it: the velarum, his brothers dying, his family getting mauled. He put his hands down on either side of the basin and heaved for air.

He'd visited Elodae and Alden in the hospital wing. They

were both hurt, but alive. They would be all right. Irelia, thank the gods, hadn't been harmed. Her prince, though . . .

When Warren had seen the prince's face, his ears had started to ring. Radford had saved the Prince of Dolannish's life, and it had cost him his own. He was one of hundreds who had lost their lives that fateful day.

Warren had spent most of his time in his room, trying to calm his mind. He only left to run the grounds of the castle. Elodae and Alden had come to see him once, but Warren's mind had been distant. Empty. They had asked him questions he couldn't answer. Wouldn't answer. Not yet.

They had left him that night with worried looks on their faces.

A noticeable tension had eased from his brother's shoulders, though. As though Alden had been relieved to hear that Finn had been chosen to be Captain of the Guard and not him.

Running his fingers through his still-damp hair, Warren made his way out of the tiny bathroom and into his bedroom. It was on the lowest level of the castle, which meant the only window he had was a tiny one in the upper corner of his bedroom. No foyer, no balcony. Only his bed, dresser, and a worktable.

He didn't mind, though. He'd never needed much. Had never wanted much. He rarely spent enough time in his room to care how big it was or how much it held.

Warren had always enjoyed being outside. Roaming through the redwoods to the west, or swimming in the sea to the east. But ever since the Veiling—he had been scared. Scared of the trees' shade or the endless black of the sea. Scared of the night. Scared of his own shadow.

The sounds of his people dying morphed into the screams of his mother and father being burned alive in that house.

Warren clenched his eyes shut and forced his mind to empty. He couldn't think about that right now. He needed to check on Elodae and Alden. Hel, even Fornax.

Finn was wandering the halls, the new head of Irelia's personal guard on his tail, when Warren finally emerged to make his way to the hospital wing. He nodded in acknowledgement to his new captain and kept walking.

"Warren," Finn called.

Warren ground his teeth but schooled his face before he turned around, tucking his hands behind his back. He'd chosen regular clothes today, black pants and a matching tunic. Vanor had suggested he take a week or two off from duty to recover. He wasn't injured, and he'd said as much to the king.

To which Vanor had replied, "It is not your body that needs rest, my boy."

"The princess has requested your presence in the Hall," Finn said with a nod in that direction.

And with that, the captain turned and left.

Irelia so rarely left the hospital wing these days. She liked to spend her time by her people's bedsides, helping the healers tend to them.

With a furrowed brow, Warren made his way toward the Grand Hall. When he rounded the last corner, he saw Elodae and Alden a few paces ahead.

"Brother," Warren called and jogged over to Alden's side. Elodae smiled at him. "Did Irelia ask for you, too?"

They exchanged a confused look.

"No," Elodae said. "*We* actually called for *her*."

Warren suppressed his confusion and followed them into the Hall. Irelia's peach-blonde hair was easy enough to spot, but it was the stunning gold cloak she wore that caught his attention.

Alden let out a low whistle.

Irelia blushed. "It was a gift."

Warren snorted and the princess shot him a glare.

"Ready?" The princess asked them.

"And what exactly am I ready for?" Warren asked carefully.

"I'm going to the Astronomers," Elodae said. "And I need an escort."

Warren went still, and Irelia furrowed her brows at him.

"Warren?" Alden asked.

"I don't think I should go."

Elodae turned to face him fully. "Why?"

He swallowed hard. "Vanor said I should rest."

Elodae raised an eyebrow.

"What happened out there, Warren?" Alden asked softly.

Warren forced himself to smirk at his brother. "I didn't get a fancy new scar like you lot, if that's what you're asking."

"It wasn't." Irelia frowned. "And not all scars are visible."

Elodae laid a hand on Warren's arm. "Come with me."

He looked at her for a moment. At the girl who had become like his sister over the years. Her pine-green eyes were gentle. Understanding. She knew what was storming inside him. What kept him awake at night and caused him to run and run and run during the day. She knew what it was like to have lived through horrors. He supposed they all did now.

If she needed him, he would be there.

After a moment, Warren nodded.

Elodae offered him a quiet smile before turning to Alden, who had once more taken hold of her hand, uncertainty worrying his lip.

"Here's the plan," Elodae said quietly.

She explained to them that Warren and she were to go to the Astronomers in search of answers to what these books meant. It was the first time Warren had heard anything of these four mysterious books with the long-lost language, but he tucked that information away and kept listening.

Alden and Irelia were to stay behind because of the injuries they both had received, for Elodae could not risk them getting hurt any further or falling behind if they needed to make a quick escape.

When his brother made to argue, Elodae had simply placed a gentle kiss to Alden's lips, quieting him. Warren ignored the ache that built in his chest at that hint of a loving touch. He was not jealous of his brother for the duchess' affections, but more so the affection at all. He longed to have someone look at him like that, to love him so fiercely they would do whatever it took to keep him safe.

Warren listened to Elodae's plan, his mind flying through all the possibilities on what could happen to them out there. The dangers that threatened at every single corner, that lingered in every shadow. Especially now that the sun had set.

He knew it was a dangerous mission, everyone knew that. But if these books could somehow help them save their people from this darkness and the demons that accompanied it . . . then they had to take that chance.

So, when Elodae made her way to the front doors of the

Castle of Cronanth, Warren followed in suit. Ready to protect her with his life if it came down to that.

Though he prayed it wouldn't.

ALDEN STARED WIDE-EYED AT ELODAE IN FRONT OF the castle gates minutes later.

"I still don't like this plan," he said, looking back and forth between Warren and Elodae.

"I'll be fine," Elodae said gently, and rose on her toes to kiss him.

When she pulled back, Alden clenched his jaw and looked at Warren. "You keep her safe."

Warren bowed his head. "Always."

"I can take care of myself, too, you know," Elodae said, slipping her hands into Alden's pockets and pulling him toward her. She kissed him again, deep and loving. He wrapped his arms around her.

Warren cleared his throat and turned away, walking over to Irelia, who was impatiently waiting by the gate door. As though already itching to return to the hospital wing to check in on a certain red-haired royal.

"I love you," Alden whispered.

"I . . . I do, too," Elodae whispered back.

His heart skipped a beat. He brought his mouth down onto hers once more before pulling away.

"When I get back," Elodae breathed, "I hope you'll be waiting for me. In bed."

Alden hardened at her words and tightened his fingers on her back. "I will wait for you. Until you are ready."

"Are you done yet?" Warren called from behind them.

Elodae laughed, and the sound sent his heart leaping in his chest.

"Promise me you'll come back," he whispered onto her lips.

"I'll come back," she breathed.

"I love you."

She smiled and pressed a quick kiss to his lips before joining Warren to walk down the street toward the Astronomers.

She'd asked Alden to wait for her—and he would.

Until his dying breath.

CHAPTER FOURTY TWO

Elodae and Warren hurried through the nearly empty streets toward the Astronomers, *The Veiling* tucked beneath her cloak. She didn't know what she expected Byron to say, but she would not leave without answers of some sort. Anything to put the running thoughts in her mind at ease.

It was the dinner hour when they arrived, and Elodae smelled cooking food the moment she burst through the front door, Warren on her heels.

"Byron," she called, heading toward the kitchen down the narrow hallway.

Pots and pans crashed to the floor.

Elodae pushed the kitchen doors, but they were shut tight. Locked. She knocked. "Byron? Daphne? It's Elodae. Are you all right?"

Low murmurs sounded inside, but no one answered.

She raised her eyebrows at Warren, who motioned for her to knock again. Byron and his wife were weird folks. Not in the way the Magicks were, but still odd.

Elodae knocked again. "Hello? I really need to speak with you, Byron. It's urgent."

"One moment, dear," Daphne called.

Byron grumbled something at his wife, but it was too muffled for Elodae to hear.

Minutes dragged by, and crashing pots and pans continued to sound as the couple hissed at each other.

Finally, Daphne yanked open the kitchen door. Her red curls were a wild mess around her head. She wiped her hands on a kitchen rag tucked into the front pocket of her apron and smiled at them. "Elodae. Warren. What a lovely surprise, but you should not be out this late at night."

Daphne lifted an arm, allowing them to pass into the kitchen. Elodae nodded her thanks and went straight over to Byron, who was stirring a large boiling pot of something that smelled delicious next to his son Pollux, a spitting image of his father. They cooked the best food in all Samarok. Food like no other.

Elodae breathed in deeply, the spices and herbs warming her body. "Byron, I need to speak with."

He grunted.

"I need to speak with you in *private*," she said in a hushed voice as Warren began chatting with Daphne about what she'd been up to today.

"Can it wait until after dinner, dear?" he asked, not looking at her as he took the pot off the stove and over to the large sink in the corner.

Elodae followed him and could feel Pollux's gaze burning

her back. His husband was nowhere to be seen, but she knew he was not far behind. The pair never went anywhere without the other.

"Not exactly."

He sighed and looked at her over his shoulder. She kept her face firm, and he sighed again and set the pot down on the stone counter. "Daph, Pollux, can you finish this? Elodae and I will be right back."

His wife blinked her big blue eyes at him, her curls bouncing as she nodded her head. "Help me, Warren?"

Warren gave Elodae a slight nod, and she followed Byron into the hallway. He led her to a private library along the hall and closed the wooden door behind her when she stepped in. She blinked at Castor, who was lounging on one of the brown settees. "Byron, I really need to speak with you alone."

Castor made an appalled sound and Elodae reined in her eye roll.

"He is my heir," Byron said, and sat across from his son on the matching sofa. "Whatever it is, you can say it to both of us. You know that."

"This isn't about astronomy, though."

Both men blinked up at her.

"Then what is it, dear?" Byron asked, leaning forward so his arms rested on his knees.

Elodae looked back and forth between Byron and Castor. She didn't want to involve anyone else, but he clearly wouldn't talk without Castor present. It usually wouldn't bother her, but this was—personal. The betrayal of Byron stung at the wounds in her soul.

She closed her eyes and took a deep breath, then sat on the settee next to Castor. "Someone's been following me.

They want my necklace. And Irelia found four books in the castle library that have the same text as my necklace. I don't know why he wants it, but . . . his name is Orion. And I don't know for certain where he's from or what he wants with me besides my necklace, but I'm obviously tied up in this somehow. And—and so are you."

The father and son sat in silence for a minute. Castor's mouth gaped open, but Byron was as still as stone. Elodae couldn't read his face. He exchanged a look with his son, who nodded and got up to leave.

Byron leaned back in his seat and rubbed a hand over his chin. He said nothing until his son returned with a large book in hand. He set it on the table that separated the two settees and began flipping through the pages.

Elodae leaned forward and peered over his shoulder. Her heart stopped dead in her chest.

It was in the same language as her necklace. As the other books.

With a heavy heart, Elodae reached inside her cloak, pulled out her own book and flipped to the last page where Byron's name was scrawled in delicate blue ink. She laid it down on the table, turning it toward the Head Astronomer.

"Where did you get that?" Byron breathed, leaning forward, brushing his fingers over the words he clearly wrote.

"The library at the castle. It was also one of the books that Orion was searching for, I'm sure. And it's in the same text as my necklace."

"They are not the same text."

Elodae blinked. "What?"

Castor is the one who replied, "These books are written in Lunalian."

"But the symbols—"

"Are not the same as the ones on your necklace, Elodae." Byron closed his eyes for a second before closing *The Veiling* and handing it back to Elodae. "Similar, yes. But not the same."

Elodae's mind went quiet. "Then what language are these?"

"Lunala."

No, that can't be right.

"Orion said the symbols in *The Night of Day* were not Lunalian, but something else."

Byron shrugged. "I don't know anything about *The Night of Day*, but I can assure you that these symbols," he waved a hand toward the book Castor had brought and the book in Elodae's lap, "are most certainly Lunalian."

Castor handed his father the large book, still saying nothing to Elodae. She tried to meet his gaze, but he wouldn't look at her.

As a young boy, he had done that only when he was hiding something. Elodae narrowed her eyes at him, but he still wouldn't acknowledge her. No flirty words or witty comebacks today, it seemed.

Byron read the page. *Read the page.*

"So, you can read that?" She breathed.

"Some of it." Castor's brown eyes were filled with apologies when they finally met hers.

"Why do you have that guilty look on your face?"

He gave her a half smile. "I don't know what you're talking about."

"Please. Just—if you know anything about any of this . . ." Elodae turned back to Byron. "I really need your help.

Why do you have a book titled the very same thing we've named these demon attacks? Why do you have Lunalian books that Orion is so desperately searching for? And how am I tied to all of this?"

Byron sighed, the weight of his years becoming more apparent on the aged man. "There is a prophecy," he began, pulling the book back toward him.

"Prophecy? I thought only the Magicks did stuff like that."

"The stars tell prophecies too," Castor said.

She frowned but nodded to Byron. A silent agreement to listen.

"There is a prophecy," he began again, running a finger over the symbols on the page. "That a child with black hair will bring evil upon this world. *A child of the stars with hair black as the void—the world will birth new scars, for all good shall be destroyed.*"

Elodae's heart pounded. She reached for her necklace, spinning the circles.

"We're not sure what it means, or how the child will destroy all the good in the world," Castor said, leaning back in his seat. "And that's all there is."

"It feels incomplete," Elodae said, looking over at him.

"It does, doesn't it?"

"There is another, however," Byron said.

Elodae whirled back toward him.

Castor sighed, leaning his head back.

"*The one with an eye of pine and an eye of sky—our divine will forever rely,*" Byron read, once more tracing his fingers along the symbols. The symbols that looked so similar to the ones on her necklace.

But that first line . . .

Elodae shot to her feet.

The one with an eye of pine and an eye of sky—

An eye of pine, an eye of sky—it begins.

Her mind raced.

The one.

It was one person. One person was responsible for all this terror.

It begins.

The Veiling had started shortly after the Magick told her that prophecy.

After she'd met—

Orion. With his one eye of blue and one eye of green.

Our divine will forever rely.

The divine could be evil, she supposed. Perhaps the divine and the child of the stars were the same person. And Orion needed Elodae's mother's necklace to find them somehow.

Elodae ran a hand through her hair and paced in front of Castor and Byron, who silently watched her.

The language these prophecies were written in was Lunalian. Orion had to be Lunalian. She had the hunch, but it was never confirmed. Alden certainty thought he was. It made perfect sense. And their prince would arrive soon. It wouldn't be unreasonable for him to have sent spies to Samarok before he arrived to make sure everything would be safe for him.

Was Orion a Lunalian spy?

Holy fucking gods.

"What does this have to do with me?" Elodae breathed.

Byron stood and approached her. "Elodae?"

"What does Orion want with me?" she asked him.

"I don't know, but he's left you alive. Thank the gods. When will the prince arrive?"

His question pulled her from her racing thoughts. "Five months. Why?"

"He is Lunalian, no? And your necklace is of a—similar script," Byron said, waving a hand toward the book on the table.

Elodae narrowed her eyes, not quite understanding. Then she looked at the man before her and asked slowly, "How do you know how to read Lunalian, Byron?"

It Castor was who said, "Where did the Astronomers come from, Elodae?"

"Lunala."

Byron put a hand gently on her shoulder, but the weight of the world around her was suffocating. "And what do the Astronomers call Lunala?"

"The Moon Kingdom, because of its shape."

Castor nodded. "And they've spent millennia not allowing anyone in or out of their kingdom. Hiding their land from the outside world. Concealing themselves, if you will."

Elodae's hands began to tremble.

The look on Byron's face was almost sad. "What's another word for concealing something, Elodae?"

The air whooshed out of her lungs. "Veiling."

Orion was the cause of the Veiling. But the Prince of Lunala claimed to have the answers to stop the Veiling. Why would they . . .

The perfect way to have someone agree to your demands would be to create a problem only you know how to solve.

Elodae's breaths came in quick, rushed pants. She was going to marry the Prince of Lunala. The monster that killed and tortured her people. She was going to be trapped with no escape.

And her necklace . . . the thing Orion so desperately wanted.

A terrible thought entered her mind. One that now she thought of it, would never leave.

Was *she* Lunalian?

WARREN WALKED BESIDE ELODAE DOWN AN EMPTY street. The lights from the castle ahead shone along with the moon up above.

"You're quiet," he said, looking sidelong at her.

"I have a lot to think about."

She was stalling.

He nudged her with his elbow. "You want to tell me what you and Byron went to talk about when you left me to fend for myself with Daphne?"

A hesitant smile touched her lips. "She's not that bad."

"No, she's not. But she is *something*."

"Indeed."

Daphne was a vibrant, eccentric woman. Her curly hair had kept whacking Warren in the face as he tried to help prepare dinner. Her bright purple dress had clashed with the green apron she wore. The stick kept falling out of her curls and onto the floor, making Warren jump every time it made a loud clacking sound. She rambled to herself and sometimes laughed at whatever the voices in her head said.

He adored the woman—everyone did—but being alone with her for long periods of time was . . . a lot. Even for him.

Elodae had been gone with Byron for nearly an hour before Warren finally went to retrieve them. She'd been uncharacteristically quiet ever since.

Byron had acted no different. He laughed and sang with his wife while they all ate dinner. But their son, Castor, kept shooting Elodae confused glances. Worried glances. Like he was uncomfortable with her in the room. Pollux and his husband had eaten their food in silence, only murmuring soft nothings to each other every now and then.

Warren knew little about Castor. He had only met the man a few times in the past, but he and Elodae were close. Especially when they were younger and Elodae had spent every waking moment at the Astronomers.

From the first time Warren had met Castor, he had known right away the man was a terrible liar. Which made for an interesting evening. Every time Elodae asked him a question, he had avoided her gaze and mumbled some vague response.

Warren didn't want to push her, but the distant look in her eyes was hard to ignore. He opened his mouth to tell her about his theory on the disappearances and the velarum. He hadn't been able to talk about it—think about it—since the attack.

Looking at her, though . . . She seemed so sad. So lost.

So instead, he asked, "Did you get the answers you needed?"

Elodae only shrugged.

He sighed in resignation and remained silent the rest of the walk back to the castle.

Cronanth had all but gone to sleep around them, so it was a silent trek. Warren walked Elodae back to her rooms and made sure she was inside before leaving. Even with guards stationed out front, the weight of anxiety stood on his shoulders until the door locked behind her.

Dipping his head in acknowledgement to the six guards outside her room, he turned and left. He was exhausted, but his mind was still reeling.

He needed to get away from the castle—from the city.

So, Warren made his way to the western side of the castle and walked down the stairs leading to an empty courtyard facing the Tyrian Peaks in the distance. He kicked off his boots and pulled off his shirt, leaving them in a pile by the gate.

And then he ran. Ran toward the wilderness that called to him. Away from the city. Away from the terrors that had befallen Cronanth these last two months. Away from himself —from who he'd had to become these last eight years, ever since his parents had died that night long ago.

He ran until the sun brought its light back to the world.

CHAPTER FOURTY THREE

I relia's eyes drooped as she returned to her rooms. Fornax had insisted that she sleep in her own bed tonight. She was so exhausted from everything that had happened, that she didn't even try to argue him on the matter.

She nodded absently to the guards outside her door as she pushed them open. It was still strange not to see Finn standing there, although the new captain still lingered occasionally.

Yawning and stretching her arms over her head, Irelia turned to head into her bedroom when a blur of black moved in her periphery.

Lady Astrid spun her and pinned her against the wall.

Irelia gasped. "What're you doing here?"

Lady Astrid's smile stumbled slightly, and something like

fury flashed across her features before her smile returned once more. "Do you?" she asked, tilting her head to the side.

"Do I what?" Irelia breathed.

"Love him?"

Irelia blinked. Love was such a strong word. She cared for the prince, that was for certain. And maybe, one day, she could grow to love him. The thought scared her and she felt her cheeks blush a bright red.

Astrid let out a low laugh. "I knew it."

Irelia had never heard that sound from her before. She looked up at the lady and blinked at the anger on her face.

"You *care* for him?" Astrid asked in a voice that sounded nothing like hers. She took a stalking step toward Irelia.

The princess backed up and bumped into the wall. Her knees went wobbly, threatening to buckle beneath her. What was going on? Astrid had behaved like this in the garden that day, but Fornax wasn't here to help her now. She had to use her voice, the way she did with him, and be stern.

"I do," Irelia said, her voice coming out stronger than she felt.

Astrid's sapphire blue eyes looked almost black in the dim candlelight as she stood directly before Irelia. "Oh, you do, do you?" the lady drawled.

Irelia hissed, "I don't know what you're playing at, but you need to leave before I call for my guards."

Something in Astrid's face changed. Her eyes brightened and the color Irelia hadn't realized was absent returned to her cheeks. The lady stumbled back a step, blinking at Irelia. "He'll come for you."

Irelia stared at her. "What?"

"He's coming for you."

"Who?" She took a step toward Astrid, but the lady held up a hand. It trembled in the air between them. "Astrid."

Astrid shook her head, then she straightened her back. The color drained from her skin, and her eyes darkened once more. She turned to leave, pinning Irelia to the spot with three simple words before she disappeared.

"He's found you."

CHAPTER FOURTY FOUR

Elodae awoke with a gasp, bolting upright in her bed. She clutched at her chest, at the necklace that rested above her heart and below the one Alden had given her.

Alden sat up and wrapped his arm around her. "Are you all right?"

Her breaths still came in sharp pants and sweat beaded on her forehead. The sun was just rising beyond her windows. She ran a hand over her face and forced herself to take a deep breath.

Alden ran a comforting hand up and down her back. "Tell me about it," he whispered, kissing her temple.

Elodae shook her head.

Alden nuzzled her neck, pressing slow, sleepy kisses there.

She tilted her head to the side and leaned into him. "Alden," she breathed.

Real. This was real. Not the dream. The nightmare. The memory. She didn't know which it was at this point. But Alden was real, and she needed him right now. Needed him to calm her racing mind.

His arm tightened, pulling her closer. He gently nipped at the base of her neck, and she sucked in a sharp breath.

"Do you know how in love with you I am?" he whispered into her skin.

"Show me," she breathed, closing her eyes and letting every thought except for Alden fade from her mind.

"Hmm," he said, and gripped her hip with his other hand. He slid the one that was stroking her back up and brushed her hair out of the way, cupping the nape of her neck.

Elodae ran her fingers up and down Alden's arms and felt him shiver.

She smiled to herself.

He gently lay her back on the bed and settled himself over her, pressing kisses up her neck and along her jaw.

She let out a breathy moan when he softly bit her earlobe. The hand on her waist slid up her side, pulling her pink nightgown up above her hips.

"Alden," she breathed again.

"I love the way you say my name," he whispered in her ear, and then claimed her mouth with his.

Elodae wrapped her arms around his neck and her legs around his hips, pulling him down onto her. He tried to prop himself up slightly, probably to spare her shoulder, but she didn't care about the pain right now.

She wanted him. Wanted all of him.

She reached between them and tugged up his shirt. He

leaned back onto his knees and pulled it off over his head. The sun's rays hit his body through the gap in her curtains, and Elodae moistened her lips.

In the morning sun—he was even more beautiful.

She sat up and ran her hands over his chest, marveling at the sight—the feel—of him. Alden stayed still, letting her trace the muscles along his stomach, his arms. She met his blue eyes as she reached the ties of his pants and began undoing them. His mouth parted slightly, and she tilted her head up.

A silent invitation.

Alden cupped her jaw with one of his hands and kissed her deeply, eliciting a moan from her. His other hand went down to help her with the ties of his pants. She would have blushed at the struggle to undo them, but something about it felt right.

Everything felt right in this moment. With him. Like she could conquer the world. All she needed was him.

The ties came loose at last and Elodae pulled the waistband down, not breaking the kiss.

His hand caught her wrist.

Elodae pulled back then and gazed up at him. "I want this."

His eyes shuttered, and he opened his mouth to say something she was sure would ruin her mood. So, she put her fingers over his mouth.

"I want this," she said again. She removed her fingers, and he didn't open his mouth again. Just kneeled there. Watching.

Elodae kept her eyes locked on his as she pulled the band

down his hips. She slid her hands up his bare thighs and a shiver went through his body.

"Kiss me," she whispered.

And he did. His other hand went to her jaw, and he kissed her. It stole her breath, that kiss.

She gently ran her fingers along the length of him. He tensed under her touch, but then his fingers fisted in her hair.

"Elodae," he whispered against her lips, his hand going for her wrist again.

"Don't."

"Elodae, we don't have to do this."

She scooted back and lifted her nightgown over her head, tossing it in a pile on the floor by the bed.

Alden's lips parted slightly again as he took in the sight of her. All of her. He'd seen her before, but this was different.

He knew it was. She knew it, too.

"Do you want me?" she asked, lying back against the headboard.

He nodded as his blue eyes dipped to her breasts, which peaked in the chilly morning air.

"Say it," she whispered.

His eyes met hers again.

"Say you want me."

"I want you," he ground out.

Elodae's throat bobbed. "I want this, Alden," she said quietly.

He slid off the bed and stepped out of his pants. When his eyes met hers again, her heart skipped at the heat in his gaze. The love that shone there.

"If you want to stop, or feel uncomfortable in any way, tell me immediately," he said, climbing back onto the bed.

She nodded and slid down until she was lying flat on her back. He moved his body over hers again. She sucked in a breath, and Alden immediately stilled.

"I'm all right," she assured him.

He brushed away a strand of hair that had fallen across her face. "Tell me when to stop," he said, and reached down to help guide him into her.

And once he was fully inside, once they were joined completely, she wrapped her arms around his neck and kissed him deeply. "Never," she whispered.

Alden slid out of her and kissed her jaw as he thrust back in.

Elodae tilted her head back, letting out a breathy moan, her fingers digging into his back.

He moved at the same pace as his mouth. Slow. Agonizingly slow. She lifted her hips into his, sliding him deeper as he tried to pull out again.

Alden breathed a laugh against her collarbone. "Do you want something, princess?"

Elodae bit her lip and moved against him again. He breathed a hiss as he slid all the way in. "I want you to show me how much you love me," she breathed, undulating her hips over and over.

He looked down at their joined hips. And when hers rose again, he shoved into her. She had to clamp a hand over her mouth to silence her moan.

She squeezed her eyes closed when he did it again.

"Look at me," he whispered. "Elodae, look at me."

Elodae opened her eyes and met his gaze. He thrust into her again and she bit her lip to remain silent. She didn't want the guards outside to hear.

He continued to pump in and out of her, and she reached a hand down to start moving her finger over herself. Alden's pace quickened the louder her moans grew.

"Don't stop," she breathed.

He hooked a hand under her backside and lifted. At this angle, he hit the very back of her and she threw her head back, calling out his name.

And then he brought his mouth down onto hers as her pleasure exploded through her. His thrusts grew uneven and then he was moaning her name. The ache of him inside her, her name on his lips, was almost too much.

Once they were both spent, Alden collapsed on top of her. Their ragged breaths the only sound in the room. He laid his head on her chest, and she didn't care that they were both drenched in sweat.

She thought he'd fallen asleep on her until he whispered, "I love you," and kissed the spot over her heart.

Elodae opened her mouth to reply, but he slid off her and got out of bed. He brushed his knuckles over her cheek and smiled at her before disappearing into the bathroom.

Elodae propped herself up on her elbow and watched him for a moment before she whispered, too quiet for anyone but her to hear, "I love you, too."

CHAPTER FOURTY FIVE

Warren made his way back into the castle, sweat dripping down his face and bare torso. It was finally beginning to be warm, hints of summer in the breezes off the ocean waves.

Pulling his shirt out of his back pocket, he wiped his face with it and ran it through his hair.

"Aren't you a sight for sore eyes," a woman's voice drawled from behind him.

He turned and smiled at Elodae as she approached. Something about her had changed. She looked more open. More relaxed.

"Your Grace." He bowed low, sweeping out his arms.

She laughed and fell into step beside him. "There's a ball tonight. Something to give the people joy in a time of sorrow or something like that," she said as they walked up the steps and back into the castle.

"Because those have gone so well these past few months."

"Truthfully." She laughed lightly.

They walked in silence for a moment before he asked, "What were you doing out here?"

"Alden and I just finished our training session when I saw you running through the halls." When he said nothing, she asked, "What were you running from?"

"Everything."

She hummed her agreement. "It's crazy to think that just a few months ago, everything was normal. And now . . ."

"A lot of things have changed in a short amount of time," Warren said. His words came out sadder than he'd meant them to. He slipped on his shirt before they stepped through the doors and into a hallway that led to the Grand Hall.

"Indeed, they have," she said softly and smiled down at her feet.

"What's got you in such a good mood?"

Elodae shrugged.

"Could my brother have anything to do with it?"

"He has everything to do with it." She said with a quiet smile.

He studied her for a moment and then asked quietly, "Did you give him a key?"

"Not yet."

He put his arm around her shoulder. "You'll get there one day."

"Gods, you need a bath." She shoved him away.

Warren barked a laugh and wrapped her in a bear hug. She shrieked even as she laughed and shoved him away again.

THE CLOCK IN ELODAE'S FOYER CHIMED SEVEN times before going silent. The sun had begun to set.

She stared at herself in the mirror. At the dress that had been left at her door. No note had accompanied it, but by its sheer beauty, she knew it had to be Irelia. She'd nearly cried when she first opened the box.

The dress was a blue so deep it was almost black, like the sky at night. And on it, in hundreds of jewels that sparkled and shined in the setting sunlight, was an exact replication of the night sky.

The Astronomers knew the stars' movements well enough now that they could pinpoint what was where on any given day of the year.

She would have to go searching for which day her sister had chosen to put on the dress.

Elodae twirled back and forth in the full-length mirror, admiring herself. She ran her fingers through the glittering fabric over the skirts. The neckline rested just below her collarbone. The sleeves were the same sheer fabric as the outer layer on the skirts—the layer that held the diamonds.

Elodae had carefully slipped on the elegant dress, surprised at how light it was despite the weight of the diamonds.

She felt a slight smile curl her lips as she looked over the familiar constellations.

Then her fingers froze and the air whooshed out of her as

she saw what had been laid across her heart. What lay beside her pendant.

The Warrior.

Elodae couldn't fight the tears that formed in her eyes. She laughed as she cried. Ever since she had opened and let Alden in that morning, she had been a whirlwind of emotions.

She touched the star necklace he'd given her, then her mother's.

Her mother.

If only her mother were here. If only she could see Elodae in this dress. Had she shared Elodae's love of the stars?

Lillianna had not been here to help Elodae into the dress or do her hair and cosmetics. It mattered little to Elodae that she had to get ready alone. She liked the silence. It gave her time to let her emotions wash over her, and then away, instead of shoving them all down. She could cry, like now, and not be judged or asked why.

Elodae sat at her vanity and began doing her hair in her preferred style, lightly curling her already wavy hair. Then she made two braids on either side of her face, leaving out her front pieces, and tied half of her hair in a knot atop her head.

She had just finished lining her eyes with kohl when a knock sounded on her door.

Slipping on her matching gloves, Elodae got up and rushed over. She pulled the doors open, and her smile faded as she saw who stood there.

It wasn't Alden. Wasn't Warren. Wasn't even Fornax or Finn.

But Hadeon. The Dolannish lord she'd danced with at the welcome ball for his prince.

"Lord Hadeon." She dipped her head slightly. "To what do I owe this pleasure?"

"I'm here to escort you to the Grand Hall," he said, lifting his arm for her to take.

"That's very kind, but I am waiting for someone."

"Lord Einar is already at the Hall. He arrived with Lady Astrid mere minutes ago."

Elodae's heart sank into her stomach. "What do you mean?"

The lord raised his brows. "Alden Einar escorted his fiancée to the ball. Why would he not?"

"Their engagement was broken off weeks ago."

Hadeon shrugged. "That's not what it appears like. But why should it matter? You're all but engaged to the Prince of Lunala, no?"

Elodae's throat bobbed, but she said nothing more as she lifted her skirts with one gloved hand and took the lord's elbow.

One of her guards shut the door behind them as they made their way to the Hall.

The sound of the slamming door echoed inside her.

CHAPTER FOURTY
SIX

Elodae allowed Lord Hadeon to lead her across the castle and through the towering doors of the Grand Hall. She scanned the gathered crowd for Alden and Astrid. They were standing by a table along the other side of the room.

Alden was smiling at whatever the lady was saying.

They're just talking, Elodae told herself.

A voice in the back of her head just laughed at her.

Irelia and Fornax were on the dais. She was smiling into her glass of wine as he said something in her ear. The princess was doing her best to ignore the prince, but Elodae knew her sister was failing miserably.

For all she knew, Alden had escorted his old fiancée out of a sense of duty. Or maybe she'd asked him. She didn't know, so she couldn't assume. Right?

Elodae made her way over to the dais, leaving the lord by a group of Dolannish men in red uniforms.

"E," Irelia squealed when she saw her.

Fornax let out a low whistle. "That is quite a dress, duchess."

"Thank you. Irelia, it truly is beautiful."

"Where did you even get that thing?" her sister asked, running her fingers over the skirt.

Elodae frowned. "Didn't you leave this for me?"

Irelia shook her head.

She looked over her shoulder at Alden, whose eyes were already fixed on her. Her cheeks heated. "Excuse me," she said absently to Irelia and Fornax.

Irelia chuckled behind her as Elodae made her way back down the dais and across the room. Alden met her halfway, and to her surprise, he cupped the nape of her neck, tilting her head back, and kissed her deeply.

Her stomach did a flip.

"You look . . ." He shook his head slowly and pulled back, looking her up and down.

"Why did you bring Astrid?" she couldn't help but ask.

He narrowed his eyes. "I didn't."

"What?"

"I was told you were already here, so I came alone. But you weren't here yet, and Astrid came over to talk about my mother."

None of that made any sense. Why would Hadeon tell her Alden had brought Astrid?

She looked around the Hall, searching for the lord, but he had all but disappeared. And where was Vanor?

The sun outside the windows dipped lower in the sky, stars winking into existence.

Elodae shook her head, looking back at Alden. "It doesn't matter now. You're here."

"I'll always be here," he whispered and kissed her again.

"Dance with me," she said, taking his hand.

He smiled and let her lead them onto the dance floor.

"Where's your uncle?" he asked, resting his hand on her hip and swaying slowly to the music. His shin was still healing and though he wouldn't show it, she knew it still ached. Her shoulder did the same every time she moved it.

"I'm not sure." Elodae looked around the room for him again. The king had been away a lot lately. In meetings—secret meetings with Lunala no doubt.

They'd find a way for her to get out of the marriage, even if it meant she and Alden had to run away and never return to Cronanth.

That thought stuck in her mind.

"Let's leave." The words escaped her before she could stop them.

Alden blinked down at her. "Leave?"

"Leave."

"And go where?"

"I don't care." If she was with him, it didn't matter where they went.

They could travel all the way to Snowria, the northernmost city in Samarok, or down to Selenehold in the Moon Rainforest. She just wanted to be with him and only him. For the rest of her days.

A small smile appeared on Alden's face, then bloomed into a grin. "All right."

"Really?" Her heart leapt in her chest.

He lifted a hand to tuck a strand of hair behind her ear. "I don't just want you in my life, Elodae. I want to have a life *with* you."

Elodae couldn't fight her own grin as he continued to lead her through the music.

"We'll pack our things tonight and leave in the morning," he said, his eyes becoming heavy-lidded as he gazed at her.

She let out a shallow breath and rose on her toes to kiss him. He wrapped his arms around her, still swaying them to the music, and kissed her in the middle of the Hall.

A throat cleared next to them. They pulled apart to see Hadeon smiling at them. Elodae clenched her jaw and gave him a tight-lipped smile in return.

The lord held out his hand. "May I have this dance?"

"Thank you for asking, but I–"

The lord swept her out of Alden's arms and into the surging crowd.

Elodae clenched her teeth. One dance and then she and Alden could escape. To hel with the ball.

They were leaving. Tomorrow.

Her stomach did another flip.

"Beautiful couple, aren't they?" Hadeon asked, looking over at the dais where Fornax was whispering something in her sister's ear.

Elodae nodded. "They most certainly are."

The lord spun her around once, pulling her a little too close for comfort. She loosed a breath and placed her hand on his chest, pushing slightly, but he didn't release his grip.

"Your grip is a little tight, my lord," she said through her teeth.

"We're no closer than you and Lord Einar were moments ago." He leaned in. "Or this morning."

Elodae's nostrils flared, and she tried to pull out of his grasp. "Let me go."

But he didn't listen. He just kept leading her through the dance.

"What would the king say if he found out his niece was sleeping with a common castle guard? Ruining his chances at an alliance with the most powerful kingdom in Eldonia." He brushed a hair out of her face.

She swatted away his hand and pushed at his chest again. His eyes darkened. "Let me go."

"Why don't you open your eyes and realize this love of yours—it will never last. I give it a month. Five weeks, maximum." He leaned in and whispered in her ear, "Why don't I show you what it's like to be with a real man? Not some common dirt. Don't soil your pretty little self with someone like him."

Hadeon ran his hand down her back and grazed the top of her backside.

"Alden is everything you wish you were. Now let me go." She spat in his face.

A cruel smile spread across his face. "Soon, there will be a choice in who you obey. I pray you choose wisely. Where is the king?" He made a show of looking around the room.

Elodae followed his gaze. She had no idea where her father was.

And that was when she noticed that the guards around the room—they were not Samarokan. Nor Dolannish, it seemed. They were in all red uniforms with black masks covering the lower half of their faces.

She looked back at the lord in terror, and he just grinned. A chill snaked down her spine. "Let me go," she said again.

Instead, the lord crushed his lips to hers.

She pushed at him, but he wouldn't move. Her heart pounded and tears rushed to her eyes, but his grip on her hand was too tight for her to reach for her dagger.

"Don't fucking touch her." Alden shoved the lord away from her.

Warren was instantly at her side. The dancing continued around them, but people looked in their direction.

Tears fell from Elodae's eyes. Stumbling back a step, she stopped seeing the dancing people around her. Stopped seeing everything.

Everything except shattering glass.

"If you ever touch her again, I will skin you alive," Alden growled in Hadeon's face.

"El," Warren said, gently touching her shoulder. She flinched and whirled on him. He caught her wrist before she could strike him. "It's me," he said softly, releasing her.

The sound of shattering glass still echoed in her mind. "Get me out of here," she choked out.

Warren didn't hesitate before he rushed her out of the Hall.

Warren led Elodae out of the ball and through the winding hallways. She gradually increased her pace until she lifted her skirts and sprinted through the castle.

He raced to keep up with her, fighting everything inside of him not to turn around and slit the lord's throat in the middle of the Grand Hall. He wasn't sure his brother would show the same restraint.

She bounded out of a doorway and into the clear warm night. She didn't stop until he felt sand beneath his shoes. Warren shoved down his shock at her going to the sea.

Finally, Elodae slowed, then fell to her knees in the sand. The crescent moon above cast the sand in a glistening glow.

Warren slid to his knees by her side and lifted back her hair as she vomited.

She fell forward but caught herself with one of her hands, the other one clutching both necklaces she now always wore.

"El?"

Elodae vomited again.

Warren looked away, begging himself not to get sick at the sight. Her body started to shake, and he shrugged off his jacket and draped it around her. Only then did he realize it wasn't from her being cold, but because she was sobbing.

"El?" he tried again and put a hand on her shoulder.

She flinched and moved away from him. "Please don't touch me."

He held up his hands.

"Something's wrong, Warren," she said between sobs.

"Alden will take care of—"

"No." She turned to look at him. The black lines around her eyes streaked down her face with her tears. "Something is wrong. Vanor. The guards. Didn't you notice none of them were our men?"

Warren wracked his memory. Finn had not been there. He'd assumed the captain had the night off, but that wasn't like Finn. Warren had thought the king had given the men new uniforms to celebrate the coming solstice—red for the sun—but they'd all worn those masks so he couldn't see their faces. He and Alden hadn't been given one, but he had figured it was because they'd been invited to the ball as guests, not guards.

"Hadeon." She bit out the lord's name. "I think he's planning something."

A preternatural growl ripped through the air.

Warren whipped around, but darkness did not follow. The stars still shone above, and the lights from the city glowed brightly. But there—in the shadows of a sandbank, he saw it. A velarum. It stood on its back legs and roared to the moon. It looked like a man.

The demon fell back onto its front legs and prowled away, toward the Tyrian Peaks. Where he had been running earlier that morning.

"Warren," Elodae breathed.

He held up a hand, silently urging her not to speak. Not to make a sound.

"There's another one," she said, barely more than a whisper.

Warren followed her gaze, and his mouth fell open as a demon—a man—stalked toward them. And although he knew it was impossible, although every logical thread within told him it couldn't be . . .

It was Charon.

Alden's father.

CHAPTER FOURTY SEVEN

Irelia sat on her seat atop the dais and watched as Fornax tried to pull Alden away from a Dolannish lord that had kissed Elodae. She would tell their father immediately and have him exiled from Samarok forever.

But as the prince tried to grab the lord and take him from the Hall, the guards slammed the double doors shut. The music stopped, and the crowd went silent.

Irelia's heart beat faster in her chest.

Two guards grabbed Fornax and yanked him away from the lord.

"Unhand him," the princess shouted, standing from her seat.

"Afraid they won't listen to you, little bird," Hadeon called back, and made his way toward the dais.

She looked around the room. With those masks over

their faces, she couldn't tell who the guards were. Where was Finn? He wasn't here.

Oh, gods . . .

The lord stepped up on the dais and smiled at her. Something deep inside told her to run. That if she didn't get out of this room, and soon, she may never make it out alive.

She turned to do exactly that when a guard wrapped his arms around her. She thrashed against his hold, but he wouldn't let go. His grip was ironclad.

"Let her go," Fornax yelled, but it was cut off when a guard punched him in the gut.

The lord lifted his arms, encompassing the room. "Cronanth is mine now. The king is no longer fit to rule, and he has named me his heir."

Chaos broke out. People began racing toward the doors, shoving each other, trying to get out. And that was when the bloodshed started. The Blood Guards began cutting down anyone who tried to escape the Hall.

Irelia screamed as her people died. Only one demon stood in this room, and he wore the skin of a man.

The crowd stopped trying to escape as they saw what had happened to their friends. Their family.

"Now," Hadeon said, clasping his hands together as though he didn't just witness the murder of countless people. "Where is our dear Elodae?"

The room remained silent.

The lord craned his neck, looking around. Rage flashed in his yellow eyes as his smile faded. "Find her," he ordered.

Four guards left the room.

"Hadeon, you bastard," Fornax shouted. "Let them go."

Hadeon slowly turned toward the prince, a savage smile

stretching across his face. "You should mind your tongue, *prince*." He put a possessive hand on Irelia's shoulder.

"Don't touch—" Fornax roared, but a Blood Guard knocked him unconscious with the pommel of their sword.

Hadeon sighed. "If only I didn't need him alive."

Irelia was frozen in place, staring up at the demon before her.

You'll be a good bird. Won't you?

She sucked in a sharp breath at the voice that sounded in her mind. It was both young and old. Near and far. And it did not belong to her.

The lord's yellow eyes held hers, and his pupils flared slightly. She couldn't look away. Couldn't move her body. Dread washed over her. She was no longer in control of herself.

Something entered her mind—her soul—and shackled it.

And then, the voice that had once belonged to her said, "Let the shadows reign."

The demon lord smiled.

Irelia thrashed within herself, screamed and yelled, but darkness swarmed inside her, clawing and shredding at her soul. Chaining her inside herself.

She screamed and screamed and screamed, but that thing inside her pounced.

And the darkness swallowed her whole.

Elodae ran as fast as she could from the creature that was both Charon and not. The thing that was both human and demon. Warren raced beside her as they headed toward the castle.

They didn't dare look over their shoulders to see if the demon that had once been Alden's father, was chasing them. But then a black figure appeared ahead.

Warren grabbed her elbow, steering her in a different direction.

"Warren," the figure yelled.

Alden.

Elodae skidded to a halt, her breaths coming in wheezing pants. She looked over her shoulder. The velarum was not following them. She thanked the gods for that small mercy.

Alden approached and doubled over.

Warren was instantly at his brother's side, wrapping a supportive arm around his shoulders. "Alden . . ."

Alden held up a hand. "Hadeon."

Elodae's blood went cold. "What happened?"

He looked her in the eye and shattered her world with a single sentence. "He's taken over Cronanth."

Warren let out a string of curses and ran his fingers through his hair, pacing.

Elodae just gaped at Alden. "How did you—?"

"When chaos broke out, I snuck out the same passageway I got you out of during the first Veiling."

"Irelia?"

Alden's eyes grew sad as he finally stood straight again.

Irelia was still inside. She was with Hadeon. Her sister.

"We need to save her." Elodae started heading back toward the castle.

Alden grabbed her elbow, stopping her. "Elodae, they said the king isn't fit to rule anymore. They slaughtered half the people in that room. I heard him ordering some of his men to find *you*." He shook his head. "You can't go back."

"Alden, Irelia is in there. I will not abandon her."

A growl came from somewhere behind them.

"What was that?" Alden asked in a low voice.

"About that . . ." Warren said, but Elodae shot him a look and he snapped his mouth shut.

Elodae started toward the castle again, once more lifting her skirts in her hands.

"Elodae," Alden called.

"I'm going to help her and the people of Cronanth. You can stay out here with the velarum if you'd like, but don't you *dare* try to stop me."

"And what are we going to do if we manage to get back inside?" Warren asked, coming up beside her.

Alden appeared on his left.

Elodae set her sights on home. "I'm going to kill them all."

ELODAE AND ALDEN CRAWLED BACK IN THROUGH the trapdoor in the castle's side.

Warren had left to find where Hadeon had put Samarok's guards. To find aid. Any aid. Elodae had written three letters, and they'd found a messenger in Cronanth. The city had been blissfully quiet. None of the guards dressing in blood trolling around. She had begrudgingly handed over the necklace Alden had given her as payment—Alden's idea.

"I'll get you another," he had vowed.

The three letters were addressed to King Malum of Dolannish, Queen Nadia of Callumere, and the ruler of Lunala. She didn't know his name—no one did—but she still sent a letter. It would take weeks for the letters to be delivered, and she had no idea what would happen before help finally arrived.

Orion and Lunala may be responsible for the Veilings and the demons, but they clearly needed Samarok for something, needed *her* for something. She prayed that need outweighed whatever their plot was to save Samarok from their darkness and come and *actually* save them.

But she couldn't think about that right now.

She needed to find Irelia. And then Vanor. The lord had not said the king was dead. Just no longer fit to rule.

Elodae felt her dress tearing as she crawled along the stone floor through the undergrounds of the castle. It was so dark she couldn't see Alden in front of her. Her mother's necklace heated against her skin, and she prayed whatever else was coming would hold off.

It took them what felt like hours to wind their way back into the castle. Alden didn't want to lead them to the kitchens or to the Grand Hall, so he had to take a route he wasn't entirely familiar with. He'd learned these tunnels as a young boy, but over time the information had faded from his memory.

Time, such precious time, ticked by like the sound of a war drum in Elodae's mind. She counted the minutes as they climbed up a steep staircase and prayed to Nath that Warren had found the other guards and soldiers.

Light leaked through a crack in the wall, and Alden slowed. Elodae stepped up next to him and tried to peer through it. The war room. It was empty.

Alden looked over his shoulder at her, and she gave him a curt nod.

She was ready.

He shoved against the wall with his shoulder, and it budged ever so slightly.

"Help me push it," he said, and moved over so she could get next to him.

Elodae placed her hands on the wall, her shoulder barking in pain, but she ground her teeth and shoved through the ache that shot up and down her arm. Then the door gave way, and they tumbled out of the passageway and into the war room.

"Sorry," Alden whispered, helping her to her feet.

She would have laughed if it weren't for the impending doom looming over them.

They quickly made their way out of the war room, and Alden held up a hand as he pulled back one of the towering doors and peered out into the hallway.

"Clear," he whispered over his shoulder.

But Elodae was staring at the map in the center of the round table.

Alden rushed over to her side. "Elodae, we have to move . . ." His words faded as he looked down at the table.

It was a map of Eldonia. Red pieces were stationed throughout Asiva and now Samarok.

Hadeon. Hadeon's men had overthrown Asiva. But that was impossible.

Elodae's mind was racing too fast for her to think clearly.

"We have to go," Alden said again and grabbed her hand.

She let him tow her out of the war room and into the hall. They kept to the shadows as much as possible. The doors to the Grand Hall were wide open, and no one was inside.

No one *alive* was inside.

With a quick scan of the space, Elodae took in the sight before her. A dozen bodies were scattered on the floor. The pools of blood around them seeping out into the hallway. Her eyes searched through the carnage; hand clamped over her mouth to keep from releasing the scream that built in her throat. It wasn't until she confirmed that her sister was not among the corpses that now littered the Hall that she could take in a breath of air.

"Holy fucking gods," Alden breathed, stumbling back a step.

"We have to stop him. Now," Elodae whispered.

He nodded, pulling her away from the horrifying sight.

The bodies of those people had been left as a sign—a message—of what would happen if anyone tried to disobey.

The man who ordered this would burn in hel. Elodae vowed that she would be the one to set the pyre ablaze.

Alden slowed as they turned a corner. The castle was eerily quiet, as if everyone had left. Even Hadeon and his Blood Guards. They reached the lord's bedroom, but not a single person was stationed outside.

What the hel was going on?

Alden looked at Elodae, a silent question in his icy blue eyes.

She pulled out the dagger she had strapped to her thigh and nodded at Alden.

He shoved open the door and went completely still.

A velarum sat in the middle of the room. Not just any velarum, though.

The demon that had once been his father.

Rage burned inside her as she looked at his father. Even if it wasn't really him—not anymore, at least—he had hurt Alden. And now his master was hurting her sister.

The blood drained from Alden's face as he stared at what was left of his father.

Elodae felt her mask stumble for a second as she stared at the demon crouched before them. Her heart lurched as Irelia followed on the lord's heels. Another form stayed in the shadows behind them. She could just barely make out the midnight black hair and sapphire eyes that pierced the darkness. Astrid. What the fucking gods was going on? Irelia wore a smile on her face as she looked between Alden, Elodae, and Charon.

"Irelia," Elodae breathed.

"She's mine now. Isn't that right, little bird?" Hadeon purred, running a hand down her arm.

Elodae saw red. She threw her dagger at the lord.

Hadeon lifted a hand, and the dagger halted midair. As if a phantom hand had caught it. He flicked his wrist, and the dagger pivoted and soared through the air, embedding itself in Elodae's thigh. She screamed and fell to the floor.

Alden rushed toward her, but the velarum roared and pounced on him, knocking him to the ground.

Irelia didn't so much as blink.

Elodae bit her lip as she yanked the dagger out of her leg. It clattered to the floor and blood seeped out of the wound and through the skirts of her dress.

"That wasn't very nice," Hadeon chided, walking over to Elodae. He dropped so he was level with her, resting his elbows on his knees, and cocked his head to the side. "I said you'd have a decision to make, didn't I?"

Elodae clasped a hand over her thigh, trying to staunch the bleeding. Hadeon stroked her cheek with one hand, and she tried not to flinch away.

"Don't fucking touch her," Alden snapped.

The velarum—his father—roared in his face and dug his claws into Alden's chest. Blood spilled out from beneath those nails.

"I would kill you right now," the lord said to Elodae, "but I need you alive." He hummed to himself, his face blurring as Elodae's vision grew fuzzy from the blood loss. "I think a lesson is in order, though. Don't you agree, my bird?"

The girl who had once been her sister smiled at Elodae and said, "Yes, my dear."

Hadeon walked over to the princess, wrapping his arm around her waist, and purred into her ear, "Who first?"

Irelia looked from Alden to Elodae and back to Alden. "Him."

CHAPTER FOURTY EIGHT

Irelia fought and fought and fought against the chains around her soul. But that darkness swirled inside her. Every time she tried to regain control of her body—it chipped away a piece of her soul.

She screamed. Screamed, but no sound came out. Not even a twitch of her muscles. She could've sworn the darkness laughed at her attempts.

And when the demon in the lord's body ordered the guards to drag her sister and Alden from his rooms and to the dungeon, the thing inside made her follow.

It carried her down into the cold depths of the castle. Made her watch as the Blood Guards chained Alden to a wooden post in the middle of a large room. The scrape of a whip echoed, and Irelia tried to turn, to stop it from happening.

But the darkness seized the reins and forced her again to watch.

Forced her to watch as one of Hadeon's men ripped open Alden's shirt and another unfurled the metal-tipped whip.

Elodae was yelling and thrashing in the corner, but a large man had her arms pinned behind her back.

The whip cracked through the air, and Alden arched at the impact. A gash immediately appeared and blood ran down his back.

Her sister screamed, but that thing in Irelia laughed. Elodae whirled on her, and she realized it had laughed out loud. *She* had laughed out loud.

"You're a monster," Elodae roared.

Irelia didn't know if it was directed at her or the demon lord by her side.

She yanked at the chains around her soul again, but the more she fought, the more she frayed. The more she felt herself slipping away.

The darkness wrapped around her soul, waiting for her to give up. To welcome it in.

The whip continued to crack until Elodae was sobbing in the corner, no longer fighting the guard that held her back. Alden was unchained and tossed to the ground next to her.

"Your turn, dear," the demon next to Irelia said with a smile.

"May the gods have mercy on your soul, because Hela knows you'll need it." Elodae spat at his feet.

The guard holding her punched her square in the jaw, and she crumpled to the floor.

Irelia could do nothing but watch.

Alden was shouting something, trying to get to his feet.

But the velarum, his father, clamped its jaws around his shoulder and pulled him back.

"How many lashes do you think will do?" Hadeon asked Irelia.

That darkness inside her purred, "Thirteen, I think."

"Thirteen it is." The lord smiled and nodded to the guard who held the whip.

It was still dripping with Alden's blood when the first crack sounded.

Elodae screamed as it struck her back, tearing clean through the dress she still wore.

Irelia begged the gods, anyone, to save them. To stop this. To spare her sister.

But no one came. No one listened.

Not even as the thirteenth strike landed.

ELODAE STAYED CONSCIOUS LONG ENOUGH TO know she had been tossed into a cell.

Her back was in so much pain she didn't even bother to catch herself as she crashed to the floor.

Distantly, she heard Alden being dropped into the cell next to hers.

"Alden," she croaked, her voice raw from her screams.

"Quiet!" someone yelled from outside her cell door.

That was the last thing she remembered before her world went dark.

CHAPTER FOURTY NINE

Fornax had been locked in his room for nearly five days now.

He'd had no word on Irelia. Or Alden. Or Elodae.

But the Samarokan guards had been let out of wherever Hadeon had kept them locked up, because Finn knocked on his door on the morning of the fifth day.

The locks had been moved from the inside of his room to the outside, because Finn let himself in, and the lock clicked back into place when the door shut behind him.

"Where is she?" Fornax asked, walking up to the Captain of the Guard—former captain, he supposed.

"She's fine," Finn said, his eyes shuttering. "She walks around the castle, usually trailing Lord Hadeon. But she's—she's fine."

Fornax shook his head. "She's not fine. Something happened to her. She's not acting like herself."

Or she hadn't been the last time he'd seen her. In the Grand Hall, the night everything had happened.

Irelia had been standing on the dais, terror written across her face. And then the next moment she was smiling at the crowd, her hand in Hadeon's. Her eyes had gone blank and distant. She hadn't batted an eye when he had ordered her dead people to be left for whenever Elodae and Alden returned. Not even when they found her friend Warren sneaking around the castles and threw him in with the other Samarokan Guards.

Finn cleared his throat. "The lord says you are permitted to leave your room, but only if you stay within the walls of the castle." Fornax tried to hide his shock. The first chance he got, he would sink a sword through Hadeon's throat. "But he advised me to warn you that if anything happens to him or if you act out in any way, Irelia will be executed."

Fornax went completely still. "Very well," he bit out.

He needed to get out of this room. Needed to see Irelia. To find out what Hadeon had done with Elodae and Alden.

Finn gave Fornax a curt nod and knocked twice on the door. It immediately opened, and Finn led the prince out of his rooms and down the hall.

"Irelia," Fornax choked out.

Before Finn could even answer, the prince turned in the direction of the princess's room, and started to run.

Pounding footsteps followed behind Fornax, the only tell that Finn followed. The prince had the feeling the guard was calling his name, but he heard nothing. Nothing but the roar of his heartbeat, of being out of his rooms for the first time in too long, for the idea of finally seeing Irelia after these too long days.

No guards stood stationed outside Irelia's double doors when they came into view. Fornax didn't even question it as he turned the door handle and the doors gave way. Fornax practically sprinted inside. But she wasn't there. He searched her bedroom, bathroom, terrace, the game room. She was nowhere to be found.

He stormed back into the hall in time to see Finn reaching the princess's room, the guard's breaths coming in heaves.

"Where is Irelia?"

Finn, still panting, stood up straight and adjusted his chest plate.

"Where is Irelia?? Fornax pushed, his voice taking on a desperate edge.

"She's been moved," Finn finally answered. "If you hadn't rushed off like that I could've—"

"Where?" Fornax cut him off.

A muscle ticked in Finn's jaw. "Lord Hadeon's rooms."

The prince's eyes shuttered, but he turned on his heels and walked as fast as he could, without running this time, toward the lord's bedroom.

Finn caught up to him with ease. "If she dies because of your temper, I will kill you," the guard muttered under his breath as they approached Hadeon's room.

Fornax reined in his growl of frustration.

Finn knocked twice sharply on Hadeon's door. His lock remained inside his room, it seemed. Of course it did. This was his castle now.

Irelia answered the door, and Fornax's heart cracked in his chest. His queen was in a sheer grey sleeping gown.

"May I help you?" she asked with a smirk and looked from Finn to Fornax. When her sea-green eyes met his, no warmth lay within. No playfulness. They were ice cold.

His heart cracked further. "Irelia," he breathed, taking a step toward her.

A nearby Blood Guard stuck out his arm, stopping him from reaching her.

Fornax glared. "Remove your arm."

"Unless you've come to play with us, you're not allowed in," she purred.

"Us?" Fornax dared ask.

Hadeon appeared over Irelia's shoulder and draped an arm around her. He was wearing nothing but his underclothes.

Fornax's vision blurred red. He took a step toward the lord, but Finn blocked his path this time.

The lord dragged his eyes up and down Fornax. "No," he drawled in Irelia's ear. "You don't want that, my bird."

"Hmm," she hummed and turned to face the lord. He pressed a kiss to Irelia's cheek.

Fornax lurched forward. "Don't touch her."

"He does more than that." Irelia winked at him and closed the door in his face.

Fornax gaped at the wood. A clot formed in his throat as he finally turned away and walked down the hall.

Finn followed closely behind.

"Leave me, Finn," Fornax growled.

"I'm afraid I can't do that."

Fornax whirled on him. "How can you just stand there

and let him do this? How can you serve him? Watch him touch Irelia in that way?"

Finn's nostrils flared. "This isn't the first time this has happened to me, *prince*."

Fornax studied the man in front of him. "How did you get out last time?" he asked quietly.

Finn's shoulders bowed. "Not all of us did."

WARREN HAD JUST TAKEN UP HIS POSITION IN THE dungeons when Prince Fornax and Finn came down the stairs.

"Where's Elodae?" Fornax asked him.

Warren ground his teeth but nodded toward the second door down the hall.

Finn took up position beside Warren as the prince walked over to the door. A Blood Guard pulled out his ring of keys and unlocked it. Warren tried to peer inside, to see her, just once. He was not permitted entrance into her cell, but apparently that privilege had been extended to the Prince of Dolannish.

He could barely make out the prince's muffled voice saying Elodae's name. He wasn't sure she'd been conscious these past few days. His brother was tough; occasionally, he had called out for Elodae and a Blood Guard had gone into his cell and beaten him. Warren had attacked the guard in charge of Alden only once. He was still sporting a black eye and busted lip from the encounter.

Hadeon had warned him that if he did it again—if he so much as spoke—Irelia and Elodae would both suffer. And then he had thrown Alden into the mix of threats.

Just for fun, the sick bastard had said.

Fornax appeared in the dungeon's hall a minute later, running a hand over his face. Warren wanted to say something—ask something—but he held his position as the prince and his captain made their way back out of the dungeon.

Hours passed, and finally, Elodae let out a pained cry. A Blood Guard immediately shoved open her door, and Elodae's cry turned into a scream.

The leash Warren kept on himself frayed even further.

He would get his family out, even if it cost him his own life.

And then he would burn this place and everyone in it to the ground.

Elodae awoke to the sound of her cell door opening. Hadeon stepped in and kicked her shin, rousing her. She heard Alden stir in the cell next to hers. "Bring the guard, too," Hadeon ordered one of his men.

Elodae was too weak to do anything but comply as he hauled her to her feet. She couldn't walk very fast due to the shackles around her ankles, but Hadeon didn't seem to care. His grip on her elbow tightened every time she stumbled or tripped over her chains. His nails dug into her skin, and something warm dripped down her arm.

A set of chains rattled behind her, and she knew Alden must be close by. She didn't know why Hadeon wanted them both. Her heart pounded in her ears, but she was so tired. So weak. She couldn't do much else besides limp alongside the lord. The beautiful gown she was still wearing was now tattered and frayed beyond recognition. Her feet and hands, all her body, was covered in dirt and grim from her days in that cell.

They made their way up from the dungeons, and Elodae had to blink against the sunlight that hit her. She had spent weeks in the dungeon now, the only light being the lamps in the hall outside her door that she glimpsed occasionally when one of Hadeon's men came in to give her a tray of food.

She didn't know how long she'd been down there. She'd tried to track the days with her meals, but the men came randomly and the sun never shone in the dungeons. They could've been down there two weeks; it could've been three. A month. Elodae didn't know. The only semblance of time she had was the constant itching of the fresh skin on her back, meaning it had been long enough for the wounds to start healing over.

Fornax had visited her once. Or had tried to.

He'd come down one day—or night. She didn't know why he'd come. But he had walked into her cell, waking her from a fitful sleep, and said something. She couldn't remember what it'd been. Something about her sister.

Elodae had been too weak and tired to stay awake for long.

The prince hadn't stayed for more than a minute or two, and she hadn't seen him since.

The only assurance she got of Alden still being alive was his yelps of pain when one of the guards tortured him. She had tried to talk through the stone walls to him once. Only once. Because the moment she had spoken, one of Hadeon's men had stormed into her cell, whip in hand.

The last thing she remembered before she passed out from the pain was Alden screaming at them to stop hurting her. Elodae had awoken a while later, not knowing how much time had passed, with a split lip and a swollen shut eye, the wounds on her back open once more.

Alden had still been shouting when she'd awoken, but his yells of anger had ebbed into screams of pain as a whip cracked through their cells.

That had been days ago. Her lip still throbbed, but the swelling in her eye had gone down. She reached up a hand to touch it and winced at the pain. Not that long ago, then.

Her back ached, though. The rub of her shredded dress against the wounds hurt so bad that the first time she'd woken after a lashing, she'd vomited from the lingering pain. Someone had then come into her cell and doused her with a bucket of seawater. Her screams had echoed down the stone halls of the dungeon.

The Blood Guards by their sides led them through the halls of the castle.

Once a place of comfort and joy, now it was a reminder of what had happened. She didn't know what had become of her father. Or of the prince. Or Warren and Finn. And every time she thought of Charon, of Alden's father who had died six years ago, she was filled with a burning rage. She would kill him all over again for harming Alden, demon or not. A man she once considered a father. He'd hurt the one she loved.

Hadeon led them into the Grand Hall. Her heart stopped dead in her chest at what she beheld.

Irelia sat on the dais. The throne to her right was empty. Still no sign of their father. Fornax stood behind Irelia's chair, arms behind his back. Finn and Warren were amongst the guards around the walls of the Hall—Vanor's guards mixed with Hadeon's, but they all wore the same red uniform.

Elodae was too weak to call out to her sister, and Irelia wouldn't even look her in the eye.

They reached the center of the Hall, and Hadeon shoved her to her knees. Alden went down beside her. In her periphery, she saw Warren's gaze snap to the lord. Rage filled his brown eyes, but he seemed to be all right. He had a couple of bruises around his left eye and cheek, but he looked whole at least.

Elodae looked away from the guard and over to her sister. Irelia still wouldn't look at her. She wanted to scream, to shout, to beg her sister to do something. To say something. To just look at her. But Irelia just sat there, frozen in her chair.

"Isn't this nice?" Hadeon drawled, walking around so he stood in front of Elodae and Alden.

"You're a fucking bastard," Alden spat.

The guard that had hauled him up here, a large, rugged-looking man, punched Alden straight in the gut.

He bowed over his knees, heaving.

Both Fornax and Warren took one step forward, as if they'd intervene. Finn laid a hand on Warren's shoulder, but Warren shoved it off and glared at him.

Hadeon held up a hand. Both Fornax and Warren immediately halted.

"What do you want?" Elodae rasped, her voice raw from not being used—from her screams.

"You." Hadeon smiled down at her, his golden eyes raking over her body.

Alden snarled at him, still bent over his knees, trying to regain his breath.

Hadeon's grin only widened as he cooed, "You still haven't learned your place, have you?" He waved a hand at the gathered royals behind him. "Perhaps you can learn from them. Or do you need to be reminded of what happens when you disobey?"

He stepped forward, fist raised. Elodae braced herself for the blow.

Alden was still trying to catch his breath, but he growled, "Touch her again and I'll kill you."

"Stop!" Warren yelled at the same time. He shrugged Finn's hand off his shoulder when the captain tried to halt him again.

Hadeon paused, his grin turning cruel, and turned to look at Warren. "Do I need to remind you what happens if you step out of line, too, guard?"

Warren went still and his nostrils flared. A muscle ticked in his jaw. He looked from Hadeon to Elodae and then back to the lord. And then he stepped back into line next to Finn.

"I believe I've been rather generous," Hadeon said. "Allowing you all to remain free. Able to wander about the castle as you please."

"Free?" Fornax shouted, an incredulous look on his face. "You call this freedom? Look at them. Look at this city. *Look at what you've done.*" He said the last with a glance toward Irelia, agony etched on his face.

Hadeon turned to face the prince. "Yes. Free. Are you currently in chains, my friend?"

"You've taken over this court," Fornax roared, taking another step forward.

Hadeon waved his hand as though that were not even noteworthy and turned back to Elodae and Alden. The guards in red herded the prince away from the edge of the dais. Away from Irelia.

The lord stared down at the pair of them still kneeling on the floor and sucked on his teeth. Then he nodded at Alden. "Bring him."

The large man grabbed Alden's shirt and hauled him to his feet. He shoved him forward to follow Hadeon toward the dais, but Alden tripped over his chains, nearly falling back onto the ground.

Elodae made to stand, to follow him, but a rough hand clamped down on her shoulder, shoving her back onto her knees.

"I think you all need to remember where your place is in this court now," the lord said, a smile on his face.

She tried to get to her feet again, to go to Alden. To protect him somehow. She couldn't watch him get hurt again—couldn't see him in pain.

The lord snapped his fingers, and a door behind the dais—the one Alden had led Elodae through to help her escape the first Veiling—opened. That memory felt like years ago, not mere months.

Elodae's heart stopped as a man emerged from the shadows.

Her father walked into the Hall.

He was not harmed; he showed no signs of discomfort at all. He even had a slight smile on his face as he made his way onto the dais and sat on his throne.

Irelia did not so much as look in their father's direction. She didn't even blink.

A hooded figure emerged from the shadows behind the king and walked over to Hadeon.

Vanor crossed an ankle over one of his knees and motioned at the lord to continue.

Elodae gaped at her father. She pulled at her chains again, and the guard at her back dug his fingers into her shoulder. She couldn't fight the whimper that escaped her lips.

A low growl came from the corner of the room. Whether it was Warren or Fornax, Elodae didn't know.

Her focus was entirely on Alden.

The large guard shoved him to his knees before the dais. Elodae flinched at the crack of his bones against the tile.

The hooded figure that had emerged behind her father unsheathed his sword. It glistened in the sun's rays pouring in through the windows.

Elodae's heart lurched in her chest. "What are you going to do?" she blurted, not bothering to hide the panic in her voice.

Hadeon looked up. Those golden eyes held nothing but pure evil within. He looked back down at Alden, at the man who held her heart. A slow, vicious smile crept across the lord's face.

"Kill him."

Elodae began screaming then.

She pushed off the floor and tried to run toward the dais, but she was too far away. The chains at her feet kept her from reaching him. The guard behind her wrapped his arms around her middle, picking her up and dragging her away.

Elodae begged her father, her sister, anyone, to stop him. To help. She prayed to the gods, any of them, to help. To stop this. To spare him.

Fornax began shouting at Hadeon, but Elodae couldn't hear it. She heard nothing but that command. It echoed in her mind like a death knell.

Kill him.

Warren lurched forward again, yelling at Hadeon to stop. No one had come to offer aid. The gods hadn't spared them from Hadeon's wrath, and they weren't listening now.

So Elodae offered the only thing she could. "Kill me instead."

"No!" Alden roared.

The entire room paused. Hadeon held up his hand to the hooded figure, who had lifted their sword, and cocked his head in her direction. "You would give up your life for this guard?"

"Yes," she said without hesitation. No doubt crowded her heart. She would take his place happily. If it meant he would live, she would do it.

Hadeon threw his head back and laughed. The horrid sound echoed through the Hall.

Fornax fought against the Blood Guards' hold on him, but they put a gag in his mouth to silence his shouting. She saw Warren take a step forward, reaching for Alden, but Finn stopped him with a hand on his forearm.

Alden looked over at Elodae. When his glacial-blue eyes met hers, she found nothing but love and light within. Love for her. He smiled and mouthed the words: *I love you.*

And she—she felt the same.

She stared at the man before her, his eyes pouring into hers. Into her heart. Her soul. She wanted to leave this place. Wanted to see the stars at night in the Moon Rainforest or witness a sunrise in the Sun Desert with him by her side.

Wanted to grow old with him. To live an ordinary life full of laughter and love.

Elodae tried to stand, tried to go to him, but the Blood Guard shoved his boot into her back, keeping her down. So, she opened her mouth to finally voice the words she knew were true, the words that had been in her heart all these years.

But then the hooded figure's sword plunged into Alden's chest. Into his heart. The heart he had offered her so freely.

Elodae's world shattered as Alden's limp body slumped to the ground in a pool of his own blood.

CHAPTER FIFTY ONE

Elodae's screams were the most horrifying sounds Warren had ever heard. They etched into his mind, a sound straight from the depths of hel, and he knew he would never forget them for as long as he lived.

Something in the world shifted as she screamed and screamed. As the man who had been his brother fell to the floor.

She kicked at the guard who had his hands around her chest, hauling her away from Alden's lifeless body. She bucked and thrashed, throwing her head back into the guard's nose. He roared in pain and dropped the duchess, who scrambled across the floor, her chains scraping against the stone.

Elodae screamed at the king, her uncle, to do something. But the king just sat there on his throne, staring down at his daughter. The princess's face was unreadable, too.

Emotionless, like she had been every time Warren had seen her around the castle these past few weeks. She hadn't even flinched when the executioner had killed her friend.

Finn grabbed at Warren as he lunged for one of the Blood Guards near him, reaching for their sword.

The world shook when Elodae reached Alden's body and rolled him over. She clung to him, her white hair staining red with his blood.

The world outside the windows of the Hall darkened, but it was much too early for the sun to have set already.

The guards lining the room all took one step forward.

Toward Elodae.

Warren looked over at her. She was clinging to Alden's body, sobbing into his frozen chest.

Terror rooted deep in Warren's stomach as he stared down at his brother, at the eyes, still open and shining with tears. He pulled his gaze away from the body and back to the windows behind him. Darkness was still pooling at the horizon.

A velarum attack was coming.

This darkness felt different, though. It wasn't the sudden sheet of black that had fallen over the world before the demons began terrorizing the people of Cronanth.

No, this darkness vibrated with agony. Pain.

He felt it surround every inch of his body. The hairs on the back of his neck stood on end.

Fornax shot forward, reaching for Elodae, who was screaming and screaming and screaming. But the guard whose nose she had broken recovered. He shoved the prince down to the floor and grabbed Elodae's arm.

All Warren could do was watch. He was frozen in place

with shock. The pain was so intense he thought someone had shoved a thousand hot iron pokers into his body.

Two guards stepped off the dais and hauled Fornax back behind Irelia. They twisted his arms behind his back as the prince fought to dislodge their grip.

Elodae whirled around. An animalistic growl escaped from her lips.

Everyone in the room went still as they gazed at the white-haired woman clinging to her love's body. Her eyes were no longer a deep emerald green, but silver. Glowing like the stars at night.

Warren lurched forward then, finally shaking free from his shock, and fought against Finn's hold. The captain had wrapped his solid arms around Warren's middle, pinning his arms against his sides. Warren bucked and trashed, but he couldn't get out of Finn's grasp.

"Let her go," Warren roared at the man trying to haul Elodae away. Hadeon held up a hand, and Warren finally broke free of his captain's grip. He stormed over to the guard still gripping Elodae's arm. "I said, let her go."

Elodae's eyes were still glowing. He tried not to think about that. Tried not to think about the puddle of blood he was standing in, or the person to whom it belonged.

The guard spat in his face.

Warren's vision went red.

"Stand down, boy," Hadeon drawled from behind him.

Anger boiled inside him, but a warning rang through his thoughts. The lifeless body of Alden—his brother—burned in his mind. Warren slowly turned toward the lord, his body trembling. Not with fear, but with rage. A vicious smile spread across the demon lord's face. Taunting him. Challenging him to fight back.

But the body on the floor . . . the person to whom it belonged—

Warren couldn't lose someone else. Couldn't risk his family. So, he stepped back, fighting every urge in his body to kill them all. Everyone in this room. For what they'd done to Alden. For what they'd done to his family.

"Bring the henbane," the lord said to no one in particular.

Three guards at the entrance of the Hall turned and walked from the room.

Irelia's hands twitched.

The lord stopped and turned to look at the princess. She did not move again. Nor did she blink. She just stared at some spot on the distant wall.

Her hand had moved. Only a fraction of an inch, but it'd moved.

Warren studied the princess, waiting. Nothing happened.

The lord narrowed his eyes slightly at Irelia and then turned back toward Elodae, who was once again sitting in the pool of blood. She'd even hauled Alden's limp body onto her lap.

The guard that had been holding her was passed out on the ground.

When had Elodae rendered the man unconscious? *How* had she rendered him unconscious?

Another one of those preternatural growls sounded from the duchess as the lord took a step toward her. Her silver eyes locked on the lord's golden ones.

Hadeon tilted his head to the side and purred, "Who do we have here?"

Elodae gripped Alden's body closer to hers. The green was coming back to her eyes.

The lord leaned forward and rested his hands on his knees so that he was at eye level with Elodae. He lifted a hand, ignoring her snarls this time, and brushed a strand of her blood-stained hair out of her face. "You are going to do so well, my pet."

Warren dug his nails into his palms, glaring at the man touching Elodae. He would cut that hand from the lord's body and feed it to his demons.

"Someone clean that up," Hadeon said, pointing at Alden's body and standing upright again. He returned to the dais.

"Don't touch him!" Elodae screamed at the guard who made to approach them.

Hadeon stopped and turned back toward her.

Warren saw the promise of death in the duchess's eyes as she looked at the lord. "I'm going to end you," she growled through her teeth.

Warren felt the world shift beneath his feet again at her threat. Her promise.

Thunder rumbled in the distance, shaking the entire castle. The chandeliers rattled, the crystals hanging from them clinking together as the thunder continued.

Finn rushed to the windows. "A mountain just collapsed," he breathed.

The air in the room went cold.

Warren wasn't sure he'd heard him right. But then he peered out the windows on the far side of the room, the ones that faced west toward the Tyrian Peaks, and sure enough—one mountain no longer stood there. A cloud of dust was all that remained.

Hadeon turned from the window and looked down at Elodae. He stalked toward her, a smile on his face, and lifted his hand to brush a hair back from her face again.

"Don't touch her," Warren said with a lethal calm, stepping forward and grabbing the lord's wrist.

All the guards around the room took one step toward them.

Hadeon slowly tore his eyes from Elodae and looked at Warren.

"Don't. Touch. Her," Warren repeated.

The lord raised his brows. "Was the reminder not clear enough?"

Warren dug his nails into the lord's wrist. To hel with all of this. He would end them all, even if it was the last thing he did.

The executioner stepped forward, toward Elodae. With no weapon to defend her, Warren had no choice but to stand down. He released the lord's arm but made no move to back away.

King Vanor simply sat there, head propped up on his fist, and stared down at his daughter.

Elodae turned pleading eyes, which were once again completely green, on Fornax and then finally Finn. Finn, who was standing next to Warren again. Tears streamed down his captain's face as he stared at the body on the ground. He dragged his eyes from the body to Elodae. Opened his mouth, then closed it.

Warren saw the life drain from Elodae's face. Saw that last ember of hope within her flicker and then go out completely.

Her eyes shuttered and then shot to the body still in her lap.

Warren wanted to get her as far away from this place as possible—but he was helpless. He couldn't do anything. No one could.

"Don't touch him!" she screamed again, her voice breaking entirely, as that same guard took another step toward her.

The three guards returned and handed Hadeon a small pouch.

Irelia's hand twitched again. But with his back turned, the lord did not see it this time.

Warren fixed his eyes on the princess, silently begging her to move again. To prove the woman he loved as a sister was still there. Somewhere buried deep inside.

Hadeon sniffed at the bag and then nodded his approval. The three guards returned to their positions against the entrance doors as the lord approached Elodae. She crawled away, smearing the blood in streaks as she hauled Alden's body with her.

Warren couldn't just stand there like a fool any longer.

He lunged forward, too fast for Finn to stop him, and grabbed Elodae. He would get her away.

It didn't matter if he died in the process. He would welcome the darkness if it meant he could see his brother and the rest of his family again.

Elodae started screaming again. Screaming and clawing at Warren. The guards along the wall rushed forward to stop them as Warren lifted Elodae into his arms, causing her to lose her grip on Alden.

"No!" Elodae screamed as she reached for Alden. "I won't leave him!"

Warren could tear the world apart with his rage.

Elodae whipped her head toward Warren when he didn't put her down. Her eyes had gone silver again.

The guards were closing in on them, but he kept running. He begged his legs to move faster than they ever had before.

Wild heart, his mother had called him as a young boy. Warren had always loved to run through the woods, trying to go faster than the birds that soared above his head. Tried to outrun the deer and wolves that ran alongside him, barefooted and trudging through the dirt and sticks that littered the forest floor. He would be gone for hours at a time, simply racing through the towering oak trees of the Tyrian Peaks.

Warren channeled those inner wolves now and vowed that if one more person touched her, he would shred them apart with his teeth and claws.

But then darkness exploded throughout the room.

CHAPTER FIFTY TWO

"Stop her!" Elodae heard a voice shout through the darkness.

It was not the same darkness that had come before the demon attacks, nor the darkness that embraced her while she slept.

No. This was the bone-chilling, soul-crushing darkness. Like the gaps between the stars. And she knew—somewhere deep down—that it belonged to her. The void within her soul come to life.

All the light within her had gone out when the man who held her heart had died in front of her very eyes. Everything left inside her was darkness. *This* darkness.

Elodae heaved herself out of Warren's arms, somehow able to see through the darkness, and yet also not.

Strangled, choking noises sounded around her. The blackness was stripping the Blood Guards' air from their lungs. Crushing them from the inside out. But whatever lurked within these shadows, they did not touch her. They did not make a sound, either.

She didn't know how, but she made her way through the Hall, back toward the dais. She reached out and grabbed a sword from a Blood Guard's sheath. It was almost as if the void was helping her. Guiding her. They showed her where to move through their destruction.

Then something tugged, deep in her soul. Something else was coming. Something had felt the ripple of her magic and had answered it.

But that didn't matter. Nothing did.

Not as she charged at the man atop the dais. The man who stood beside her sister, a claiming hand on her shoulder.

His men were yelling. Shouting. Choking.

Dying.

She wanted the air sucked from their lungs. It happened. She wanted their hearts crushed into nothing but mist. It happened.

The darkness remained, and she could've sworn stars flickered throughout the void. A part of her—some small, broken part—marveled at the twinkling lights in her darkness. But she didn't have time to think about that.

The void wrapped itself around her soul, curling around her heart like an animal protecting its prey. She didn't care about that either. Let it devour her. She had nothing left to give of her heart anyway. The only thing that mattered was the body of the man on the floor at her feet.

Elodae rushed toward Hadeon. A roar erupted from her, and the sound encased all her pain, her shattered heart.

She lifted the sword, ready to make the killing blow, but something as hard as a stone wall barreled into her.

Elodae slammed into the ground, dropping her sword.

The shadows whispered to her, but she couldn't understand what they were saying. She clawed at the man on top of her—except it wasn't a man. It wasn't even human. She'd felt this kind of flesh before. The roughness of it. The stench of the breath that puffed onto her face as a low growl vibrated in its chest.

It was a velarum, but it was not attacking her. And this darkness . . . it belonged to her. Not the demons. This was not the Veiling.

Who are you, my pet? a voice both old and young whispered in her mind.

It wasn't the shadows that spoke to her, nor the darkness. It wasn't the tug she felt occasionally, deep within her soul.

No. This thing—this voice—was from the depths of hel itself.

And Elodae knew exactly to whom it belonged.

Before she could shove the demon off her, a hand pressed over her face, and a sweet, smoky scent filled her nose, her mouth. Choking her.

And the surrounding darkness pounced.

CHAPTER FIFTY THREE

One day since

Elodae awoke in a dark room.

She didn't know where she was.

She didn't care.

Her body was no longer drenched in blood.

Chains rattled around her wrists and ankles as she rolled over on a soft mattress.

She didn't care about any of that either.

Elodae closed her eyes and let the darkness sweep her away again.

CHAPTER FIFTY FOUR

Three weeks since

Elodae sat on the carpet in her foyer, holding her knees to her chest. The cool chains pressed against her skin; her cheeks stained with tears.

The furniture that had once been in the room lay broken around her. Shattered, like her soul was.

Someone knocked on the door.

Once.

Twice.

Footsteps sounded as they walked away.

No one had forced her to speak. No one had even come to haul her back to the dungeons.

Elodae continued staring into nothing as the footsteps grew ever quieter.

CHAPTER FIFTY FIVE

One month since

Elodae walked beside Fornax on the beach. She looked over to the waves that roared and grabbed for her shackle-less feet.

At one point, she would've been stricken with fear and unable to bear the closeness. Would've been confused by who was in her company. Or wondered where her restraints had gone.

But today—nothing.

The warmth of the sun didn't even heat her skin as its rays landed upon her face. Or the warm sand beneath her toes. She didn't notice that the trees up the shoreline were no longer blooming with flowers, but vibrantly green. Or care that a horde of Blood Guards followed closely behind.

The Elodae who noticed such things had died one month ago.

Not that anyone had realized, because none of the blood that had been spilled was hers.

Her heart, however—her heart had been slaughtered in front of her very eyes.

She turned away from the sea and sent up a prayer to Amphia to let the water swallow her whole. She knew the goddess wouldn't listen, though. None of them had listened a month ago. They certainly wouldn't now.

Thankfully, a moment later, her mind went blissfully empty again.

ELODAE DIDN'T REMEMBER HOW SHE'D GOTTEN back into the castle, or where the prince had gone. She closed the door to her bedroom and crawled into her bed, pulling Alden's shirt out from under the pillow next to hers.

For weeks, she had refused to let her new lady's maid change her sheets. The smell of *him* had still clung to them.

It was why she'd hidden the shirt.

She knew it had long since lost his oak and spice scent, but she didn't care.

In her dreams, she would wake next to him and he would smile and tell her that he loved her.

The man who had always been there.

The man who had loved her in silence for so many years.

The man who would never know that she loved him back.

Elodae cried herself to sleep, wishing she could tell him. If only once.

CHAPTER FIFTY SIX

Elodae's pain had ebbed into rage. A fire had ignited in her soul. In her heart. And she was angry. So fucking angry that she wanted to tear the world apart.

Elodae would be forced to attend a dinner that night in the Grand Hall. She had thrown up twice already thinking about the last time she'd been in that room.

Her nightmares no longer consisted of shipwrecks or demons or swelling darkness, but of the man she loved toppling over, a pool of his blood spreading over the marble floor.

Tears streaked down her face as her thoughts spiraled and spiraled and spiraled.

She looked up at her reflection in the mirror behind the

sink in her bathroom. Her face had hollowed out. Black circles lay beneath her eyes, and her hair was dull and limp. Her cheeks and lips had lost their color, too. She barely recognized the person staring back at her.

Elodae swiped away the wetness on her cheeks and walked into her room. She pulled out the remnants of the midnight blue dress with constellations scattered across the skirts and waited for the joy of the stars and moons to hit her. Nothing came, not even as she stared at the Warrior stitched into the fabric. She wasn't sure she could be happy anymore.

Hanging the dress back up, she pulled out a simple black one and tucked her necklace inside her slip. They hadn't been able to remove it for whatever reason. She couldn't be bothered to care. The dress hung awkwardly off her malnourished body.

Her new lady's maid entered a moment later. No knock. No announcement. Just entered. She pushed Elodae over to the vanity and pulled out some pins.

The new attendant pinned the back of Elodae's dress so it was once again fitted to her torso. The woman then pinned Elodae's hair in a half-up fashion, with random braids throughout, and tears rushed to her eyes at the familiar hairstyle Lillianna had done so often for her. Without a word, the lady's maid left her room.

Alone again, Elodae rummaged around her armoire, looking for her daggers. After tonight, all of this would end. She didn't care who crossed her path. She would find the ones who had done this to her, to the people she had cared for, and she would end them.

Slowly. Brutally. As they had done to her heart before her eyes.

She growled in frustration at the lack of weapons. Hadeon must've had them removed long ago while she was in the dungeon. Before *he* had—

Elodae shook her head. She couldn't think about him now.

The last two months had been eerily quiet.

No demons. No Veiling. And no Hadeon.

He had all but vanished from Cronanth. She knew that wasn't true, and that she had most likely been lost in her sorrow, but something deep within her tugged.

In her solitude, Elodae had allowed the darkness within her to consume her heart, had allowed it to control her mind, control every thought she ever had. She had been unable to conjure the darkness like she had on that fateful day again, but she could feel it in her very bones that it was there. Waiting for her to figure it out and wield it once more. Like now, as she stared and stared at her necklace.

Elodae wanted to scream, to cry, to roar her rage to the stars. But she was so tired. So fucking tired.

She shoved the tears back from her eyes and swallowed her feelings. She could get through tonight.

And then—then she would bring the stars crashing down upon the world.

Warren stood behind the princess on the dais, looking out over the gathered crowd. Every time he entered the Grand Hall, he wanted to burn the place to the ground.

The bastard that was currently strutting around, welcoming the guests, had defiled this castle. Defiled Warren's home.

The only thing that kept him nailed to his spot was the lord's threat that if any of them stepped out of line, Elodae would be next. And if any harm should come to Hadeon, Irelia would follow.

No one had been able to figure out why Irelia was so lifeless. They didn't know if she had retreated into herself to cope, or if Hadeon had done something to her. The old king had promised she was not poisoned. No visible signs of harm appeared on her body.

Warren could barely look at his old king, who sat on Irelia's right. Perched on his throne, a smile across his face, the man looked out over the Hall. He hadn't been seen for too long before that day, and then he had shown up and just —sat there.

"Warren," Finn's warning voice came from behind him.

Warren had been glaring at the king, a hand on the pommel of his sword. He released his grip and tore his gaze away from the man on the throne to look at Finn.

Something growled in the shadows behind the dais; the velarum that had been Alden's father, *his* father in so many ways. Lord Hadeon had been keeping it—him—like a pet these last few months. It never showed itself, but Warren could swear that late at night, he could hear it stalking outside his door.

Finn shook his head and said quietly, "Do not step out of line tonight."

Warren ground his teeth but gave his captain a curt nod and turned back to face the crowd.

A woman with moon-white hair stepped through the towering double doors, escorted by five Blood Guards. The black dress she wore hung off her too-thin body.

Elodae.

Gods, when was the last time he'd seen her? Cronanth had been uncomfortably silent these last few months, and Hadeon had made no move toward Elodae or anyone else in their court. The sight of her now—it took all of Warren's self-control to remain on this dais and not run to her side.

He hadn't been able to protect her all those months ago. Tears burned Warren's eyes, but he blinked them away. He hadn't been able to protect his brother, either.

Fornax's heart broke over and over in his chest as he stared at the princess, stiff-backed in her chair, atop the dais.

He wanted to yell and scream at her, wanted to shake her from this stupor. One day she had been fine, the next she was a pet to the demon that had taken over this city. The woman before him now was a stranger, and it terrified him to his core.

He didn't know how to save her. Or if she even could be saved.

Elodae walked past Fornax's line of vision then. He blinked at her. It was Elodae, but at the same time, it wasn't her at all. She was but a shell of her former self. She made her way over to the dais.

Fornax headed in that direction as well.

Hadeon jumped up onto the raised surface and lifted his arms as soon as Elodae took her seat beside the princess. Neither of the two women so much as glanced in the other's direction.

The entire room went still. Silent. The former king smiled, sitting up straighter on his throne.

"The Crown Prince of Lunala is due to arrive soon," Hadeon announced. Murmurs broke out amongst the guests but were silenced quickly after as the lord continued, "The marriage between our dear Elodae and the prince will take place the day after their arrival."

Fornax's mouth dropped open.

The man was sick. He had murdered Elodae's love mere weeks ago, and now he planned to marry her off.

Fornax looked over at the king, the man who had raised her as his own, and silently begged him to do something. To stop this madness. But the king just nodded in approval.

Elodae's expression, usually aloof and unreadable, burned with rage.

Hadeon turned toward her and grinned.

Elodae smiled back at the lord. Such unyielding rage shone in the slight uptilt of her lips. It was a smile full of promise. She would devour this world.

The sight sent chills down Fornax's spine. He prayed that the gods would save them from the wrath of the white-haired woman sitting next to his queen.

Elodae stood on the terrace off Irelia's room as the sun lowered beneath the horizon.

She had no idea where the princess had gone after the dinner. Wasn't sure she even cared anymore. Irelia had just sat there and let *him* die. Had done nothing except moved her hand.

The rage in Elodae's heart swelled. The air around her matched her anger as a storm brewed across the vast sea before her. She'd let that darkness—*her* darkness—curl around her heart, and her soul had faded from the light of the stars to the endless void between.

If they wanted a villain—she'd give them a villain.

Nothing mattered to her anymore.

Elodae turned her back on the sea and let the darkness twine around her fingers, veiling her in shadows. Something had snapped in her at the dinner, at seeing the room where it had all happened. Seeing the stain on the floor that no one deigned clean up. Something far, far inside of her, broke. And the darkness in her veins were suddenly there at the tips of her fingers.

No one knew. She had hidden herself in her sorrow, letting them think she was too broken. Beyond repair. And maybe she was. But instead of wallowing in her despair, she forged it. Made it anew.

Wielded it.

Nothing could prepare Cronanth, Samarok—all Eldonia —for the rage that burned and burned inside her. *The Ending*, Irelia had once told her Fornax called the Veiling. The prince was right—and wrong. The Veiling was the beginning of the end. The end of peace. The end of light. But what they did not know was that Elodae would be the one to drive out the light with darkness. She would be the one to end it all.

She left the room and strolled through the halls of the castle, calling forward her darkness, wreathing herself in it. Jumping from shadow to shadow, nothing more than a whisper in the wind, she made it out of Castle Cronanth and into the bustling city beyond.

Her hunt began now.

For the people who had taken everything from her. She'd start there, leaving the lord who had made her worst nightmares come true for last. So he'd know she was coming. So he could try to run. But he'd never be able to hide. Not from her. Not from who she was now.

She smiled as she lifted the hood of her cloak over her head. Her shadows retreated but remained around her face, concealing her from the light of the lamps above. Like a man with a constellation's name she'd met long ago. A man who had disappeared without a trace. Probably returning to his prince to aid in their coming arrival.

Stalking down the streets, she shoved her hands into her pockets and prepared to unleash herself upon the city.

Elodae had made a promise to herself the other night. *Make them all pay*. Every last one who was responsible for the loss of her heart.

No mercy remained within her.

Everything good and pure within her had been snuffed out by the void that now gaped like an open maw in her soul.

And like the walls of this city, forged to keep the world out—Elodae built a fortress of darkness around her ruined heart.

# BEFORE

The Dark One had traversed mountains and valleys, rivers and seas, to find the child of the stars. He could still hear the ancient prophet's eerie voice.

> *A child of the stars with hair black as the void—the world will rid its scars, for all evil shall be destroyed.*

He had snuck into the mind of the prophet, tampering with their memory, and had them change it to:

> *A child of the stars with hair black as the void—the world will birth new scars, for all good shall be destroyed.*

And then he'd forced them to drink an elixir that allowed him to control their minds. Their bodies. He could access their thoughts from even across the oceans.

The Dark One would not let the prophecy come to pass. He and his Kingdom of Darkness had worked endlessly to reach this world. To find the Star Bringer and feed off their magic.

But the old crone had died before they could reach her.

So, they waited. They bided their time in the shadows and in the depths of the sea. Lurking. Watching. Waiting. For a new Star Bringer to be born.

And one day, nearly four thousand years after they'd torn into this world, the Dark One had felt the shift in the universe. The tug of something great. Something so powerful that even his magic trembled at the hint of it.

A Star Bringer had been born.

His people worked tirelessly to find the black-haired child, convincing the Eldonians they were helping to save their world from the Harbinger of Darkness. *Scrios*, they called the child.

Ruination.

The Dark One forged demons from mortals to hunt the child of stars.

And there—beyond the veiling of the moon kingdom— he found them.

ABOUT THE AUTHOR

Caitlin Zura was born in Richmond, VA, but currently lives outside of Dallas, TX with her family. Being an avid reader herself, Caitlin decided to take a leap of faith and write the book she had always wanted to read. And *The Veiling of the Moon Kingdom* was born. When she's not reading or writing, you can find her with a coffee in hand (or Dr. Pepper), and hanging out poolside with her corgi, Boone.

instagram.com/authorcaitlinzura

tiktok.com/authorcaitlinzura

goodreads.com/caitlinzura

ACKNOWLEDGMENETS

This story is so near and dear to my heart. It has lived in the chaos of my mind for far too long, and I am so thankful to share it with the world. It would not have been possible without some very important and special people in my life.

I want to start by thanking my wonderful friend and alpha reader, Sarah. From staying up until the odd hours of the night while I read aloud to you my very first drafted chapters, to pushing me when I wanted to give up—this book would've never gotten completed without you.

Thank you to my two dearest friends: Emma, a beta reader, and Morgan, my second alpha reader. Without you two, these characters would not be half of who they are today. Morgan helped create the depth and tragic beauty that is Elodae. Emma was the one to help shape some of the sharper characters and add a little spice to each of them.

To my other betas, Purva and Gabby. Thank you so

much for your input and feedback. The emotions I saw you guys go through made this process so entertaining.

The art—not just for the book itself, but the map and character art—is so incredibly beautiful and I am so thankful I got to work with some amazing artists.

Ella, my cover/dust jacket/chapter header artist. This book didn't really come alive until I had the solidity of the cover. You did such a beautiful job! I could not be happier with the outcome.

Oakleaf Arrow Studios, the beautiful upgraded map design artist. The new map in the second version of *The Veiling of the Moon Kingdom* is one of my absolute favorite new additions. I'm so happy with how it turned out!

To the countless artists I have worked with over the years, this story would be nothing without all of you. You bring these characters to life and I am beyond grateful for your continued support of me and these characters.

To Faye, my lovely editor and one of my best friends. Thank you so much for putting all of your time and hard work into making *The Veiling of the Moon Kingdom* the best version it could possibly be. I'm eternally grateful to have someone like you in my life.

Thank you to the friends who supported me in ways they probably didn't even realize. Jill, Grayson, Taylor, Astera, and so many more. You not only supported me throughout this journey by simply being a positive light in my life, but by inspiring me to do what I'm passionate about. Regardless of what others may think or say.

A big, huge, enormous thank you to all of my fellow indie authors that have been a shoulder to cry on and have been there for me time and time again. E.C. Garrett, K.B.

Elizabeth, L.C. Emerson, Mindy Pettengill, S.T. Trubiano, Kyra Hinton, and so many others. All of your support has truly been life changing during the writing and publishing process. Words cannot do my appreciation and love for all of you justice.

I want to thank my parents. Your support, not only with writing a book, but my entire life, has been . . . there are no words. I truly could not have accomplished half of this without your help and support. From my mother sparking my love of reading to my father never letting me give up—their love is at the heart of everything I do.

And last, but certainly not least, to you, dear reader. This book is nothing without you. During my darkest days, I found light again in reading, found my home in the worlds I escaped to. I hope some of you saw a piece of your soul within these pages, and perhaps even found a home. So, thank you. From the bottom of my heart. May the stars always guide you home.

And always remember: Even the moon has scars.